When his estranged father  returns to the ancestral estate on the Scottish moors, desperately wishing to recover his missing childhood memories. Once there, he is swept up in a set of odd occurrences that make him question his sanity. Something other than his half brother Andrew is waiting for his return....something ancient and unnatural.

Noah's assistant Gavin is suspicious of the sudden circumstances that have lured Noah back to Scotland, and sets about uncovering a dark family legacy filled with sinister implications. Noah and Gavin have been friends for years, but each man suffers from a damaged past that has placed definite boundaries on their relationship. An ominous storm triggers a night of passion and terror, bringing the two men face to face with the unimaginable truth on the dark and menacing plains of Noah's ancestors.

Featuring a roll call of some of the best writers of gay erotica and mysteries today!

Derek Adams	M. Jules Aedin	Maura Anderson
Victor J. Banis	Jeanne Barrack	Laura Baumbach
Alex Beecroft	Sarah Black	Ally Blue
J.P. Bowie	Barry Brennessel	Michael Breyette
Nowell Briscoe	P.A. Brown	Brenda Bryce
Jade Buchanan	James Buchanan	Charlie Cochrane
Karenna Colcroft	Jamie Craig	Kirby Crow
Dick D.	Ethan Day	Diana DeRicc
Jason Edding	Theo Fenraven	Angela Fiddler
Dakota Flint	S.J. Frost	Kimberly Gardner
Roland Graeme	Storm Grant	Amber Green
LB Gregg	Drewey Wayne Gunn	Kaje Harper
Jan Irving	David Juhren	Samantha Kane
Kiernan Kelly	M. King	Matthew Lang
J.L. Langley	Josh Lanyon	Anna Lee
Elizabeth Lister	Clare London	William Maltese
Gary Martine	Z.A. Maxfield	Timothy McGivney
Lloyd A. Meeker	Patric Michael	AKM Miles
Reiko Morgan	Jet Mykles	William Neale
Willa Okati	L. Picaro	Neil S. Plakcy
Jordan Castillo Price	Luisa Prieto	Rick R. Reed
A.M. Riley	George Seaton	Jardonn Smith
Caro Soles	JoAnne Soper-Cook	Richard Stevenson
Liz Strange	Marshall Thornton	Lex Valentine
Maggie Veness	Haley Walsh	Missy Welsh
Stevie Woods	Lance Zarimba	

Check out titles, both available and forthcoming, at
www.mlrpress.com

SONS OF
THE WOLF

REIKO MORGAN

mlrpress
www.mlrpress.com

Published by
MLR Press, LLC
3052 Gaines Waterport Rd.
Albion, NY 14411

Visit ManLoveRomance Press, LLC on the Internet:
www.mlrpress.com

Cover Art by Deana C. Jamroz
Editing by Amanda Faris

Print format ISBN# 978-1-60820-389-5
Also available in ebook format ISBN#978-1-60820-390-1

Issued 2011

For Sonya
Who loved Scotland and all things Scottish.
You were loved and you are missed.

Here is a plot with a vengeance...
It seems to me as if a vast, incomprehensible
Power has suddenly, silently begun to weave a net round us...
The beginning of some tragic drama in which we are each forced
By an invisible psychic force to play our respective parts.

The Heart of the Moor, 1914
—Beatrice Chase

ONE

The cruelest lies are often told in silence.
   —Robert Louis Stevenson

It had been an unusually warm day near the end of autumn, one of those days that fool you into believing that changes were farther off than the moment implied, a lull of the senses that caught you unaware. Such days could also be the harbinger of worse things to come. At any rate, that glorious sunny morning he certainly did not consider that his semi-orderly existence was about to dissolve into chaos not entirely of his making.

To Andrew Bainbridge it seemed that most of his life was not of his making. He had set about in his youth like most of the clan did, with a reckless abandon that often courted disaster as much as accolades. He had been a normal boy set loose on unwitting society; an imp of a lad out to terrorize the household with practical jokes and a less than firm upbringing in his early years.

Those days could be forgiven. His doting father had allowed his only son full privileges as only the child of a dead mother could garner, a complete freedom that had translated into the brash, headstrong folly of youth. That initial whirlwind of childhood was barely a memory. It had been replaced with other things. Darker, more oppressive things.

Lord James Wallace Bainbridge, Thirteenth Laird of the Estate and Andrew's doting father, had brought about those changes. Whether he had been aware of the scope of his actions on his then still young and impressionable son, no one dared guess. Maybe there were things at work that even he had never dared imagine. It had descended one dark and stormy night in the middle of winter and after that nothing had ever been the same. The reason why became irrelevant. One simply did not question the Laird.

Andrew's childhood had ended that night. Much of his memory regarding the event was unclear, but he knew one thing; his father had been unable to bear it. In the years that had passed since, Andrew had somehow managed to endure the depth of his father's penance. Its unyielding estrangement had shaped their existence, strangers in a self imposed prison of artificial familiarity borne out of routine.

It was beneath the guise of that familiarity that Andrew had first noticed his father's unusual absence at the hour for tea, an unbroken tradition that the house still clung to amid the disintegration of so many other things. The days of visitors, parties, and far reaching clan gatherings were long gone, banished into the silence of that night along with Andrew's childhood. Yet his father still cultivated the amenities of a Lord, at least in appearance and habit. For him to be absent when the tea was ready for pouring was as glaring an oddity as if he had been doing cartwheels through the main hall.

Knowing his father's habits, Andrew sent the servants off to fetch him from his room, thinking that perhaps he had nodded off while reading. When his discovery was not forthcoming, Andrew sent them off to search the house in earnest, the strange tingle of foreboding he had felt earlier in the day taking on a new urgency at each passing moment of silence. With the tea cold and forgotten, they split up to search the grounds next, each filled with their own dreadful excitement.

Like all major events in his life seemed to operate, it was Andrew's fate to find him. There was no reason for his father to be there, but there he lay, on his back in the center of the old pathway that led from the rear stables through the edge of the nearest woods and out into the meadow. The grass out there was long and golden, whispering in the breeze. It moved with life where his father had not.

Andrew's initial run of discovery turned into a walk of numb shock that took him at last to where his father's body lay in the fading dappled sunshine. He knelt beside the body, reaching out to confirm what he already knew—the need for urgency was gone. He remained kneeling, unaware of the passage of time.

Perhaps his father had been lured out for a walk on such an abnormally warm sunny day. Even with that change in his routine, Andrew still found it odd that he would have taken that particular path. It led to nowhere…and to the one part of the estate that his father had forbidden, the crypts and graves of the ancient family cemetery with its long unused chapel in ruins.

Andrew could see it from where he knelt, its partially tumbled gray stones scattered about on the ground, broken and motionless like his father's body. Hearing his name called brought him from his reverie and he rose to his feet. His eyes caught something stirring the tall grass at the edge of the forest but it quickly faded into the shadows, dark and low to the ground. Then his gaze spied something he had failed to see before, almost beneath his boot. He picked it up.

It was a gold crucifix, lying in the path where it had no doubt fallen from his father's dead fingers. Andrew stared at its simple detailing, nestled in the palm of his hand. His father had never struck him as a religious man. Secretive, unyielding, and reclusive, but not religious. It seemed just another incongruity in a life both strange and short.

He placed the crucifix in his pocket and called out to Duncan, who was coming down the path at a trot. Andrew merely waited, silent and tearless. Once again his life was about to undergo a drastic change with little warning or compromise.

❧ ❧ ❧

The next few days came and went in a blur. The weather turned along with his fortune, bringing a steady rain that rattled off the windowpanes and a bone chilling wind that moaned through the old house like the wail of a banshee. Andrew was mostly oblivious to the comings and goings of the local constabulary, too lost within himself to hear what they had to say. He was, for the first time in long years, directionless.

They said his father must have died of stroke, not unheard of in a man of his middle years. They gave condolences and bemoaned the state of the weather. He shook their hands and nodded. Anything beyond that was out of his control.

A few days later—a week?—he could not say, they buried the dead Laird in the old churchyard of the village, beside the graves of his first and second wives, both dead in their youth. The rain had stopped, but there in the graveyard beside the sea a cold wind lingered, cutting through their overcoats.

No tears fell from Andrew's eyes, standing there, fingering the crucifix in his pocket. Perhaps the shock of finding his father like that had not worn off, but he knew there were other reasons. When had he become such a bitter old man at the age of twenty-eight?

Andrew didn't want to think about what was in the blue painted coffin. Who had chosen blue? Blue, the color of tranquility and innocence. Duncan probably, the man who had taken care of everything beyond Andrew's ability, even the arrangement of the private funeral with its pitiful gathering of mourners. Duncan now stood just behind Andrew's shoulder, appropriately respectful and solicitous.

What possessed Andrew at that moment to glance up at the shadowy woods at the edge of the cemetery was anyone's guess. His heart almost stopped beating. His breath froze in his throat. An empty coldness rushed up into him, taking away the sound of the priest's voice, taking away awareness of anything around him but the coldness and the single spot of blue that dominated the center of his tunnel vision.

It was a strange feeling, like no longer being in his body, tied to skin and bone and earth. Andrew's startled mind simply could not comprehend what his eyes were telling him. Standing there at the edge of the trees was a boy. A young, blond-headed boy of about eight. Who looked exactly like Noah had looked all those years ago, the first day they had ever met as children.

For that instant, that immeasurable moment in time, Andrew's world ceased to move. Then a gust of wind whispered through the distant trees and ruffled the boy's fair hair, hair that faded into nothingness, disappearing along with the figure in the moving breeze.

Blue, the color of the apparition's eyes, filled with sorrow and unknowable things.

Blue. The color of innocence.

The first clump of earth from the priest's hand landed on the lowered coffin with a thud of finality. Andrew felt the wreath of flowers he had been holding fall from his nerveless fingers. He slid to his knees and would have toppled over into the grave if Duncan had not caught him in his silent faint.

Almost a week later, Andrew sat at the desk in his father's study.

The study looked as you would expect such a room to look in a house the size of Bainbridge Hall. It was large and imposing, a room designed to showcase the man who sat at the desk amid the towering twelve-foot bookcases, flanked left and right by heavily draped windows of the same height. The ceiling was ornate plaster from which a single large chandelier hung suspended by heavy chains. Sturdy, uncomfortable chairs faced the desk, made to give no comfort to whomever the Laird and master of the house regarded from across the expanse of wood.

Andrew held the legal document in his hand. It was all there, clearly spelled out in black and white; like anything his father did could ever be explained by words on a page. He looked up at the two men sitting opposite him, his father's attorneys from an Edinburgh firm as irreproachable as it was officious. They were very serious and very accommodating, wondering no doubt how their information might be taken. Beyond them stood Duncan, leaning against a bookcase with his arms crossed over his chest.

"Did you know about this?" Andrew asked, looking over the heads of the lawyers.

Duncan had been his father's butler and manager of the house for over a decade. He had been a father to Andrew more than his own father had been for years. More than a servant and less than family, he resided in the not always comfortable space in between.

"I was never privy to the inner workings of the Laird's mind," Duncan said with ambiguity. "Where Master Noah was concerned there was simply no room for discussion."

Simply no room for discussion. That pretty much summed up his father's view of everything regarding his life and, more especially, that of his sons. While Andrew had no idea how Noah would react to the stunning revelation, he had no doubt about his own reaction; pure rage. For a moment he simply shook from the amount of control it took not to lash out with blinding anger at the others in the room. They were not the object of his black fury.

He dropped the paper on the desk. It was an impressive double secretary desk, its shiny dark surface worn down with age from countless years of use. Its many drawers were stuffed with letters, ledgers, books, and papers from his father and his grandfather's time as Lord of the Estate. The heavy bronze seal, official family symbol of right and privilege, set in its time honored place to his right, used by countless hands in duty to the estate for hundreds of years. At that very desk, in that very room.

"Lord Bainbridge," one of the lawyers said, using Andrew's new title. "This hardly changes anything."

Andrew kicked himself back from the desk with such vehemence that both of the men almost jumped from their seats. He stood slowly, trembling with rage.

"It hardly changes anything?" he repeated in a voice that dripped sarcasm and venom. "You are correct. It will not give either of us back twelve years of our lives. It does not offer a single reason for any of these…these…" He stopped himself, almost apoplectic with rage and grief.

Andrew could still remember the shy little boy peering at him from behind his mother's skirts that first day when Noah and his mother had come to live at the ancient manor house. Andrew accepted his new brother and for a while they enjoyed each other's company, the very picture of an ordinary, happy family. When Noah's mother died in a tragic accident everything changed almost overnight. For reasons of his own, Lord Bainbridge sent Noah away to boarding school and then a special private music school, where the years passed while the boy grew into adulthood. Andrew never understood why his step brother had been sent away, and although he had pressed his father for answers, he never received any that he considered sufficient.

Time passed and their relationship became one of inconvenience, practically strangers. While he imagined that Noah's life had been lonely, his own had faired little better. His father had pushed the both of them away and turned into a recluse of sorts, a haunted secretive man until the day he died. On that day the estate and the title passed down to Andrew, current Lord of Bainbridge Hall.

"Sir, your father's will provides for your brother. If he agrees to the stipulations, I see no—"

Andrew turned on him with a snarl. "My *father* was a cruel, controlling tyrant who liked to play with other people's lives. He liked it so much he is still trying to control things from his grave. He didn't know either of his sons but he made certain that both of our lives have been hell."

The men cringed at his words, refusing to look him in the eye. His father no doubt had paid them more than enough money to keep his secrets all these years. Now the title, the estate, and the secrets were Andrew's.

"Stipulations," Andrew spat, sending the papers flying with a sweep of his hand across the desk. "I know exactly what Noah will say. He will tell you to go hang! Now get out of my sight!"

They scurried to comply without another word, Duncan opening and closing the door with their exit. He remained in the room as Andrew collapsed into his chair with an exhalation of disgust. With the objects of his ire removed, the rage that had crackled through the air moments before faded into depressive silence. Andrew shook his head.

"What happened to us, Duncan?" he asked without expecting an answer. "Where did it all go so wrong?"

"You are not responsible for your father's decisions," Duncan told him. "You are the Laird of the Estate now. Your own decisions will shape your future."

Andrew sighed. Somehow he still doubted that. "I suppose Noah will be getting this filthy thing soon enough."

"The will and its supporting documents have already been dispatched, I believe."

Andrew shook his head again. God, what a way to be told such things. Lawyers really had no idea of the effect of words on people's lives. He could hardly imagine being in Noah's shoes.

"Find out where Noah is, will you, Duncan?"

"What are you going to do, sir?"

"I'm going to ask him to come home, if he wants to. Do you think that selfish of me?"

Duncan's thin lips twitched. "No, sir. I shall set about it, right away. Anything else, sir?"

Andrew looked at him. Impeccably dressed in a dark blue suit with one manicured hand resting on the doorknob, Duncan looked every inch the well trained, reliable butler that he was. His black eyes were unreadable, but the hint of a smile still curled the corner of his mouth.

"Can you stop calling me sir?" Andrew asked with a smile.

Duncan's lips widened only slightly but a spark flashed in the dark eyes. "No, sir," he replied and with a twist of the knob was gone from the room.

The smile slid from Andrew's face as if the muscles were unfamiliar with such an expression. He bent and retrieved the scattered documents from the floor. Alone, he began reading the last wishes—commands—of his father in their entirety, aware that he had already set into motion the very thing that his father had tried to prevent.

TWO

I am not of your element.
   —W. Shakespeare

The charity event was one of the most grand in Tokyo that season, an invitation to be garnered at all cost if one wished to be among the upper crust of the country's elite. Held at the large and impressive Museum of Modern Art at the request of one of the wealthiest families in Japan, it would boast no less than four hundred guests and several of the world's leading performers to entertain them. Food and drink flowed freely amid the chattering voices of high society, the air crackling with the energy of their ambition.

Amid the crowd of finery three event directors scurried about guiding the various parts of the occasion; nonstop delivery of food and drink, containment of the crowds to the areas assigned to them, timing of the auction and the cajoling of bidders, the stroking, dressing, and staging of the various performers. Kabuki was the theme of the night, the stylized form of ancient Japanese theater. Along those lines the performances included colorfully costumed dancers, acrobats, and singers; each coming and going from mezzanine to main level staging area where the orchestra sat ensconced along one side of the huge main rooms.

Costumed servers weaved their way through the gathering, brightly colored kimonos blending perfectly with the array of party dress and the loud primary colors screaming from a great many of the paintings displayed on the large gleaming walls. It was a kaleidoscope for the senses, an orgy of color, taste, and sound that somehow seemed to work, as such a blend of ancient and modern always seemed to go hand in hand in the bustling, sight blowing, mind bending mixture that was Tokyo.

It was a voluptuous scene, that masquerade. At least Edgar Allen Poe had it right, thought Gavin Moore, watching the tumult unfold around him. Mostly it just gave him a headache.

A large flowing red and gold dragon wound through the path, the eight pairs of black clad human legs giving it life on the way to the stage for the next performance. The high soprano notes of an opera singer rang through the open air, managing to overcome the undercurrent hum of voices and activity. At the far edge of the dressing area the staging manager motioned for Gavin's attention, waving his arms and pointing. Gavin got to his feet and walked over to the makeup area where his employer was being transformed for the evening.

Noah Westerhaven was decked out in the most fabulous of costumes, an authentic silk Kabuki ensemble of elaborate embroidered kimono, with long trailing sleeves, worn over a dark tunic and black trousers. A bright red sash encircled his slender waist, bringing out the red, deep blues, and greens of the dragons on the gold background of the kimono. With his feet encased in white tabi socks and high-bridged sandals, he was easily three inches taller than usual, almost Gavin's impressive height. He clacked around in the sandals like he had worn them all his life, testing them out on the hard wood flooring and the interspersed rugs. Satisfied, he sat down in the makeup chair for the dresser to finish his costume.

Gavin watched the process from start to finish, amazed at the transformation. The Kabuki makeup was a covering of thick white foundation over which the character's facial expressions were painted. In this case, Noah was the Demon King from the new opera *The Jade Empress*. His eyebrows were elongated in black paint; the same lined his eyes with deep red eye shadow filled in between, from his eyelashes to the curving sweep of his eyebrows. Two red lines spanned the narrow vertical bridge of his nose and his lips were painted black and gold. The lip paint was in need of constant retouching as he kept marring its line by drinking from a water bottle, irritating the makeup artist.

Gavin reached over and did what the makeup artist could not, took the bottle from Noah's hand and sat it down out of his reach. Meeting Gavin's gaze, Noah stuck out his tongue, the action changing the makeup into an evil grimace.

"Your time is almost up," Gavin told him. "Sit still and let him finish."

They had braided part of Noah's long silver hair with red and black silk cording, and now looped it with red and black lacquered picks to hold it and a small black silk cap in place. The artist retouched his lips with gold and stepped back to admire his handiwork. The overall image was both terrifying and physically stunning. Gavin thought Noah looked even more exotic than usual.

"Wow," Gavin told him. "You look...beautiful."

Noah laughed, getting to his feet. "I think it's supposed to be scary."

"Yeah, maybe that too. Sure you can walk in those things?" Gavin asked, indicating the elevated Japanese sandals.

To prove the point Noah demonstrated, even managing an odd looking pirouette. Down the corridor two Geisha in expensive antique kimonos watched him, giggling appreciatively from behind their fans. Noah, who had been chatting with them earlier, bowed in their direction and reached to take his violin from Gavin.

"First time I've come close to your eye level," Noah said, flexing his fingers. "I could get used to it."

"I'd say break a leg but I'm afraid you might. You should braid your hair for the next album cover," Gavin said off hand. "This could be a good look for you."

Noah just looked at him with those wildly painted eyes. Gavin laughed and took Noah by the arm to help him negotiate the distance down the sloping, curving walkway leading to the performance stage below. It was a lot trickier than it seemed and once or twice Noah would have gone sprawling had it not been for Gavin's strong arm. When they finally arrived at the set up curtained area, Noah took a deep breath and let it out with an explosive sigh.

"I have a new respect for these shoes," he grumbled. "Thank you."

"Told you so," Gavin said. He knelt to rearrange the long tunic and flowing lines of the kimono. Then he stepped back to watch Noah prepare for his performance.

Noah did the same thing every time. He brought the violin to his shoulder and gently plucked the strings to make sure that it was still tuned to his liking, having tuned it himself only an hour earlier. Then he lowered it into the crook of his arm at his waist while he stood with his head lowered and the bow in his opposite hand held straight down by his side.

To Gavin it always looked as if he were praying. Noah lifted his head and waited, like a knight holding helmet and sword, until it was his time to take the stage. It was odd to see him standing there in that colorful garb, holding the bow instead of a sword.

The stage had been set, lights fully blazing on the seated orchestra as the singer finished and the audience applauded with pleasure. Noah stood waiting in the wings, a slight, unmoving figure in the shadows. The sounds of an eagerly waiting audience murmured in the lull of his introduction; he was the reason for their anticipation. Walking out into the warmth of their adoration he stood alone in the front center of the stage, his mere presence enough for them to hold their collective breath as they waited for him to begin.

Noah should have been used to it by now, but that moment, that shimmering silent gathering of energy, always terrified him. He did not look out at their shadowy faces but held the instrument at the ready, bow poised in the air like a sword. They waited with him for that first blow, a hushed and straining impatience that brought its own expectation of terror. The moment teetered on the edge of the abyss…and then came to life on its own, a sweeping building crescendo of light and color and sound that filled the slender form with the illusion of another life as it spilled from him into the night.

They knew it would always be so. He played with his soul in the strings, the music rising up through his blood and flesh so that he and the instrument were of one mind and one heart, each indistinguishable from the other for those moments of magic. That such passion could pour forth from one so young was always a shock. His long silver hair flew about his slender shoulders in motion to the exalted life of the music, the light glinting off the sweat of his brow as every cell of his body transcended the mortal world and dared to reach the sublime.

The piece, so difficult for others, seemed to flow from him like the air he breathed, rising and falling with his heartbeat. He played that night without once opening his eyes, afraid perhaps of what he might see if he did so. If the crowd breathed, they never knew it and if he was never aware of their existence, they forgave him.

Then as Gavin watched, something strange happened. Noah did something he had never done before once he was on stage. Noah's blue gaze swept in his direction, just one glance, barely a second in duration. Gavin's heart froze in his throat at what he thought he glimpsed in that alien painted face. He had seen that look only a few occasions before during his time with Noah. It was always bad.

When the music ended abruptly, the audience sat spell bound in a long moment of protracted silence, realizing at last that something unplanned had happened while they were holding their breath. Slowly, like a puppet whose master had merely put down the strings after the performance, Noah folded up at the knees and simply collapsed with a crash in the middle of the stage, his long silver hair and red ribbons flowing out around him like water and blood.

❧ ❧ ❧

When Gavin came into the room three days later, Noah was sitting on the cushioned window seat of their hotel suite, barely home from hospital. It was raining outside, a seemingly constant drizzle that permeated the city with gloom. It had been raining that night too, the night they had taken him from the museum by ambulance. He did not look up at Gavin's entrance but remained staring out through the dark, mirroring window with his knees drawn up to his chin and his long arms circled around his legs.

He had been unconscious for over a day, lying in his hospital bed like a ghost. When he awoke he said nothing, refusing to answer questions put to him by the doctors and when they had done every test they could think to do, they had released him. Gavin brought him back to their hotel just that afternoon, fed him and tried to make him lie down. Noah still looked like a ghost, dressed in black pajama bottoms and a black T-shirt beneath a turquoise blue and black kimono. His right wrist was in a splint, hospital bandages still covering the needle marks in the crook of his left elbow and the back of his hand.

Noah William Westerhaven. At least that was the name that Gavin knew.

The papers he now held in his hand told him otherwise, and came as something of a shock. Gavin had been Noah's personal assistant for four years. He thought nothing about the twenty-two-year-old virtuoso could surprise him, but this did. While Gavin stood there, wondering how to convey his thoughts, the bright eyes of his employer turned and looked straight at him, scoring him to the spot where he stood.

Noah William *Bainbridge* was a study in contrast. He was the newest reigning star of the classical stage, a violin virtuoso whose young talent had catapulted him into the stratosphere at the age of fourteen and held him there still.

Gavin knew from first-hand experience that Noah's attitudes and eccentricities were often misinterpreted by his fellow musicians. He rarely attended society parties and he shunned the press like the plague. He preferred to spend his time working, either with the symphonies that begged him for appearances or long hours at his own practice. Noah did what he wanted to do and let things sort themselves out. So far that had seemed to work in his favor.

Gavin would be the first to admit his looks went a long way in his favor too. Noah came about his good looks naturally, in no way arrogant or even conscious of his appearance. Slender to the point of girlishness, Noah seemed even younger than his twenty-two years. His was handsome, even beautiful, and wore his silver-blond hair long, a curtain of silk that whipped around his face as he played. It was an effective prop, his calling card, like the silk suits with oriental collars he now wore at every performance. The body beneath those suits was whipcord taunt, muscles honed by yoga and Tai Chi.

He was reserved but his aloofness was not conceit. His manner was gentle but he was not soft. When the music transformed him on stage, he was nothing less than magic. Women and men fell over themselves just to get a glimpse of him yet Noah remained an enigma. His eyes were perhaps the most magical thing about him; blue, the azure blue of a Norwegian ocean. Deep, filled with undercurrents and mystery.

Those eyes were burning a hole through Gavin while he stood there staring back in silence.

"I don't believe it," Gavin finally said in a tone of awe. "I don't believe it."

Noah looked away from his assistant and sighed. Since getting out of the hospital, he had already been threatened, cajoled, brow beaten, mollified, and ordered about. Now he was simply tired, too tired to deal with Gavin's constant energy and overprotective concern.

"What don't you believe, Gav?" he asked in a mumble.

"That you knew," Gavin said. "You already knew your father was dead."

Noah frowned but then again he should have expected something to arrive announcing his step father's death. Even away from England such news would manage to locate him. He knew it, yet hearing it stated aloud seemed different somehow, more permanent, actually real.

How Noah knew it came as something of a shock, even to himself. After all the years and all the miles, for it to resurface at that moment had been almost too much to bear. When had he come to think he was immune, walled off from his strange history and his perceived personal curse? It was a lie. Most things about him were lies. It was his particular weakness, an aberration he tried to keep hidden, even from himself. It crept out at the most inopportune times and sometimes it simply slammed into him with force like it had that night on stage with a crash of horror and the sudden, immutable knowledge that his father was dead.

Whatever it was—that flash of teeth and fur—the image had almost knocked him down on stage. It had come crashing into him with the unmistakable awareness of his father, as shocking and breathtaking as it was terrifying. As the wave of darkness struck him in the middle of the stage, there had been little Noah could do about it. In the aftermath of such a powerful revelation he was always left feeling empty and exhausted, less able to focus.

He looked at Gavin, who had been with him for years now, solid and trustworthy. He counted on Gavin for so many things, not the least of all discretion. Many times his assistant had rescued him from despondency by sheer force of his presence, an insatiable energy for life and living. Gavin put up with his idiosyncrasies, shared his love of music, and had a brilliant mind beneath his cultivated scorn at most things he considered hypocrisy.

Noah had learned when to trust Gavin's advice regarding his career, and Gavin knew when to offer it and when to be silent. His intuition, like his quick acerbic tongue, could cut through almost anything. Noah and Gavin shared other things too, like a parentless childhood directed at the whims of others and a distinct distrust of the outside world. They simply hid their similar wounds with different camouflage; one with biting sarcasm and the other with retreat into a more controllable world of his own making.

At least Noah had thought he exercised some control over it.

Looking now into Gavin's dark open gaze, he wondered if that were true. And he wondered why he could not share with Gavin this thing that he was sure Gavin already suspected, the gaping flaw in his person, the terrible secret that haunted his life and now sat between them unspoken like a traitorous lie.

Because Noah could not. Unwanted, uncontrollable, his psychic nature was his personal terror, his private unseen mark of Cain. He had lived with it all his life but he had never shared it with anyone. Fear also held his tongue, fear of derision and yes, even from Gavin who knew him so well and whom he trusted with his life, fear of abandonment. So he chose yet again to suffer in silence.

Gavin saw all those things in the eyes of his young employer and because he understood that terror when he recognized it, Gavin allowed the secret to remain unspoken. He had seen that *look* and its consequences too many times now not to understand its implications.

"You never told me that your name is Bainbridge," Gavin said smoothly.

Relief flooded Noah's face. "It was my step father's name, not mine."

"I guess you guys didn't get along or something," Gavin continued softly.

Noah made a small sound of derision and angled his face toward the window. The curtain of pale hair slid over his shoulder to conceal his expression.

"Something like that."

"I'm sorry, Noah. I didn't know about your father. You've never spoken of him."

"It's okay, Gavin. Not many people knew." He had almost forgotten himself. Apparently someone had taken the trouble to locate him with the news. He looked up. "Did the attorney send his obituary? Is that what you have in your hand? Read it, please."

Gavin had forgotten the outrageous letter he held in his hand. He took the glasses from where he had shoved them to the top of his forehead and put them back on his nose, holding the papers in front of his face. He had a nice face, high cheekbones and a straight nose beneath dark brown hair. The glasses were for reading only, especially the tiny lines of contracts that were part of his job.

"'Mr. Noah William Westerhaven *Bainbridge*,'" he read aloud, emphasizing the name. "'We regretfully inform you of the untimely death of Laird James Wallace Bainbridge, Keeper of the County MacLearen, and your Esteemed and Honored Father. To you, the younger son, we offer our deepest condolences and respect. The Laird, your father, has made provision on your behalf with his final words and dispense. We would like at this time to offer any services we might render on your behalf with probation of the Laird's final Will and Testament which will be rendered in full by special courier to the place of your permanent address within a week of the dispatch of this letter. Until such notice, let us assure you that your Rights and Property will remain inviolate and under Trust of the Sovereign Laws of Scotland. May the Almighty grant us Peace and Wisdom.' Your servant, blah, blah, blah Esquire. What a way to talk."

Gavin looked over his glasses at Noah's shocked face and felt immediately like a heel. It only then occurred to him that when you were rich, death meant wills and while he had no idea of Noah's family history, he had apparently had a father at one point. A wealthy, *titled* father.

"Noah, I'm sorry, I didn't think…"

Noah unfolded himself from the window seat and reached to take the papers from Gavin's hand. He was trembling as he scanned the lines of the letter, printed on crisp white linen with the heading of the legal firm in bold black and gold lettering.

"God, I'm an idiot," Gavin berated himself. "I was so surprised that I didn't even… I'm sorry, Noah. Please, sit down."

Noah allowed himself to be ushered to the sofa. He sat down, holding the papers but no longer looking at them. Gavin very gently eased them out of his clutching fingers and put them down on the table beside him. Noah did not hear what Gavin said until he felt the glass in his hand and Gavin's warm fingers curled around his.

"Drink this," Gavin ordered, alarmed at Noah's white, expressionless face.

Noah did as directed even though his hands shook. He swallowed and coughed, the brandy scorching down the back of his throat. He did not usually drink alcohol, but the amber liquid seemed to bring some life back into his dim thoughts. He looked across into Gavin's worried dark eyes.

"Thank you," he said. "I'm okay now."

Gavin had his doubts. He took the glass and placed it on the table with the papers that had precipitated the whole scene. He simply sat where he was on the floor in front of Noah, his legs tucked beneath him.

"You weren't expecting to be in his will," Gavin surmised from the reaction and the open shock on Noah's young face.

It *was* as a shock. After so many years Noah had had no idea his stepfather even knew where he was. To be considered in his will was…it had to be a mistake.

"I don't understand. We have not spoken for years, most of my life."

"But you *are* in his will. *Lord* Bainbridge."

Noah recognized the tone of surprise and disdain. Gavin, for all of his forays into the circle of high society and his acceptance of the perks of such a life, still viewed the titled elite with something less than hospitality. The idea that his employer might be one of the perceived enemy gave him pause.

"That will be my step brother's title now, not mine."

"And a brother too," Gavin said thoughtfully. "I find it hard to believe you are the black sheep of the family. I bet whatever you get will buy a lot of white wash."

Noah laughed slightly. "I wonder if that is how Andrew will see it."

"Andrew is your step brother? I recognize that name. He phones or writes every now and then, doesn't he?"

"The only one, for twelve years now." Even though it had been more than two years since they had last spoken.

"Twelve years?" Gavin repeated in amazement. "Wow. What happened?"

Noah shook his head. "I don't know. I don't remember much about...it was a long time ago. My mother died not long after we went to live there, at the estate in Scotland. After that Andrew's father sent me away to school and I never went back."

"It's Scotland," Gavin said with a shrug. "What's to miss?" He knew of course. Family. Roots. Belonging. He understood the same feelings for the same reasons. "I guess your step father regretted what he had done. Enough money will cover a lot of guilt."

But it was only money. Noah made upwards to a million pounds a year and he was just getting started along a lifetime of possibilities. He had not expected anything from his estranged family. At least his conscience was clear.

"Did Andrew send a letter? Anything?"

That question alone let Gavin know that the money meant nothing and that the twelve year banishment had left its secret, hidden wound. Something else occurred to him as he sat there looking at the naked emotion on his young employer's face. He had accepted the fact that Noah knew about his step father's death at the moment it happened, three nights ago when he had collapsed on stage. Noah simply *knew*. The years and the miles made no difference.

"No," was all Gavin said in reply. "I'm surprised the lawyers even found you this soon, this far away. He must be doing a million things, Noah." *Like counting his money*, he thought darkly and then felt shame at the thought. "I'm sure he will call when he has a moment."

Noah sighed and rubbed his forehead with the back of his splinted wrist. He didn't need to worry over such things when Gavin was perfectly capable of taking care of it. They would be awhile yet in Japan, two more concerts and several appearances within the next two weeks.

"I'm going to lie down for awhile," he said. "Wake me in a couple of hours."

"You should cancel the rest of the tour," Gavin said again. They had already had the same argument at the hospital yesterday. "Your wrist is injured and you are obviously exhausted."

"It's my bow hand and it's fine."

"No one will hold it against you once they know your father has died."

"No one is going to know, Gavin," Noah ordered, getting to his feet. "You are not going to tell them."

Gavin also rose, watching Noah remove the splint from his wrist to prove his stubborn point. Noah allowed him a wide leeway in regards to doing his job, but he understood without being told that crossing certain lines would not be tolerated. Opening the legal envelope clearly marked "Private and Personal" was not an issue. Prying open Noah's past or trying to tell him what to do, was. Noah was very much in charge of his own life and career, yet when he turned to leave the room, Gavin took a breath and dove in anyway.

"Don't you think you should take some time and get through this?" he asked, taking the splint Noah shoved at him. "You aren't in any condition—"

Noah wheeled on his heel, his silver hair and untied kimono sweeping out around him from the force of his turn. "How much time do you think, Gav?" he snapped back. "Twelve years not long enough for you?"

"Sure, it's long enough," Gavin admitted darkly. "But a lifetime is longer. Sometimes you have to stop running from things long enough to actually look at what's chasing you."

Noah blinked. Something in that simple choice of words triggered a long repressed memory, or the shadow of one anyway. It rose up within him like a crashing wave and knocked him senseless, catapulting him into freefall. He recognized the initial shift in his awareness but this time was different; it came from within himself as much as from without. The crack in his psyche shattered into a million bits of color and he fell into it, able to go only where it took him, like a twig in a roaring river.

Gavin jumped to catch Noah when he toppled over like a sapling in the wind. He went down on one knee with Noah's unconscious body cradled against his chest. He had watched that incredible change in expression with horror, knowing it now for what it was, not just some kind of spell but a trance, an enchantment.

Beneath the silken robe Noah's arms felt like ice. Gavin pushed the inert form up on its knees long enough to readjust his grip and stagger to his feet with Noah in his arms. He walked straight to the bedroom and eased the unconscious man down on the bed.

Sitting there in the dim light with Noah's cold hand in his, Gavin did not know what to do. Those blue eyes were open but what they saw Gavin could not begin to comprehend. He knew enough to realize that this time was different from the usual spells he had witnessed in the past, something more like the incident a few nights ago. If he were to believe that, it could go on for hours yet, even days for all he knew. The thought of that terrified him. His heart was pounding so hard in his chest that he could see the edge of Noah's robe tremble with every beat.

What could he do? He was as useless as the doctors at the hospital. Their diagnosis had been emotional exhaustion, the splint on the sprained wrist the extent of their expertise. They had sent Noah home with a bottle of blue pills that he had promptly dumped down the toilet. The only thing Gavin could do was keep him warm and wait for the attack to pass.

He rose to fetch some blankets. Noah's hand reached out and grabbed him around the wrist, so startling him that he gave a little bleat of fright. He turned and looked down at the figure on the bed.

Noah's eyes were closed now but that did not make the episode any less horrific. The fingers clamped around Gavin's wrist were biting into his flesh with icy force. His hair stood on end at the eerie sound that issued from Noah's lips, a sound that he hoped to never hear again from any living creature.

"Noah!" Gavin exclaimed, again sitting on the edge of the bed and placing his free hand over the icy fingers. "Noah, you're safe, do you hear me? I'm here. You are all right."

Was he all right? Noah was unsure where he was, at the mercy of whatever power had held him in its grasp. Without Gavin's warm, living energy to anchor him in his body, Noah had no idea what might have happened. There was no knowing how long the episode had lasted, only how much it terrified him. He was afraid to open his eyes and risk seeing the horror he heard in Gavin's voice reflected on his face. He gasped when Gavin's trembling hand passed across his forehead.

"Whatever you saw, Noah," Gavin told him quietly. "It can't harm you. I'm here with you. I promise nothing will hurt you."

Noah opened his eyes. He was in his hotel bedroom. Gavin was sitting right beside him, holding his hand. Steady, dependable Gavin, his eyes still glittering with fear in the dim light, shook up for probably the first time in his life.

"I'm sorry," Noah whispered.

With an inarticulate sound of agonized relief, Gavin pulled Noah into his embrace and held him there, pressed against his pounding heart. He almost groaned out loud when Noah's hands slid up his back. The rush of heat over his skin made him momentarily self-conscious, aware of his reaction to Noah's touch.

Gavin shuddered. He had realized only recently that he was in love with Noah, had been in love with him since their first meeting all that time ago. His emotions were a living, breathing thing that sat in his heart like a dragon, slowly devouring him, but Gavin could not risk his professional relationship with Noah to admit those feelings. They trusted each other, but trust was a delicate thing, easily damaged without intention.

So Gavin swallowed his desire, unable to say the three little words that would change their relationship forever. Now he would simply have to live with it, no matter how much it might crush him in silence. His suffering would be worth it, if only he could save Noah from himself, from a perceived world without love or trust.

"Can you tell me what happened?" Gavin finally asked in a hushed voice.

Noah shook his head. Gavin's familiar aura enveloped him; he could smell the scent of Gavin's skin. It felt good to be held by a warm, living body. After a moment, Gavin shifted, his hand rising to gently stroke Noah's hair. Noah sighed at the comforting gesture, actually allowing his muscles to relax against Gavin's hot, solid body. Slowly the horror he had felt eased away, cell by cell.

"Do you *know* what happened?" Gavin asked in the silence.

No reply at all that time, simply flexing of arms. Gavin nodded and moved his hand back to Noah's shoulder. He could understand the reluctance to share such things.

"I'm sorry, Noah, I didn't really understand until now. You don't have to keep things from me. You don't have to live with this kind of thing alone. Do you hear me?"

Noah squeezed his eyes shut and nodded. "You can let go of me now, Gavin."

Gavin gave a short snort of a laugh. "You think so? Maybe you are the one holding me up. You gave me quite a fright."

"Sorry," Noah apologized then giggled in Gavin's ear. "You should have seen your face."

"You should have seen yours," Gavin told him seriously. "Lie down."

Noah released Gavin and did as he was told, stretching back out on the bed. He lay there silently while Gavin disappeared into the front room and returned holding the wrist brace. Noah merely held up his arm and allowed Gavin to put the thing on his hand. With that done, Gavin took both of Noah's hands and crossed them over his waist, reaching across to pull the bedspread up over his body.

"Try to get some sleep. I have a lot of phone calls to make and then we are packing."

Noah said nothing. He knew Gavin was going to cancel all of his performance dates out until who knew when. Just as well. There was no way he could risk another public display so soon after the one at the charity event. People would talk.

Gavin was right about other things too; his troubled past was coming back into focus, whether Noah wanted it to or not. His step father's death made it inevitable. There was only one thing to do about whatever lurked in the unknown shadows of his mind.

Stop running and let it catch him.

❦ ❦ ❦

They had been back in London for three days. Those three days were filled with some sense of normalcy within the familiar walls of Noah's spacious park-side flat they called home when he was not travelling for various performances. It was modern and comfortable, an eclectic combination of furnishings and art. A piano graced the corner of the open living area, there to provide accompaniment whenever Noah practiced with fellow musicians. The main instrument of his livelihood currently sat in its open case on the top of the piano; his treasured violin.

Gavin went about making tea without really paying attention to what he was doing. Tea was a habit about which Noah was *most* English; he liked his afternoon tea hot and dark, served with tiny sandwiches and biscuits. It was also a necessary meal, especially on performance nights where often it would be close to midnight before they had a chance for dinner. The life of a performer was not all glamour. It often came with heavy sacrifices, including odd hours and long stretches away from home. A few routines were necessary comforts amid a life in constant motion.

Another of Noah's routines was underway in the room beyond Gavin's activity in the kitchen. The yoga instructor had toned down the usual practice in deference to her pupil's wrist injury, but even then Gavin was amazed at the contortions they managed to hold. His muscles ached in response to the sight of slender twisted limbs and taut stomachs, teacher and student in silent mirror image.

His own method of exercise was a more common touch; he jogged through the park during the early morning hour and occasionally did some kickboxing at the gym when he had the time. While he had at first sneered at Noah's far eastern approach, he now knew that although the younger man was smaller in stature and slight in build, he was by no means soft. Those long, lean muscles were honed to perfection, perfectly capable of self defense or keeping up with anything Gavin could manage.

Gavin put the loose tea and steaming water into the teapot, leaving it on the bar to steep while he finished laying out the items on the tray. His gaze once again crept up from what he was doing to look at the large legal envelope sitting on the counter in front of him. The thing practically demanded his attention, announcing its importance with its red and black striped exterior securely holding the secret documents within. Gavin knew—more or less—what it contained, having expected it for days and having signed for it before taking it from the courier almost an hour ago.

That did not lessen its obsessive hold on him. Because of that burning curiosity he had not opened the thing. It sat there mocking him.

Annoyed at his own unrepentant snooping and that fact that Noah was taking longer with his workout than usual, Gavin carried the tray to the coffee table in the living area beyond. Right on cue the yoga teacher came through the door with her bag in her hand and her black ponytail swinging, in an excessively good mood for having undergone an hour of torture.

"Hi ya, Gav," she called, heading for the front door and her next flexible client. "I'd stay for tea but I'm late. Keep Noah from using that hand for a while yet, eh? See ya!"

Gavin barely had a second to wave goodbye but that was how Evie was, a charged bit of girl somewhat like a lightning rod. He wondered how on earth she stopped that effervescence long enough to practice yoga, a slow and supposedly calming technique. It certainly never seemed to slow her down.

Noah followed in her wake, toweling off his damp face and arms, his hair too in a ponytail. He came over to the tea service and plopped down in the oversized fabric arm chair instead of the suede sofa, dropping the towel on the floor. He put his head back with a groan.

"God, I thought she was going to kill me."

"That's what it always looks like to me," Gavin said while he poured tea. "I thought she was going easy on you today."

Noah reached for the offered cup of tea. "Easy? I don't think Evie knows the meaning of the word. There are a few others she doesn't know, like 'that hurts,' 'I can't do that,' and 'can we stop now?'"

Gavin laughed, taking his cup and sinking down onto the sofa. "You wouldn't do it if you didn't like it. Nothing like being tortured by a cute young thing in the privacy of your own home."

"Unless of course you are the one being paid to do the torturing."

They laughed together, at ease with each other's company. It was the uncomplicated everyday things that seemed to ease the memory of their hurried flight from Japan and the reasons for it. Yet as they went about eating, drinking and talking about nothing, Gavin knew that the big padded envelope and the information it contained would tarnish their efforts. With that in mind, he waited until Noah was almost finished before getting to his feet to fetch the dreaded thing from the kitchen counter.

The moment Noah saw it, slowly proffered unopened in Gavin's hand, he put down his tea cup and sat straighter in his chair. The fact that his assistant had left it unopened was a statement in itself. He sat chewing his lip, staring at it. He could ignore his past and go on with his life in its strange state of disequilibrium…or he could face the truth—whatever it was— and try to find a way to live with it honestly. Gavin was right; the past could not hurt him anymore.

Noah took the envelope. It was heavier than he anticipated, whether that was a good or bad thing remained to be seen. Gavin turned to leave.

"No," Noah called out, stopping him. "No, you don't have to go."

"Noah, if you'd rather…"

Noah shook his head. "It doesn't matter, Gav. Whatever it says about my past, it's my *past*, ancient history. I can't imagine what my step father would have left for me. Even if he did mention me, it doesn't mean anything."

Gavin sat down. Those were big words but he could already see that splinted hand trembling. All of a sudden his curiosity was gone. He would rather see the thing thrown away, its secrets unknown, than to witness what it might do to his friend, but the choice was not his.

Noah pulled the zip cord that opened the package with a hollow echoing rip. Three things spilled out into his hand; two letter sized envelopes, each with a description written in flowing cursive hand, and one larger, almost square envelope with no label at all. Noah stared at them as if trying to decide which one to open first. He opted for the one marked *Will and Testament*, placing the other two on the table in front of him.

The document was several sheets of parchment paper that crackled with import when he unfolded them. While Noah read, Gavin watched his eyes get larger and larger in his white face. So much for it not meaning anything. Even expecting it, knowing he was mentioned in the will, it was clearly a shock. Unable to speak, Noah simply handed the document over to Gavin.

Yanking his glasses from where he kept them hooked over his shirt collar, Gavin took the sheets like being handed a particularly loathsome piece of trash and scanned the legal mumbo jumbo with expertise. His eyebrows rose so high that they almost disappeared into his hair. He looked over the edge of his glasses at Noah.

"This says he is leaving you half of everything," he said in disbelief, looking back down to find the unbelievable paragraph and reading it aloud. "'To my younger son, upon my death I bestow one half the sum of all my private accounts, subsequent business holdings, investments and property, with the exception of the inherited family Title and the residence known as Bainbridge Hall, its contents and its contingent land holdings in Trust. These aforementioned cash and properties, after proper accounting and sale if necessary, shall come to an amount somewhere between three and four million pounds sterling.'"

Gavin frowned at the next set of instructions.

"'This amount I do bequeath, without prejudice or malice, with only one governing stipulation; that from this day forward, Noah Bainbridge, my younger son, shall never again set foot on the property known as Bainbridge Hall, neither for the purpose of residence nor for any other reason, including dispensation of this Will. For him to do so will represent a flagrant disregard for his Father's wishes and will cause the immediate withdrawal in the aforementioned bequest and constitute the voiding herein of his right to claim any portion of My Estate.'"

Gavin stopped and stared across at Noah's ashen face. It was an unexpectedly large amount of money attached to an unimaginable command. But that was not what held Noah's attention with horror. He had opened the second letter and held the single sheet of paper in his hands. Gavin's heart plummeted into his stomach.

"What is it?"

Noah stared at the paper with tears rolling down his face. How could such a thing be possible and why would his father— *his father*—have done such a thing to him? He heard Gavin's voice rising with worried concern and looked up. His hands were shaking so hard that he could hear the sound of the paper rattling, or maybe it was his bones.

"He is not my *step* father," Noah exclaimed in a voice that shook. "He is my...*was* my *real* father. How can that be? How could he do this to us, to Andrew?"

Gavin jumped to his feet and took the paper from Noah's wavering hands. Noah leaned back into the chair with his hands over his face in distress and disbelief. Alarmed at the reaction, Gavin had no idea what Noah was trying to tell him. He scanned the odd looking document with growing comprehension.

"Why would he have done this?" Noah cried out. "How is it even possible? Poor Andrew. What must he think?"

Gavin was slowly putting it together. Andrew and Noah were really *half* brothers. However shocking it was to Noah, it was true. The legal firm had the proof to back it up; Gavin was holding the cruel damning truth in his hand.

What a thing to tell someone without any preparation! And to do it after a promise of an inheritance where you could get the money but never again see your brother or your ancestral home if you wanted to keep it. It was controlling and vindictive and evil. Had Bainbridge just been a crazy old man? Did he enjoy terrorizing both of his sons? That was certainly what he had ended up doing, was still doing as only the long arms of the rich could.

A flash of distrust went through Gavin's mind. Did Andrew perhaps know the reason? He had certainly been an older child when Noah's mother died and Noah was banished from the estate. He had remained silent all those years while his father was still alive. Had he been threatened with disinheritance, warned to keep his distance from his only brother? It made no sense and they were going to get no answers from lawyers.

"Noah, I…I'm sorry."

Gavin sank down again onto the sofa, at a loss for words. What could he say that would change the horror that Noah clearly felt, the shock of it all? Nothing. The only thing worse than believing you had no family at all was finding out that the family you wanted with all your heart did not want you.

Noah took his hands from his face. "Poor Andrew, my *brother*, Andrew."

Gavin ground his teeth together to keep from saying what

was on his tongue. It was just like Noah to think of others before himself, even then. Dear half brother Andrew had managed to keep his distance, leaving lawyers—strangers—to deliver such shattering news instead of offering it himself. He had made no effort to ease his brother's torment over the years. He had the title and the estate. Gavin was almost certain that poor brother Andrew was beside himself that half of the money was gone, handed over to the young half brother he barely knew.

"What are you thinking, Noah?" he asked, watching the grief stricken mask of a face.

Noah shook his head. His brain was numb. He had always thought of Andrew as his brother so the news of a blood link between them changed nothing. He had long ago been banished from the estate, cut out of their lives as if he had never existed, so why had his father found it necessary to *emphasize* the fact after all those years? And why would he offer half of Andrew's inheritance to ensure that banishment?

In all of that twisted, curious scheming by a man he barely remembered—his *father*—the most devastating fact of all was that his *mother* had told him lies. That cut Noah to the quick, sucked out his breath, tore the shallow bleeding wounds of his soul wide open.

"I'm too numb to think," he said with a voice that sounded dead to his ears.

"Let me check into this," Gavin offered, the only thing he could do. "There has to be more to all of this…scheming."

"Leave Andrew out of this," Noah said, knowing Gavin's thought processes. "He didn't know about any of this."

"How do you know that, Noah?"

Noah sighed, a sound of infinite weariness. "We might as well look at the last envelope," he said, seeing its unmarked surface lying amid the tea items on the table where he had placed it. "Maybe it's a letter from Andrew."

Somehow Gavin thought not. He sat silent as Noah picked up the smaller tan envelope and pushed up the metal tabs of the clasp holding it shut. The contents spilled out into Noah's waiting palm, caught between his thumb and fingers.

They were photographs. A collection of ten to fifteen photographs, some in color, some black and white. An assortment of memories that Noah had long since forgotten, of a family to which he had never really belonged, in a childhood that was based on deception and abandonment. It was his face staring up at him from those photographs; a young face caught in an unguarded moment of happiness that would soon be gone forever, the face of a stranger to the skin he now occupied in the adult version of that innocence.

Catching his breath in a sob, Noah dropped the photographs from his nerveless fingers, scattering them on the floor. The wave of grief, free from the corner of his mind where he kept it contained, was crushing him. He vaulted to his feet, unable to face himself, and fled from the room while he could still manage to move at all, fled from their immovable expressions, faces frozen in time.

Horrified to see Noah tear from the room in an incoherent stumble, Gavin jumped to his feet, the photographs raining down onto the floor like shrapnel from landmines. The loud gasping sobs nearly wrenched his heart from his chest. Without thinking, afraid for Noah's state of mind, Gavin followed.

The trail of discarded clothing never registered to his brain; he was merely responding to the sound of wretched anguish. By the time he had crossed through the large bedroom and reached the wide open doorway to the luxurious bath, the sound of the roaring shower penetrated his mind. He stopped at the muted sound of desperate weeping, blinking his eyes to bring his thoughts back into focus.

Noah had retreated to the shower. He stood with his hands flat on the wall as if to hold himself up beneath the deluge of thundering spray. His dripping head was bowed low with the weight of his grief, the silver hair a curtain hiding his despair. He was at the mercy of his shadowed memories, devastated by a truth that was far more bitter than the lie he had believed for his entire life. The anguish poured out of him like the water running over his naked skin, wild and uncontrollable.

With his breath stuck in his throat, Gavin slowly backed out of the doorway and retreated from the moment; some revelations were too personal and too intimate to witness, much less to share. He closed the bedroom door behind him. Standing with his hand on the doorknob, he gazed out into the room beyond where the fallen photographs lay like pieces of Noah's shattered life. Gavin let his breath out in a rattling sigh. Tea was simply not going to be enough if they had to go back into that room and face those ghosts.

Gavin went straight to the cabinet under the kitchen counter where he kept the liquor and yanked out the bottle of Irish whiskey, sloshing some of its amber contents into a glass and swallowing it in one gulp. It burned its way down his throat and when it hit his stomach it hurt. He was shaking. He poured himself another one and downed it just as fast. Then he went through the automatic motions of making coffee before he walked back out into the mind field.

In some weird sense of irony most of the photographs had landed face down on the rug, their secrets yet waiting to be unveiled with individual impact. He ignored them, picking up cups, plates, and napkins and dumped everything they had scattered about during tea back onto the tray. The red and black striped courier packet that had precipitated the whole mess went with the tray into the kitchen, out of sight for the moment, its damage done. That accomplished, Gavin set his jaw and returned to the task at hand.

The photographs were not what he expected. As he picked them up one at a time to view their mute faces, the horror of their silent revelation began to take a hold over him. They were family photos, what most people would consider harmless enough. Simple family photos of an ordinary sort, some posed and some not, taken over what Gavin knew had to be a short period of time. What made them so devastating was their normality, the run-of-the-mill family caught with the lens of the camera, single bits of their lives forever frozen against the wheel of time.

Noah was easy to recognize; the same bright white hair and large blue eyes Gavin knew were looking up at him from the glossy paper. The family—and they had *looked* like a family then—was easy enough to identify but harder to comprehend.

Noah looked like his mother, an exact copy in masculine form; same soft silver-white hair and blue eyes, same slender figure with pale skin and long limbs. To see her young face in the adult face of her son was something of a shock. There was a photo of them sitting together on the lawn, young Noah in her embrace with their faces turned partially away from the camera. It was a moment caught unawares, mother and son, their bright heads close together. Looking at it made Gavin's chest constrict.

The other photos were equally hard to look at. Andrew and his father were just as ordinary in all of them. There was one of the two boys together, obviously caught in a moment of play with the older brother holding down the younger; Noah's mouth was open with laughter, his face glowing with happiness while an equally laughing Andrew tickled him relentlessly. A posed shot of the four of them showed a family that Noah could probably no longer recognize; a family that had at some point been like any other family. In it they stood in a row of descending height— James, Helen, Andrew—each holding onto a section of Noah, suspended horizontally in front of them by shoulder, hip and legs. They were all laughing.

Gavin could only shake his head. He stared at the handsome laughing face of Lord James Bainbridge, unable to reconcile that image with the cruelty of the man who, it seemed, had purposely devastated Noah's young life. As he looked at them, the photos grudgingly gave up the secret of time's passage, with subtle hints he had first failed to recognize. Andrew grew taller and more broad shouldered, dwarfing his little brother's reed thin form, while Noah grew more serious, the laughter gone from his penetrating gaze even though his lips still curved in a smile for the camera.

What terrible, unimaginable tragedy had occurred that had

removed that light from his innocent eyes, a gaze that still regarded the world around him with a veiled introspective wariness? Gavin shivered, placing the stack of photographs down on the table. He felt sick with his own share of guilt in the aftermath of Noah's breakdown.

He had told Noah to face his past, that it could not hurt him. God, what a stupid fool he was! He could kick himself now, wishing that he had ripped that bloody package open when it had arrived and thrown the contents away before they had the power to wreak their terrible truth. It was too late now. Maybe it had been too late all along.

Gavin went into the kitchen to fetch the coffee—and the whiskey. Seeing the cursed envelope still sitting on the abandoned tea tray, he snatched it up and stuffed it into the rubbish bin. He put the bottle and carafe on the tray and carried it around the corner to the living room.

He almost dropped the entire service when he looked up to see Noah already there, having silently reappeared while he was clinking around with the coffee. Without saying a word, Gavin carried the service over and put it down on the table.

Noah was sitting on the sofa with his legs tucked beneath him and the stack of photos on the table directly in front of him. His hair was still damp and he had wrapped himself in his heaviest robe over dark blue flannel pajamas, no doubt trying to warm his blood, frozen with shock. He looked up at Gavin without expression, but his eyes were red rimmed and bloodshot from his tears.

He seemed so young and so vulnerable that Gavin felt the familiar tightening in his chest almost paralyze him. To keep from doing what he wanted to do, Gavin sat down instead, sliding to the edge of the chair and reaching for the coffee carafe.

"Would you like your coffee plain or Irish?" he inquired in what he hoped was a normal voice. His hands were shaking.

Noah knew how much it took for Gavin to pretend that things were normal. There was nothing about him or his life that was normal, including his reaction to those ordinary photographs. He held them in his hand now without seeing them, unable to focus on anything but the sound of Gavin's voice.

"Whatever you want," he replied in monotone.

Gavin looked at him but said nothing. He poured sugar, cream, and a dribble of whiskey into the cup of coffee, stirred it and handed it across to Noah. In his own cup Gavin poured a shot of straight whiskey and slugged it down before pouring more whiskey and then coffee, black. He stared at the second cup without touching it.

Noah drank his coffee, the slight bite of alcohol barely noticeable with the sweet cream and sugar. He thought he might get used to the taste eventually, especially if he continued to allow Gavin to pour it down his throat with consistency. He was cold in spite of the scalding hot shower and the layers of warm clothing, and his hands shook with sporadic trembles. They sat there in the silence for another few minutes while he drank in tiny sips and Gavin avoided looking at him.

When he was ready, Noah put his feet on the floor, set down his coffee cup and took the stack of photographs in both of his hands. Looking at them one by one was the hardest thing he had ever done in his life. He was trembling when he replaced them on the table but the overpowering wave of grief did not return. He felt hollow, an empty shell, yet something in his chest ached with every breath.

"It's funny, isn't it?" Noah said, looking at nothing, speaking mostly to himself. "They look almost normal, the people in those photos."

Gavin cringed hearing Noah refer to himself in the third person, having earlier thought the same thing. "Yeah, funny," he replied in a dismal tone.

Noah poured more coffee and then splashed a liberal amount of whiskey into the cup, adding the cream and sugar. Gavin watched with a raised eyebrow and said nothing. If his boss wanted to get drunk now, he had plenty of reasons to do so.

The silence was like knives scoring his flesh. Someone had to say something soon or they might just both have a heart attack from the tension.

"You look just like your mother," Gavin said without looking at Noah or the incriminating reflection of her features in the black and white photograph near his elbow. "Exactly like her, even more than Andrew resembles…"

He could not say the words—*your father*. Gavin groaned silently, taking a swallow of his coffee to cover his ineptitude.

"I suppose I do," Noah said quietly.

Noah looked at her long dead face staring up at him, gentle eyes and soft yielding mouth. He remembered very little about her, which he had long thought was due to his young age at the time of her death, but now he began to wonder if there was some other reason for the wide black gap in his memory. Most of the moments captured in the photos were of someone else's memories, not his. It was oddly disturbing, as if someone had simply cleaved him in two, before and after, forever to remain apart.

"I don't remember a lot about her," he admitted. "We look… we looked happy, didn't we?"

Gavin nodded. That was the odd thing; they had all looked happy. They had loved each other once. What had happened to those smiling people that had torn the family apart, shattered into pieces that still had the power to wound deeply?

"You said he sent you away after your mother died," Gavin said, finally having the nerve to speak. "What happened? Did she die in an accident?"

"That is what they told me. I have no memory of the accident…or the funeral…nothing. Father… My last memory of father is of him standing over my hospital bed. I never saw him again or went back home after that."

Gavin frowned. "Hospital? You were in hospital?"

Noah blinked, unaware of the importance of that particular

memory. "I was in a hospital. Yes, I was there for some time. I don't know why. Do you think I was there...with Mother...when she...?"

"It could explain a lot, if you were both involved in an accident. Maybe it affected your memory. Maybe he blamed you in some way. You look so much like her, Noah. What if he simply could not endure seeing her reflection every time he looked at you?"

Noah put his hands over his face. He had never thought of that. What if his father had suffered all these years with as much grief and guilt as he felt? Maybe he had regretted his actions after a time only to realize that he could not easily undo such a terrible thing. Was the unexpected inheritance his way of assuaging his guilt and trying to make amends for the terrible injustice he had done his youngest son?

"That is too terrible to believe," Noah said, lowering his hands. "All of this is my fault."

"Stop that," Gavin snapped with a flash of anger. "You were a child. You were not responsible for the events around you or the whims and weaknesses of the adults in charge. If that was what happened then your father is the one to blame, not you. If he wanted to show his regrets he picked a strange way of doing it, telling you never to set foot in his house again. Money does not cure everything."

Noah smiled sadly. "I don't want his money...Andrew's money."

"Andrew. What has he been doing in all of this mess? He certainly didn't take your side of the argument, did he?"

"What could he do, Gavin?" Noah defended. "At the time he was a child too. Worse, he was the heir to a title as old and venerated as that of Scottish royalty. People like that don't get choices. They are expected to do what their family has always done; respect and obey."

Like you have done all these years, Gavin thought but did not say aloud. *Never once questioning your father's decision, merely accepting the punishment without even knowing the crime of which you were supposedly guilty.*

"Maybe that's why he decided to give you half the money with that threat attached to it; he was afraid that you would try and take the estate as well. He had no way of knowing the depth of your animosity after all these years. This way you get some of the truth and part of the money but none of the respect."

It was a cruel thing to say and the moment it was out of his mouth Gavin wanted to take it back. He watched the single tear slip from Noah's eye and slide down his cheek.

"I apologize. I didn't mean that. I just don't want to see you hurt anymore. Maybe you were right. Maybe twelve years of your life is enough."

Maybe it should have been but looking at Noah's face at that moment, Gavin knew otherwise. That damn package had opened a huge gaping hole, a cavernous expanding pit into which Noah was preparing to leap without aide or restraint. It terrified him, what he saw in those damp blue eyes.

Noah poured more whiskey into their cups, no coffee at all this time. The conversation was over. Whatever fears or reservations Gavin might entertain, whatever reasons or pleas he might put forward, none of it would alter the course of action already decided upon. How much was stubborn curiosity and how much simply fate, he had no idea. Gavin merely drank his whiskey in silent protest.

One day later the call came.

Gavin had considered refusing it, but that would have done nothing in the long run but delay the inevitable. The voice on the other end of the telephone sounded pleasant enough. Andrew had placed the call himself, not relying on a servant to make the connection first. That alone gave him a momentary reprieve in Gavin's eyes. He had placed the caller on hold and gone to find Noah.

The sound of intermittent violin music was a dead giveaway, leading him to the corner of the living room where Noah was practicing a new piece. He was standing beside the piano on which his sheet music resided, alternately playing and then stopping to make notations on the pages. He had taken off the wrist brace. Making him wear it was a constant battle that Gavin lost most of the time.

Noah looked up when he heard Gavin enter the room. Without saying a word, Gavin handed him the phone and retreated to the kitchen, only to stare at the clock for fifteen minutes until he heard the door of Noah's bedroom open again. Noah walked directly to him and put the phone down on the counter between them.

Then he said the words that Gavin knew were coming, three little words that set off the biggest fight they had ever had up to that point.

"I'm going home."

THREE

Our separated fortunes shall keep us both the safer.
—W. Shakespeare

Funny how things worked out. Stranger still how they didn't.

That was what Noah was thinking, waiting for the train to reach its final destination in the filtered light of a fall afternoon. He sighed and pulled his jacket collar up around his neck, feeling a chill. He was nervous. He could not remember the last time he had felt anything close to what he was currently experiencing; a strange combination of excitement, fear, and nostalgia. He was going home.

With a sigh of exasperation Noah shoved his hands into his jacket pockets in the effort to release some of the pent up tension he had held bottled inside for hours now. The train was late. He had no idea what to expect when his half brother met him at the station. It had been two years since they had really spoken, even longer since they had seen each other.

He had told Andrew that he had been hospitalized while on tour with what doctors had called *mental exhaustion*, returning to England recently only to be greeted with such terrible news. Admittedly, that double blow had taken its toll. No doubt Andrew had heard it in his trembling voice when they spoke only a couple of days before. At least the two of them had managed to survive their separate difficult childhoods to emerge as relatively unscathed adults—more or less.

Andrew had offered a refuge, a place for reconciliation and recovery. Noah jumped at the offer without much thought, the forfeiture of an inheritance not the slightest consideration. It was only money, lost to the both of them the moment Noah set foot on the Estate. Even coming under such difficult circumstances it was a chance Noah felt he had to take.

The train was finally pulling in to the station, almost an hour late. Noah smoothed his palms across the fabric of his trousers. He took a deep breath, released it slowly, and grabbed his bags. With a lump in his throat, he waited for the passengers to begin pouring out onto the platform. He spilled out of the side of the train with the wave of people, an overwhelming jumble of sound and color and unfamiliar bodies rushing by.

Then Noah found himself standing outside on the chilly train platform, terrified that Andrew would not be there to meet him. He stood motionless in the scurry of people, clutching his violin case in one hand and a small valise in the other, scanning the crowd for a familiar face. When their eyes met, Noah felt his heart leap at the flicker of recognition.

They walked toward each other without a doubt, dodging people, baggage, and children. Where Andrew would have thrown his arms around his brother and lifted him off his feet in a bear hug, he checked himself at the last minute. Too much time had gone by for such a display, too many ugly things in between. Their father's death stood between them, that and the expression of terror in Noah's face.

"Noah, welcome home," Andrew said warmly. "I…it's so great to see you."

Noah tried to smile but it came out as more of a grimace. He dropped the larger bags and shifted the small valise beneath one arm so that he could at least shake Andrew's offered hand. "Is it really you, Andrew?" he asked, almost in disbelief.

"Same Andrew that used to tease you because you were afraid of the dark," Andrew said with a wide grin.

"I still am," Noah replied without thinking.

"What?"

"Afraid of the dark."

Releasing his brother's hand, Andrew allowed the comment to go untouched, not knowing quite what to make of it. Noah seemed distracted, uncomfortable in his skin. That should hardly be a surprise after having been away for so long.

"Come on then, let me grab your luggage and get you home," Andrew said, thinking that Noah's condition could be more fragile than the attorneys had led him to believe.

"Home. It still sounds funny." Again Noah made an effort to smile. "Drew, I am glad to see you. I have missed you."

Andrew laughed at the use of his nickname. "I missed you too."

Noah relaxed a little after that, allowing Andrew to grab his larger bags and carry them to the car. The sun was warm in the cool autumn breeze, the fresh country air enlivening after the stuffy train ride. The shock of seeing each other after so many years made them both a little nervous. It had been a long ride out from the edge of the city, leaving no doubt that Bainbridge Hall was a country house.

The open countryside flowed by, fields of green and brown extending out from the roadway, broken only by the occasional stone fence and rocky hills. Small copses of trees tucked here and there provided a break from the empty meadows. Andrew was an excellent driver and the convertible purred along the well-remembered road with ease. They spoke in intermittent spurts of conversation, not exactly knowing what to say after so many years apart. One could hardly be expected to pour one's life out to a virtual stranger. They kept it safe for the moment; chatting about the train trip, the weather, the growth of Edinburgh's suburbs.

Before long Andrew turned the car off the main highway, down a side road that would lead farther out into the countryside. Long stretches of empty space increased the sense of being far removed from the modern world, an alien landscape of bracken covered hills and sharp gray mountains. The forested areas increased as the road turned off yet again, offering only a glimpse of the ocean in the far distance.

Noah peered at the road that wound ahead of them. The house could not be much farther down the curving path. In his mind's eye he conjured up the old image of gray stone and tall windows that a child of seven had called a castle. Was it true that things were never as grand in reality as they were remembered from childhood? He was not aware of it, but he was holding his breath.

The house came magnificently into view, stepping out of a storybook to grace the colorful hillside for a moment before disappearing again into the forest. Bainbridge Hall was a large manor house set in a green space between acres and acres of deep, dark forest and the sharp craggy coast of Scotland's unrelenting sea. The road to it was narrow and curvy, leaving the modern world of Edinburgh far behind and reaching into a world that was part of a past awash in blood and mystery. It had been the impressive stone sanctuary for generations of Andrew's ancestors, a lineage that reached far back in history.

The first time seeing it upon exiting the oppressive forest was stunning and awe inspiring and it sent Noah into instant paroxysms of fear and trepidation. Andrew had left the top of the car down for Noah's account, to get some fresh air and a better feel of the countryside. Now it merely gave him nowhere to hide. His shaking must have been visible, for Andrew glanced at him from the opposite seat.

"Are you cold? I can put the top up."

Noah shook his head. "No, it's nothing. It's all so overwhelming," he tried to explain. "I feel like…like this is a dream. I'm afraid someone will pinch me and I will wake up."

Andrew reached over and pinched him, lightly on the arm. "I assure you, this is real. Just relax. There's nothing to worry about, Noah."

Noah smiled in spite of his queasy stomach. He felt out of place, adrift on the ocean of emotion, afraid of where it was taking him. The car moved ever closer to the imposing house with every beat of his heart. He stopped watching the landscape go by, keeping his gaze down on his restless hands or on Andrew's profile as he talked in an amiable ramble.

Why was he so afraid? Why did the thought of setting foot in the stone structure he barely remembered from his childhood chill him to the bone? It was a house, stone and wood, nothing more. It was the place where he and Andrew had played as children and where Andrew had grown up into the seemingly caring adult now sitting beside him. So why was he shaking like a child?

He was being an idiot. Noah closed his eyes and kept them shut for the remainder of the short drive down the private road and up to the stone and ivy monster.

Andrew parked the car in the circular drive that wound around a huge fountain before the main entrance. The sculpture of the fountain was frightening enough; a frozen stone tableau of wolves tearing at a stag, the creature's terror almost palpable as the bared teeth of the wolves slashed at it from all directions. The deer's head was raised above the gentle splashing of water falling around it from the open jaws of the wolves, its mouth opened in an eternal cry, its stone eyes rolled down to meet its death.

Stepping out of the car and clutching the handle of his violin case, Noah stood looking at the grim thing. Andrew closed the door for him, placing his hand lightly on Noah's arm for reassurance.

"Dreadful thing, isn't it?" Andrew said, seeing the look of revulsion on his brother's face. "I guess you don't remember it. Unfortunately you will see it all over. The scene is more or less a family crest of sorts."

Noah looked at him with an expression of dread. To him, Andrew's smile looked very much at that moment like the gleaming teeth of a wolf and Noah felt too much like the terrified deer, out of his element and surrounded by things he could not control.

"Welcome home, Noah."

Noah turned away from the fountain and felt the shock hit him, meeting the towering facade of the house that dwarfed them in its shadow. It had been a mistake not to watch its size increase as they drove nearer. The sudden shift of its dimensions from small object in the green distance to massive stone far over his head and yards in each direction was a jolt that he could not take in.

Before he understood what was happening, darkness rushed up at him and he fell down into nothingness.

❦ ❦ ❦

He had fainted.

Noah had crumpled at Andrew's feet like a rag doll, narrowly missing cracking his skull open on the hard fountain only by Andrew's quick reflexes. The staff had come running at the shouts for help, finding him crumpled in the driveway like a piece of old newspaper. They carried Noah upstairs to his room where he awoke to find himself stretched out on a huge, antique bed.

What an entrance. To faint at that moment was a humiliation almost too much to bear. Noah made a quick movement to get up but fell back into the heavy damask pillows when Andrew's face and the dimensions of the room seemed to spiral away from him.

"Lie still," Andrew ordered, placing his hand on Noah's chest to ensure compliance. Noah was pale as a ghost and his skin was clammy with cold sweat.

"I feel like an idiot," Noah mumbled.

Andrew's hand moved to his brother's forehead to check for fever. Noah closed his eyes, opening them again when the warm hand left his skin.

"I am all right, really."

Andrew did not look convinced. Frankly, neither was Noah. A cold sinking dread seemed to permeate his bones, nausea swirling dangerously in his stomach.

"You are going straight to bed," Andrew told him in no uncertain terms. "Duncan, run a hot bath and then tell Mary Katherine to fix a tray, nothing heavy. Oh, Duncan this is Noah. Noah, this is Duncan, my right arm around here."

Duncan was somewhere between fifty and sixty, a lean whip

of a man with thinning dark hair and a carriage that clearly announced him as a presence to be heeded by others. His eyes were sharp piercing black above a hawk-like nose. Noah tried to smile, what could only come across as pathetic embarrassment. Duncan smiled what did pass for sincere welcome and concern.

"Welcome home, Master Noah. We will have you up and good as new come morning. Not to worry."

Duncan finished closing the casement windows and disappeared across the large room. Noah looked helplessly up at Andrew, who seemed to alternate between being concerned and being amused at the situation. Water could be heard running from the bathroom taps.

"I am sorry," Noah said, dropping his hands down on either side of his body for emphasis. "I blew it I guess."

Andrew laughed quietly. "Hardly," he said, reaching again to brush strands of hair from Noah's forehead. "You made quite an impression on the two house maids, fair fainting youth and all that."

Noah groaned and put his hands over his face. Andrew laughed even more and Noah felt a warming connection between them even if it was at his expense. Still, his reaction to the house was unusual, if not alarming.

"Just too much excitement for you," Andrew said. "I should have realized you were working yourself up on the drive. It was a long train ride and you are just out of hospital so, into the bath with you. It will warm you up. Supper will be up in awhile and then to bed young man."

"Thank you, Drew…for having me here."

"Don't be silly. You belong here. I will have your things brought up and put away while you are in the bath. Are you sure you are all right, Noah?"

Noah nodded and slid slowly from the huge bed, standing up without any ill effect. He put his arms out, palms up to emphasize the fact.

"I will be fine. I will never live this down, but I will be fine."

"Good. Be careful getting around if you are still shaky."

Andrew closed the door and left Noah to recover his bearings. It had to be a shock for him, coming back to the house from which he had been so unceremoniously banished those years ago. The house had always frightened him, something Noah seemed to have not outgrown. The news of their father's sudden death had left him nervous.

When Andrew returned with a food tray somewhat later, Noah was more comfortable in robe and pajamas, sitting in a large, upholstered chair beside the fireplace. Duncan had started a fire while the maid unpacked Noah's belongings, secreting items off to drawers and closets. His violin case set on the dresser along with his valise filled with sheet music and his smaller case filled with personal items. He seemed at home in the room, much more relaxed than he had been earlier.

"Ah, I am glad to see you partially recovered," Andrew said, carrying the tray over to the small table. He removed the covering cloth and viewed the dishes with a smile. "Dinner is served. Do not feel like you have to eat everything. Mary got a little carried away. Shall I have tea with you?"

"Yes, please. I am sorry things started out…"

"Forget about it. The staff knows that you have been ill and you need time to recuperate. We are prepared to do anything necessary to see you get well as soon as possible. So stop worrying and eat."

The smile on Andrew's face made Noah feel somewhat better, and the warm delicious food did wonders for his shaky disposition. By the time he had a cup of tea and a bite of quiche, he felt much better. Andrew nibbled thoughtfully on a piece of toast while he watched Noah eat with more appetite than he had thought he possessed.

"Feeling better now?"

"Yes, thank you," Noah replied, remembering that he had eaten only a few crackers on the long train ride from London.

"The food really is excellent."

"One of the saving graces of living in this prison—Mary is an excellent cook. I hope you will be comfortable and feel as much at home here as you did once."

Noah looked away, into the fire flickering in the hearth. Why was it so painful to look his brother in the eye? "I…I am sorry about our father. I should have tried to get in touch with you when I…when I first heard the news."

Andrew shrugged. "You had no reason to be bothered one way or the other. In fact you have every reason to despise our father."

"Don't say that, Drew. Father made it possible for me to have the career I enjoy. I don't hold any ill will toward him or you."

Andrew smiled weakly. "I'm glad. I understand you were in Japan at the time father died. I guess you travel a great deal and see a lot of fabulous places with your career."

"Yeah, one symphony hall to another. After awhile all the cities start to look alike when you see them between the airport and the concert hall."

"I caught one of your performances in London, a year or so ago."

Noah's eyebrows rose. "You did? Why didn't you come backstage and let me know you were there?"

Andrew shrugged, looking slightly embarrassed. "I was…I wasn't sure how you would feel about it. Besides, you seemed to have enough people around you all the time. It is not an easy life, I am sure."

"No one has an easy life, Drew. I am sure you know that as well as I. Anyway, I cannot imagine doing anything else. The music is in my blood, you know?"

"I know. You play brilliantly. It gave me chills to hear it."

"I will play for you one day soon, a private concert."

"That will be great but don't overdo things too soon. I should let you get some sleep. I'll send someone up to check on you in an hour or so, all right?"

Noah set his teacup down. "I am really not that much of an invalid. I do not need someone checking on me like a sick four-year-old."

"All right."

Andrew gathered up the things on the food tray. Noah walked to the bed and ripped back the bedcovers, sending a shower of small pillows flying in all directions. He managed to catch the one that flew toward the vase of flowers on the night stand and then he sighed in defeat.

"Okay, so maybe I do need a babysitter."

Andrew laughed while Noah climbed into the huge, high bed. "And don't fly out of bed if you hear someone in the room or the hallway. The servants will be coming and going to check on you and the fire. Remember, it is an old house and you are not accustomed to the sounds of the country."

"Is this place haunted?" Noah asked half joking.

Andrew did not smile but rather looked down at the floor. "Not much," he replied and left, turning out the light as he went.

Noah stared at the closed door in the dimmest of light coming from the fireplace and around the edge of windows, now draped against the setting autumn sun. The silence immediately grabbed his imagination, the gentle crackle of the fire the only noticeable sound. He wanted to leap out of bed and run downstairs where he knew there were people, not lie up there in the huge empty room full of silence and the unknown. He hopped out of bed and went into the bathroom to brush his teeth.

They had, at least, not put him back into the room of his childhood. He momentarily wondered if it was Andrew's old room and then decided it was not. Surely Andrew had not already moved into his father's suite, not so soon after his death. It would be…too creepy. Noah rolled his eyes at his reflection in the mirror.

Why had he made that inane comment about the place being haunted? Like he needed that suggestion in his head, already filled with questions and misgivings. Maybe Gavin had been right. Maybe there was no way he could go back.

The image of Gavin's dark, cynical gaze swept into Noah's thoughts and he almost groaned out loud. Their parting fight had been ugly, made longer and more emotional by his stubbornness and Gavin's skeptical disposition.

They had shouted the roof down and he had said some things that anyone other than Gavin would have taken as a personal affront. Gavin had merely winced and kept his argument on track, at the top of his lungs, until he realized he was not going to win. Then he had retreated into forced submission with a cool civility that his flashing eyes betrayed at every glance.

Noah knew that look. While he had won the argument, he had lost the war. He had no doubt in his mind that Gavin was quietly doing what he had threatened to do; find out everything he could about Noah's odd little family, from the moment of his birth down to the laundry mark on Andrew's underwear. Well, what could it hurt? Noah certainly knew very little about them. He felt his mouth quirk up at the corner.

Less upset about it than he was before, Noah crawled back into the huge comfortable bed and snuggled down into the soft sheets. He left the bathroom light on for his first night back in his father's house, a house filled with empty memories and shadows of his childhood. He lay there in the silence, trying to remember that first night, long ago, when he had been a terrified child left alone in a similar cavernous room in the dark.

Fortunately, worn out from the tension of the day's travel, it wasn't long until he was fast asleep. He never heard the housekeeper open the door to check on him or the strange sounds that the night breeze stirred in the darkness outside.

Noah slept on, in a deep, dreamless sleep that soon enough would be only a wish and a memory, like his life before he had returned to Bainbridge Hall, the scene of his lost childhood.

And the secrets waiting in the darkness.

FOUR

Memories of childhood are strange things.
—Floyd Dell

The following morning Noah walked with Andrew down the magnificent staircase to the lower floor and his first day in the country. At least he had been correct in his assumption; Andrew was still in his old room across the hall and one door down. Their father's compartments were unoccupied at the moment, closed and silent. The entire house had the feeling of unnatural stillness about it, a veil of something unfulfilled.

The upper wing was one of two, separated into family rooms and guest wing, each meeting at the upper landing where a huge stained glass window proclaimed the family in residence with its colorful depiction of the same dreadful scene as displayed in the courtyard fountain. Up close the scene blended into a disjointed mural of color and light. Only from the foot of the staircase could one see the shocking spectacle in its colorful entirety; the bloody allegory of brutal English and Scottish conflict in the resolve of the bleeding stag and the equal determination of the bared fangs of the encircling wolves. The family motto was there as well, written in ancient Gaelic in blood-red script.

Noah stared at it in stupefied amazement, having made his first entrance unaware, so to speak. The place was monstrously huge, as large as his childhood memory, like a palace or cathedral. The grand staircase curved down into an entrance hall with a circular design of stone in the floor and two crystal chandeliers the size of small automobiles hanging from heavy chains some forty feet overhead. The stone inlay gleamed in multicolor; rusty red, gold, green, blue, purple, and the ceiling overhead mirrored the same colors in a large stained-glass rotunda. From the foot of the staircase, the place opened to the left and right where a large wreath of mourning flowers draped with black ribbon stood like a sentinel.

Right was the way to the front living areas, music room, and ladies parlor. Left was the direction they headed, to another drawing room, the study, dining areas, and kitchen compartments that angled off of the rear of the house. The entire place was filled with antiques, museum quality paintings, tapestries, rugs, and artwork, and the walls sported hand-carved woodwork and delicate plaster detailing from another era. The main hall had two huge hearths, a necessity for heating a space so large.

The house seemed to fit Andrew in an odd sort of way, but Noah was accustomed to hotel rooms and his memories of the house were playing tricks on him. Some things he remembered. Other things, like the family crest in all of its glory and horror, he did not. With a shiver, he felt the place overwhelm him again and Andrew's arm moved around his lower back for reassurance.

The formal dining hall was a vast echoing room that struck him as a cross between the old library halls of his school days and a scary musty museum of nature with its dead, stuffed animals and articulated skeletons. It was a huge long room with floor-to-ceiling windows that turned out to actually be French doors along the exterior wall. Large medieval tapestries covered half the opposite dark paneled wall. The table was large and heavy, probably oak and ancient enough to have the dark shiny patina that antique furniture often acquired with age and use. It could easily seat forty people in narrow high-backed chairs, and two gigantic silver candelabras and overhead chandeliers would provide a minimum of lighting on special occasions.

There were no dinosaurs, but the heads of many stuffed and mounted animals stared down from their places on the walls above; various deer, antelope, a particularly evil looking water buffalo, boars, the head and skin of a large ferocious looking lion, and the skins of other spotted or striped cats. Even the head of an African elephant looked alive enough that it might lift its trunk and trumpet at any given moment. That in itself made the row of heads even creepier.

The large, carved panel doors at each end of the room were

black with age and never closed due to their unwieldy weight and rusty hinges. Two crystal bowls of fresh flowers stationed on the table at evenly spaced intervals did nothing to alleviate the atmosphere of the room.

"Oh God," Noah intoned, stopping in his tracks. "How can you eat in here?"

Andrew stopped beside him and looked up as if he were seeing all the floating heads for the first time. The morning light coming from the wall of glass barely made a dent in the shadowy darkness that seemed to permeate the space.

"I don't really. This place is too large for one or two people to feel comfortable. We will be dining in the breakfast room."

"Any dead animals in there?" Noah asked with a shiver.

"Only the ones on your plate," his brother assured him. "Hunting was a grand passion for several of our bored and noble ancestors. The stag and wolves you saw on the fountain and large window are the family crest as well. Our family motto, roughly translated, is *Our Blood, Our Fate*."

"What is that supposed to mean?"

"I'm not sure. The entire thing is written down in a book somewhere. I guess you do not remember much of the house after all these years. Do not worry about it. There is another way to the back of the house without going through this room. I will show it to you later. I am sorry it has upset you."

Noah realized that he was shivering almost uncontrollably in the dim light of the house. This room, this house, it fascinated and repulsed him in equal doses, although he never knew what reaction it would provoke around each new corner and doorway. This room of death clearly had a negative influence on his suddenly delicate psyche.

He sighed. "I'm sorry, Drew. You must think I am half crazy."

Perhaps it was a bad choice of words considering Andrew knew of his recent collapse and hospitalization. Even with his brother's strong unflinching presence standing beside him, Noah felt the eyes of the many disembodied heads watching from above. A cold silence permeated the room, enveloping their living energy in a vast dead space that seemed to press against his skin, wanting to touch him, to connect with his energy. He could feel the house drawing it from him as if he were a battery it could use to recharge itself. Noah mentally pushed at the feeling and it subsided a little.

Andrew watched him shiver. "I realize now that I should probably have prepared you for the house instead of plunging you head first into another century. You are used to the unceasing sound and motion of large cities and you have been away since you were a young lad. Nothing is ever as you remember from childhood."

"I guess not," Noah muttered.

Andrew took him by the wrist and led him out of the dark room without saying another word. They passed the closed door to the study. Then they were in a bright and airy room that seemed open to the outside, the breakfast room with its wall of glass looking out to the gardens beyond. Andrew took Noah straight to the windows where he could see outside and feel the sunlight on his face while he stood shivering.

"Put this on," he said, helping Noah into the jacket he had carried down.

Noah consciously took in slow, deep breaths and gradually regained control of his body. His thoughts were another matter entirely but he chose to ignore them. Andrew turned him around and walked him to the table, pulling out a chair for him to sit down. Once seated, he placed a freshly poured cup of coffee into Noah's cold hands.

"Are you all right?" Andrew asked quietly while one of the staff entered the room behind him to begin serving breakfast.

Noah nodded, not yet trusting himself to speak. The young woman began setting food onto the table from a serving cart. She glanced at him shyly and he suspected that she had witnessed his humiliating entrance of the previous evening. She had very thick, long black hair that overshadowed her delicate features. Her eyes were light blue and her skin even whiter than his.

"Noah, this is Moira," Andrew said in way of introduction. "One of the house staff. Moira, this is my brother, Noah."

"Good morning, sir," she said with a bright smile and local accent. "I hope you like your breakfast. Mary Katherine did it up special for the occasion."

Noah smiled as best he could, which seemed to be enough because she blushed. "I'm sure I will, Moira. Thank you."

"Thank you," Andrew echoed.

She smiled even brighter and finished serving the amazing assortment of items. Then she refreshed their coffee and left them alone. Noah stared at the food, his stomach doing odd little flips and feeling none too hungry at the moment.

"Are you sure you are all right?" Andrew asked again.

Noah sighed and picked up his fork. "I suppose it's just stress." He managed a feeble smile. "You know we artsy types, high strung and impressionable."

Andrew frowned. It was the first time Noah had seen his face darken with what looked like anger...or distrust. Then the expression was gone so quickly he thought he had imagined it along with everything else that seemed to be going on in his spinning head. Andrew was smiling with affection.

"Eat your breakfast. Since you never had a chance to know much about the family I will tell you about the house while we eat."

Noah nodded, glad for the option of silence.

The sound of giggling caused them to turn and catch two young women peering out from behind the far doorway. Once their cover had been blown, they gasped with alarm and practically shoved each other out of the way to escape. They skittered away in a dash of bobbing red blond hair and dark blue maid's uniforms, their muted high pitched giggles fading in the distance.

"That would be Caroline and Ester," Andrew commented with a grin. "I think you made quite an impression on them earlier."

The reported two house maids. Noah groaned and Andrew laughed until Noah had to laugh with him. It felt good to laugh, to see his brother laughing like the Andrew he remembered, always up to one thing or another. Relaxed, Andrew then proceeded to tell him the history of Bainbridge Hall.

Their family had made their money like most of the titled elite, off the backs of their fellow countrymen and the riches of far away lands. They had holdings in timber, mining, shipping, and real estate, to name just a few. The civilized ancestral home had been set apart in the wilderness as a tribute to man's dominion over nature, at least it had been so back when the land was truly wild. The house held onto its mystic atmosphere and grandeur in the face of modern life, filled with loving details and treasures gathered from many lands beyond the sea.

The family history was a bit more bleak; successions of tragedies that no doubt left their indelible mark on the darker atmosphere of the house, generation upon generation of lives lived out within the isolated stout walls of the Hall. There were deaths in childbirth, lives given in far away lands in service to Her Majesty the Queen, men who lived to ripe old ages and children who died young. Through it all, the Hall existed unchanged and the family continued to pass it down from one son to another through countless wars and an endless succession of royal families.

Listening to this litany of Andrew's lineage that he had no doubt learned at his father's knee, Noah had no wonder that the house affected him so. How could it not, given to his unpredictable and mostly unwanted psychic nature? Andrew did not know about his half brother's hidden *talents*. Noah had told no one, often even chose to hide it from himself.

He had no desire to inform Andrew of it now, would rather be considered weak or just plain crazy instead of having someone know that he was malformed in that way, somehow not like everyone else walking by him in the normal world. It had returned with a vengeance only lately, an annoying bubble in his blood that he had thought, incorrectly, under his control. It would pass, it always did with time.

At least Noah hoped that it would. The Hall seemed to be plugged directly into his system somehow, an alarming awareness that had begun even before Noah set foot in the place. Already it was a constant hum in his blood, like static energy crawling just beneath his skin. He was unsure if perhaps his own worries about the past—about his newly formed place in Andrew's life—had set off something hidden within the walls of Bainbridge Hall, or perhaps the house itself had simply been waiting for someone like him to bring it back to an unnatural life.

Noah felt none of the dread or warning from Andrew himself. He did not connect his brother with the dark energy coming from the place. Yet it unnerved him. He wondered if it had more to do with the sudden, crushing psychic wave that had brought him the knowledge of his father's death from half a world away. That incident had certainly shocked him, leaving him emotionally drained and battling a physical lethargy that hung on with dogged persistence.

Their father had died less than three weeks earlier of a massive stroke while he was out walking the grounds. One disadvantage of living in an isolated area was that any immediate illness requiring medical intervention might easily result in death; assistance of that nature some distance removed. His father was dead long before help arrived, finished with life at a somewhat early age of fifty-six.

Andrew would be twenty-nine in another few months, almost seven years older than Noah. Of course Noah's mother had also died many years ago, just another tragedy at the ancient brooding house.

"I never realized that history could be so depressing," Noah said after a moment of silence. "My mother… They were both too young to die."

Andrew shrugged. "Things happen that are beyond our

control."

Especially in this house, Noah thought. One more tragedy added to the burgeoning list. What would be the next?

"I guess all we have now is each other," Andrew added, reaching to refill his coffee and then Noah's.

"I guess so," Noah replied.

"Getting enough to eat?" Andrew asked.

Noah looked up at his brother's laughing dark eyes, aware that he had indeed been enjoying the immense plate of food once he had started to eat.

"I will be getting fat. I need to meet this Mary Katherine," Noah stated, wiping at his mouth with a napkin and groaning his appreciation. "No one should be able to make ordinary food taste like this."

Andrew laughed. "You should meet the rest of the staff then. Since you enjoyed her cooking so well, we will start in the kitchen with Mary Katherine."

Noah was not sure if he was up to staff introductions on the heels of his unconventional arrival, but he had to meet them all sometime. Moira certainly seemed sweet enough, and they had all worked hard behind the scenes to make his arrival as easy and uncomplicated as possible. He did appreciate that, although it made him no less nervous.

The kitchen was large, appropriate for a kitchen in a house the size of the Hall. It was both old and new, filled with commercial-size stainless steel appliances including a stainless preparation counter of about eight feet in length. A large wooden table and chairs marked where the staff ate their meals in warm cozy comfort before an ancient, smoke-darkened fireplace large enough to easily roast a whole side of beef. The stone wall reached up to darkened timbers of the ceiling high overhead, from which hung heavy iron chandeliers that had been converted from gas to electric lighting. Unlike the hideous dining hall beyond, the kitchen for all its size and gleaming metal surfaces felt comfortable and homey.

Upon their arrival a murmur of greetings met them. Three women and a man were present. Moira, whom Noah had met briefly earlier, and two older women, one of whom resembled an older Moira. The other was gray haired and thin, standing ramrod straight like some of the older nuns Noah had known from school. The young man also resembled Moira, her thick black hair and delicate features startlingly handsome in their masculine form, obviously her brother. Unlike Moira, his eyes were a deep, stunning green flecked with gold. They seemed to leap out from his smooth white skin and very dark hair.

"Good morning," Noah said, suddenly ill at ease beneath their scrutiny.

Andrew performed the introductions. Moira, her brother Seth, and their mother Mary Katherine. The three lived in a small cottage on the property and had ties to the village almost as far back as the Bainbridge family. The other woman was Rose Marie, who ran the comings and goings of the kitchen and staff. There was nothing immediately rose-like about the woman, whose hand gripped his with every bit of the strength of a man. She looked Noah over with blue eyes the color of cornflowers, eyes every bit as sharp and cynical as those of Gavin.

Quite the opposite was the smooth plump hand of Mary Katherine that squeezed Noah's fingers with both hands and a mother's familiarity. Noah returned the open smile on her round face and the warmth he felt from her with sincere warmth of his own.

"Thank you so much for the wonderful breakfast," he told her. "Your oat cakes and jam were the best I have ever tasted."

She chuckled with good humor, releasing his hand. "Ah, I bet you say things like that to all old ladies, but you can say it to me as often as you like, young man. I am right pleased you enjoyed it." She then looked him over candidly. "I might say you could use the best cooking there is to be found."

"Mother!" Moira replied in a tone of shock.

Andrew laughed and put both of his hands on Noah's thin

shoulders. "Do not get carried away Mary Kate, he is already worrying about getting fat."

She snorted. "City boys, they are getting as bad as the girls. You just do what makes you happy and everything else will fall into place."

Best advice anyone could ever get and Noah told her so. Once they had escaped from the kitchen, Andrew showed him the back stairs, used mostly by the servants, and the remaining rear of the house that ran parallel to the front rooms, joining the two upper wings beneath the staircase landing. It was a room without a purpose, a long, seemingly endless corridor thirty foot wide with a few floor-to-ceiling windows along the exterior courtyard wall that did little to alleviate the gloom. The Hall was named for that long, impractical corridor and the collection of long-dead founders who occupied it, their grim portraits bearing silent witness to the passage of time.

Noah felt the procession of painted eyes follow them while they walked along in silence. His ancestors had been a formidable lot if their portraits were any indication; steely-eyed men with hard jaws and stout shoulders, shown dressed in the family tartans of old. Each was pictured with sword, armor, or medals attributing them with the honor and respect deserving of a Laird of the Realm.

A few suits of armor stood guard at regular spaced intervals. Many a lance, sword, and battle axe were displayed on the walls along with faded war banners. The odor of dust was heavy. Apparently the maids chose not to clean the rugs regularly and he could hardly blame them; having those hard men watching your every move would be as unnerving in death as they must have been in life.

"This room used to terrify you," Andrew said while they paused before a life-sized portrait.

"It does not do much for me now either," Noah admitted uneasily. "They were a serious lot."

"Haughty. They thought so much of themselves that they

created a separate room dedicated to their vain glories, as if this horrendous house was not enough. They expected their descendants to walk this Hall with pride and terror, maybe stopping to sit and converse with their memories, worship at their feet."

Andrew's bitter voice made Noah aware that their father had treated them both with contempt. Perhaps it had been harder on Andrew all these years, in their father's immediate presence yet accepted as merely part of the scenery. How were either of them ever going to get over such things?

Even feeling sadness for Andrew, a shadowy part of Noah's veiled mind recalled being locked in some place cold and dark and frightening. The memory itself did not resurface yet the emotion left him shivering, aware that too many things remained out of his reach. They exited the hall of ancestors on the opposite side of the house near the music room. Light and air poured into the space, dispelling the gloom. Andrew looked much like Noah felt, oddly affected by the house and the memories it held.

"Are you up for a stroll outside?" Andrew suggested suddenly.

It was a beautiful day for autumn, sunny and bright. The gray highland winter was coming soon but there would be weeks yet of the colors of fall, the yellow of ripening grain, the red and orange of changing leaves. The house came alive in the autumn, its stately gray walls gleaming against the backdrop of the temporarily colorful hills, blue sky, and fog laden valley. The air was filled with the scent of evergreen and heather.

The gardens were formal in design and immaculately maintained like everything around the Hall seemed to be. It had to cost a fortune to keep the place. The moss covered path from the rose garden became a stone path leading to another fountain, with a seating area of stone benches around it.

At least the fountain was less gruesome than the one in the front of the house; a whimsical scene of mermaids, sea horses and fish. The garden branched out from the circular fountain into the rose garden, then a short maze formed of perfectly trimmed hedge rows and topiary, and into a wilder looking English garden filled with a variety of flowers, herbs and shrubs.

"Very beautiful," Noah said, taking in a deep breath of the perfumed air.

Andrew stood looking at his brother's bright hair in the morning light. "Noah, I am sorry—"

Noah raised his hand to stop whatever Andrew was about to say. "It wasn't your fault. You have never done anything wrong, Drew."

Andrew stood looking down at his feet.

It was hard, harder than Noah had anticipated, to talk about things they both seemed more comfortable forgetting.

"Can you show me where father…where you found him?"

Andrew started at the request but he should have expected it. Even though Noah had been elsewhere for years and not a part of their lives, James had been his father too. He had a right to know such things. Without a word Andrew led the way, the path through the gardens and out beyond the stable area.

It was a horse trail and walking path that went in the direction of the shadowy woods, eventually forking off to an open meadow, where it then led across the field to another section of forest. The crashing sea lay two miles or so beyond those distant woods. At the edge of the woods, just where the golden grass began to give way to brambles and undergrowth, Andrew stopped.

They were some distance from the house, the line of sight broken by fencing, loose groups of smaller trees, and a thicket of mulberry bushes at the end of a small tor. Ahead of them the woods covered the path in shadow. To the right the open meadow beckoned; the smell of dry grass and the barely detectable tang of ocean brine in the air.

Noah did not need Andrew to tell him when they had reached the spot of their father's sudden misfortunate death. The place still held the overpowering impression of his presence. It rose up from the ground like a hidden assassin, crashing into Noah's body with the force of a tidal wave. For a moment he was blind and deaf, swept away by the shock as he had been that night on stage.

Whatever it had been, it moved there still, just beyond the edge of his vision; a quick furtive shadow that was there and gone before he could grasp its importance. When Noah came back to himself, Andrew was staring at him suspiciously. Then a veil moved across his brother's face, hiding his thoughts.

"Here," Andrew indicated unnecessarily. "By the time we located him there was nothing anyone could do."

Noah stood there without looking down where he knew his father's body had lain. Instead he looked back along the way they had come, a winding path not often traveled, overgrown with grass and brambles in some places. It was not a path someone would walk just to be taking a leisure stroll. He shielded his eyes from the sun to look out into the meadow and the scattered collection of dark objects in the distance.

"What is that?"

Andrew followed his brother's gaze. "It's the old family cemetery and chapel ruins. No one has been out there for years. Father forbade us from even setting foot in the meadow, remember?"

Noah lowered his hand. "Why would he be out here, Andrew? Did he often walk out here alone?"

"I wondered the same thing. No, this was not a usual path for him to take."

"Can we go out there?"

Andrew's eyes narrowed. "What are you thinking?"

"Nothing. Just curious. Did you ever disregard his order about that place? You were always the braver of the two of us."

"Braver? Most foolhardy, you mean. Remember that time I jumped off the roof of the stable? Anyone else would have laughed themselves silly but you…"

"I cried," Noah said.

"Yeah," Andrew said softly. "You cried. I broke my arm, but you were the one that cried."

They regarded each other in the silence. Noah again had that feeling of being out of sink with the fabric of time. For a moment Andrew was again that boy holding his broken arm at an odd angle while he tried to comfort his little brother. Noah's breath caught in his throat with the lump of emotion.

"Drew…did you know?" he asked in a whisper.

Andrew looked into his brother's face. There was that young, frightened child that he remembered, looking back at him. "No. Father kept his secrets well."

Noah allowed the tears to flow, as much for Andrew as for himself. His brother's arms went around him, warm and comforting, yet there were no tears in the dark gaze. After a few moments, Andrew released him and stepped back. Noah wiped at his eyes with the back of his hand.

"I am not sure I could have done what you have," Andrew stated in a hard flat voice. He rolled his shoulders as if to toss off some imagined weight. "Time to get back. You should be getting some rest, not out here wondering about such things."

"You never wonder, Drew? Do you not want to know why father did such things?"

Andrew stood with his hands in his pockets looking at the ruins of the family chapel in the distance. Its broken stone walls were a representation of their lives; destroyed by the ravages of time, worn down to the point where they would never again fit together the way they were intended originally. Even though he tried to keep the bitterness out of his voice, it was easy enough for Noah to hear.

"I have wondered all my life, but he is dead, dead and buried, and now I do not have to wonder anymore. I refuse to give him another second of my time or allow his arbitrary decisions to have one more hold on my life. You should do the same."

When Andrew turned his head, Noah felt his blood run cold at the dark, bitter expression. A gust of wind blew up from the meadow, ruffling their hair.

"Why *did* you come back?"

The tone of the question as much as the words shocked Noah, sending him into an unexplainable shiver. Then the cold hard gaze shifted, becoming again the brother that he thought he knew. The change was subtle and yet startling.

"You are shivering," Andrew said with a frown of concern. "You need to lie down, after all, you came all the way out here to get some rest. You will find that is about all you can do out here in the country."

"Sure."

"Come on then. I have some work to do. Maybe you would like to go into the village later, have a look around. It's certainly not London, but there are a few nice pubs and a couple of decent shops. We will have to find you some more sensible shoes if you want to do any walking around here."

Noah looked at his feet clad in expensive loafers and then at Andrew's well worn riding boots and heavy wool jacket. Andrew laughed, back to normal.

"Yes, brother, you look like a city boy. Not to worry, we country mice will not hold it against you. MacDaughtery can fix you up with the country squire look in no time."

"All right," Noah agreed. "Just one thing."

"And what is that?"

"No kilts."

Andrew looked at him with an appraising glance. "The family tartan is a necessity on some occasions and who knows? You might look good in a skirt."

They laughed uneasily, turning to go back to the house. Noah regarded his brother's profile as one might appraise a stranger. They were brothers but they had little to nothing in common, including looks. Andrew was the perfect picture of a strapping country lad; light brown, slightly wavy hair, strong chin, wide shoulders and large hands. His cheeks glowed with red patches from the cold wind and when he smiled his teeth were strong and white.

Beside him Noah felt like a child. He had a more pointed chin and slender, almost delicate hands. He was very much smaller but then he was used to that; a great many men towered over him by several inches, including Gavin, whose throat was barely at eye level. Maybe it was the unintentional regression back to childhood that was the cause of Noah's unease. Or maybe it was that his memories of Andrew could be as faulty as his memories of the house seemed to be.

"I would rather you not go walking or riding too far on your own," Andrew said when they neared the back of the house. "With your health as it is, it could be dangerous. Ah, there is Duncan. I must be late for my meeting. See you around lunch then."

Noah watched his brother walk off and Duncan come forward to greet him.

⚜ ⚜ ⚜

The local village was as picture perfect as any good Scottish borough from a guide book on the countryside; that is to say, it was "picturesque." The main road was narrow cobblestone winding through a collection of ancient stone buildings and wooden structures set up and down a steep and rocky hillside overlooking a river where it ran to the sea. Whitewashed houses with thatched roofs sat in individual patches apart from the timbered-and-stone row houses that spread down the few streets of the town. The main road was marked with a large fountain at one end that had once served as the village water supply, but now paid homage to some man forgotten in history with a life-sized statue of weathered bronze.

Dating back to Viking times, the village had an ancient pedigree to which it clung with a tenacious pride. The two and three-story structures were mostly original, and a few boasted claims to historical figures and events, some Noah even recognized with surprise. Thick glass windows, wavy with age, looked out over a road that had once been more than wide enough to allow passage of two horse-drawn carts; now it was barely wide enough for vehicle traffic between well-worn sidewalks. Along that sidewalk were heavy shop doors painted with bright colors and window boxes of flowers beckoning shoppers to enter. Uneven stacks of chimneys crowned the steeply slanted roofs, some puffing a hearty welcome of smoke into the autumn sky.

Several wooden fishing boats were nestled at an ancient pier along with piles of lobster pots announcing the village connection to the sea. There were a couple of low stone buildings used for the preserving and storage of fish. Farther along and set back away from the village proper was a church, its timber tower visible from the hill or the sea. The town had a semi-retired doctor, an apothecary shop, and a small modern schoolhouse, along with the taverns, shops, and market that populated the downtown area. A bright red phone box stood outside the apothecary, its once ubiquitous sight now a rarity in Britain.

Overall it was a quaint, busy little place making its living from the sea and the ever present tourist trade. There were several cars parked along the streets and people walking up and down the sidewalks. Andrew pulled the vehicle into a parking spot near a shop with an ancient wooden sign that simply said "Haberdashery." Next to it was a smaller shop that sold books, maps, and souvenirs.

"MacDaughtery first," Andrew was saying as he killed the engine. "Depending on how fast he is today, we might have time to amble about a bit afterwards."

Noah was already out of the car and peering in the connecting shop window. "I would like to get a few books."

Andrew slapped him on the back. "There are tons of books in the study but if you want the touristy kind, I am sure you will find something that catches your fancy. Come along then."

The haberdashery was warm, quiet, and slightly dark inside. While Noah waited for his eyesight to adjust to the gloom, he looked around at the contents that filled the place from floor to ceiling; boxes and racks and piles that would no doubt fulfill every wish. Bolts and bolts of tartan plaids were stacked and piled along one entire wall, along with wools, velvets, broadcloth, and tweed. Hats and gloves were piled on a table. The air was filled with the scent of cedar, leather, and polish.

An older man dressed in a white shirt and dark vest appeared out of nowhere and came forward to greet them. He had white hair, wire framed glasses, and a cloth tape measure hanging around his neck.

"Gentlemen, may I be of service to you this morning?"

"I hope so," Noah said with enthusiasm.

The man was smiling and about to reply when he noticed and clearly recognized Andrew. The smile froze on his face. "Your Lairdship, it is good to see you about. I was very sorry to hear about your father."

"Thank you, MacDaughtery," Andrew replied, reaching to shake the man's offered hand. "It was rather a surprise to all of us."

"I imagine so, I imagine so. What might I do for you this morning, Laird Bainbridge?"

"I brought my brother in for a fitting. He comes from London so of course he has no appropriate clothing for country living. Fix him up, will you? Some boots, a family tartan, and a jacket or two perhaps."

Noah had watched the man's face change during Andrew's speech. The anticipated gleam of a large sale never materialized on his pale wrinkled visage. Instead he clasped his hands together nervously and glanced at Noah with what resembled shock and fear. He tried to hide his reaction but it was more than obvious to Noah, who could only wonder why his presence was so upsetting to a man he had never met.

They wandered about the shop looking at various materials and talking about the history of the Scottish tartan. The first purchase was a new set of boots and heavy wool socks. Noah decided he needed some new trousers and a sweater. He stood ill at ease while MacDaughtery took his measurements and jotted the figures down on a small pad of paper. The tailor produced a tweed jacket trimmed in beige leather, which was a perfect fit and Andrew said they would take it without looking at the price tag.

They argued a bit over the tartan but Noah finally relented and stood still while Andrew and MacDaughtery dressed him like a mannequin in the regalia fitting a highlander. A black jacket would be made to order, but for the sake of demonstration they put him in one three sizes too large. The clan tartan was a royal blue plaid with black, red, and gold threads. Worn properly it draped across the body over one shoulder, secured in place with a round metal pin, and hung to the knees along that side of the body. It was heavy and Noah had no doubt that in the old days it was more than useful for any purpose; clothing, coat, carry all, blanket.

The shop had a large amount of that pattern on hand owing to the clan's association with the village and the local area. In the past the Lord of Bainbridge Hall had owned the village and most of the land, the men and women under his protection and answering to his will. For a place as remote as the Hall, that was still partially true in modern times; the Bainbridge family paid for the school and the library and with their support for local events could make or break the livelihood of most of the village.

Finished with dressing him like a doll, they led Noah over to the set of triple mirrors near the corner dressing rooms. Andrew positioned a hat on his bright hair, an extravagant thing with the long feathers from a ring-necked pheasant as decoration curling out from the side. MacDaughtery turned on a small light switch. It could have been one of the family portraits staring back at him from the mirror. The only thing he needed to complete the picture was a sword.

"Wow," Andrew said from beside him. "You look like a picture from one of those tourist books. Must be the long hair."

Noah gazed at his reflection with some amount of shock. He did indeed look like one of his ancestors, regal and haughty. Maybe it was the hat or maybe it was just the old world appeal of the tartan. Whatever it was, he was not certain he liked it and he reached up to slide the hat from his head, noticing that MacDaughtery refrained from meeting his gaze in the reflection.

"I am suffocating in this," Noah stated, twisting his collar. "I had no idea it would be so heavy."

"Maybe that explains why they wore kilts," Andrew said with a grin. "A bit of air conditioning below."

Even MacDaughtery managed a smile as he took the hat.

"No kilts," Noah reiterated.

With that accomplished they waited while MacDaughtery wrapped the items they were able to take with them. Andrew then ordered two suits and a new pair of boots for himself. They even took the hat. The rest of the order would be delivered to the Hall when they were finished in a day or so. It amounted to a fair number of parcels and a staggering amount of money.

Noah thanked the man and turned to leave. In the reflection of the front window glass he watched the man cross himself, a motion well known to Noah, having grown up in a Catholic school. Outside on the sidewalk, Noah shook his head. Then he looked up to see Andrew beckoning him into the connecting book shop and forgot about what he was thinking.

Spending money must have been on Andrew's mind because he seemed to take pleasure in buying whatever Noah lingered over. They left the book shop with several items; books on local history, tartans, Scottish myths, and three paperback novels. In another shop they bought tea and chocolates. Andrew walked Noah down to one of the three pubs on the street and ushered him through the ancient black-timbered doorway.

Inside the pub was warm and friendly, the initial noise of the lunchtime hour quieted down to a hush of a few voices and the familiar clatter of glasses, plates, and telly. They had barely settled in the ancient high-backed wooden booth when a young man came over to take their order. Noah garnered the usual once over that all out-of-towners received, this one lingering no doubt because he was with Andrew.

"What will it be, your Lordship?"

"Bring us two of the usual," Andrew ordered without need of a menu. He turned to Noah, rubbing his hands in anticipation once the man was gone. "Wait until you taste the steak and kidney pie. It melts in your mouth. It's even better than Mary's but do not tell her I said that or I will deny it."

Noah smiled and did not have the heart to tell his brother that he really did not eat meat, at least not often and definitely not organ meat. He supposed it would not kill him to try it. He was even more dismayed to see the drinks arrive, two large foam covered glasses of dark beer. Andrew must have seen the look on his face.

"What's the matter?" Andrew asked. "Don't like stout?"

"Do not drink at all, I am afraid. I really do not eat meat either."

Andrew rolled his eyes with a groan. "Aye, saints preserve us. You are going to give the family name a black eye. I suppose it would be tea you prefer?"

"Coffee would be good. I am really not very hungry."

Andrew shook his head but called out across the room to order coffee. "I suppose I should tell Mary Katherine of your city sensibilities before she puts down a sheep's head in front of you for dinner. We will buy some fish at the market as we leave."

Noah actually cringed. "Well, I could try the pie I guess but I draw the line at heads."

Andrew laughed. The coffee arrived, carried to the table by the owner, who had been behind the shiny black bar when they first came in. As Noah considered tasting the beer, the man's large hand reached out to take the glass of stout from beneath his fingers.

"We will have none of that," he said in a voice with an Irish accent. "Cannot have the local Constable citing me for corrupting a minor. Here is your coffee." With that said, he turned his attention to Andrew. "Andrew, good to see you out. I had to come over and see who was with you turning down my stout for coffee at nearly two o'clock in the afternoon. Doesn't look old enough to be drinkin' in the first place."

"He is old enough but turns out he does not drink."

The man shook his head in disgust. "What is the world comin' to, I tell ya."

Noah stared at the two of them. They were clearly friends, on a first name basis. The man was close to Andrew's age, maybe in his early thirties. He wore his thick black hair pulled back in a ponytail that hung down past his shoulders. His black eyes appraised Noah with a candid gaze, something that Noah was getting used to from the locals. Andrew made the introductions.

"Barry, this is my brother Noah. He has come to the Hall to stay for a bit. You two have a lot in common." They regarded each other with doubt. "Noah is a classical musician from London. Barry plays too. Even though you have lived here for years, Barry, you are still considered a city bloke and a foreigner."

Barry laughed heartily. "True enough. The only reason they allow me to stay is that I brew a good stout."

"That you do." Andrew took a deep draught of his beer.

As he continued to regard Noah, Barry's frown turned to recognition. "I know you. You are that chap that could play the Devil's Trill at thirteen. I have the CD of your concert in Prague. I still get chills when I hear that piece."

"Thank you," Noah said, almost ashamed at the awe in Barry's voice. "You are a musician as well then? What do you play?"

"The fiddle but I sound like you only in my dreams. I do folk music, ballads and such. I have a few CDs out but mostly I play at the local festivals like the one coming up. You should play for us since you are here. I know it's asking a lot, but we never get the chance for your caliber of artist out this way very often."

"He is talking about the Harvest Festival," Andrew explained when Noah looked lost. "It is coming up in a few days. Dora Finsterwall has already been in my face about it. She wanted to hold it at the Estate this year."

"That would be a great idea," Barry chimed in. "You've not

had the place open for years. Why not? It would mean a lot to the town's folk and with your brother here it would be the perfect opportunity."

"I don't know. Noah is kind of here to rest."

"Come on," Barry said to Noah. "I will fill in for you before and after, just a couple of pieces. It does not have to be the Trill. Next to me anything you did would seem like music from heaven. Man, you are really Andrew's brother? This town has a claim on the likes of you and never even knew it?"

Andrew's good will seemed to be wearing thin. "We will have to think about it. Keep this under your hat, Barry. I do not want Noah bothered with all this…celebrity stuff."

"Sure, sure. Whatever you are having, it is on the house. Let me know if you need anything else. Very good to meet you."

Noah shook his hand and watched him disappear back behind the bar.

"I guess you are a bigger name than I am, even around these parts," Andrew said.

"In many ways it is a small country," Noah replied with a sip of coffee. "This festival, what all does it entail? Would it be too much trouble to have it at the estate on such short notice?"

Andrew drank his beer and wiped his lip. "Not really, I guess. The committee will do all the work, setting up tents, food service, all that stuff. It is basically fun and games. Caber toss—that is log tossing—axe throwing, dancing, drinking…the usual excuse for a party before the long winter comes."

"Log tossing?"

Andrew laughed quietly. "Highland games are a connection to our past glories when the land was wild and so were the people. It would give you an excuse to wear that new tartan. I have not worn mine in several years I guess."

"Father was not the partying type," Noah said quietly.

Andrew's smile vanished. "I guess we should try and open the place up once again after all these years of isolation. That Trill he was talking about…I think I know the one. Were you really able to play that at thirteen?"

Noah nodded. That piece had set him apart and made his career. He viewed it in many ways as the creator of the piece had no doubt intended, with reverence and trepidation. There would be no way he could play anything complex in two days time with his wrist still bothering him, but he could play something.

"I would not turn down the idea," Noah ventured as their meat pies arrived, steaming hot. "I could do something. If it would help you get back in the town's graces, you should consider it."

Andrew smashed the flakey crust of the steaming pie with his fork, releasing the heavenly aroma. Even Noah had to admit it smelled appetizing. He held his fork suspended for a taste if he felt brave enough.

"We will see," Andrew said, taking a mouthful.

Noah had no doubt what Gavin would think of the idea. No way, no how, uh-uh. Well, Gavin did not have to know, did he? What would it hurt? The truth about his real name and his past would leak out eventually, even if it started in such a backwater town in the middle of nowhere. It had been Noah's choice to return and tie himself to such a place. All the same, he should probably call Gavin, if for no other reason than to find out what he was doing left to his own devices.

The pie was nauseating. Noah managed to nibble the crust until Barry's watchful eyes caught him and sent over a salad in its place. Noah waved in thanks when they got up to leave and Barry waved goodbye and winked. Only as they were going through the doorway the second time did Noah notice the figure carved in the stone lintel, the same figure he had seen cut into the stone entranceway at the clothing shop. It was the outline of a wolf, cut deep into the worn stone facing, where it had obviously been for hundreds of years.

Outside they turned to head back to the car. Several people, friends of Andrew, waved in their direction and Andrew waved back. They were connected, the village and the Bainbridge family, part and parcel as the land and the sea. These people had watched Andrew grow up. They had helped him bury his father. They were more a part of Andrew's life than Noah would ever be.

When they reached the car, Noah quietly asked what he had been dreading to voice out loud in Andrew's shifting frame of mind. "Drew, can we go to the churchyard? I would like to visit mother and father's graves."

Andrew stopped with his hand on the car door. His expression was unreadable but he merely looked down at his watch and then opened the door.

"Sure. Get in."

They drove the short distance in silence. The church was a medium sized building, ancient stone and timber set at the edge of the encroaching woods on the lip of a hill overlooking the sea. The churchyard itself spilled out across the stony land between the building and the forest, a wide lawn filled with jumbled Celtic stone crosses and dark moss-stained crypts hundreds of years old.

While the Hall had its own cemetery, no one had been buried on its land in over a hundred years. The latest of the family Bainbridge lay in repose under the soft green lawn of the churchyard, the family plot a large space of iron fencing and mausoleum reserved for them alone in the far desolate corner.

Noah stood looking down at the graves, the latest yet covered with a mound of soft brown earth. To the right was his mother Helen, dead and buried some twelve years. To the left was Andrew's mother, whom he had never known, dead even longer. Noah had been to none of their funerals and even though he knew it was his mother buried there, it still seemed an impossibility, some cruel trick of fate. A tear slid down his cheek and he reached to wipe it away with the back of his hand.

"Andrew, I want you to tell me how mother died."

Andrew made a small sound of displeasure. "I knew it was a mistake to come here."

Noah closed his eyes. "Andrew, I do not remember...I don't remember most of my life here. I need to find myself, that part of me that died that night and lies buried here in the ground with her. Do you understand?"

Andrew came up behind him. "I understand that our father did us a great injustice but I cannot bring back the dead, Noah. After all this time, is it not better to leave the dead as they are?"

As they are? Silent and holding on to their secrets? Noah knelt down and put his hand on the cold headstone of his mother's grave. There were none of the usual platitudes carved there, no words of comfort or carvings of angels or crosses, simply her name and the dates of her birth and death. As of yet there was no stone marking their father's grave.

"Andrew...Andrew, did I cause her death?"

"Good God, Noah!"

Andrew grabbed his brother by the arm and pulled him to his feet, wrapping his arms around Noah's shivering body. Noah squeezed his eyes shut to keep the past from getting too near and pressed his face into the hollow of Andrew's shoulder.

"Noah, how could you think such things?"

"Is that why my father hated me so much?"

"He did not hate you," Andrew said quietly. "He was indifferent, to both of us. I don't know what happened, truly. When I awoke that next day, you were both gone. He never told me why although I asked him for years. I do not understand any more than you do, but I know that you had nothing to do with her death. That is simply not possible. Put that out of your mind. If nothing else, know that you were not responsible for any of this. Maybe not remembering is a good thing."

Noah turned his head to wipe at his eyes. He felt exposed in the open, ripped apart by the grief over which he no longer seemed to have any control. Even his brother's strong arms did not seem to give him shelter. A sound nearby caught his attention and he looked up into the edge of the shadowy forest.

It could not have been what Noah thought he saw there in the dappled light; a crouching figure with scowling green eyes. He felt the now familiar rush of his soul leaving his body, the ghost at the edge of his vision vanishing in a flash of subtle fur and movement. Noah's body too gave away, leaving him lost once more in the unrelenting darkness.

Andrew tightened his embrace when he felt Noah slump against him. Clearly Noah's illness was more mental than physical, a weakness that could take him without warning during times of stress, an illness that made him easy prey to strong emotions. Caught unprepared, Andrew started to ease his brother to the ground.

"Here now, do you need assistance?" a voice called out.

It was Father Perrine hurrying their direction through the crosses and headstones as fast as his long vestments allowed him to scurry. With help to arrive at any moment, Andrew held Noah upright as best he could, staggering a bit at the unbalanced dead weight and his footing on the uneven ground.

"Thank you, that would be most helpful."

The priest came to a halt and offered to lift Noah's legs while Andrew repositioned his brother's inert body so that he could grip his upper half. Together they managed to carry their burden out of the churchyard and up into the quiet, semi-dark building, laying him down on one of the wooden church pews. Andrew took his brother's smaller hand and held it between his rough palms.

"What happened?" the priest asked with concern. "Should I fetch the doctor?"

Andrew shook his head. "It's just a faint. He will be all right in a moment or two. Just too much excitement lately."

"Who is he?" the priest asked.

"My brother, Noah. He is here from London for a visit."

"Your *brother*?"

The tone as much as the question caught Andrew's attention.

He raised his head to look across at Father Perrine. The priest was a fixture of the community even at his relative young age, watching over the religious health of his flock for almost a decade since the retirement of the previous priest. Father Perrine had buried Andrew's father with a memorial service in the same church a couple of weeks before. Now he sat with his white hand on Noah's forehead, looking every bit as ill as Noah.

"Your brother?" the priest repeated.

"Yes. I understand your shock. You came only after Noah had gone off to school. That is his mother, Helen, buried in the plot beside my mother and our father. I am afraid father's death has struck him rather hard."

"Well, I have no doubt. Let me fetch a cold cloth."

Father Perrine seemed to have recovered a bit from his shock. He went to find a cloth and dampen it with cold water, the quiet church amplifying the sound of his quick footsteps. He brought it back and folded it neatly across Noah's forehead.

"Will he be living here, at the Hall with you, Andrew?"

"I doubt that. It would be too difficult for him to live here with his busy career. He came to catch up with family things after father's death. Why?"

"Oh, no reason," the priest said. "It is just a surprise, that's all. Are you sure he does not need a doctor?"

As if to answer him, Noah's eyes flickered and opened. He reached to take the cloth from his forehead and wipe his face with it before looking up at the two serious expressions peering down at him. The hard wood beneath his back and the cold bits of colorful light coming from the stained glass windows let him know he was in the church even before he recognized the priest's vestments.

"Was I out for long?" he asked with a sigh.

"Not long," Andrew replied. "How do you feel?"

"Foolish."

"No sense for that," the priest said gently. "Dizzy? Did you hit your head?"

Noah slowly sat up, swinging his feet to the floor and feeling no immediate ill effects. The priest was regarding him with curious interest.

"No. I...I have spells," Noah admitted reluctantly. "Sorry Andrew. I know you tried to keep me from coming here."

"This is Father Perrine, Noah. He is the town's conscience."

"Hardly that. More like sounding board. I wish we could be meeting under a happier occasion. Please accept my condolences on the death of your father."

Noah nodded. He felt strange, as if everyone he had met was judging him somehow. Maybe it was his own conscience doing the judging. "Sorry to have interrupted your day."

"Not at all, young man. I was simply preparing for a meeting with Dora when I noticed you needed assistance."

Andrew groaned out loud. "Oh no. Do not tell me that woman is about to make an appearance next."

A slight smile twitched at the corner of the priest's mouth. "No, I was just leaving to meet her but I will be sure to tell her you said good day."

"I for one have had enough excitement for today," Andrew said. "Noah, do you think you can make it to the car?"

"Of course. Thank you, Father Perrine."

"Don't mention it. Please take it slowly."

Noah rose with Andrew's hand on his arm. They had only carried him in as far as they needed to put him down on the first pew of the back row. On the way out he dipped his finger in the basin of holy water near the door and, touching it to his forehead, crossed himself. It was habit after years of life in a school run by nuns. It seemed to startle Andrew but he remained silent, reaching to pull the heavy door open.

In the brighter light outside, Noah squinted and raised one hand to block the sun from his eyes. He was tired and every step felt like walking underwater. Safely in the car he buckled his seatbelt and leaned back in his seat. Father Perrine waved and headed off down the walking path toward the village. Andrew remained silent for the drive back to the Hall, forgetting to stop at the market for the promised fish, and Noah did not remind him. He had been enough trouble for one day.

When they arrived at the Hall and spilled out along with their packages, Noah was ordered to his room to rest. For once he did not argue; it took all his energy to climb the staircase and collapse into bed. Seth's dark form walked by carrying the parcels into the room before Duncan closed the drapes and chased everyone out. As his eyes closed with exhaustion, Noah heard Duncan's voice telling him dinner would be served in his room.

The last thing he remembered was Seth's green eyes flashing with unguarded contempt. Green eyes flecked with gold.

FIVE

It is far harder to kill a phantom than a reality.
  —Virginia Woolf

Noah awoke to a dark room and for a moment did not remember where he was. The scent of freshly turned earth lingered in his mind, causing his heart rate to jump for a moment. He slid out of the high bed and made his way into the bathroom, seeking the reassurance of light, which sprang to life the moment his hand touched the wall switch.

Even though he had slept for hours there were dark smudges beneath his eyes and his head ached with every thump of his heart. Digging around in his bag for an aspirin, he downed two with a small glass of water before turning on the water in the tub. Maybe a nice hot soak would help. Walking to the windows, Noah drew back the drapes and looked out across the countryside. It was late. Although the setting sun was painting the sky pink and purple, there was a large black cloud encroaching on the horizon. They were in for a rain storm that night.

Looking down, he could see a dark figure walking along the grass covered path that led from the garage areas at the side of the house to the gardens beyond. It could have been anyone. The figure stopped, half turning to look up where Noah stood at the window. He shrank back into the shadows on reflex, but there was no way anyone could see him there. After a moment, the figure continued out of sight.

Noah shivered and switched on the lamp at the bedside table. The golden glow did little to alleviate his mood so he walked around the bed and turned on the second one. At least there would be light when he came out of the bath later. Returning to the tub he added soaking salts and settled himself down in the steaming bath. His stomach rumbled with hunger and by the time he was drying off the rumbling came from outside, the storm growing nearer. It began to rain.

Dressed in jeans and a sweatshirt, Noah stood looking at his violin. If there was a chance that Andrew would relent and allow the festival to be held on the estate then he should practice, just in case. He wasn't in the mood. His small travel clock said it was 7:18 p.m. As his stomach grumbled unhappily he wondered if he would be eating any time soon; his lunch had been small and the hour for tea long past.

He proceeded to dig into the pile of items he had brought home from the village. The small package of chocolates was tempting but he left the box unopened and set them along with the tea on the dresser. When he reached for the boots another package tumbled out instead, books sliding across the floor at his feet. He bent and picked them up, carrying them to the bedside table. Looking at the cover proclaiming *Scottish Myths*, he forgot about the rest of the packages and sat down on the bed with the book in his hands.

Noah half smiled to himself when the first chapter was dedicated to the monster of Loch Ness, but then again "Nessie" was modern big business if not honest fun. The author included it tongue-in-cheek, stating that if ever a creature did exist that many a drunken Scotsman would have gone missing over the years. The rest of the book was dedicated to more scholarly discussions of ancient religious practices and folk mythology. Ancient myths of nature and cults of fertility goddesses abounded, some still practiced in modern times.

One story told of a human child stolen from its crib and replaced with a faerie child, parents none the wiser at the switch. What became of the human child was never told, but the "changeling" grew up often possessing unusual powers. Noah shivered at that tale, regarding it with an unsettling parallel to his own life. The entire litany of myths and monsters gave him the creeps and made him wonder about every "harmless" fairytale he had ever heard.

When a knock came at the door, it startled him.

"Come in."

It was Duncan with the dinner tray at last. He came inside and closed the door before moving to place the large tray on the table in front of the fireplace. He glanced at Noah, who tossed the book he had been reading on the bed as he rose.

"I hope you are feeling better, Master Noah."

"I'm starving," Noah admitted on smelling the tantalizing aroma of food.

Duncan smiled, lifting the lids from the plates. "An appetite is a good sign. I see you enjoyed your excursion to the village."

"Oh, I was just getting around to putting those things away."

"No bother, sir. Allow me."

Noah put a bite of poached salmon in his mouth, where it practically melted on his tongue. He sat back and sighed with delight. Duncan went about carefully unwrapping each item from the shopping spree to put them away. Thunder rolled in the distance and the lights flickered slightly. Duncan stopped what he was doing long enough to walk over to the dresser and light a couple of tall candles, placing them safely inside glass covers.

"Does the electricity go out often?" Noah asked, watching him.

"Every time the wind blows," Duncan replied with a smile. "We keep candles and flashlights in every room for just such an occasion. If the winter is bad enough we sometimes have to break out the oil lanterns for days on end. Not to worry. This is a small quick moving storm."

Noah returned to eating the salmon and creamy potatoes. Duncan put away the trousers and set the heavy boots just beneath the bed. Then he discovered the newly purchased tartan and shook out its heavy folds.

"Do you plan on wearing this anytime soon?"

Noah swallowed his mouthful. "Maybe. Andrew is considering allowing the autumn festival here on the grounds in a couple of days. I might wear it for that."

Duncan's eyebrows lifted in surprise. "The festival? We

haven't had a gathering on the estate since…for many years. If that is the case, I will leave this out to air. It has a certain slight smell of mothballs to it."

Noah nodded; that was the strange odor he had failed to recognize in MacDaughtery's odd little shop. He watched Duncan carefully drape the tartan over a large padded hanger and hang it on a hook at the side of the armoire.

"I didn't really see the need for it but Andrew insisted. I could have just worn Father's for the festival."

Duncan glanced at him. "That would be impossible, sir. He was buried in it."

Noah remained silent. Of course they had buried his father in his tartan; he had been a Scottish Laird. The tales and traditions were part of Noah's ancestry yet he felt so alien to the house and the landscape that he could have been from China instead of London. He was never going to fit in.

Duncan placed the hat on an empty top shelf and closed the armoire. He glanced at the books that were piled on the bed and table. "If it is Scottish history you are interested in, there are several excellent scholarly books in the study, sir."

Noah shook his head. "I am more interested in the myths. I wish I knew more about the family history though. I didn't even know about the specific tartan until today."

"Well, in that case, perhaps you should look in your father's room. He kept several such books and papers there. There is even an old genealogy written on parchment somewhere."

Noah tried not to gape. "Father's room? Is that allowed?"

Duncan seemed surprised. "I do not see why not."

"It is locked. I just thought…"

"It was locked for privacy during the wake and funeral dinner. Your brother has avoided going into that room for his own reasons. When I suggested he move into the suite after your father's funeral, he declined."

"I can understand how it might be hard for him this soon

after…"

"Yes, sir. I can unlock the door if you wish but I should warn you, it might be difficult for you too. Are you certain you are ready for that step so soon, Master Noah?"

Noah looked up into the butler's black, intelligent eyes. The sound of the rain spattering on the windowpane was the only sound in the room. He felt cold again. "Do you think my father haunts this place, Duncan?"

Duncan's expression did not alter. "Not in that room."

Noah shivered. This was his chance to get to know his father. Wasn't that what he wanted? His father had spent the last months of his life closeted in that room. It would be filled with his presence, his belongings, his memory. So why did that suddenly seem so daunting a chore?

"All right," he said with false bravado. "I would like to see father's room."

Duncan nodded. "I would suggest you wear a sweater. The room has been closed off and unheated for some time."

Noah did as suggested and pulled on a jacket. He also found a small flashlight in the dresser drawer and put it in his pocket, just in case. Closing the door to his room, he stepped across the hall and waited for Duncan to unlock the door to his father's room. A gust of frigid air greeted them from the darkness. Stepping inside first, Duncan switched on a light that rested on a small table just inside the suite. Lighted by the small golden glow, the room expanded out in front of him.

The entrance was a sitting room or small parlor with an upholstered sofa and chairs before a small stone fireplace. Round-top tables held up fancy Victorian lamps and a couple of straight backed chairs were pushed against the wall. A tiger skin rug covered the floor at the foot of the sofa and several walking sticks occupied an umbrella stand near the door. A large piece of furniture overpowered the space; an ancient hall tree that held three heavy jackets hanging from brass hooks and whose mirrored center was lined with age.

From where Noah stood in the doorway he could just make out the edge of the huge four-posted bed draped with curtains in the dark paneled room beyond. It was separated from the parlor by a partially open sliding pocket door. Beyond those doors the room was cold and dark and silent. With some hesitancy, Noah stepped into the front room.

"I will leave you alone," Duncan told him. Noah nodded. "Take as much time as you need. There are lamps on the table beside the bed just there," Duncan said, pointing them out. "I will see to heating your room for the evening."

With that he was gone, closing the hallway door behind him.

Outside the thunder rumbled. In the cold silence Noah stood alone with the memories of his dead father. The jackets hanging on the hall tree tickled his mind with their human shapes. There were stacks of magazines on the floor by the sofa and an old knitted throw blanket draped over its back. The room smelled of cold ashes, tobacco, and the slight mildew odor of age that permeated the entire ancient house.

Noah moved over to an old worn bookcase full of odds and ends, the shelves sagging under the weight of too many books. The worn spines of books told him that his father had liked spy novels and Agatha Christie mysteries. He quirked his mouth in a half smile; he liked mystery novels too. There were some history books, some political biographies, and a collection of smaller books of poetry.

English figurines sat on the mantel and table alongside empty shotgun shells; apparently his father was a huntsman, like so many country people. He had not seen the guns but they were probably downstairs in the study or one of the rooms off of the kitchen. A stuffed owl stretched its wingspan across a corner space. There were small stone figures and broken ceramic objects that looked like they should be in a museum, along with a couple of smoking pipes stacked in a jade bowl. A bottle of Scotch and two glasses resided on the floor next to the chair.

Sweeping his gaze forward into the next room, Noah hesitated. That huge cloth draped bed already unnerved him. He hated beds like that, beds that looked like they could swallow you up, hiding all sorts of spiders and monsters within their concealing shape. He closed his eyes to get that image out of his head. Another image popped in unwanted; had they carried his dead father up into that room, put him down in that bed?

Noah groaned out loud and shook himself. Everyone including Andrew would be laughing at him if he ran screaming out of the room now. To further jangle his nerves the lights flickered again but did not go out. He felt the hard cold flashlight in his pocket. Setting his jaw, he moved forward to the pocket doors and pushed them open. Without looking at anything else, Noah reached to turn the toggle on the bedside lamp and was relieved when more welcoming light flooded into the space.

The monstrously huge bed was covered with a green velvet spread and some kind of fur throw that looked like beaver or mink. The ancient posters were hung with the same dark green velvet, held in place with gold tasseled ties and falling to lie in puddles of fabric on the floor. He looked up into the space beyond the bed and felt his heart leap into his throat with enough force to almost strangle him. A flash of lightning lit the far end of the dark room with a moment of eerie blue light.

Noah stifled a scream by clamping one hand down over his mouth, falling to one knee in shock. A loud rumble of thunder momentarily covered his startled exclamation and echoed off across the sea. Reaching out to grab a handful of the bedcover for support, he climbed to his feet without taking his gaze from the painted eyes of the portrait staring back at him from across the floor. It was a face he barely remembered, one he had seen again only a few days ago in an aging photograph of a family he hardly knew.

Helen Westerhaven Bainbridge. His mother's lovely blue eyes stared into his while a knowing smile curved her painted lips. Standing there looking at her, Noah trembled violently. That was what Duncan must have meant when he said it was not his *father's* ghost that haunted the room. With an effort Noah slowed his shallow rapid breathing and regained control of his emotions.

It had been a shock to see her there.

The painting was huge, close to life size in an ornate gilded frame that took up a third of the far wall. Stepping deeper into the room, he was startled by other things. At the foot of the portrait was a desk, a long narrow fancy piece with golden pulls and curlicues, probably French and centuries old. The things on top of the desk held his rapt and stunned attention, drawing his gaze from his mother's laughing eyes as he again gasped for breath. With his legs shaking and his mind reeling, Noah collapsed into the chair and stared at one object and then another.

His face stared back at him from a picture frame. Next to that was another of him as a young child, maybe two or three years of age, in his mother's arms. The most startling one of all was the most recent, probably taken at one of his concerts since in it he was wearing the now trademark dark silk suit. In the photo he was tilting his head at an odd angle, a habit he had picked up at some point. He was doing the same thing at that moment and forced himself to sit straight.

Sitting in that room filled with ghosts, Noah did not know what to think. He had no idea that his father had kept up with him or his career over the years. The reality of those photographs certainly belied the actions of a man who hated his son. Noah looked up at the painted face of his mother, rendered forever young and vibrant on canvas. His father had closeted himself in that room with his memories, unable to face the world or his own sons.

Noah looked down when his fingers touched something metallic. It was a golden crucifix about four inches long, its delicate filigree work of Celtic styling and fine workmanship. He had seen no other religious symbols in the house to lead him to believe that his father or Andrew practiced any particular faith. Like the photographs, it was an incongruity.

Noah opened the upper desk drawer. It held writing pens and paper, reading glasses, a measuring tape, a glue stick, a small stapler, and a white binder. The binder contained his life, at least, scraps of it. There were newspaper and magazine clippings of his concerts and performances dating from the beginning almost up to the last trip to Japan. The few letters he had written to his father and which had gone unanswered were there also, tucked neatly inside plastic sheet holders. It gave him chills. He closed the book and replaced it.

There were other drawers filled with folders of papers that he gave only a cursory glance. His father had been corresponding with several people he had apparently known from his university days. The letters were oddly cryptic, talking about something that seemed to be heavy on his father's mind in the last few months of his life. Noah could make no sense of it. There was a small book that looked like it was hand bound in leather, almost black with age. He very carefully lifted it out and cracked it open.

It was the genealogy that Duncan had referred to earlier, carefully written out in flowing script, drawn in lines of black ink on brittle yellow parchment. Noah handled it carefully, afraid of damaging its ancient pages. The words at the beginning of the book were in a language that he could not read. As far as he could tell, the Bainbridge line was far older than he had imagined, perhaps even older than the first date written in the book of clans. The pages crackled and snapped as he slowly closed it and slid it into its place.

The next thing he found was a thin book of prayers. As he looked at it he recognized that they were prayers of protection in Latin, a language he had learned in school and could read almost as well as Italian or French. Two were prayers of intercession to the Archangel Michael. One dog-eared page was an ancient rite of exorcism. He looked again at the cross and a long rumble of thunder made the hair on the back of his neck stand on end. Against his will, he glanced uneasily over his shoulder.

There was nothing there of course, only an empty room and an empty bed. He chewed his lip in thought. The overpowering presence of his mother daunted him. Her portrait dominated the space, commanding attention from any point in the room. It was almost like his father had intended it to be a shrine; the photos of them at her feet, the desk like an altar. Maybe Gavin was right.

Maybe his father had simply come unhinged at Helen's death and could not stand to look at her son, the living reflection of her image in Noah's delicate features.

He shivered and again looked around the empty room. It gave him the creeps thinking of his father locked in that room with *her*, watched by her painted eyes whether he was sitting at the desk or lying in the bed just beyond. The dead should stay dead, but in that house with its many ancestral portraits and dark memories, he doubted whether many of them did. He could feel the press of the house gathering in the gloom, the storm outside moving into the distance.

What did Andrew think of the shrine and the ghost his father had chosen to live with instead of him? He had to know it was there, just as Duncan knew. A new depth of sorrow for his brother stirred in Noah's chest.

Andrew's bitterness was understandable. Noah's mother had replaced the memories of Andrew's mother when they came to live at Bainbridge Hall. Even after Helen's untimely death she had still managed to supplant his father's love, the Lord choosing to turn away from both of his sons to live with the memory of a dead wife. That Andrew had offered him brotherly affection or could even stand to look at him filled Noah with sadness and gratitude.

He sighed, a deep exhaling of emotion. It made his father seem an even more pathetic figure. Gavin was right. He could not go back. He could not even fathom the twisted emotions that had formed their miserable lives. He could only feel sorrow and pity for the children they never were and the adults they would never become.

Noah looked up at his dead mother's painted face. "I wish I knew who you were," he said out loud. "I wish I knew who I could have been. But I am no long certain I am willing to face my fear long enough to find out. Is that disloyal of me, Mother?"

A loud crash startled him, making Noah whirl in his chair. The lights chose that exact moment to go out. The plunge into blackness was even more unnerving than the sound had been, raising the hairs on his scalp and sending his pulse thundering in his veins. His fingers scrabbled with his pocket to find the flashlight, the time between the thought and the action seeming to take an eternity. The meager beam of light shot out across the room and promptly went out. With rising terror he clicked it on and off and thumped it across the palm of his hand, but it refused to cooperate.

Out of the corner of his eye Noah caught a glimpse of what seemed to be a dim greenish light. He had thought the drapes were closed when he came into the room. Holding his breath in his throat with the useless flashlight clutched in his fingers, Noah forced himself to slowly turn his head. The drapes were slightly open but the dim misty light did not come from outside.

A sound of surprised exclamation made him jump. He jerked his gaze toward the door as footsteps became audible in the front parlor. Noah realized that the sliding pocket doors were closed only when someone yanked them open with a mumbled curse. A beam from a flashlight moved across the floor, someone stepping into the room. The tiny light and the presence of another living human broke the spell that had held Noah under its power. He was on his feet when the narrow beam of light hit him full in the face.

Noah heard a jagged intake of breath, and then an eerie, hair raising sound that scared him even more than the darkness had. The person dropped the flashlight and turned with a stumbling lurch that sent them crashing into the edge of the partially opened door, bouncing back into the bedside table and lamp. With a second deafening crash whoever it was hit the floor amid splintering wood and shattering glass and lay still. The flashlight rolled to a stop, its light aimed beneath the bed, but it was enough for Noah to see and recognize the dark sprawling figure.

"Andrew!"

Noah jumped into motion, dashing across the span of floor between them and dropping to his knees amid the glittering field of broken glass. He grabbed the flashlight and turned the beam on his brother's face.

Andrew had fallen back onto the insubstantial bedside table with all his weight, and it promptly collapsed beneath him, sending him reeling headfirst into the heavy wooden bed frame with the lamp crashing down on top. He lay with his head at an angle and his arms and legs sprawled in all directions. A trickle of dark red blood made its way from his hair down the side of his ashen face, his eyes closed in unconsciousness.

"Andrew?" Noah asked with uncertainty. His brother did not move when Noah touched him gently on the arm. "Andrew can you hear me?"

More blood flowed down from the head wound, seeping into Andrew's collar. Noah tugged on his brother's much heavier body, managing to move him from beneath the edge of the bed and straighten the angle of his neck. The splinters of the destroyed table creaked beneath Andrew's back and legs. At least their clothing kept the broken glass from cutting into their skin.

"Duncan!" Noah turned his head and shouted at the top of his lungs. "Duncan, help me! Andrew is hurt!"

He had no idea where Duncan was or if anyone could hear him shouting through the heavy walls of the old house. The prickling sensation returned on the back of his neck and he twisted himself around to look behind him, scanning the dark silent room with the flashlight. Nothing moved. The earlier green mist was gone. Noah turned the beam back on Andrew's face with dismay and then scrambled to his feet to go for help.

"Duncan!" he shouted, reaching the hallway door and stepping out of the room. "We need help!"

To his immediate relief he saw the butler hurrying in his direction down the dark hallway, his progress lit by the golden glow of a candle lantern. Noah stood in the doorway until Duncan had reached him, the butler's sharp face and dark eyes alive with flickering light.

"What is it, sir? What has happened?"

"Andrew is hurt. He hit his head pretty hard."

Without need for further explanation, Duncan followed him

into the dark room and assessed the situation with a sharp exhale of breath. The broken glass crunched beneath the soles of their shoes. Duncan set his light down on the floor and knelt beside his master to check the severity of the injury.

"Please go into the bath and fetch a towel or two," the butler directed with a grim expression made grimmer by the flickering light. "That door there, to the left."

Noah noticed the closed door for the first time. Taking Andrew's flashlight with him, he grabbed two towels and managed to dampen a washcloth before hurrying back to Duncan. He handed everything over without a word and crouched down on his heels, holding the light. The butler's hands were gentle and precise, wiping aside the blood and probing the thick wavy hair for lumps and bumps. Satisfied, he pressed one of the towels onto the wound and held it in place.

"What happened?" Duncan inquired at last.

Noah shook his head. "The lights went out. I was sitting at the desk when I heard him come into the front room. The pocket doors were closed. They had been open, I swear. Andrew came into the room and…he dropped the light and ran into the edge of the door. Then he fell backwards onto the table."

Duncan looked at him with an odd expression. Noah had no idea what he must look like in the candlelight but he certainly felt strange, shaking and breathless. As they contemplated each other Andrew began to make gentle moaning sounds and move his legs. When he tried to move his head, they both sprang to hold him down.

"Lay still, sir," Duncan said with authority. "You have a head injury."

Andrew groaned louder and then his eyes flickered open with dull awareness. "Duncan?"

"You are bleeding," Noah told him, still pressing his shoulder down gently. "Don't move yet."

Andrew's eyes shifted to look at him. Noah watched the dullness lift and some amount of awareness return to the dark eyes. Beneath the glare of the flashlight, Andrew looked as pale as wax.

"Noah," he said in a flat voice. "Noah?"

Noah nodded his head, tears threatening to spill from his eyes. He was as rattled as Andrew. "I didn't mean to scare you like that, Drew."

Andrew closed his eyes and sighed. When he opened them again knowledge of what had happened along with embarrassment and annoyance resided in his gaze.

"Noah," he said again.

"You have soaked the towel," Duncan said with the same grim voice. "If you can sit up now I need to see to your wound."

They carefully assisted Andrew to sit amid the field of destruction. He groaned with effort but managed to remain upright. He reached up to hold the fresh towel in place on the side of his head and they pulled him to his feet, where he stood swaying and cursing. Noah slipped his brother's free arm around his shoulders to hold him up.

"Let us get him into the bathroom if we can," Duncan suggested. "At least we can keep him from bleeding all over the rugs."

Andrew gave them both a disagreeable look but managed to walk as they directed him into the bathroom a few feet away. Once inside the dark space, Duncan hauled him over to the toilet and made him sit down on the cushioned lid. Noah ran back to fetch the candle lantern so they could better see what they were doing, and returned to hold the flashlight for Duncan to inspect the wound in Andrew's scalp. Andrew alternated between cursing and moaning with pain at the older man's probing fingers.

"An impressive gash," Duncan said, once again pressing the cloth to the wound and holding it in place with pressure. "You could use stitches."

"Forget it," Andrew grumbled. "Just slap a bandage on it."

"We must get the bleeding to stop first. Hold still."

Noah met his brother's steady gaze with guilt. They both knew what had happened now and it was both embarrassing and revealing. Noah could well imagine what it must have seemed like for Andrew to see his face coming out of the darkness—Noah's face that was so like his mother's—in that room that was dominated by her presence.

"I am sorry, Drew," he apologized again.

Andrew gave an odd little laugh. "It's all right. I just was not expecting...I was not expecting something to move in the darkness. My fault."

"I guess it is my fault," Duncan stated. "I should have told you I had left Master Noah in this room."

"So we are all to blame," Andrew said with a grimace. "That does not make this any less embarrassing. Duncan, don't you dare tell anyone about this."

"My lips are sealed, sir. I believe the bleeding is under control. I will fetch the first aid supplies if you will sit here and keep pressure on the wound."

Duncan took the flashlight, leaving the two brothers looking at each other with guilt and embarrassment. The darkness was not so frightening in the clean porcelain space of the bathroom even though they both looked like terrified children. Andrew's face was ghastly white with dark smudges of blood on his skin and shirt. Some of his blood stained Noah's hands and the knees of his jeans.

"It wasn't your fault," Andrew said quietly. "It was just so... startling."

"I am sorry. I should have called out to you, but I was so—"

Andrew made a small sound. "Forget it. It is that room. It is bad enough in the daylight."

"Yeah," Noah agreed. "I can understand why you do not want to be in there."

Andrew fell silent. Noah squirmed slightly beneath the scrutiny. He realized that his hands were hurting and looked down at them in the candlelight. There were probably bits of broken glass imbedded in his skin, but beneath the stains of Andrew's blood he could see small half-moon shaped indentations in his palms. At some point he had clenched his fists so hard his fingernails had dug into his flesh. He turned on the water and washed his hands, grateful for hot water even as it stung the small cuts.

"I guess I should have asked your permission before…"

"Don't be silly. I heard the crash and came to investigate. The door to the room was open or I would never have thought of looking in here."

Noah frowned at his brother's pale face. "That's strange. The door to the hall should have been closed. The pocket doors were open, at least, they were when I went into the bedroom. Do you think…?"

Andrew's eyebrows rose slightly. "What? You think the crash was the inside doors being slammed shut? I guess we will have to wait for daylight to inspect for any other obvious cause of the noise." He gave an odd little shiver. "You really scared me witless, Noah. I thought…well you know what I thought. Stupid, isn't it? A grown man behaving like that. I don't think my heart rate is back to normal yet."

Noah did not smile at his brother's misfortune. "This house, Andrew…"

Noah stopped on the verge of spilling his guilty secret to Andrew. He could hear Duncan approaching and his lips sealed themselves shut, trapping the words inside. How could he possibly tell his brother about his own version of a mental defect? Andrew would no doubt think he was as crazy as their poor father must have been in his last years.

That the house seemed to be responsible for unleashing his hidden talent was only a guess at best, yet it was his only answer. Noah could feel the shadowy undercurrent even then, swirling just beyond his awareness in the dark recesses untouched by the dim golden light of the candle flame.

"Here we are," Duncan stated, setting the first aid box and its contents on the counter.

Noah moved out of his way, allowing the butler to perform the necessary actions. Andrew winced and sucked his breath in when the cold burning antiseptic touched his wound. His mouth pressed into a tight, grim line, his gaze never leaving his brother's face. Several minutes later Andrew was a shade whiter and swaying slightly as Duncan finished wrapping the bandage around his forehead to hold the gauze pads in place over the cut. When that was accomplished, Duncan stepped back and held up one hand.

"How many fingers, sir?"

Andrew scowled. "Three. I will be fine."

"That may be but you will certainly have a headache in a few moments and probably suffered a concussion. Take some aspirin and we will keep you awake for the next couple of hours."

Andrew continued to grumble. Duncan shook out two pills and handed over a glass of water. His patient swallowed them with a single gulp and put the glass down on the counter. The lights chose that moment to come back to life, noticeable only because the room beyond had been in total darkness. The lamp that had been turned on in the parlor sent a sudden glow onto the green bed, enough to see the dim outline of objects through the door of the bathroom.

Duncan reached over and flipped on the bathroom light.

"Good heavens," he said with dismay.

In the bright white light the damage was clearly visible. Andrew looked even more ghastly; his face was tinged with a sickly green color. The blood staining his shirt was bright red and there were red spatters down the entire front of it and on one sleeve. A good size bump stood out just at the edge of the bandage.

Noah looked only slightly better because the blood staining his clothing was not his. His face was as white as Andrew's and his long hair gave him away; they could see it trembling as it hung half over his face.

"I dread to see what the room looks like," Duncan said without much sympathy.

"Have a look at Noah's hands," Andrew said with the same grim expression.

Duncan took Noah's hands one at a time and removed several bits of glass from the cuts with tweezers. Finished, he then dabbed the cuts with alcohol and applied a few necessary bandages.

"Please change your clothing, both of you. Leave the bloodstained garments on the bathroom counter of your room so the girls can treat them tomorrow. I will clean this room once we get you taken care of. I suggest we meet again in the small drawing room as soon as you two clean up."

They nodded in agreement, too embarrassed to argue. With the lights on, the space between the bed and the pocket doors was indeed a small disaster. Shiny bits of glass were scattered everywhere amid the splintered remains of the night table. They skirted around it as best they could, with Duncan shaking his head and sighing at the damage.

Rose Marie was standing in the hallway, wringing her hands, when they emerged into the light. She was the only other person who stayed in the house at night besides them, her rooms just beyond the kitchen.

"What is going on in this house?" she asked, her eyes widening at the sight of them. "Good heavens, have you been fighting?"

The two brothers looked at each other and started laughing, further alarming her. Noah shook his head, finding it amusing that she could think he would get the best of Andrew in a fist fight. Duncan was not amused and tightened his grip on Andrew's arm, propelling him down the hall toward his room while issuing orders.

"Please make some tea, Rose, and take it into the small drawing room. I will see to the injured party and do the cleaning up. Master Noah, go to your room and change."

Noah jumped to obey. Something about Duncan gave him the impression of a military man; no nonsense, accustomed to giving orders and expecting action without question. How he had ever chosen such a subservient role as butler was a mystery. They left Rose Marie standing in the hall looking perplexed, but she too scurried away to do Duncan's bidding.

In the safety of his room, Noah closed the door with a sigh and leaned against it for a few moments to gather his thoughts. The room was comfortably warm, the fire glowing in the hearth and the lights on as he had left them. He pulled off his jacket and inspected it for bloodstains, finding none. His jeans had faired the worse, from the knees down spattered with blood. There were smaller drops on his shirt front, no doubt from his wounded hands.

Noah left the clothing out on the counter as Duncan had requested. He took a moment to inspect his hands and brush his hair. Dressed in black sweatpants and a soft turtleneck shirt, he pulled on a woolen zippered sweater and stuck his feet inside loafers. Warmer, he headed downstairs.

There was no one in the drawing room when he arrived, but he turned on the lights and made a space on the coffee table for the tea service. Noah considered making a fire in the hearth but he was useless along those lines; he had never had to start a fire at home, or even do laundry or cook for himself. As he thought about it he was rather useless in general. He stuck his lower lip out in a pout of self discovery and irritation. Once he got back home he would tell Gavin to stop babying him and maybe even take cooking lessons.

Rose Marie entered the room carrying a large tea tray and eyed him with silent suspicion. She put it down on the table he had cleared. He withered beneath her scrutiny, reaching up to twist a strand of his hair like he often did when upset.

"Really," he said in defense of the accusation in her eyes. "It was an accident, nothing more."

She said nothing in reply but turned her back on him and left the room, the sound of her bedroom slippers flapping in her wake. He sat down on the sofa with a groan of defeat and contemplated the tea tray. She had managed easily enough in her outrage; the tray was overflowing with tea cakes, biscuits, cold cuts and cheese. Noah looked up when the others came into the room.

Andrew looked somewhat better in dark clothes under a heavy green robe. Duncan had managed to wipe the blood from his hair, and even though Andrew came into the room under his own power, Noah had no doubt that Duncan had been holding onto him until that point. Noah felt his lips twist in a half smile. Apparently stubbornness was a family trait.

"How do you feel?" he ventured to ask when Andrew sat down across from him. "Dizzy? Stomach okay?"

Andrew groaned. "It was until I saw all those sweets. How about some brandy?"

"No alcohol," Duncan replied, checking to see if the tea was ready to pour. "Not a good remedy for a possible concussion. Have your tea, sir."

Andrew's hand trembled only slightly taking the proffered cup and saucer and he sat back to sip the hot calming liquid. It did seem to do him some good, as he released his breath in a deep sigh and some color began to return to his cheeks. Noah downed his first cup in a few gulps and Duncan poured more. Without asking or being instructed, Duncan then turned and began making a fire in the fireplace while Noah watched over his shoulder with interest.

"I'm sorry, Andrew," Noah said again.

"Stop apologizing. It just makes it worse."

"She thinks I hit you."

Andrew groaned. "Okay, that makes it worse."

"I will explain to Rose," Duncan volunteered. "I will come up with something plausible."

Andrew scrunched down into the cushions. "Does she really think I could get beat up by my little brother? If this gets out I will never live it down."

"As you will be wearing a bandage for a few days, we can hardly keep it quiet. Which is worse?" Duncan asked over his shoulder. "The supposed beating or running into doors in the dark?"

Noah laughed at the look on his brother's face and made a karate chop motion with his hands. Andrew burst out laughing, almost spilling his tea. Duncan turned to see the two of them roaring with laughter. He crossed his arms over his chest and stood up.

"I am glad you now find it so amusing," Duncan stated.

They managed to stifle their amusement, subsiding into snickers. Andrew let his breath out in a sigh at the look on Duncan's face.

"We will stick to the door story," Andrew agreed. "I tripped over my feet in the dark and fell down. Perfectly believable to anyone who knows me."

"Very well, sir. I will go clean up the mess."

They watched Duncan leave the room with the stiff dignity of a man wronged. They looked at each other and shrugged, turning to their tea in silence. The house was very quiet, as the storm outside had rolled away, leaving only a gentle rain in its wake. It was barely noticeable against the thick windowpanes some distance from where they sat near the fireplace.

The small drawing room was hardly small; it only seemed small in comparison to the cavernous space of the main room, so large it was arranged into multiple seating areas with all the ambiance of a grand hotel lobby. The small drawing room was a fourth its size, arranged in a more livable space of over-stuffed chintz sofas and arm chairs. The oriental rugs were thick and well cared for and the various tables held an assortment of flower arrangements and art pieces.

A large and formidable piece of furniture against one wall hid all the modern electronics that filled every household; television, DVD player, stereo speakers, etc. It seemed to be the Hall's one concession to the fast moving modern world. Few of the rooms had private telephone access and even in a house the size of the Hall, there was no intercom system. One still called to servants the old fashioned way by mean of bell pulls or, as Noah had done, shouting at the top of one's lungs.

The electrical wiring was fairly modern but the location of the Hall made the delivery of reliable power difficult. For the same reason there was no cell phone coverage, something else Noah had discovered on arrival; all calls had to go through land lines. While the Hall had conceded to modern plumbing at some point in its past, the heat still came from wood-burning fireplaces and a collection of old boiler style radiators that had their own set of problems. Any necessary air conditioning in the summer came from open windows. It was almost like three hundred years had gone by without anyone noticing.

"Does it hurt much, Drew?" Noah inquired with some amount of guilt.

"Not too much. My hip hurts more. I guess I bruised it when I so gracefully obliterated the table."

"I'm sorry."

"Stop apologizing! This is my own bloody fault. I should be apologizing to you for making you stay up late to keep me company."

Noah shrugged. "I am used to late hours. My usual schedule is sleep late, stay up late."

"I guess that's right. You are accustomed to the scurry and noise of city life and late night entertainment. You must find it totally boring out here with nothing to do. Even the village shuts down by eight."

"Well, I am here to get some rest."

"We have done a poor job of that so far, have we not?" They regarded each other in silence that Andrew was the first to break. "Noah, I should have prepared you for that room. Why didn't you just ask me to see it?"

"When I first arrived I was surprised that you had not moved into father's rooms. The door was locked so I just ignored it until Duncan mentioned some of the books that might be there. I'm sorry, I should have waited."

"What books?" Andrew asked, perplexed.

"Nothing in particular. He saw that I was interested in local mythology and such."

Andrew's face was expressionless. He reached over and poured himself more tea, settling back on the cushions. His lips were slightly pale. "I guess finding her there was kind of a shock."

"You could say that," Noah admitted. "I had a similar reaction to yours…only the lights were on at the time."

Andrew grimaced. "I guess you were right to question father's state of mind. That room kind of opens a lot of questions."

"Drew, was father…unbalanced?"

Andrew raised his eyebrows. "Unbalanced," he repeated. "That might be a good word for it. At least it sounds better than mad as a hatter. No, he was not crazy, not any usual form of insanity, I mean."

Noah felt his blood chill. "What do you mean, Drew?"

"He talked to her, like she was alive and in the room with him. Gradually it just…took him away from the rest of us. In the last six months or so he seemed to be working himself up to something. He was delving into the family history, looking for obscure texts, digging up old documents that I had never even seen before."

"I found the old genealogy in his desk," Noah admitted.

Andrew nodded. "Stuff like that. He started mumbling things in Latin and Gaelic. I don't know either language so I have no idea what he was saying. I think he might have had secret meetings with Father Perrine, why I have no idea. I found a crucifix next to his body that day, on the path. Before that, to my knowledge, father had no ties with religion of any kind. We give money to the church but never go there to worship. He started to lock himself in his rooms for days on end. That is when he changed his will."

Noah's eyes widened at that information. He had no idea his father had been so isolated and so intense. He could see in Andrew's eyes the toll it had taken on him. Dealing with mental illness was never easy.

"I am sorry Andrew. I didn't know."

Andrew shook his head and grimaced. "I chose to ignore him, like he ignored me. You had no way of knowing. You were gone… You had no ties to either of us and your own life to lead. There was no reason for me to burden you with worry over things beyond your control."

"I still do not understand the will," Noah stated, at a loss to understand a lot of things.

"That makes two of us. I truly had no idea, Noah, that you were a Bainbridge by blood. I found out like you did, when the attorneys read the will."

Noah shook his head. The shock of that had still not worn off.

"It infuriated me, that father could do that to you, to us," Andrew continued darkly. "And then to include that stupid clause. I can only imagine what that did to you."

Noah blinked tears out of his vision. Maybe they would never understand it. How could you understand the reasoning of an unbalanced mind? Perhaps everything he had feared was an illusion, a warped misunderstanding of cause and events.

"I guess father never figured you would have the guts to turn down the money."

Noah smiled weakly. "The money is the furthest thing from my mind. I hope you know that, Andrew."

"Yeah, I guess I always knew that. You never struck me as the kind of bloke to hold grudges. So, here we are. What do you say that we just put everything behind us and start out fresh from here?"

"Sounds like a plan."

"Good," Andrew said with a grin. "Then due to the lack of anything to do around here but eat, I will—on account that the hit to my head has given me strange ideas—consent to the use of the grounds for the Harvest Festival. God, did I just say that?"

Noah laughed. "Yes, you did."

Andrew groaned. "Dora will be in my hair every moment once I give her the go ahead."

"Don't worry. I will help."

"*You* will no doubt be the star attraction and you may change your mind once you meet Dora. Think you are up to it?"

"I am not the one with a head injury."

"Thanks for reminding me. Ouch. I am not much up for reading or chess. How about some plain old television for a bit?"

They made themselves comfortable in front of the newest drama on the BBC and spent the next couple of hours engaged in small talk and mind numbing programs. Duncan came and went several times and finally agreed that Andrew could go to bed without much worry over his head injury. They retired to their separate rooms in the huge silent house.

Although Noah was tired, it took a long time for him to get to sleep and even then his dreams kept him from a peaceful night. He tossed and turned in the soft scented sheets, muttering to himself in Gaelic, his closed eyes seeing the image of his mother's painted face trying to tell him something he could not hear.

Six

Could be worse—could be raining.
—*Young Frankenstein,* Mel Brooks

London awoke to a chilly autumn day hinting at rain. The wind blew with a noticeable rawness across the Thames and the rustle of leaves was an ever present background noise when Gavin Moore went for his morning run through the park. He had gotten out of bed in a bad mood, and the draining four mile jog in the cold wind took some of the dark humor out of him. Some, but not all.

Back at the flat he showered and breakfasted by 8:15 and sat drinking coffee and reading the *Times* without really paying attention to anything more than headlines. The flat was quiet and dark beyond the room where he sat. The lack of Noah's presence was a gaping emptiness that affected him more than he wanted to admit. Without the near constant music and the flurry of activities, all of London seemed less than it was.

And Gavin hated waiting. Worse, he hated waiting with nothing to do. He had errands and activities—he had picked up dry cleaning, done some shopping, read over several contracts and proposals—but none of them took his mind away from what was really chewing at him. He had to trust other people to find the information he wanted to dig up himself, and the indeterminable wait was driving him crazy.

He had gone out with a group of friends the night before in an effort to distract himself. The clubs seemed impersonal, his friends uninterested, and the dinner mediocre. He had run into Marjori, one of Noah's fellow symphony violinists, and she was sporting a new ring and a new fiancé, both of them so excited and filled with life that it was almost nauseating.

In the end all the evening accomplished was a dismal realization that he was alone in the world and most likely going to remain that way. Gavin had then proceeded to drink his frustrations away and lived to regret it that morning. He was also annoyed that Noah had not rung up to let him know how it was going at the old homestead. He was damned if he was going to be the first to phone, especially considering the way they had left it.

Why did it have to be Scotland to cause such a rift between them now? Gavin took another swallow of his coffee, his thoughts drifting away from the newspaper. It wasn't *Scotland* he disliked, per se. Gavin had been to Edinburgh and Glasgow and they were large, charming cities filled with industry and culture, much like London or any other major metropolitan area. It was the miles and miles of *nothing* in between that he disliked.

Maybe it was the fact that he had spent two months stuck out in the windswept nothing in the cold and the rain while scratching through a peat bog with a dental pick that had brought about the aversion to Scotland and all things Scottish. That had been the last thought Gavin had given to a career in archeology before he gave it up for law.

That early fall—it had been early September surely and not the dead of winter—had been both miserable and glorious for as long as it lasted. The dig itself had been a wretched experience, one Gavin now equated with what hell must be like. If hell was cold instead of hot surely it could be no worse than the wet, windy nothingness of the Scottish Highlands while trying to sleep in a soggy tent and kneel on the spongy cold ground raking furrows in the stinking earth with a dental pick. He shuddered to think about it still.

The change of career study had been an immediate epiphany as soon as he found a warm bed. The fact that the bed had been in Edinburgh in the rooms of his archeology professor's assistant had been immaterial at the time; that had been an eye opening experience for Gavin in more ways than one. That man had known every sexual position in the book and every bar in the city and they drank themselves into a stupor that had taken all of winter to overcome.

During that long, dark winter Gavin had discovered some

things about himself that he didn't like. He had been young and foolish. Somewhere between the drinking and the sex he had fancied himself in love and stated it out loud. That had been the beginning of the end of his relationship with his first real lover, and with Scotland. He had been used and tossed away like a bottle in a long line of empty bottles of Scotch. The last three weeks had been as terrible as the first two had been glorious.

Gavin understood only much later that it was all part of the plan: seduce and destroy. The drunken binges became filled with caustic, biting words and sometimes stinging blows that he had at first simply accepted in shock. When the cursing and punching had not done the trick, the truth delivered in the most calculated manner possible certainly had; he caught his lover in the act with someone else. The circumstances were intentional, as were the parting words, spoken in barely disguised contempt with that sexy Scottish burr, from a man stone cold sober.

Perhaps the reason he hated Scotland had more to do with the man than the country, but in Gavin's mind the two were indistinguishable. That winter had changed his life. He had grown up. He had gone back to school with a vengeance borne of the need to prove himself worthy, if only to himself. Gavin had learned to guard his true nature at the hands of a master manipulator. It was a hard lesson to learn at nineteen.

Somewhere down the line, Noah seemed to have learned the same lesson. Gavin still thought of his employer as a kid even though there were only four or so years between them. When he had first been interviewed at the agency for position of personal assistant to Mr. Westerhaven, Gavin had not known who Noah was and had not been expecting a musician, much less a kid. At the time Noah was barely eighteen years old and if he still looked like a kid at twenty-two, he more resembled a child then…at least, until you looked him in the eye.

Gavin had passed through the first and second round of interviews and background checks and had finally been allowed to meet his prospective employer face to face in, of all places, the symphony hall. That had been his first clue that the position was going to be different from what he expected. The second clue was sitting in the vast empty hall with the few other job candidates while they listened to Noah's practice with the single pianist on stage. It had been an oddly disconcerting experience.

Gavin was certain that he was not the only one of the applicants who thought they would be interviewing with the thirty-something gentleman playing the piano. While Gavin sat there in the semi-darkness listening to the music, he had been aware of seeing and hearing only the boy with the violin, the man at the piano fading into the background.

The sound coming out of that violin had transfixed him with a magical spell, reaching some place inside that he had never known existed until that moment. Time had ceased to move while that slip of a boy had stolen his soul with those strings, binding him surely as gravity held the earth in its orbit.

When the rehearsal ended and they were ushered up onto the stage, they had all been shocked when the one who turned toward them had been the boy and not the man. The agency woman had introduced the four of them, one by one, to the boy even though two of the candidates clearly viewed him with arrogant dismissal. Noah Westerhaven shook their hands without speaking, holding his violin in the opposite hand as if it were part of him. Noah had shown no emotion, which Gavin thought odd and extremely controlled for a kid.

Only when the boy shook his hand and looked him in the eye did Gavin understand; this boy had learned through the school of life to show no part of himself to strangers. The long slender hand held his for no longer than the accepted length for a handshake, yet the startling blue of Noah's eyes had lingered with a nearly imperceptible awareness. Gavin had held his breath until that gaze moved on.

The final interview process was unlike anything Gavin had ever gone through, but then again, he had never met a celebrity or been interviewed for such an exalted position. They each gave a small summary of their schooling and experience, then expanded upon by the agency woman, while Noah sat halfheartedly playing the piano and occasionally asking what seemed at first like totally immaterial questions.

In reality he was performing a discreet personality test in a totally natural and unassuming manner. When it was over, Noah no doubt knew a lot more about the four of them than they knew about him. They left none the wiser and Gavin had been completely in the dark.

He had spent the next two days doing research on Noah Westerhaven only to be astonished at what he found. Noah really was a kid, although a genius it seemed. He had been in charge of his own career since he was sixteen and the world of classical music was agog over his talent. Gavin's experience with classical music was limited but he understood genius when he heard it. That was about all he could find out. It was like Noah had fallen from the sky with a violin in his hand and channeled music straight from the heavens.

What on earth would a genius want with the likes of him?

Gavin didn't have a chance. His experience with law was limited—he had no license to practice yet—and he had never been a personal assistant to anyone. The agency had explained that the position would include travel, contract negotiations, scheduling arrangements, and all the duties included in waiting on Noah hand and foot. Celebrities were expected to be arrogant and demanding. There would be no personal life with this job, at least not much of one anyway.

So why had he wanted it so badly he barely slept for two nights? It was crazy. Getting the invitation for a front row seat for Noah's symphony performance on the third day had been a shock. Holding it with shaking hands, Gavin had stared at it and the handwritten note accompanying it. Noah had written in precise flowing script; *I thought you might like the performance. If you wish, meet me backstage afterward.*

It had been a truly memorable experience. Even though he had enjoyed many such performances since that night, Gavin still looked back upon the first one with a sentimental chill at the terror it had given him. He had understood as he watched Noah's performance what a challenge it would be to be caught up in that light and never be able to really know the creator behind it. Only once during the height of the performance had Noah looked directly at him, a blue laser beam straight into his heart.

And he had been lost ever since. Four years later Gavin was only just beginning to understand the chance that Noah had taken on him. Slowly, bit by bit Noah had revealed himself as more than just a pretty face with a talent for music. He was witty but shy, loyal to his friends, fearless about music, smart and generous. Noah was also damaged in a way that left him unable to trust anyone beyond a certain point, vulnerable to the isolation that created, and the depression that he often suffered because of it.

Until recently Gavin had considered that flaw to be similar to his own. Now he understood that it ran much deeper and was bound up in another unexpected talent. Noah's true vulnerability was as unique and disturbing as the insights that came with it.

Gavin looked back on certain events with a new awareness in the light of that hidden talent. Noah went out of his way to avoid touching people. Perhaps it was merely a defense mechanism in order to protect himself from the unwanted intrusion of other people's emotions. Gavin shuddered.

Had Noah been able to look into his soul from the first touch of his hand? That was a thought that was both terrifying and exhilarating, yet it made a certain sense; Noah kept himself aloof because he had to in order to survive. That he had grown to trust Gavin was a miracle in itself. He remembered the feeling of Noah trembling in his arms and closed his eyes with a sigh. It was a trust that Gavin would go to any lengths to preserve, no matter what the cost.

Gavin nearly spilled his coffee when the telephone rang; the circle they travelled in knew better than to call so early. Dropping the newspaper, he jumped up to grab the phone off of the kitchen counter and tried to answer in a cool, unbothered voice.

"Good morning, Westerhaven residence."

It wasn't either of the calls he was hoping for. It was Mr.

Takamura, the Japanese business tycoon who had orchestrated Noah's last interrupted tour. The man had the power to move empires; it had been his private jet that whisked them home in luxury after Noah's public collapse. The image of the man formed in Gavin's mind as they spoke; refined, cultured, darkly handsome.

"I was phoning to inquire about Noah's health," the man said with perfect English, using Noah's first name without pause. "I hope it was nothing serious and he is recovering quickly at home."

"Thank you for your concern. Noah is making a steady recovery but it will be some time before he is able to perform again."

"I am glad to hear he is making progress. Your sudden departure left many disappointments I hope to soon redress."

"I am sure that Mr. Westerhaven feels the same way," Gavin said formally. "If there is a problem with the symphony contract, I am sure we can work something out at a future date."

"There is no need for worry. I have a personal interest in seeing to Noah's future reception in Tokyo. I look forward to a more…private arrangement. Please have Noah phone me as soon as he is able."

"As soon as he is up to it, Mr. Takamura," Gavin replied stiffly. "Thank you again for your assistance and concern."

"Of course, Mr. Moore. One must see to one's friends. Please give Noah my deepest regards. Good day."

Gavin disconnected the line without another word and stared at the phone with outrage. Had that man really the temerity to insinuate that Noah would…that he might…? Gavin actually made an audible sound of annoyance. Then he felt his eyebrows rise with suspicion.

Noah had been difficult to locate on more than one occasion. Could he really have been with Takamura? It would not have been the first time that a rich patron had made sexual advances. As far as Gavin knew, Noah usually turned them down, but Takamura was handsome and radiated sensual charm with that cultured voice. The fact that he had a wife and grown children had no bearing on the matter.

Annoyed that he thought it should be any concern of his, Gavin swore to himself. He was losing his objectivity. Noah was an adult who could do what he wanted; he had proven that often enough. Gavin was an employee, nothing more. If he could not get himself under control, he might not be that for much longer. He ground his teeth.

He was still grinding them an hour later when a private courier hand delivered the large package from none other than Mr. Takamura. The "gifts" to "a unique young man" included a slim, silk-bound volume of Japanese poetry along with a silk kimono worth well over a thousand dollars, a delicate jade carving of a Shinto deity, and a large paper wrapped package of expensive tea that Gavin knew no one outside of the country could get through normal channels. He laid the kimono out on Noah's bed, somewhat awed at the extravagance. Clearly they were flattering gifts intended to entice if not to indicate appreciation.

Women and men often sent Noah gifts and love letters, to no avail; he seemed outside the reach of most admirers. Gavin had seen plenty of them quietly yet firmly denied. This could simply be yet another extravagant attempt. He felt his mouth curl with an evil grin; it would be difficult to court someone from half a world away. When the telephone rang again he answered it without concern.

"Mr. Moore? This is Anthony McKewen."

About time, Gavin thought upon hearing the voice of the man he had hired to find the answers he was looking for. McKewen ran the highly respected and extremely private investigative firm of McKewen and Weatherby. McKewen was a fastidious man of about fifty with pure white hair and piercing blue eyes. He was a former Scotland Yard detective and his partner was a lawyer; together they ran a large multifaceted business whose clientele reached far and wide, yet remained untouchably secret.

"Mr. McKewen, what do you have for me this morning?"

"Good morning, Mr. Moore. I have a pitiable offering as of yet, I am afraid. The depth of the information you requested is proving to be a bit elusive."

"I see."

"However, I do have some things to report regarding Helen and Noah Westerhaven. This information will be included in our final report or I can send it over by courier now if you prefer."

"Talk, McKewen." Gavin had been informed that the firm did not use postal, fax, or email as a delivery system regarding their business transactions. Security was insured the old fashioned way; person to person, secure landline telephones, or hand courier packages only.

"Very well. You were correct in your assumption that Noah Westerhaven probably did not know who his father was up to this point. His birth certificate was filed indicating his father as 'unknown.' While that is not unusual in such circumstances, it certainly opens more questions after the fact, wouldn't you say?"

"That's what I hired you to find out. What do you mean, in such circumstances?"

"An unmarried woman of a fairly prominent family. The Westerhavens had fairly recent ties to the York area, their ancestors having immigrated to that location from Austria in the middle 1800's. Apparently they made their money in shipping and textiles and settled down as part of the gentry with a comfortable fortune."

Gavin sat down and silently rolled his eyes. At least they were thorough; he was apparently going to get a complete history lesson and that in just two days' worth of research.

"Helen Westerhaven was the only daughter of Sophia and Charles, who unfortunately died in an airplane crash when she was thirteen years of age. She was raised by her paternal grandparents at their mansion in York, a seemingly proper upbringing for someone of her class. The grandmother died when Helen was twenty, leaving her and her grandfather as the last remaining Westerhavens."

"You mean Noah is the last of the family line?"

"That is correct. Helen continued to live at the family mansion even after she apparently gave birth to a son out of wedlock. We can find no one who will say a disparaging thing about the woman or anyone who will admit they knew the father of the child. If the grandfather knew, it was an acceptable arrangement for him; he continued to support his granddaughter and her son for the next six years and left them everything in his will upon his death."

Gavin felt his mouth turn down at the corners. Even though he expected it, it was a sad and depressing tale. Noah truly was alone in the world and had been for more than half of his short life.

"That is where it gets interesting," McKewen said. "After the grandfather's death, scarcely two months go by before Lord Bainbridge is on the scene."

"Really," Gavin muttered.

"The two of them were apparently married in a small private ceremony in York. Not long after that Helen and Noah were permanently moved to Bainbridge Hall and the house in York was sold. What I do not know is whether Lord Bainbridge knew all along that the child was his and had some arrangement with the grandfather or if, after the grandfather's death, Helen came forward with the information. Either way, it seems to me that since he chose to marry her, he must have had feelings for her and the child. The photos you sent us seem to bear that out."

"I guess that makes some sense, if he didn't know about Noah, I mean. That would explain why he waited so long to marry Helen; if they had a brief affair that he ended without knowing about the pregnancy."

"There are simply too many strange things going on here," McKewen continued. "For instance, the proof of parentage, and the will itself for that matter. The will is recently dated, which means that another will preceded this one. According to your information, Lord James had nothing to do with his youngest son for over a decade. What event precipitated his altering of the will? Something important must have happened."

Gavin was nodding his head. "It makes no sense. Why would the man push away his own flesh and blood?"

"The document you provided leaves no doubt as to that fact. The odd thing about that is the date when the DNA testing was done for confirmation. According to the lab that performed the test, it was done twelve years ago. That means Bainbridge waited until after the death of his wife before he ordered the test, not when most men would have ordered it—upon being first told that he had a son he knew nothing about—three years earlier."

"Even worse," Gavin agreed. "When he then had undeniable proof that Noah was his, he turned him out, never to see or speak to him again. It's absolutely coldblooded. I'm doing my best not to judge that crazy family, but it isn't easy."

"I do understand. While Lord James did undeniably 'turn him out' as you put it, he sent the boy to one of the better local private schools and then on to an expensive music academy. According to my investigator, the boy did amazingly well, considering. The Sisters at the private school remembered him as a quiet child with a naturally quick mind and unerring talent. He excelled at his studies and proved to be a genius at the violin. There were a few incidents where he fell into ill health but recovered quickly enough. In any case, we are still looking into the Bainbridge family. They are an extremely old clan with high influence and connections."

"What did you find out about the death of Helen Bainbridge? And what of Noah's odd memory of hospitalization around that same time?"

"We have been unable so far to locate any information regarding the boy's supposed hospitalization; perhaps we are looking in the wrong places. One cannot expect private records to be easily obtained when the family in question is of the upper levels. From the public facts that I could gather, Helen Bainbridge died as the result of misadventure. Things like that do happen. As for the son, he simply disappeared from view after that night, almost like he died and was reborn later under the guise of his mother's name as the classical musician he is known as today."

"How soon before you have the rest of it?" Gavin asked with grim determination.

"A day or two, I imagine. Shall I come to you—"

"Call me," Gavin ordered. "I'll come to you."

"Very well. Good day, Mr. Moore."

Gavin sighed with frustration. Digging up Noah's past made him feel like a guilty spy but it had to be done. The more he found out, the stranger and stranger it all became. The memory of Noah's devastated white face loomed before his eyes, twisting the unreasonable premonition of danger like a knife in his gut. What the hell was going on in that family and why did it feel like he had sent an innocent lamb off to his slaughter unawares?

Gavin shivered, unable to shake the feeling.

Only a short while later, Noah finally telephoned from Scotland.

SEVEN

The eternal silence of these infinite spaces
fills me with dread.
  —Blaise Pascal

The view outside his window looked oddly dreamlike, swathed in its layers of fog, the white misty substance transforming everything below into indistinct shapes. The trees and hills were invisible. In the city even the thickest fog failed to completely obliterate the view of the tall buildings that sat close together like giants huddled against the cold. From the Hall it looked like Noah had been transported, house and all, to a world of spun sugar wisps; nothing beyond the window but white and the scary sense that the world he remembered did not exist except perhaps in his mind.

Going over the events of the night before, Noah wondered if that were not true. He took some time to do an abbreviated version of his yoga exercises before preparing to go downstairs for breakfast. Remembering the brace at the last moment, he put it on, its secure stiffness around his wrist a reminder that he should call Gavin. He slipped into a heavy sweater and picked up the morning coffee tray to take it with him.

If Andrew had any sense in that hard, damaged head of his, he would still be asleep. Noah glanced at the door to his brother's room as he turned to go down the corridor. It was fairly quiet in the house. The distant sounds of people moving about were almost impossible to hear from inside the thick walls of the bedrooms. At the last moment Noah decided to look into his father's suite.

The door was unlocked. The muted white light from outside spilled in through the open pocket doors with more than enough light to see by. Duncan had cleaned the broken pile of furniture and glass from the night before; the wood floor was spotless and the rug had apparently escaped damage. In the daylight it was just a cold empty room. Noah closed the door and made his way downstairs.

One of the housemaids was just reporting for duty and she gasped when he appeared outside the breakfast room carrying the tea tray. She yanked her apron tie into place and hurried over to him with a look of horror on her face. She took the tray away from him as if he were stealing the family silver.

"Oh no, Mr. Bainbridge," she admonished with a shake of her red blond head. "We cannot have you doing that, can we? Rose Marie would have a conniption and a half and it is too early in the morning for that. I hope you slept well with that storm and all. You look a might peaked. It is a pleasure to meet someone like yourself, famous and all and the Laird's brother, no less. Please go to your breakfast now and I will take care of this and tidy up your room."

Noah stared at her with his mouth half open. Her gray eyes were large and sensible even though the majority of her speech was incomprehensible to him due in part to the speed with which it was delivered and the country accent that accompanied it. She batted her eyes and smiled, showing two dimples on the right side of her cheek.

"My name is Ester," she said again, taking his dumbfounded expression for interest. "Caroline is my twin sister but you can tell us apart easy enough—"

"Ester!"

The girl's mouth, always moving it seemed, actually formed a silent "O" as if she had been caught doing something not allowed. She hunched her shoulders with a quick lift and drop and had the nerve to wink at him. Without another word she turned and disappeared behind the authoritative figure of Rose Marie, who stood at the edge of the room leading to the kitchen beyond.

"I apologize for that," Rose said stiffly. "Ester is…exuberant. She has yet to understand the concept that maids are meant to be unseen and unheard."

Noah blinked. He vaguely wondered about the defining characteristic that differentiated the twins, having had Rose interrupt before he found out. From the look on her face it was the reason she interrupted.

"I am sorry," he said. "I got only about half of that. I guess I will have to work on learning the local dialect."

Rose actually smiled at him, a half smile anyway, the first he had seen on her stern face. It softened her otherwise impervious image; hair twisted up in a knot from which not a single hair dared escape, light gray dress belted to accentuate her thinness.

"Ester and Caroline do try but they are simple country girls. Never bother. If this house is going to be opened again to visitors and the like, we will be hiring professional live-in staff soon enough. We cannot keep the village girls for long and the local accent is simply too difficult to be understood by outsiders." As if she just then realized how that might sound, she actually blushed. "I did not mean…"

Noah smiled to ease her sudden discomfort. "That's okay. I *am* an outsider. And it seemed a waste of time for me not to bring the tray down. In a house this size an intercom system seems long over due."

She smiled again. "Perhaps that is something you could discuss with Lord Bainbridge while you are here. Please, do not allow me to keep you from your breakfast. I will tell Moira to serve it immediately. The newspapers are already on the table."

"Thank you."

She made a slight movement with her head that passed for acknowledgement and retreated toward the kitchen area. Noah shook his head. He was not used to all the bowing and scraping from staff. While it was true that Gavin was his personal assistant, he and Gavin were more like equals. Gavin might make the tea and run the errands but Noah had not hired him to be a formal butler. The very idea of Gavin bowing and saying "yes sir" and "no sir" made him grin with amusement.

Noah ignored the newspaper and turned his head to look out through the wall of glass. The fog swirled about like a living presence but it did not seem so thick at ground level as it had upstairs. Maybe the day would not be a total loss. The idea of staying in the house all day seemed oppressive, even though he would have to spend the morning practicing his music. Noah figured that he could do that in the music room without much worry of waking Andrew upstairs.

He ate his breakfast alone. The newspaper could not hold his attention. The house was quiet but the undercurrent of invisible energy that had almost flattened him upon arriving was still there, grating on the edge of his awareness with persistence. The silence and feeling of isolation brought on by the enveloping fog only amplified the annoying sensation. Noah doubted whether he would ever be comfortable within the vast empty walls of the Hall, with its history and its secrets.

Fortified with enough sustenance to get him through until lunch, Noah went in search of a telephone. The previous Lords of the manor were apparently intent on their privacy and their dislike for modern apparatus in all forms; there were few electrical outlets in the bedrooms and no telephones. While many houses like the Hall were even equipped with things like lifts and ornamental outside lighting, the frugal Scottish masters of the Hall relied on basic necessity over the coming and going of the latest fads; they had considered electricity and indoor plumbing in the "fad" category until Noah's father's time. The modern contraption known as the telephone appeared to fit into that category as well, installed with grudging realization that times were changing whether they wanted them to or not.

There were in fact only three lines coming into the entire house. One was for the use of the staff from units located in the kitchen and Rose Marie's little office, and for use of guests from the second drawing room. The two remaining lines were private and strictly for the use of the Laird or his secretary, accessible by phones in the study, the men's parlor—now a small office/storage area—and the Laird's sitting room outside of his bedchamber.

It seemed a far inadequate number in Noah's opinion, but then again he was a product of the modern world. With a slight grin of amusement, he considered Gavin's obsession for the newest gadgets in their plugged-in, electronic-mad, modern existence. Living at the Hall for more than a day would drive Gavin absolutely crazy in more ways than one.

The study door was unlocked. As he stepped inside and turned on the lights, Noah gave a small silent whistle of awe. The room, like all rooms created to impress, was large and suitably intimidating. Hundreds of books filled the impossibly tall bookcases, shelves so high that a ladder was necessary to reach them all. There was a ladder on each side, made so that it could be moved by sliding along a heavy, polished wooden railing as one climbed up and down and moved back and forth. The heavy desk was the focal point of the room, equally impressive, a clear statement of authority. Sitting on its wide polished expanse was the magical, much maligned instrument of heathen duplicity that Noah was searching for; the telephone.

Very much aware that the desk was his brother's domain, Noah chose to sit in one of the uncomfortable chairs in front of the desk, dragging its sturdy frame close enough to access the phone, which was not a cordless model. He was more than ready to hear Gavin's voice and be reminded that there was an outside world where people flew in airplanes, talked incessantly on cellular phones, and jostled each other on busy sidewalks. Shaking his head at the incongruity of wealth and old fashioned inconveniences, Noah rang his flat in London.

Gavin answered on the third ring. "Noah, what are you doing up at this hour?" he stated with surprise.

"I am in the country, remember? They get up with the cows, or is it the ducks?"

"It is the chickens," Gavin replied with a chuckle. "How is it in bonny Scotland?"

"Fine, if you like chickens and countryside. Not your kind of place, I imagine. The local village has only three pubs."

"I am glad to hear that you are going into pubs these days. I guess your brother cannot be all bad if he patronizes such establishments. You two getting along okay?"

"Andrew is fine," Noah replied with a sigh, curling the phone cord in his hand. "I still do not remember much of this place but maybe that is okay. Hey, I have a family tartan to wear now. Isn't that cool?"

There was a pause before Gavin's reply but Noah could not tell what he was thinking. "That's great unless a kilt and bagpipes come with the deal."

"I think I will stick with the violin and Andrew can wear the skirts of the family. What have you been doing?" A none-too-subtle hint that Gavin had been up to things he shouldn't have.

"Nothing," Gavin said too innocently. "I had dinner out last night and went for a jog this morning. The wind was rather chilly. I guess winter is not far off."

"We had a storm that knocked the lights out for a bit. It is kind of like living in the good old days out here, although I never understood what was so good about them. There is nothing romantic about cold drafty castles and scary family ghosts."

"Family ghosts?" Gavin asked with alarm. "What have *you* been up to, Noah?"

"Oh, nothing in particular. I am going to get lazy and fat. They have an autumn festival coming up soon. Maybe that will be fun."

"Really? Do they eat haggis and fight with sticks?"

Noah laughed quietly. "Something like that. So nothing else is going on?"

Gavin sighed. "I haven't discovered that your brother is a worldwide criminal or anything like that, if that is what you mean. Oh. You did get a phone call and an interesting package from Mr. Takamura."

"Takamura?" Noah asked innocently, hearing the cool tone in Gavin's voice.

"He wanted to arrange some personal time with you." Silence. "The gifts are certainly personal."

"Don't worry about it," Noah said quietly.

"So, do you need anything out there in the woods? Are you wearing your wrist brace?"

"When I think about it," Noah said, looking down at it on his hand. "I guess I am good for now. Gavin, I…"

"Are you sure you are all right?" Gavin asked in his deep, resonant voice. "You aren't missing me, are you?"

Noah sighed. Gavin seemed to be able to read his emotions, even over the distance. It made him feel even more guilty…and lonelier.

"Gavin, I want to apologize—"

"No need for that, Noah. I understand. Family comes first."

Family. Noah sighed again. What he wanted to say stuck in his throat.

"Call me in another couple of days, okay?" Gavin directed.

"Okay," Noah agreed with a smile. "Maybe something exciting will happen between now and then."

"I certainly hope not," Gavin replied in a mysterious tone. "Bye, Noah."

Noah replaced the phone and sat staring at the desk.

It had been a strange conversation about nothing. Gavin kept it polite and simple, too polite. Noah remembered Gavin's artificial smile as he waved at the departing taxi. He had no doubt Gavin was doing things behind his back. Oh well, he had not volunteered much information either, even though some strange things had been happening at the old house. It was a temporary truce between them in regards to Andrew, probably the best Noah could hope for.

The cold silence of the room closed in around him. He started scanning the bookshelves with half interest, absentmindedly humming an aria as he fingered the spines of an assortment of books, both old and new. There seemed to be little organization to the collection; biographies were mixed in with histories and stacked up against romance novels and books on photography. It was an eclectic mix. At least some of his ancestors had a variety of hobbies and took reading seriously.

Noah looked up over his head, noting the books nearer the high ceiling were older, bound in cracked leather with fading gold-stamped titles. Many of them were bound collections of the household accountings from generations past, when such records were handwritten. No doubt there were diaries and family letters, maybe even maps and copies of deeds from the time when the Laird of the Hall ruled the surrounding lands with an iron fist, or at least with the absolute right of a monarch.

Those days were long gone. Noah was not interested in ancient history, at least not his family's version of it; he had no intention of climbing up on those scary floating ladders. He pushed at one just to see how stable it was and grimaced when it rattled and moved slightly. Returning his attention to the more recent collection at eye level he had his hand on a book about modern Celtic ballads when the title of another book a row down and a foot over seemed to leap out at him; *The Symbolism and Ancient Art of Heraldry.*

Noah moved over and pulled the book out from between one on pottery and another on bronze weaponry. It was heavy, a seriously in-depth tome of scholarship printed by the Cambridge Press. As he flipped through its heavy pages, a group of folded sheets fell out and landed on his foot. Bending to retrieve them, he saw they were individual sheets of thin paper that had been folded and stuck within the pages of the book.

Noah walked back to the desk, where he laid the book down to the place it had opened and slowly unfolded the papers. There were four separate sheets; one covered with words scrawled out in black ink in shaky handwriting, and three others that looked to be some kind of charcoal rubbings, although the images were unclear from a glance. He turned his attention to the words, recognizing the layout as a pattern of verse, a poem or such. It was written first in Gaelic and then transcribed in English on the lower half of the page.

> From yea sacred standing stones, o'er blackened sacrificial bones,
>
> The eldest knee bowed to seal, ancient power his to wield,
>
> The youngest forfeit life to give, in order that the Clan shall live.
>
> Let nay reason stay your hand, or yours shall be a troubled land,
>
> Blood the only sacred sorrow, his or yours or ne'er a morrow.
>
> The Cursed Path on which ye kneel, one son each, to close the Deal.

Noah felt his hair standing on end and glanced around the room to verify he was still alone. The poem certainly called up an eerie sense of imagery that had him shivering in spite of himself. He had read such things before; ancient poets seemed to revel in dark and mystical verse, often speaking about things like blood, curses, and the like. Why had someone kept this particularly odd poem hidden away in a book?

Looking at the book in question, Noah was surprised to see the family crest displayed on the page opened before him. It was somewhat different but still singularly unappealing with its allusion to violent struggle and death. In the muted colors and thick inked lines rendered by the ancient artist, the wolves had a more human-like appearance. Their muscular bodies stood upright and reached out with human hands, extremely unsettling as they ripped away at the stylized deer. Curling his lip in distaste, Noah looked at what the authors had to say about the drawing.

The usual stuff about the allegory to English-Scottish conflict was there but the authors believe that the reference was a new interpretation upon a much older and long forgotten theme. Cults of all types abounded in ancient Britain, the most well known being the highly romanticized Druids. Thanks to the publishing of a fabricated tale entitled "The Golden Bough," the modern idea of the robe-wearing mystics was now almost entirely associated with Stonehenge.

Other, lesser known "religions" were popular, from fertility cults to prophetic divination, but the wolf cult was unique. It had somehow escaped scrutiny by the rulers of the time and quietly faded into myth. The authors discussed the human-looking wolves at length in regards to ancient tales of shape-shifting demons and the worship of a pagan demi-god in the local area. They proceeded to exonerate the Bainbridge family from any and all possible suggestions to witchcraft, no doubt out of fear of legal action at such absurd academic musings.

Noah's gaze slid to the whispery sheets of black charcoal over white paper. Given his full attention, their shadowy shapes made more sense to his eyes; the charcoal rubbing outlining the carved images in broken lines of darker black. The same human looking wolves from the book were looking back at him from the rough black rubbings, their elongated limbs ending in human hands, holding daggers or short swords. The intentionally startling combination of human and animal into such amazing creatures repulsed him even as it fascinated him.

He wondered who had done the rubbings, where they had come from and why they were in the book along with the strange poem. Rubbing was a technique often used in archeology to record carved images at historical sites or cemeteries. Noah thought about the old family gravesites and the ruins of the chapel that were probably as old or maybe even older than the current standing Hall. The wolf carvings he had seen in the village came back to him, but they in no way resembled the eerie etchings he was holding in his hand.

The flash of a moving image came to him unbidden, that of a glimpse of fur and a glinting of teeth. Noah shivered, aware that the room was cold and empty, yet the impression of something unseen and uninviting lingered in his perception. Maybe he should have told Gavin about his—

Tendencies to over dramatize things, he thought with annoyed self incrimination. It was an empty room. It was an old family house. Maybe his father or grandfather had been interested in family history. Noah refolded the sheets with the intention of replacing them but decided at the last moment not to, instead tucking them into the waistband of his pants just beneath his shirt.

Resigned to the fact that little else could be done in a thick fog, Noah decided to follow through with his plan to practice that morning. It was only as he was turning to leave that he noticed the portrait of his father on the wall to the left of the doorway. He stopped to examine it, recognizing the artist's style from his mother's portrait in the bedroom. Unlike Helen's painting, this one was not life size, but it was still enormous in its gilded frame with a bronze plaque preserving the identity of the subject for all of history; James Edward Wallace Bainbridge, Thirteenth Laird of the Hall.

Noah's first impression was that the painting of his father was different than those ancient men lining the ancestral walk. The artist had painted him in a sitting position, reclining in one of the medieval armchairs from the main drawing room, the heavy brocade drapes drawn across the window behind him. Dressed in the full regalia of a Laird—pleated kilt, sporran, velvet coat, draped tartan, and buckled brogues—James presented the perfect image of a modern Scottish Lord, relaxed and smiling, the same slight smile that graced Helen's face upstairs.

It wasn't only the sitting position that made this portrait different; there was no weaponry of any kind visible in the painting, no *skian dubh*—Scottish dagger of stag horn worn in a sheath against the leg—or claymore or spear. His father's hand held a pipe and on the ground beside his chair was a stack of books and a walking cane. The portrait had been painted while James was in his early thirties, a much younger man than Noah had known but somehow more the man that he remembered. It was impossible for Noah to reconcile the two; the man in the portrait and the man who had abandoned him.

Closing the door of the study behind him, Noah headed off to his bedroom to fetch his violin and music, with the idea of stashing the purloined sheets of paper somewhere in his room for the moment. Coming up from the landing into the corridor,

Noah caught a glimpse of a male back disappearing down the servant's stairs at the far end. Assuming it to be Duncan on one errand or another, he gave it no thought.

The signs of Ester's announced visit to his room was evidenced by the newly made bed and the spiriting away of the bloodstained clothing from the night before. A stack of fresh towels sat on a shelf and the bathroom sparkled with a clean lemon scent. Whatever flaws Rose Marie saw in Ester's character were clearly made up for by the girl's cleaning abilities.

Noah tucked the papers inside his book of myths. He wasn't really concerned that anyone would look for them. Rounding up his violin and the case of sheet music, he went back downstairs without seeing another living soul. The entire right wing of the house was probably uninhabited most of the time outside of the small drawing room. The music room was just another empty, unused reminder of the Hall's grand past, which seemed to have no place in the modern world.

The pocket doors opened upon what Noah vaguely remembered as his favorite room from childhood, and the reality did not disappoint. The walls were covered in pale green silk trimmed with white woodwork, and the two large windows were draped in silk brocade of the same pale green color, the long trailing curtains pooling on the floor like water. The floor was imported teak covered here and there with custom woven oriental rugs of pale green, cream, powder blue, and gray. A white plaster ceiling curved upward from the walls to meet a crystal chandelier held in place by plaster sea shells and mermaids, a theme carried over to the room's corners and lintels by beautifully carved sea horses and scallop shells.

A grand piano dominated the room, flanked to the left by a golden harp and to the right by a cello leaning on its stand. Velvet cushioned wooden chairs had been pushed back to the far wall, lined up like soldiers in front of built-in cabinets that hid other instruments and piles of sheet music behind their closed panels. It was a room meant to be used and enjoyed, at one time the heart of entertainment for family gatherings. Now it was like most of the house; a museum more than a dwelling.

Noah sighed and closed the doors quietly behind him, walking to the piano to place his violin case and items on its glossy top. At least the girls took the time to dust; the piano gleamed with newly polished luster. He sat down and opened the keyboard, taking a moment to play a bit of Beethoven on the ivory keys; it was only slightly out of tune. With a sad smile he recalled bits and pieces of sitting at that very piano; some of that time spent with his mother, some of it in solitary enjoyment. The carpeted space beneath the piano had also been one of his favorite places, a safe little hideaway for reading or drawing or playing with his toys.

He removed the violin from its velvet case and plucked at its strings until it was tuned to his liking. Noah ran himself through a warm up of simple lilts and small arpeggios, stopping once to fine tune the strings and remove the brace from his wrist. It somewhat hindered his ability to play so he tossed it on the piano and flipped through his sheet music until he found the new piece he had been practicing before he left London.

Tucking the violin beneath his chin, he began to play, a soft yet serious start that became a wild and difficult middle before falling once again to a haunting, melodious finish. It still needed some refinement but overall he was pleased with the outcome. He played it through for a second time, changing a bit here and there, holding the ending note out for an extra count. He glanced over at the closed door when he heard a sigh followed by giggling.

Pretending he had not heard them, Noah smiled to himself and started on a piece he knew by memory. Barely a few bars into it, the doors slid open abruptly, depositing not one girl but two head first into the room in a less than decorous manner.

Noah stopped with his arm raised in surprise and his eyes wide at the sight of twin maid outfits spilled on the rug. Twin faces looked up at him with very different expressions, one with shocked embarrassment and one suffused with fury. Behind them in the doorway stood Seth, a hand on each door panel and a smirk on his handsome face.

"I guess the new resident genius has a following," Seth

drawled. His local accent was barely noticeable compared with that of Ester. "If you are going to make a habit of listening at keyholes, maybe you should learn to stop giggling first."

While Noah jumped to help the nearest girl to her feet, the other one launched herself at Seth, who made her even madder by holding her off with one lazy hand on her shoulder while she swung at him and swore. It took only a second for Noah to realize that the girl he had hold of must be Caroline, while the "exuberant" twin with the mouth like a sailor's had to be Ester. He released the red faced girl and stepped back, embarrassed himself.

"You didn't have to do that," he said to Seth, trying to defend the two eavesdroppers.

"Aye, maybe not but it was so much fun. Now stop it Ester before you hurt yourself. If you wanted to listen to Master Noah's music you could have sat down in the parlor and kept quiet. Rose Marie would have a heart attack to walk by and see you both with your eyes to the door crack and your backsides exposed to the world."

Caroline made a pained gasp and fled from the room, darting past the two in the doorway without a word or a glance. Ester gave Seth one last dirty look and took off after her sister, whose loud wails of distress could be heard echoing across the grand hall. Seth remained standing where he was, arms crossed over his chest.

"So you sneaked your way into the Laird's room, did you?" Seth said, turning the question into an accusation.

Noah felt the flush burn his cheeks. "I did not sneak."

"Sounds to me like you did. He find you in there and you two get into it?" The green eyes looked him over with cold appraisal. "You do not look big enough to take Andrew. Crack him over the head with something?"

Noah felt his mouth open with outrage but no sound came out.

"I guess you are pretty used to getting your way, mister high and famous, but don't get too used to it around here. We have our own ways."

They stared at each other. What could he say to a speech like that? Noah was once more aware of his place as outsider and because of that, swallowed his anger and kept his thoughts to himself. Unlike everyone else he had met, Seth had remained aloof up until that point, judging from a distance. The more vocal and menacing Seth was one that Noah could do without.

Seth smiled a crooked smile. "I will make certain that your practice is not interrupted before lunch," he said, reaching for the doors. "It sounded worth the effort."

He closed the doors with a bang, leaving Noah alone to ponder the incident; it was a household filled with strange encounters. Noah stood there staring at the closed doors with annoyance. His creative mood was shot. He picked up the violin anyway, tucking it under his chin, then stood there whipping the bow in the air with indignation.

How dare Seth accuse him of snooping! He remembered the etchings at that moment hidden in his bedroom and turned his mouth down at the corners. So maybe he was snooping, but he had the right to look into his father's death. There were things going on in that house that no one seemed to realize. Noah dragged the bow across the strings and started playing, totally unaware of the notes that flew from his fingers.

Everyone seemed ready to believe that he had attacked Andrew. That was not only ridiculous, it was…was it? Did they think he held his brother responsible for the last twelve years? They all surely knew what was up in that room. Why had no one, including Andrew, told him about it? Noah whipped his shoulders back with a hard movement on the bow.

That would have been a good reason to fly off at Andrew but it had been his brother who had come unglued in the dark. Could it be that Andrew really had something to hide? Noah gave his head a little shake. No, he could not believe that Andrew had anything to do with it. Yet the longer he was in the house of his childhood, the more he felt its dark secrets. Not only the house, he realized, but in more subtle ways, the house residents and the village too.

The crescendo rose in the air like the undercurrent of warning in Noah's blood. Was he the only one to feel it? His father's death had been no accident, he was certain of that now; James had been lured out onto that trail to meet his killer. What he could not fathom was the reason why. The dark rubbings of human-like wolves jumped back into Noah's mind. Wolves on the crest, wolves in the village, wolves everywhere. Was there, perhaps, a wolf in sheep's clothing amongst them all?

That was the image that haunted him still, that subtle flash of fur. Noah had seen it on more than one occasion. The accidental discovery of the rubbings with the poem made the connection all the more curious. Noah closed his eyes, trying to recapture the memory of the night on stage. Whatever his father had been trying to tell him was lost in the horrific emotions that came with the vision. The fact that his father had chosen to call out to him at that moment was shock enough; it still unnerved him when he thought about it. And so did the house, dark and silent and locked in time.

The music pouring out of him came to an end, along with his half angry musing. Noah stared at the pile of sheet music without seeing it, unaware of what he had just been playing. The tendons in the back of his wrist hurt and a trickle of sweat rolled down into his eye and stung. Blinking it away he replaced the violin in its case and reached up to wipe the sweat from his face. That he could be sweating in the chilly room made him wonder and when he looked at his watch he felt his eyebrows rise in surprise; almost two hours had gone by since he first came into the room.

While he could occasionally lose track of time during practice, he rarely lost himself. He flexed his fingers and again felt the twinge of strain in his wrist. Gavin would not be happy if he came back from his "convalescence" with a greater injury than when he had left. Noah strapped the brace onto his aching wrist and gathered up his things.

He walked into the space of the grand hall and turned toward the staircase, headed for his room. Seth was there, sitting on the third step of the stairs with his elbows propped on the fourth step and his right ankle resting on his left knee in a pose of relaxed nonchalance. He had been listening.

Noah stopped directly in front of him. Neither of them spoke, but after a moment Seth drew in his lanky limbs and slid off the steps out of Noah's way. Winner of the contest of wills, Noah walked past him and up the stairs to his room, but not before he had seen the crooked, contemptuous smile and the half mocking bow that went with it.

According to Rose Marie it had been the dark ages since a true dinner party had been held at the Hall, and she intended to have everything just right. Moira had been dispatched earlier to the nearest decent market a village over to fetch the things they did not have on hand. The girls cleaned like miniature whirlwinds while Duncan polished the crystal and silver. Andrew disappeared into the study to catch up on neglected business matters and phone calls. Since no one would let him do anything, Noah followed Andrew's example and made himself scarce.

The fog had finally lifted, leaving the day partially sunny, always a pleasant interlude with the rains and snows of winter not far off. In his room, Noah thought it a perfect time to go about some snooping, and prepared to do so by changing his clothing into something more suitable. He pocketed a flashlight—making sure beforehand that it worked properly—and went quietly down the back stairs and out of the house.

Noah walked around the hedgerow separating the gardens from the garages and down the path heading for the stables. There was a touch of chilly wind in the air, but it was a fine enough day for what he had in mind—a little archeology session with the ancestors. On his own for the afternoon, he had decided that the secrets of the old family chapel were well within his scope of investigation.

There was the possibility that his father had been going there or coming from there on the day he died. Why else be on that forlorn little pathway? He also had the rubbings to consider. If his father was responsible for them as well, there seemed to Noah only one place on the estate where they might be found.

While his father had forbidden anyone from setting foot in the ruins, Noah doubted Andrew had taken that rule to heart. The Andrew that Noah remembered would have more likely than not done the exact opposite of what he had been told; for little boys, tumbled down ruins beckoned exploration even at the risk of punishment. Now it was Noah who was curious and Andrew had not forbidden it.

It had to be less than a mile or so through the meadow once he turned off the path at the edge of the woods. Noah was ready for the walk, wearing his new boots and heavier jacket. What he was not ready for was the sight of Seth brushing down a large black horse at the edge of the enclosed paddock. For whatever reason, Noah hesitated.

The animal noticed his presence first, turning its head to look at him with interest. Seth looked up from the animal's back, holding the curry brush suspended for a moment while a smile curved his lips slightly. He leaned forward against the horse's body, crossing his arms over its broad back.

"Well, good afternoon to you Master Noah."

Noah felt his mouth pull into a thin straight line at the greeting he was getting accustomed to but not happy with. The way Seth said it more than hinted at the contempt clearly visible in his green eyes. His current candid appraisal made Noah uncomfortable.

"Afternoon," Noah answered curtly.

Noah was prepared to walk past with nothing more when Seth's voice stopped him again. Turning, he saw Seth duck beneath the horse's neck and come to the fence, standing with his arms dangling over the top rail and one knee bent at an angle. The same slight twist of amused disdain curled the corner of his mouth.

"Are you planning on walking somewhere? I see that your brother has gotten you fitted up proper for the part."

Noah blinked at the comment, unaware where the hostility came from or how to respond to it. What business was it to Seth where he walked?

"Maybe it's a ride you are looking for," Seth continued. "I just finished up with Echo. I could saddle him for you, just take a minute."

Noah looked at the now prancing horse with apprehension. He didn't much like horses…or large dogs for that matter. Small dogs did not bother him much. Well, they were more like cats weren't they? Noah had never taken the time to figure out why his particular phobias annoyed him; they were just there, like his eyes were blue.

"No thank you. I had rather walk."

Seth again waited for him to turn away and take a few steps before calling out. "If it's to the ruins you are walking, you might reconsider going alone."

Noah stopped and looked back. Seth looked serious, his expression unreadable.

"Why is that?"

"You being unwell and all," Seth replied with a slight kick against the fence boards. "It's dangerous there. The broken walls are leaning and the ground is covered with stones. You could twist an ankle or something…could fall."

"I can manage," Noah assured him. "Thanks for the caution."

He got away without being stopped again, aware that Seth's green stare was piercing a hole between his shoulder blades until he passed around the edge of the barns. It had been a strange conversation, but then again he seemed to be having a lot of those lately. Noah shivered in spite of himself and let his breath out in a sigh. It seemed that country people were every bit as hard to fathom as city dwellers, existing in a narrowly defined code of acceptable conduct. At least in the city he understood what that code was.

Once Noah had turned off the narrow beaten pathway, he was glad to have the sturdy leather boots on his feet. The grass of the meadow, looking so smooth from afar, was difficult to walk in, growing out of patches in hard raised lumps. Mixed in with the lumps were stones of various sizes, hidden within the waving strands of soggy dead grass as tall as his waist. There were cattle out in the far edge of the field, the shaggy Scottish variety along with more reasonable looking black and white animals, all chewing with exaggerated motions as they watched him with placid stares.

After a while of watching the cattle and almost twisting a knee more than once, Noah looked up at the sound of hoof beats coming from behind him. He groaned with dismay at seeing the object of his excursion still a good way off, its tumbled, dark gray walls no less lumpy and uneven than the ground at his feet. Looking over his shoulder he sighed with annoyance to see Echo covering the ground with speed and alacrity, Seth perched atop the animal's glossy back.

Noah kept walking, refusing to acknowledge Seth's presence even when the horse and rider quietly walked along beside him for a few moments. The horse had no trouble with the unruly grass clumps; its wide feet merely smashed the lumps flat with half a ton of its body weight.

"Are you ready for a lift now?" Seth finally asked after a few moments more.

Noah had to stop walking to look up at him. "What do you want?"

Seth nodded as if to say that he deserved that tone. The horse flicked its long tail, making Noah flinch in spite of himself.

"I thought maybe I had better come with you," Seth replied without the sarcasm he had displayed earlier. "If something happened to you before he can show you off at his dinner party Andrew might have my head and like I said, it's dangerous out here. Hard going, huh?"

Noah sighed, glancing at the distance he yet had to cover. The long grass, still wet from the earlier fog, had begun to dampen his jeans and his spirit.

"Come on then," Seth offered, reaching down with his hand. "Echo here won't hurt you and it is a lot easier going for him than for us."

Noah looked from the offered hand to the horse's round intelligent eye to the unbroken field of rocky, uneven meadow spread out before him. Sometimes stubbornness could simply lead to trouble. He placed his hand in Seth's and his foot over Seth's foot on the stirrup and heaved himself up behind the saddle with the young man's help.

"Stubborn," Seth said. "Must be a family trait. Hold on to me."

The horse moved and Noah stifled a cry of alarm. He had no choice but to put his arms around Seth to keep from falling off when the animal started into motion. The horse wanted to run free across the meadow instead of walk as its rider commanded; Noah could feel its muscles quivering beneath him.

He thought he could understand the allure of such an animal; all that power and beauty gathered beneath you, waiting to be unleashed at the touch of your hand. Even walking the animal's stride ate up the ground with ease and soon they were directly in front of the ancient cemetery and its long dead occupants.

Seth pulled the horse up beside a large fallen stone and assisted Noah from the animal's back, keeping hold of him until he was firmly on the ground. Dismounting by tossing his leg over the horse's neck and sliding off, Seth draped the reins over a broken piece of old fencing and looked around.

"Well, here you are."

"It's a lot bigger up close," Noah said, looking at the remaining walls of the ancient chapel towering over them. "And less sturdy."

To emphasis his words a small sound of crumbling and falling rock echoed from somewhere in the shadowy walls. There were probably mice and birds nesting within its stone sanctuary, maybe even something larger. Grass and lichens had long since taken a stronghold, breaking the manmade structure down into its original components, one tiny piece at a time. A flurry of wings as two ravens flew out from a dark nook made Noah jump. For once Seth remained silent.

They walked around the ancient graves, weaving in and out between broken headstones dark with lichens. Noah examined each one he found but almost all the engravings were unreadable, long worn away by rain, wind, and time. Seth seemed content to wander on his own, but Noah could tell he was more interested in watching him than looking at anything else, which struck Noah as more suspicious of his activities than concerned about his safety. When he picked his way through the minefield of tumbled stones that had once been a wall of the family chapel, Seth spoke up.

"What are you looking for?"

"Just snooping," Noah replied, bending to examine what had been a piece of curved archway. "Old ruins are fascinating, even when they aren't on family property."

"I suppose city people might think so," Seth replied.

The way he said *city people* made Noah grind his teeth. He climbed up on one of the large stones and looked around. The ruins were much bigger than they looked from a distance, an odd collection of dark and medium colored stones mixed with broken pieces of flat slate or granite. A few trees and bushes grew around and through the stones. As Noah slowly turned he could just make out what had been a wider structure, now disassembled and half hidden by the long grass. The chapel itself had once been part of the greater design.

"Was this where the old Keep used to stand?" he inquired of his reluctant companion.

Seth was sitting on a stone and had to look up to see Noah's face. "What do you know about it?"

Noah sighed, barely hiding his irritation. Could the man not respond without making every sentence sound like an invitation to a brawl? He decided that the best way to deal with Seth's near permanent mood was to ignore it.

"I know that we are an old clan and the house is nowhere near old enough to be the original. Most chapels are not placed so far from the main residence. In fact they were usually built within the house or attached to the castle. That makes this one kind of odd, stuck off out in the field by itself. Besides, I can see the faint design of an older foundation not quite hidden by the grass."

Seth stood up on his stone and looked around as Noah pointed out his discovery. Difficult to see from the ground, standing on the large stones gave just enough of an elevated position to make out the hint of ancient barrows and barely visible foundation rock. Archeology was one of Gavin's hobbies and quite a bit of his knowledge had rubbed off on Noah over the years. Even Seth seemed slightly impressed, once again sinking down to sit on his stone.

"So you guessed as much," he condescended. "They dismantled most of the Keep when they built the manor; all that stone made for a fine foundation I expect. The house is in a much better place halfway up the hill. No worry about drainage when the winter rain turns this field into a bog."

"I guess they left the chapel because of the cemetery," Noah mused, hopping down from his stone. "They could have built a new chapel at the house."

"Yeah, but they didn't, did they?" Seth muttered.

Noah looked at him knowing that he was right. There was no chapel in the current house. "The Reformation made for tough times. Situated where they are, the clan had to be very careful, I imagine."

"Are you insinuating that the Clan was beholding to that pig of a King?" Seth asked, the words whistling through his clenched teeth.

Noah raised his eyebrows. He kept forgetting that many people did not consider ancient history to be that far removed from current history.

"I only meant that after the war they had to be cognizant of the danger from either side. They were a clever lot or the house would never have remained standing during those times. Better for the chapel to lose a few stones than you to lose your head."

That seemed to mollify Seth slightly. Noah made his way toward the remaining walls of the building in question, his curiosity peeked by Seth's remarks. He was sure that the keep and adjoining chapel had never been particularly ornate; they would have been far too old for anything other than the most rudimentary decorative touches.

The moment Noah set foot in the shadow of its ancient walls he was stuck by the sensation of dread. The dark stone beneath his boots was covered with a soft carpet of dirt and moss that swallowed up any sound of his presence. In places across the mossy green carpeting there were broken stones, scattered about like pieces of a board game.

Three partially standing walls were green and brown with moss and lichens, ivy twining its way up through the broken corners and open ceiling above. The heavy, woody vines of a giant lilac twisted its way across the gaping irregular shape of a window, barring the opening with dark, rough branches. Where before there might have been stone or wooden benches there was nothing but emptiness.

It felt at least ten degrees colder in the shade than outside in the sun. A soft scurrying sound caused Noah to turn his head. A hare near the edge of one cracked wall quietly departed, its brown eye taking only a moment to inspect the interloper. The sun caught its form, casting an odd elongated shadow across one wall. The stories of brownies and goblins popped into Noah's mind and he did his best to squash the fears that the shadow called forth.

Heedless of the stone towering over his head, Noah inspected the wall a little more closely. He was slightly disappointed that nothing even resembling a wolf was present, not a carving to be seen. To prove it to himself, he crept farther inside, smoothing his hand along the stone wall. The musty odor of decaying matter and clearly recognizable scent of earth permeated the space, bringing back to mind the hazy memory of a dream he had recently.

The space was larger than Noah thought. Moving toward the far interior wall, the stone beneath his sliding fingers was cold and damp, bumpy with organic growth. He glanced up at the open space of ceiling and the irregular outline of broken stone edges against the bright sky. When he looked back down the dark shadows looked blacker to his eyes and he stopped for a moment for his vision to readjust.

"What are you doing?" Seth called out, having only then come to the edge of the wall opening. "Be careful! The floor is not sound in there."

Frankly it had never occurred to Noah that he should worry about where he put his feet; the stones over his head were of more concern. That was before Seth's warning and the ominous crumbling sound of earth and stone combined into a perception of danger just a heartbeat too late.

Noah looked down to see the floor giving away beneath his left foot. It was a strange sight to behold; an opening crack growing larger and larger while the toe of his boot seemed to be floating over space as black as ink. The black hole was quickly expanding outward with the rumbling of a small avalanche. When Noah moved his foot back, the ground beneath his right foot moved abruptly, causing him to suck his breath in with surprise and fear. The wall under his hand would offer no purchase to keep him from falling into the stygian depths that seemed to be opening to swallow him.

Noah shifted his body and bumped into Seth, so close behind him that he stepped back in surprise. His heel sank on the edge of the crumbling hole, causing him to lose his balance for a second. Seth's hand shot out and grabbed him by the front of his jacket, swinging him away from the sheer drop of the expanding hole and slamming his back up hard against a solid wall of cold stone.

The crumbling stopped almost immediately, the echo of falling stone and earth striking a surface in the darkness far below, an unpleasant reminder of near catastrophe. For a moment neither one of them moved, the only sound in the shadows that of their panting breath. Noah looked up into green-gold eyes inches from his own, aware of Seth's hard body pressing the length of his.

Then Seth's mouth was on his and Noah felt the shock of that touch all the way to his toes. He closed his eyes in reflex, his lips answering the hot seeking passion with equal desire that came out of nowhere, rising up through his defenses in response to Seth's plundering tongue and hard grasping hands. Noah heard a moan and realized it came from his mouth. Seth's fingers slid into his hair, holding his head with both hands while they kissed in wild abandon. In danger of losing himself, Noah moved his mouth away, gasping for breath.

"I can't do this," he panted, his hands on Seth's lean hips.

Seth's hot mouth slid up his neck to seek his lips again. Noah shuddered when Seth's fingers rubbed him through the material of his jeans.

"You want to," Seth's breathy voice replied.

Seth pressed against him, holding Noah's head still so that he could catch Noah's mouth once more. That hot engulfing kiss threatened to steal his will, turning his treacherous body into something he could not control. Noah was powerless to stop the roaming hands that pushed his clothing aside, sliding beneath his shirt to stroke and caress.

The sound of cracking rock brought them both back to their senses long enough to realize where they were. Seth grabbed Noah's wrist and hauled him out of the dangerous ruins and into the sunlight, where they collapsed on the damp solid ground. Panting for breath where he knelt in the sunlight, Noah regained some control over his senses. He staggered to his feet, shaking so hard his teeth chattered.

Seth's hands reached for him. A small scuffle ensued and when it was over Seth was sitting on his backside in the damp grass. They regarded each other with wary suspicion until Seth made a small sound that was half laugh, half a snort of surprise.

"Well, so the little brother is more than just a pretty face." Seth got to his feet in one languid motion, moving to sit on a large stone just behind him. He put out the tip of his tongue to lick the blood away from the corner of his lip.

Noah straightened from the half crouch and stood with his arms straight down by his side. Slowly he relaxed his clenched hands. The extent of his injuries was a few scrapped knuckles and wounded pride. He was also very much aware that Seth had probably saved his life.

"I guess I should thank you for that," Noah said grudgingly.

Seth's shrug was eloquent but his smile was slightly sinister. The unspoken words that went along with that smile made Noah's face burn. He simply could not figure Seth out. The man was probably his age or even younger but the chip on his shoulder was the size of Buckingham Palace. Even Seth's compliments were couched in sharp insulting innuendoes, meant to draw blood. Yet he sat there with deceptive grace and stunning confidence for someone so young.

"Keeps," Seth explained at last. "Dungeons. Cellars. Crypts. Next time, remember all of your archeology lessons."

I deserved that, Noah thought. It was a dangerous place. No wonder his father had forbidden it as an area of play; one could too easily become a permanent part of the scenery. He shivered at the thought.

It was Seth who ended the unpleasant silence, tilting his head at an angle that looked like he was listening to something calling in the distance. When he turned his head it was still there; that half twisted smile, that unmistakable look of contempt.

"I have to leave now," Seth said suddenly. He walked toward the horse that stood quietly munching on grass. "You coming with me or walking out on your own?"

When Noah remained silent, Seth shrugged and smiled.

"Suit yourself. Don't go back in there and fall into any holes while you are here alone, *Master* Noah."

Flinging himself up in the saddle, Seth was gone in a flurry of dust and a scattering of stones as the horse ran full out. Noah stood there at the edge of the shadows watching the horse and rider growing smaller in the distance with each passing second. The wind ruffled his hair and sent the long grass to swaying, the stalks whispering like ghostly voices.

Noah reached up and wiped his mouth with the back of his cold, trembling hand.

Eight

Perhaps one day this too will be pleasant to remember.
—Virgil

Noah made it back to the house without seeing a sign of Seth. The black horse was in the paddock when he walked by; it snorted at him and tossed its head as if laughing at a secret joke. Noah went straight to his room and proceeded to drown himself in the bath, trying to soak away sore muscles and dark thoughts.

He was in no mood for a dinner party and while he tried to blame Seth, the real reason for his distemper was the lingering impression left by the ruined chapel. No amount of hot water seemed able to chase the chill from his bones. Noah remained in the tub until he was waterlogged and came out into a room warmed by a fire newly built in the hearth. He stood naked, basking in its warmth as he dried his hair. He took his time dressing, although Andrew had told him the dinner would be informal.

Noah ended up wearing his olive, Italian-made trousers and the zip-neck long sleeved shirt of a slightly darker shade. Remembering the chill of the house in the evening, he decided to take the thin suede jacket to complete the ensemble. There would probably be no confusing him with the locals; from his neck to his feet everything was designer expensive and impeccably tailored to fit his slender frame.

The evening was becoming a more typical autumn night in the highlands; a chilly wind blew in off the sea, rattling windowpanes and moaning through the chimneys. Rain might follow later during the night but at least the fog would stay away. The lights of the Hall blazed in all their glory, a welcoming beacon to any fool-hearty traveler out on the soggy and windswept heath. Fool-hearty or not, the guests for the evening began arriving; the sound of the ancient iron knocker booming through the house to announce their presence.

Dreading their attention like he dreaded a room filled with paparazzi, Noah slipped into his jacket and made his way down the staircase. The blazing chandeliers gave the vast entryway and impersonal drawing room the illusion of warmth. He noticed that the mourning wreath had been removed from the foot of the staircase. That had been the one and only concession by Andrew to the memory of their father. The short and artificial show of grief was over; guests could not be bothered with such things.

There were already three guests indulging in cocktails in the far end of the huge main salon; Noah heard their murmuring voices and Andrew's laughter from the top of the staircase. A crackling fire in one of the two gigantic hearths helped to warm the open space, and Noah appreciated the heat as he walked by and approached the gathering.

Andrew turned in his direction when he entered the immediate area. Barry, the one other face Noah recognized, actually rose from his seat in polite acknowledgment.

"There you are," Andrew said in greeting. "Allow me to introduce my brother Noah, everyone. Noah, you have already met Barry Fitzgerald. This is Barry's lovely wife, Madeline. She teaches at the local school."

"Pleased to meet you," Noah responded.

Barry shook his hand and Noah leaned down over Madeline's outstretched offering, turning her wrist so that he could brush the back of her hand with his lips. The continental approach usually disarmed the ladies and she was delighted; her shapely lips, unadorned by lipstick, broke into a wide smile. She was as small as her husband was large but they were a matched set; long dark hair, black eyes, and an easy disposition. Her hair was piled on her head in a mass of curls and her petit form was covered neck to toe in a gray wool skirt and black tunic belted tight around the waist.

"And this is Doctor Reginald Montague Fox-Pitt the Third.

Did I get that right?"

The man in question made a face as he stood to shake Noah's hand. "Just call me Reggie," he said in a serious deep voice. "Like to keep the formal stuff to a minimum."

Noah smiled slightly. One would never guess that by looking at the man. He was impeccably dressed in a suit and tie that basically screamed money and position. The gray hair was still thick, and brushed back from his tanned forehead to expose a face of some fifty years of age, still remarkably unlined and conventionally handsome. The one flaw was a slightly receding chin and a chipped front tooth when he smiled; he looked surprisingly like Prince Charles.

"I understand you are partially retired," Noah commented, deciding he might as well leap into the conversation early. "What city did you decide to leave behind for country life?"

That started an amiable discussion on the disparities of country life versus city life that continued while the door knocker summoned Duncan once more. The butler properly announced the newest pair to the group after he had taken their coats. Mr. Jamis Selkirk and his sister, Claire Selkirk, came forward and shook the circle of hands.

The woman was the younger of the pair, her pale golden hair confined in a plait that fell the length of her slim back. Her skirt was short and her boots were high but no skin showed in the gap between, and the skirt was the blue/black tartan Noah recognized as Clan. A shawl of the same plaid was draped around her shoulder and secured with a large stickpin of gold, the ruby eyes of a smiling wolf at its tip.

Her companion was somewhat less conspicuous in his attire. Jamis was dressed more or less like Andrew, the picture of a country squire in soft gray tweeds and black boots. They would easily have been identified as one of the aristocracy from their speech and manners if not from their attire. The local accent was not present when they spoke and while her manner seemed friendly enough, his retained the aloof regard for which most of the upper class was famous. Both sets of blue-gray eyes met

Noah's with carefully concealed interest.

"My God," Claire said, hooking her arm through Andrew's. "This place is just as awful as I remember."

To do him justice, her brother cringed along with most of the others. Apparently Andrew was accustomed to her outspoken opinions.

"Good to see you again, Claire," Andrew said with a hint of laughter in his voice. "You are looking delectable this evening. What would I do if I did not have you around to keep me abreast of the latest fashion?"

She took the glass from his hand and downed the last bit of scotch with one swallow.

"Thank you, darling, but really, when are you going to allow me to redecorate? This one looks like the Ritz *in its day* and I assume the other still resembles Miss Marple's sitting room."

"I rather like Miss Marple," her brother commented in response.

"Here, here," the doctor agreed.

Claire pulled her bright red mouth into an unbecoming grimace and then turned back to Andrew, waggling the empty glass in her hand. Andrew took it from her and handed it off to Duncan, who had returned from putting away their coats to resume his butler duties. He gathered up the rest of the empty glasses on a silver tray and disappeared. The men all resumed their seats, all but Andrew who was still in the languid clutches of the only unmarried female in the room.

"I didn't quite believe it when Drew told me you were his brother," Jamis said, crossing his ankle over his knee and leaning back with his arms along the top of the sofa he occupied alone. An unruly lock of his dark blond hair fell across his forehead. "I knew your name, of course, but I recognize you now. You probably don't remember us, we were not around that often and you are a lot younger than we are."

Noah stared at Jamis as if he had just admitted to having two heads. Looking from him to Andrew the resemblance became obvious. It shocked him. Somehow Noah had the impression that they had no family connections. A stupid assumption, he now realized; *clan* was synonymous with *family*. Everyone in the village and neighboring countryside probably had a strain of Bainbridge genetics in their blood.

No doubt reading his puzzled expression, Andrew hurried to explain. "Claire and Jamis are your cousins, I forget how many times removed. We occasioned to play together as children. They live down the road just to the west, beyond the next forested valley."

"Our place is nothing like the Hall," Jamis tossed in. "Just a little country house. We spend most of our time in Edinburgh. Some of us have to *earn* a living, you know."

Andrew's expression darkened slightly but Barry came to his rescue.

"I guess we all can't be good at brewing beer and fiddling," Barry said, lacing his fingers with that of his wife. "Somebody has to be doctors and teachers and car salesmen."

The comment was subtle but hit its intended mark. Jamis took his arms off the back of the sofa and folded them across his chest. The irritation in his expression was only there for a moment before he broke out into a broad grin.

"Aye, that is the truth. If any of you are interested in a good deal on a Bentley, Rolls, or Land Rover, give me a call. We take trade-ins."

Everyone laughed with clear relief. Noah felt like a bit player watching an odd collection of actors on a stage. He had no idea what the script entailed, but he was certain that it would prove interesting. Barry and Jamis talked cars while the doctor and Madeline occasionally tossed in a sentence as they picked at the canapés. Andrew and Claire whispered among themselves with an occasional laugh coming from her throat in a deep sexy purr.

Duncan came at a quick walk when the door again announced more visitors; the size of the Hall made walking quickly a necessity, but Duncan still managed it with a stately decorum. Behind him, from the direction of the dining rooms, came Seth carrying the silver tray filled with cocktails. Looking the part of a servant in his dark suit and tie, Seth even bowed when offering the drinks to the guests, his face fixed with a slight smile. The offerings were sherry in delicate crystal stems; straight scotch in highballs or bourbon and soda over ice; several martinis with lemon twists…and a single glass of what looked like orange juice served up in a cut crystal tumbler.

After serving all the others, Seth came to Noah and bowed slightly so that the tray was held at his seated eye level with the glass of juice prominently positioned for him to take. Noah looked up into the smirking green eyes and felt the heat rise from his neck to his hairline when one of the eyes winked. Noah took the offered glass. Seth moved to stand to one side.

Noah took a drink and almost choked. It was orange juice all right—and half vodka. He swallowed and gasped while his eyes watered. No one noticed his discomfort amid the entrance made by the last two guests, coming at that moment across the vast stone floor of the grand entryway. Noah barely had a chance to glare at Seth, who stood with an expression of bland boredom against the far wall, before the most outrageous sight of the night was bearing down upon him.

"Finally," Barry said.

"You know she does it on purpose," Claire stated with a roll of her eyes.

"At least we can eat now," Jamis sighed. "I am starving."

Noah leaped to his feet, not so much out of courtesy, but for self preservation. She came at him like a billowing orange and purple cloud. Noah had never seen anything like it and he had seen lots of strange things. It was a caftan of some sort; at least he thought that was what robes of that kind were called, outside of one's boudoir or a few foreign countries. There was no doubt as to the wearer; the much alluded to Dora Finsterwall, queen bee of the village social set, at least in her own mind.

Noah could hear Andrew's reflexive groan as the impossible sight reached the point where he stood frozen to his square of carpeting. Stupefied would be a good word to describe his reaction to the spectacle of outré proportions. Noah stepped back out of reflex. Dora promptly invaded his space with an overpowering scent of some heavy, expensive perfume and her jingling, bejeweled hands reached out to capture his like massive jaws closing on a hapless bird.

A squeal of delight nearly shattered Noah's eardrums as she clapped him to her massive bosom and then promptly yanked him back so that she could inspect him head to toe at close range. Her eyes were large and brown and possessed a more shrewd intelligence than the rest of her portrayed in that getup. They viewed him from a height four inches or more above Noah's open stare.

Even with her height, Dora might have once been a pretty thing, but her bones were lost under an extra fifty pounds of weight and forty years of living. Her hair was brown and gray and pink and green, bound up on top of her head with coiled braids and golden cording. Every solid inch of her that was visible was covered in rings, bracelets, and necklaces, including her toes, sticking out of open sandals at the gilt-edged hem of her robes.

"Oh my God, it is you! I cannot tell you how honored I am to meet you! You are absolutely fabulous! That evil brother of yours, hiding you all this time. I've never seen such fine features. Your mother must have been a model. I think I am going to faint. Oh my God, I cannot believe we could have someone so famous agree to play for our little festival. That is what you said, Barry, wasn't it?"

Noah gaped, unable to form a coherent sentence and unable to get one out if he could in between the nonstop flow coming out of her bright pink mouth. He simply nodded in response to her exuberant pumping of his arm, his hand still clamped in both of her hands as she talked and nodded and half curtsied all at once. The curtsy might have been funny if it were not so terrifying; the mound of colored hair studded with long hair picks dipping perilously close to Noah's face.

Of all the people in the room, it was Claire who came to his rescue. She reached in between them and removed Dora's grip, taking the woman's hands and moving her firmly away to a sturdy chair.

"Now Dora, don't smother the boy. Can't you see you are frightening him? He is not used to you like the rest of us are. What on earth are you doing wearing open toed shoes on a night like this? Andrew, stop laughing." Claire turned her head to glare in Andrew's direction. "You are enjoying this entirely too much. I think you probably deserved that bump on your head."

Andrew stuck his lip out. Noah turned bright red for the second time in a few minutes. Faces looked from one brother to the other with rising eyebrows and then burst out laughing at Claire's hint. Well, squabbling and joking were what brothers did, in every family. Noah sat down again, taking up his glass, having forgotten what was in it. He promptly choked and someone behind him thumped him on the back a few times.

It was Father Perrine. No one had noticed that he had come in with Dora; her entrance precluded noticing the house on fire. They were the town's perennial odd couple. Where he was thin, she was not. He dressed in the dark suits and robes of his profession while she wore the most outlandish garb imaginable. He was soft spoken and highly critical of his own thoughts. She was...not. Yet they were often together; the pagan and the cleric.

"Excuse us for being late," the priest said after administering the last slap on the back. "Dora's group was meeting and they ran rather late. I am afraid that I simply did not give her time to change."

"That is perfectly all right," Claire said sweetly.

"I hope you don't think I go around like this every day," Dora offered in Noah's direction. "I wear normal clothes some of the time."

Noah had to smile in spite of himself. Father Perrine walked around and sat down in the chair alongside his, offering a smile of his own. The priest lifted a dark inquiring eyebrow but said nothing about their previous meeting.

"What ridiculous thing are you planning this year?" The question came from Jamis as he scanned Dora's attire. "Something Greek? The role of *Aida* does not become you and you are not exactly dressed as a Valkyrie."

Dora's features took on a decidedly blank expression. Jamis had guessed her surprise identity. Everyone in the room who knew her groaned simultaneously.

"Oh you can't," Barry intoned with a shake of his head.

"Please tell me you are not going to sing," said Claire.

"Sing?" asked the doctor with his glass half to his lips. "Sing Wagner?"

More groaning to the point that the talents discussed were considerably outside of Dora's skill. She rolled her eyes and tugged on her skirts, the trailing hem tangled with her toes.

"Of course we are not going to sing. We will mouth the music. It will only be one set for a couple of scenes and the girls are all so excited. You must admit that last year's *Pan and the Garden* was the hit of the festival. It was not my fault that poor Jules has no imagination."

"Poor Jules is still recovering from that, I will have you know," Andrew stated flatly.

"Ah, but it was something to see on stage, wasn't it now?" Barry teased.

"He should be thanking me," Dora said. "I'll bet he had more offers of marriage after that performance than he could count."

While they were talking, Father Perrine leaned over and explained the entire incident to Noah in a conspiratorial whisper. He then turned bright red. Noah laughed out loud. Dora's grin was positively wicked and aimed straight at him. Whatever she was dressed up to be, Dora had lightened Noah's mood considerably. The others laughed in spurts and waves as Seth made his way to the newcomers with the drink tray. Father Perrine shook his head and Dora went straight for the martinis, both of them.

Noah stopped Seth by catching the tail of his jacket. He replaced the spiked glass of orange juice on the tray and took a glass of whiskey and soda without a change of expression. He would be damned if a couple of women were going to chug down hard liquor as if it were water while he sipped at what they all thought was orange juice. Seth's eyebrow quirked and his lips twisted in a smirk. One swallow of the bitter, smoky tasting drink almost made Noah change his mind, but he hid his grimace behind the glass, smiling when he lowered it.

The small talk stayed on the subject of the festival, the obvious reason why Andrew had called everyone together. It was an odd little gathering, Andrew's friends. Noah wondered, not for the first time, how he was ever going to fit in with such people. Before he knew it, the main topic of discussion had been settled; there would be no setting up on the estate that year.

"Too late to make changes like that," Jamis said with a shake of his head. "Already have the main game area set up in the usual spot outside of the village."

"The tents are ready to put up tomorrow," his sister agreed. "Besides, all the merchants would like to keep the traffic close to their shops instead of way out here. You'd have to run electrical wiring and bring in portable toilets and security."

Andrew argued around the edges but gave in without much persuasion; he had entertained the idea only as a fleeting thought. They were right in any case. Such decisions could not be made or accepted at the last minute.

Dora was far from ready to give up the concept entirely. She had that look on her face that all the others recognized; she was plotting a coup d'état. She swallowed the last half of the second martini in one gulp and tossed the empty glass at Seth, who caught it out of midair as if they practiced the maneuver daily.

"What about moving our little theater group to a grander stage?" she asked. "We could perform right here. That cavernous front room would be perfect. I can see *Aida* as much more grand there than in that tiny space at the school. The staircase would be a fabulous set."

"You are banished from the school, remember?" Madeline commented with a half smile. "Jules was not the only one with no imagination."

Dora stamped her foot. "Small minds. We could use the church, I suppose…"

Father Perrine lifted his face toward Andrew. "Please, I beg you, let her do as she asks and have it here. Besides, if your brother is going to perform a concert for us, would not it be better to have that here than in the tiny church or Barry's, uh, establishment?"

Barry laughed with no hard feelings. "I guess it would at that."

"Who said anything about a concert?" Andrew inquired, seeing the look on his brother's face. "If anything, Noah said he *might* do a couple of pieces. That hardly means a private concert."

"Oh, but it would be too sad if we cannot hear such a magnificent talent." Dora stuck her lip out in a pout. "Think of the price we could get for tickets."

Noah had to speak up; Gavin was not there to do it for him, thank God. He lifted his arm with the wrist brace clearly visible. "I am physically unable to perform a concert, even if my manager allowed it. I could play a couple of pieces, nothing difficult, but no more than that."

"That would be enough. We do our little operetta…have some of the girls with their dancing…Barry and his bunch. We could turn it into a nice little production."

"No extra fees on my account," Noah added, seeing the gleam in her eyes. "I will do it, for Andrew's friends, but not for profit." He looked pointedly at Dora. "Mine *or* yours. Do we have a deal?"

She pulled in her lip and batted her eyes. "Perhaps a concert next year?"

Everyone groaned or laughed. Noah shook his head, smiling.

"No promises of return performances every year, especially if you cheat on the deal. No profits mean no inflated tickets sales, no unauthorized merchandising, no recordings. I'm sure I am leaving something out but your friends understand the idea. If you want a donation for the cause, I'm sure we can work something out, right Andrew?"

Andrew was speechless at how easily Noah seemed to handle the Queen Bee. He had actually said the word "no" and she had actually heard it. She was smiling and arranging her skirts with jingling, bangle-covered arms.

"Ahh...sure," Andrew responded. "Then it's settled."

"Night before the other activities get in swing?" Barry asked.

"That gives you one and a half days." Claire said, leaning forward. "The tickets have already been selling for the operetta which states the performance time as seven o'clock, night after tomorrow. Is that enough time for you, Noah? Barry?" They both nodded their assurance. She looked at Dora. "Aida?"

"I guess it will have to be," Dora said with an exaggerated sigh of a harassed artist.

"Great," Claire agreed, making the word sound more like a curse than agreement. "I will assist with the setting up and such, Andrew. Don't worry."

"Who is worried?" Andrew said amiably.

"I would be," Noah heard the good father say beneath his breath.

Duncan appeared at the edge of the assembly to announce dinner. They were an odd number for dinner, but that hardly mattered and everyone went in more or less in the manner they had arrived, with Noah bringing up the rear. He was unaware of Seth's presence behind him until he reached the doorway and the man leaned to whisper in his ear.

"You are looking delectable this evening," Seth quoted Andrew's earlier compliment to Claire with perfectly drawled innuendo.

Noah caught himself in time not to gasp audibly, but he was certain the lighting in the room was not dim enough to cover his blush. He looked up, straight into the dark eyes of Dora being seated by Duncan across the table. Noah sank down beside Jamis and looked down at his plate.

They were using one end of the ridiculously long table, maybe less than one quarter of the space. The women were more or less interspersed among the men with Andrew sitting at the head of the table and Noah between Barry's wife and Jamis. The room was chilly as usual, even though the large hearth held a roaring fire and the wall of long French doors had been swathed in heavy damask drapes. Both of the silver candelabras were in use at their end of the table, and the overhead chandelier was also burning brightly, yet the space seemed darker than it should.

Rose Marie had done an admirable job on such short notice. The crystal and china glowed with newly polished life amid fresh cut greenery decorating the center of the table. The hint of evergreen, flowers, and crackling fire did its best to dispel the dusty dampness of a seldom used room. Overhead the many glass eyes of the long dead animals seemed to flicker with an eerie light, giving the illusion of movement where there could be none.

Noah was aware of the presence the moment he entered the room.

That was how he described it now, a *presence*. The room filled him with dread, even in the company of laughter and the clinking of china. With the wall of glass closed off by draperies, the oppressive atmosphere seemed more intense than during the daylight hours, or perhaps it was merely his imagination due to his dislike of the disembodied heads. He almost jumped when Seth reached over his shoulder to serve the first course.

It was a fabulous meal, hardly a casual dining experience. Noah half expected to see a group of medieval musicians tucked into the far corner or a couple of knights in armor clank through the door. Instead there was only the sound of contented voices happily chatting and the coming and going of Duncan and Seth serving the evening's repast. They looked like a well rehearsed pair of dancers moving in and out between the diners; lifting and lowering plates, filling wine glasses, smoothly practiced and almost unobtrusive in their dark suits.

The wonderful smells announced even more fabulous food, a smorgasbord of local sampling that Noah could not believe Mary Katherine had managed to produce. Poached salmon and jellied eel. Oyster and shrimp tarts. Creamy turnip and sage soup. Stuffed pork loin with leeks and thyme sauce. Herb salad and scallop potatoes. Crab stuffed mushrooms in cream sauce and steamy buttered carrots. Not one sheep's head or haggis to be found.

The wine flowed as freely as the food and Noah continued his new experiment with alcohol, finding the glasses of wine to be only slightly more acceptable than the harsh taste of scotch. The richness and sheer amount of food overwhelmed his palate, and he settled down to sampling with tiny bites while he drank entirely too easily. Across from him, Dora ate with small precise mouthfuls, her jewelry jangling with every motion, her dark eyes watching everything.

Andrew's friends were an interesting group; sinners and saints, menders of bones and breakers of hearts, performers and audience. Noah had no doubt in which group he belonged. He laughed when a joke was told and when prompted, was happy to tell little stories about his music and travels. Mostly he listened, imagining how things would have gone with Gavin at the dinner table that evening. The sly little comments by Claire would not have gone untouched, he was certain of that. Gavin's witty acerbic tongue would be more than a match for the cousins. It would have been Gavin lording it over the rest of them with his haughty disregard of all things *aristocratic*.

What an addition to dinner that would have been. Once or twice Noah was brought out of his reverie by the changing of dishes or the pouring of wine. Those lapses did not last long enough to be noticed by anyone, at least, he hoped not. No one had the bad taste to bring up his sudden miraculous appearance or the recent unexpected death of Lord James.

After dinner coffee was served in the drawing room where the evening had begun. Noah was more than happy to get out of the dining room but the damage was already done. When he got to his feet the room spun clockwise and he felt himself leaning against the chair for support. Apparently Barry had been watching him too; his large hand came up to Noah's elbow and held him steady.

"I thought you didn't drink," Barry said in a half whisper. "Should have started off with beer instead of trying to keep up with Dora."

"I'll remember that," Noah said, making the effort to walk in a straight line.

"She must really like you," Barry continued as they walked along together. "She's left you unmolested all evening. Then again, you are one of the few people I have ever heard tell her no."

"But I didn't tell her no. I blackmailed her just like she did me."

Barry chuckled appreciatively. "I guess you did. I'll have to remember that."

Noah was grateful to sit down. His head ached and his stomach was feeling none too well. He accepted coffee from Duncan. He was aware that Andrew's gaze had followed him during dinner and was watching him now with curiosity. Noah drank his coffee. His were not the only hands that shook; Dora lifted her cup from the saucer to keep it from chattering like teeth.

"Can we borrow your truck in the morning?" Claire asked Barry, taking a sip of coffee. "We have to round up chairs from the school."

"And perhaps you to go along with it?" her brother added from where he stood by the fireplace. "She is using the royal *we* and that means *me*. I have no intention of being the only work horse in her stable."

Barry shook his head. "You can have the truck but not me. Got to practice with the lads and business is already picking up. How 'bout Andrew?"

"Chairs?" Andrew inquired. "How many are we talking about?"

"Enough for fifty or sixty people. Maybe more once they hear about Noah."

"Sixty? Good lord, why not the whole village!"

"You may have the whole village if you do not put a limit on the tickets available," Madeline commented as an afterthought. "That is something you left out of your deal, Mr. Bainbridge."

"So I did," Noah agreed thoughtfully. "Dora?"

Dora looked them all over with the expression of a child being asked to hand over the forbidden cookie she was about to eat. She sighed. "All right. How many do I get? Seventy? I do not see how we can go lower than that even with the performers adding another twenty to the list."

"Another twenty!" Andrew exclaimed in dismay.

"Oh Lord!" Dora said suddenly. "I have a million phone calls to make. I must tell the girls about the change of plans. We will have to set up the scenery and do our final rehearsals here."

"Scenery?" Andrew repeated.

"That settles it," Jamis said with a sigh. "Eighty is the magic number. Get yourself to the school tomorrow morning by ten, Andrew. We haul chairs. Do you know how to use a hammer? Never mind, I'll teach you."

"I'll help," Noah volunteered, seeing his brother's expression.

Jamis shook his head. "Nope. Cannot risk you hurting yourself before the big night. Your brother is perfectly capable of manual labor, even if it does not appeal to him." A wicked gleam came into his eye. "You might hang around and give the ladies pointers on their *opera*—if you are brave enough."

Half of them laughed. Father Perrine sighed. Dora sneered.

"You will require more help for the night of the performance," Madeline suggested. "I'll get a few of the girls and lads to help with the seating and coordination. Jamis, while you are in town tomorrow ask around for a couple of men to help with parking, although I expect quite a few folks will carpool. You had best designate an area out front for that, Andrew."

Andrew looked stricken. He had clearly lost control of his perceived little adventure. The look he gave Duncan was met with reserved silence; not the butler's place to give the Laird public advice. Noah watched the exchange with amusement.

"Seth can mark off the area for parking," Noah commented with a glance at the man in question. "I am certain he is capable of more than serving drinks."

Seth took the jab with a raised eyebrow and a curl to the corner of his mouth. "Anything you wish, Master Noah. Might I suggest Moira to assist you with ushering, Mrs. Fitzgerald?"

Madeline nodded her dark head. "That would be great. Please have her call me tomorrow and we will discuss what the ushers should wear."

"Then we should be going," Barry added, getting to his feet. "I need to call the lads tonight and inform them of the changes. Just come by the pub for the keys in the morning, Jamis. Good night everyone. Andrew, wonderful dinner."

Everyone got to their feet with the general idea of leaving along with the Fitzgeralds. Duncan and Seth fetched overcoats and scarves. Everyone shook hands or kissed cheeks with words of parting. Outside the wind had vanished and fog had crept in from the valley to lay at the edge of the Hall, cutting it off from the rest of the world.

Noah followed the doctor out onto the paved walkway, needing the fresh air to clear his head and giving Andrew a moment alone with Claire. Jamis thumped him on the back and walked away with a smile on his face. Noah waved goodbye to the Fitzgeralds and then turned to go inside, only to have his way blocked by Dora Finsterwall.

She slid her arm inside of his, making it impossible for him to do anything other than escort her to her awaiting vehicle. Her arm was like an iron bar and she walked with steady confidence. Father Perrine scurried ahead of them to the car.

"I do hope you think nothing ill of us," Dora said quietly. "We are all a little eccentric it seems. Too many years of nothing but the wind and the sea."

"I found dinner to be very entertaining," Noah said truthfully. "I can hardly wait to see your opera."

"Very kind of you. You are very much like your mother."

Noah could not hide his shock. They stopped at the car door but she did not release his arm and he made no move to open the door for her. She did not look at him.

"You knew my mother?" he asked after he had recovered his breath.

"She was a sweet and generous woman. James…well, he never recovered, did he?" She looked at him then, her dark eyes in shadow. Her arm slipped away. "You are a lot like her. You are like your father too, in ways you might not suspect. Take care of yourself, young man."

Noah stood with his mouth hanging open while she opened the door and slid inside with the grace of a woman half her size. He closed the door and stepped away. Father Perrine turned the ignition key and the sedan purred to life. They drove away, leaving Noah staring after them, the lights of the car disappeared into the fog.

"Is he like you expected?" Father Perrine asked his companion in the dark after they had left the lights of the Hall behind.

Dora sighed and allowed her head to fall back on the headrest. "I do not know what is going on in that house, Ian, but whatever it is, that poor child is right in the middle of it."

Father Perrine glanced across at her. She was exhausted… and frightened. "So you think getting yourself into the house will help?"

"I don't know," she admitted. "At least I can be there during the day. At night, well... At night that place has its own ideas."

Perrine said nothing. He had his own questions about Bainbridge Hall. While Dora looked and often acted the fool, she was far from it where certain things were concerned. The fact that Dora seemed to be in agreement made his suspicions all the more plausible. It did not, however, make them any less fantastic. They drove down the narrow curvy road in foggy silence, each pondering their own dark thoughts.

Back at the Hall, Noah shivered, watching the last car disappear into the darkness. The fog had sneaked in unawares, a blanket of mist so thick that he could feel it against his skin. He did not like the sensation. He entered the house with a sigh, Duncan closing the door behind him.

Andrew was standing beside the glowing hearth, its beckoning embers the only warmth in the gigantic room. He looked up at the sound of Noah's footsteps.

"Well you did it. You survived your first encounter with the Queen of Glachmourrin with nary a scratch. I am duly impressed."

"I would not say quite that," Noah replied, stopping at the hearth and holding his icy hands out to the heat.

"You did look a mite terrified clasped to her bosom in that manner. I shiver just thinking about it."

Noah grimaced. "I suppose I was a bit overwhelmed at first."

Andrew laughed. "You looked like a frightened twelve-year-old in the clutches of the largest multicolored banshee I could ever imagine. *Aida*. What is she thinking?"

Noah laughed with him. "I take it these performances are the highlight of the year around here?"

Andrew shook his head. "At least they are not going to sing. You should have seen and *heard* them doing excerpts from *Cats* a few years back. Every dog and cat in the county ran for cover at the noise."

"Ah well, I suppose it is great fun for them, a little culture way out here."

"I suppose, but why do they have to torture the rest of us? And I set myself up right for the torture this time. Get ready. Starting daylight tomorrow, we will have not a moment's peace until the festival is over. Sure you are up to it?"

Noah shrugged. "Why not? I might even join Barry in playing a jig or two."

"Do not get carried away by Dora's frenzy. Are you feeling all right? You look a little green just now."

Noah leaned against the wall next to the hearth. The heat made him slightly dizzy and the evening's stress tempered with alcohol had just hit him hard.

"Too much of everything I'm not used to I guess. If you will excuse me, I think I should call it a night."

"Of course," Andrew replied and turned to face Seth, who was in the room behind them. "Seth? Assist Noah up to his room and make sure he has everything he needs for the night. I am going out for a walk to clear my head."

Duncan and Rose were busy cleaning in the dining room; Noah could hear the clatter of dishes and the muted even tones of their voices. Seth had just returned to fetch the coffee service but sat it back down at Andrew's order. If Andrew noticed the look that passed between them, he said nothing.

They walked across the vast echoing space, dark now that the main chandeliers were switched off. Noah headed up the staircase with Seth following a step or two behind in silence. When they reached the door to his room, Noah would have barred the way but Seth stepped quickly around him to open the door, continuing deeper into the room, switching on lights. Noah hesitated, but only for a second or two.

"I'm okay," he grumbled. "You don't need to do that."

Proceeding to turn down the bed, Seth glanced at him but said nothing. Noah stood where he was in the middle of the floor watching Seth perform as he had in the dining room, the perfect illusion of obedient domestic. When Seth had the fire rekindled in the hearth, he stood up. Noah felt uneasy beneath the steady green gaze but he refused to take a single step back when Seth moved toward him.

"You drank a fair amount tonight for a man who doesn't drink."

Noah winced. He was already regretting that decision. He was also regretting following Seth into the room even though the door behind him was wide open. He could hardly turn and run; he had already seen how quickly Seth could pounce, besides, it was his room. As if Seth could read his mind, the familiar mocking smile curved his lips.

"You didn't tell him about the ruins," Seth said quietly.

Noah felt his eyebrows rise at that comment. The silence between them hinted at a variety of meanings, none Noah was willing to consider at the moment.

"Neither did you," he replied.

Seth shrugged, a slight lift of his shoulders that he somehow made look eloquent. Maybe it was the dark suit lending him an air of refinement that he lacked in his usual daytime work attire. The term "servant" no longer applied to modern service domestics and there was certainly nothing subservient in Seth's demeanor.

"Guess we are even then." Seth moved toward the door and turned to look back with his hand on the doorknob. "I see you are in no mood to accept my innocent offer to help you undress so I will just be on my way."

Noah whirled around to meet the challenging green eyes, aware that his face was burning with indignation. He had to catch himself on the edge of the bed as the room continued to spin even after he had stopped moving, ruining his chance of a witty return.

"Drink a couple of glasses of water before you go to bed,"

Seth said from the doorway. "It will keep you from being too hungover in the morning. Better yet, I will send Rose up with some soup and tea. You didn't eat much through dinner."

Noah felt a wave of nausea roll through his stomach. To his annoyance, Seth remained standing in the doorway, watching. He really did not want to be sick in front of Seth but he couldn't let go of the bed at the moment with the room spinning.

"I don't need your advice," Noah said with a groan.

"Really?"

Seth came back into the room long enough to take Noah by the arm, lead him over to the stuffed chair and drop him down in it with a thud. He pushed Noah's head down over his knees and held it there.

"Breathe through your nose not your mouth. What would they all think if they could see you now; *wunderkind* with his head between his knees about to hurl? Do not get up."

Noah couldn't have gotten up if he wanted to. The world was suddenly a very unpleasant place and he wanted to get off. That this was happening in front of Seth was a humiliation almost too much to bear. He groaned in misery when a cold wet cloth dropped down across the back of his neck followed by hands reaching for the edge of his jacket.

"Don't get up," Seth told him again. "Just move your arms enough for me to pull the jacket off before we soak it."

Somehow Noah managed. The cold washcloth made him feel a little better. Seth's long fingers sliding across his hot forehead did not. He sat up, clearly a mistake.

With Seth's help he made it into the bathroom before he threw up. It was the most unpleasant experience in Noah's memory, but when the last of the heaving was over, he recovered his equilibrium almost immediately. Unfortunately his pride was beyond hope of repair. Sitting on the tile floor with his back to the cold edge of the tub, he wiped his mouth with the washcloth.

"Feel better?" Seth asked with what seemed like genuine

concern.

Noah sighed. He felt humiliated and sick, but at least the floor beneath him was solid and unmoving.

"You look better," Seth said, answering his own question. "I guess you can blame me for this. I kind of egged you on. You're just the type to take the bait too—stubborn."

Noah shook his head. He was back to not being able to figure Seth out. "I didn't do it because of you," he admitted reluctantly. "I watched those women downing straight scotch like water and it irked me."

Seth actually laughed. It changed his face entirely, making him look like the schoolboy he should have been. He reached over and tousled Noah's hair like he would do that of a child.

"Serves you right then. The women around these parts *are* like the men. Scotch *is* water to them, you nit. Well now, you have had a busy day. If you can get around by yourself unsupervised for a moment, I will fetch you some soup and tea. Don't argue. Can you stand?"

Noah managed on his own. He was cleaned up and in pajamas before the knock at the door came. It was Rose bearing soup and tea, beaming with delight at the success of the dinner party. She chatted away, sounding more like Ester than not, as she poured and patted and left him to his business. Apparently Seth had said nothing to her regarding his upset; just another thing for which he would be beholding to Seth.

He ate some of the soup, simple beef broth with tiny bits of mushroom and barley, and carefully drank the tea. Feeling much better—damn Seth—Noah sat up reading one of the mystery novels he had purchased until the heroine's predicaments exhausted him. For the first time since coming to his brother's house, he locked his door.

After the light went out, Noah fell to sleep almost immediately, a deep black sleep that held no portent of things to come; no spinning, no running and no smirking green eyes.

NINE

All the world is a stage, and all the men and women merely players.
  —W. Shakespeare

A consecutive series of crashes woke him up.

At least Noah thought he was awake; one eye opened, unbothered by the fact that the other one did not. It was daylight, a weak watered down sort of daylight that made him think it was earlier than it was. Another crash made him open the other eye and attempt to focus on the clock just beyond the rim of his pillow. Both eyes opened wider at the realization that it was a quarter hour from noon.

Noah rolled over in the tangle of sheets with a groan. He lay there staring up at the ceiling until he decided that he didn't feel anywhere as bad as he should have…considering. He unwound himself from the bed sheets and stretched in the chilly room, turning to rummage through the blankets until he found his robe. It then occurred to him that the reason there was no fire or tray of morning tea was that he had locked the door the night before.

Another crash assured him that everyone else was up so he padded to the door to unlock it before giving the old fashioned bell pull a tug or two. He supposed that somewhere in the vast recesses of the house one of the staff would hear it and know he was awake. The dark circles around his eyes, along with the tangled sheets, hinted at a restless night, but he didn't feel that bad; some food would help. Stifling a yawn that seemed endless, Noah staggered into the bathroom and set about brushing his teeth.

Sure enough, no sooner than he had replaced the toothbrush did someone knock and enter the room. It was Duncan with a tea tray that he placed on the table.

"What is going on down there?" Noah asked with another

yawn.

"I apologize for the noise," Duncan said, drawing open the drapes to allow more of the muted light into the room. "Chairs, I'm afraid, sir. Why Mr. Selkirk feels he must throw them down, I have no idea."

Noah poured himself a cup of what turned out to be coffee. He drank it down without sugar or cream and waited for it to work its magic.

"It is the lunch hour," Duncan said needlessly. "If you are feeling up to it, the luncheon will be served buffet style in the dining room today. Or I will bring it up to you, as you prefer."

"I'll come down," Noah agreed when Duncan reached to refill his cup. "Sorry for sleeping so late. I guess Andrew has been at it for awhile."

"To the village and back, as you can no doubt hear." Another crash bore that out. "I expect Madame Finsterwall at any moment. She will no doubt arrive just as the food is being set out."

"Duncan," Noah said with slight disapproval.

"I am sorry, sir, but that woman has an uncanny ability to know such things. The rest of her 'troop' will be arriving in an hour or so I have been informed. If I might suggest, try to be out of sight and earshot by then, Master Noah."

Noah laughed silently. Apparently Dora Finsterwall's reputation was well deserved. "I guess I will have to suffer along with the rest of you. Thanks, Duncan. I'll be right down."

Duncan nodded and departed, closing the door behind him. Noah stood at the window drinking his coffee, trying not to shiver in his robe and pajamas. Outside was a mess of a day, light blue with a mist that was not quite rain and a low cloud deck that might have been fog an hour earlier. A nasty day for hauling chairs and setting up tents. Feeling more alive after the second cup of coffee, Noah went about showering and dressing as he made ready to join the circus.

By the time he walked down the stairs, a fair amount of the

destruction had been accomplished; piles and piles of folded wooden chairs lay about the grand hallway in sodden heaps. Jamis Selkirk stomped in with another load under each arm and proceeded to fling his load forward and drop them on the stone floor with an echoing crash. Andrew tried to be a little quieter about it but managed only slightly. Both men were wearing coats and hats shiny with moisture, trailing a wet grassy path from the doorway.

With some interest, Noah noticed the additional stacks of wood and boxes that were being hauled in by Seth and another man who were both coatless and hatless. When they walked by carrying a large covered item suspended between the two of them, Seth glanced his direction.

"Go ahead and have lunch," Seth called out. "We will be there as soon as we finish unloading the last lot."

"Scenery?" Noah inquired.

Seth glowered at him. The other man did not look much happier. Taking his hint, Noah headed off to the dining room and nourishment.

The room was not empty as he had hoped. Claire Selkirk and Rose Marie were in a heated discussion about something and did not even look at him when he entered on the opposite side of the room. He went about gathering some food on a plate and pouring a cup of coffee while they stormed out in mutual disagreement. Noah sat there in the large empty silence contemplating the feeling in the pit of his stomach that had nothing to do with food or alcohol.

Bringing another covered platter from kitchen to dining hall, Moira caught him in his introspection. "Is everything all right, sir?"

Noah shrugged with a delicious smoked salmon sandwich half to his mouth. "I just don't like this room very much, I guess."

Claire came bursting into the room without preamble. On spotting Noah, she stopped short of the table. "Been hiding out?"

"Just trying to avoid all the noise," he lied.

"Ahh, a little too much wine with dinner." Her smile was malicious and understanding at the same time.

"I think it was the scotch and the vodka before the wine," Noah muttered.

Her smile was beaming. She certainly looked none the worse for the night before. "Isn't that sweet? To find a man who cannot hold his liquor."

Noah had no idea how to respond to that, but was saved by the entrance of none other than the queen bee herself. Dora came barging into the room dripping water from a wide brimmed hat that looked like something Captain Ahab might own. Her trench coat was pink and covered in tabs, pockets, buttons, and folds, enough for the envy of any female secret agent and much to the consternation of Duncan, who had apparently chased her all the way from the front door. She tossed both soaked items at the butler and turned with a shiver.

"Daylight does nothing to improve this room," she said and headed straight for the food set out in silver serving dishes on the long sideboard.

Seeing both Duncan and Claire's faces, Noah suppressed a grin. Moira refilled his cup of coffee and went about pouring for the two women. As he was seated at the end of the table, both women came and sat down on either side of him.

Claire was astonishingly beautiful in her pale blue tunic over jeans, her long blond hair pulled up in a simple ponytail. Her hands were slim and sporting a French manicure and thousands of dollars worth of diamonds. Noah had no doubt she could get a man to do anything she wanted.

Dora sat her plate down with a clunk. She more substantial than Claire but as simply dressed. Her hair was totally brown today, actually plaited in pigtails like Rebecca of Sunnybrook Farm. Somehow they made her look more like a Valkyrie in combination with her spangled-covered shirt and grey wool trousers. The bangles of *Aida* were gone, replaced with a diamond bracelet on one wrist and a wide silver cuff with Celtic designs on the other. Devoid of makeup and exhaustion, her skin was perfectly smooth and white.

"Those men are certainly slow this morning," she said after taking a savage bite of roast beef with chutney and swallowing almost without chewing. "The girls will be here and not a single bit of the scenery will be up."

"It is raining in case you haven't noticed," Claire said in defense. "The truck had a flat at the school and Jamis hates having to deal with vehicular problems—weird when you know he sells the bloody things."

"Probably because he sells them," Noah added. "Besides, Dora, you knew the scenery would not be ready so soon. They will have to figure out how to assemble it and half of your fun will be in telling them."

She smiled at him with a wicked glint in her eye. "I am actually dying to tell your brother what to do with a hammer."

"I will bet he's dying to tell you the same thing." Noah smiled back.

She looked shocked and then burst out laughing so hard tears rolled from her eyes. She was still laughing when the men came into the room with the sound of scuffing boots and panting breath.

"What's so funny?" Andrew asked.

They laughed even harder.

The men went about serving themselves, griping about the weather and the things they had left to do. One by one they sat down at the table and started shoveling in the food. The array of sandwiches included smoked salmon, roast beef with chutney, egg salad with bacon, shrimp pate, and goat cheese with duck. Alongside that were mushroom and tomato soups, leftover trout/spinach puffs, scones with jam or clotted cream, and a bowl of fruit. Stuffing oneself was a full time occupation at the Hall.

Two of the small sandwiches, half an apple, and some coffee

were more than enough for Noah. He rose along with Claire, who went back for more food.

"Finished already?" Jamis inquired, looking up. "No wonder you are so little. Hardly ate anything at dinner either."

"Jamis!" his sister admonished him.

"Well, it's true," Jamis defended. "I bet he doesn't weigh a hundred and fifty pounds soaking wet."

"Then it is a hundred pounds of talent and that is more than I can say for you."

"Now see here, girl—"

"Stop it both of you," Dora intervened with a sandwich aimed for her mouth. "Remember it is not the size of the dog in the fight that counts, it is the size of the fight in the dog."

Noah and Andrew groaned simultaneously but Seth started laughing until the rest of them had to laugh along with him. Noah shook his head at the whole lot of them. He must have been out of his mind to get involved with a local gathering if these people were a fair representation of the locals.

"I don't want to keep any of you from your work," he said from the doorway. "I am thinking sunny Rome would be nice."

They stared after his departing back and then went on eating.

The offices of *McKewen & Weatherby* were on the ninth floor of a twenty-eight story chrome and glass building of modern design one block from the riverfront. Their names were emblazoned on the wall above the reception desk, the only thing you could see when stepping off the lift into the silent, official looking lobby. The offices occupied the entire floor and if you did not know what their business was, you would never guess it from the expensive furnishings and lack of any identifying signage. The tall reception desk was dark granite and from behind it the receptionist looked properly awe inspiring.

Two receptionists, in this case. Gavin stepped out into their domain with a shake of his raincoat and a glance around at the oriental rugs and Ming vase prominently displayed before two Chinese screens. Expensive real estate and expensive tastes. If all their clients paid like he was paying, they could well afford it. Gavin only hoped they were worth the money.

The male receptionist stepped out from behind the monolith to greet him. The man was young and handsome, dressed in a dark blue suit and silk tie, thick dark hair pulled off of his face in a ponytail. He did not offer to shake hands.

"May I be of service, sir?"

"Gavin Moore," he introduced himself with a slight nod of his head. "I have an appointment with Mr. McKewen."

The man smiled, a slight curve of his lips that did not reach his dark eyes. "Yes, he is expecting you. If you would follow me, please."

Gavin followed the handsome young man down a short corridor and into a medium sized room with a riverside view through a solid wall of windows. It was comfortably furnished, with a sofa against the far wall, a heavy wooden table with chairs, and the same expensive tastes in artwork hanging on the apricot-shaded walls. Gavin set his briefcase down on the table and the young man helped him off with his wet coat, taking it to a coat rack just inside the door.

"May I bring you some coffee or tea?"

Gavin accepted coffee and the man left him alone. He walked to the wall of windows and looked out over the river. It was a gray, damp day and from there he could see the outline of the parliament building in the misty distance and the coming and going of several small boats getting drenched on the Thames. He shivered with a sudden chill and wondered what Noah was doing at that moment.

"It is a dreadful day, isn't it?" said McKewen from behind him.

Gavin turned to see both men enter the room, McKewen holding the door open for the receptionist, who was carrying a serving tray. The young man put the tray on the table and pushed down the plunger on the French press, carefully pouring the coffee into two porcelain cups.

"I don't know why London couldn't have been in Spain," Gavin said in agreement of the comment regarding the weather.

"Aye well, it might have been if they had won the war," McKewen stated with a hint of humor. "Please, have a seat, Mr. Moore. That will be all, Michael."

The young man inclined his dark head and left, closing the door behind him. Gavin joined McKewen at the table, where the aroma of freshly brewed coffee was irresistible. While McKewen added cream and sugar, Gavin drank his black.

"He makes good coffee," Gavin remarked. "Sumatran?"

McKewen smiled. "Good to know a fellow connoisseur."

Gavin was unsure if the comment pertained to the coffee or the young man who had served it. He finished his drink and poured himself part of another, sparing a glance at the leather bound folder McKewen had set down near his right elbow.

"Nice offices. Your decorator has excellent taste."

"Weatherby likes to collect oriental art. I collect…other things. Well, Mr. Moore, I think you will be happy with what we have uncovered so far."

"Let's see it then."

The man handed him the leather bound folder, keeping a plain plastic binder for himself. Gavin opened the professionally organized dossier and scanned the table of contents in its sheet protector. It looked like an in-depth investigation by the number of listed items and the thickness of the pages.

"Researching the Bainbridge family must be something tantamount to searching the history of the Windsors," Gavin said. "I am already impressed."

"Hardly a surprise," McKewen stated. "They are one of the oldest families in Scotland. The Laird's coat of arms is here somewhere, wolves tearing at a stag."

He flipped the pages open to a particularly dreadful crest of sorts, detailed with the formal hand-drawn art of the fifteenth century. The blue-black wolves looked fearsome enough, their fangs barred with purpose, the red blood of the dying stag staining their thick fur. Gruesome.

"The family motto is *Our Blood, Our Fate*, a strange motto to be sure but probably taken from an older, longer version of an oath to the King or such. The name *Bainbridge* is a more civilized interpretation of the old Gaelic family name, which literally means 'Cursed Path.' They changed it in 1788, probably for aesthetic purposes in a more modern world."

"I can see why," Gavin said in distaste. The more he looked into Noah's blue-blood family, the more he disliked them.

McKewen continued with a general family history of distinguished pedigree from great-grandfather up to the last Laird of the Hall. If they had not been the smartest and most ruthless of families, then they had been the luckiest. They managed to not only survive from generation to generation through famine, plagues, wars, and economic disasters, but to prosper even through modern mishaps that ruined far more royal and well connected families. They lost their fair share of clan members to all of those miseries, but somehow they always came out ahead of the game.

James Bainbridge had been just as intelligent and adept at money making as the rest of them. He had been on the board of several international corporations and owned a lion's share of stock in many other successful ventures. He had been a veritable juggernaut in his youth, earning several degrees along with a few athletic awards. He had settled down in his late twenties with a wife at the family homestead in Scotland. Within two years of that fated occurrence, his life had turned an unforeseen corner; at least, presumably, unforeseen by him.

It began with the birth of his son Andrew and the death of his wife. For several years after that James seemed to withdraw from the business world in favor of time spent with his son. Then his father died and he inherited the title while still in his middle thirties. During that time his businesses suffered some minor setbacks but nothing spectacular. Andrew grew old enough for him to begin taking more time away from home and it was during that time that James met Helen Westerhaven.

Apparently she had been more than a slight distraction. Having seen her photograph and the living representation of her features in Noah's handsome face, Gavin could understand. She had apparently been taken by James as well because she bore him a son out of wedlock, an unheard of thing for young women of her class. For whatever reason, they had parted company and she had set about raising Noah on her own.

McKewen had included Noah's childhood history, as much of it as they could gather; the school where he had lived, the reports of his grades, the transfer to the music academy. Through all that time there was no personal contact with his father as far as they could tell. They had researched Andrew in the same manner and with limited conclusions.

Andrew had followed the route of most upper class boys; he had been given tutors in his youth and then followed to a private school in his teens. His upper levels had been at St. Andrew's University and Oxford. Following in his father's footsteps, he had developed a remarkable skill for investment. All in all, he seemed a most ordinary fellow.

Gavin had another shock regarding "the money." Twice a year since he had been with Noah, a rather large sum had been deposited into the account from which they drew for expenses. Gavin had always thought that it came from Helen's trust because he knew there was one; he saw the name and the amount on the tax filings and year-end financial papers. It had always irked him that the withdrawals were large, yet the Trust seemed to grow larger with each passing year.

Now he knew why. The semi-annual funds had come from Noah's father. Every year since his unspoken banishment, Noah's father had seen to his younger son's welfare. The amounts had not lessened or ceased once Noah was out of school and on his own; they continued still. Gavin wondered if they would cease now that Noah had voided the intention of the will, now that Andrew would have control over the money, even presumably, the accounts his father had been using for Noah's benefit all this time.

Gavin flipped through the pages, following along with McKewen's narration. The histories of both families were there in chronological order, along with copies of the appropriate birth, marriage, and death certificates. Gavin sat expressionless as he looked at Noah's birth certificate with the space for father filled in "unknown."

The marriage certificate for Helen and James was there too, along with the photocopy of the magistrate's book with their signatures. Then there was the copy of James's death certificate, the ink barely dry, with the date and conclusions in black and white; *cause of death unknown, manner of death natural.*

Gavin took all the information in with a growing, nagging doubt. He already knew that Noah had chosen to disregard the money, but what had surprised him was that Andrew had agreed to forfeit it as well. The will had not provided for it to return to the estate, naming a secondary destination instead.

What Gavin had not known until recently was that the accounts mentioned in the will were James Bainbridge's private, individual accounts, not the bulk of the inheritance, which was in Trust to the titled Lord of the Estate, never to be touched or distributed otherwise, from generation to generation.

"Was there an autopsy done on Lord Bainbridge?" he asked when McKewen stopped for a moment to drink the last of his coffee.

"No autopsy was done. The county where the estate is located is yet extremely rural and the medical authority deemed it natural causes. They did run a blood scan to look for anything unusual and found nothing. Are you suggesting…?"

Gavin sighed. "I have no idea what I am suggesting. He changed his will only a short time before his death. Do you have any idea what the old will contained?"

McKewen shook his head. "There is no way to obtain that private information except from the family's attorneys and they will be understandably disinclined to speak to us. Since you wished this investigation to be confidential, we did not approach them."

Gavin nodded. "Why do you think he changed his will?"

McKewen speculated for a moment, rotating his coffee cup on its saucer. When he had slowly turned it a complete circle, he stopped. "I would say that he did it to keep the younger son from returning to the Hall."

Gavin felt his mouth set in a hard grim line. "That's really the only interpretation, isn't it?"

"It would seem to be so. There was no way Noah could touch the main inheritance in any case. If he had gone to court to fight for anything, he would probably have gotten half or less of the remaining personal estate, exactly what James gave him."

"He probably had no idea that Noah would disregard the money. People like that, they think money is everything."

"Apparently Lord James considered it a large enough incentive to keep Noah off of the estate and out of Andrew's life permanently. The question that now leaves is, why?"

"Quite a question. I certainly can't seem to find the answer," Gavin muttered. "If someone were going to kill James for the money, they waited too long. Andrew would have gotten it all anyway. What other reason would there be for killing him?"

"None that we can surmise. Even the recently released family 'secret' about Noah seems at most an arbitrary fact. The Westerhavens certainly knew the truth, regardless of what the birth certificate says. James knew it; at least, he had no reason to doubt it by the fact that he did not order a blood test immediately on marrying Helen."

"That is what still bothers me in all this, that damn paternity test. Why did he do one at all? Noah was not going to inherit anything, whether he was blood or not. Why wait until Helen's death to do a test? It doesn't make any sense."

"It might if she died from some genetic disease but as far as we know, she died in an accident of some sort; certificate says *misadventure*."

"And yet James did the exact opposite of what you would expect a man to do once he knew for certain that Noah was his—he cut Noah out, out of his life completely."

"That is not entirely true," McKewen said, shaking his head. "As we discussed earlier, he paid for Noah's way and according to the Sisters at the school, they corresponded with him regarding the child's health and progress for years. It only looked on the outside as if he had abandoned his youngest son."

"I would call it abandoned, wouldn't you?" Gavin said darkly.

"In families of great wealth, money often substitutes for affection. In any case, James continued to provide Noah with a substantial stipend, even in the face of losing a great deal of his investments over the last ten years. He seemed to have lost interest in pursuing wealth, in living life in general. He cut himself off from every outside acquaintance, in effect, choosing the isolated life he had forced upon Noah."

"There does seem to be a family curse of sorts, oddly enough," Mr. McKewen continued in a strange voice. "Every generation seems to lose a younger son and I have gone back quite a ways now. I thought Lord Henry, father of James, had been spared but then I found the records for a younger son who died only four days after birth, leaving James, who was four at the time. There were daughters to be sure, but the deaths of younger sons seemed to be the most prominent trait in the family history. Odd, isn't it?"

Not for this family, Gavin thought unhappily. It was beginning to make a strange sort of sense to him, horrible but logical.

"Hmmm, there is one other thing about that time, the night of Lady Bainbridge's death. Lord James rolled over his entire staff at the estate, all of them, down to the cook. I have never heard of such a thing. We are looking for the old butler, but such people are difficult to locate after this many years. I have at last been able to locate the boy's doctor, retired and living here in London. He would not meet with us or provide us with any records but he agreed to see you in person. I will provide you with the name and address if you wish it."

"How did you find him?"

"We finally located a record, under the name of William Gordon, fitting the description of Noah and the dates in question. 'Gordon' was the maiden name of Sophia, Helen's mother. The doctor at the time worked for a private convalescent hospital just outside of Edinburgh. We were unable to get the complete records released to us."

Gavin's eyes widened. "He hid Noah's identity?"

"Not unheard of among the wealthy. Another thing about this doctor, his specialty is neurology. Whatever happened that killed Lady Bainbridge must also have seriously damaged her son. As far as we can assume from the dates given to us, Noah was hospitalized for an entire month. That would suggest a serious accident and perhaps some type of head injury or trauma."

"Why would you keep an accident a secret?"

McKewen shrugged. "Private people. Perhaps something embarrassing to the family or some underlying cause that might show blame."

"Like murder, maybe?"

"I would not go spouting off things like that if I were you," McKewen cautioned. "In any case, if you are accusing Lord Bainbridge of murdering his wife, we could hardly prove it or take him to court now. Slander *is* still punishable in the court system."

"But it would make sense in a way. Suppose James killed his wife, or was responsible for the accident that took her life. Maybe Noah knew the truth and to keep it quiet James had him committed or something, just long enough to get it under control and maybe help Noah forget somehow. Then he figured to keep those memories from returning he had to keep Noah away from the Hall, permanently."

McKewen shook his head with a rueful smile. "Those kinds of things happen only in films. Even if Noah remembered such an event, it would be his word against his father's and the shadowy memory of a nine-year-old would garner no support."

"You are no help here."

"You are trying very hard to find a villain in all of this. Suppose there simply is none? The truly wealthy are not like you and I. Often their reasons for doing things are totally unfathomable to the rest of us."

"I guess I am finding that out," Gavin sighed, leaning back in his chair. "You have done a thorough job in a short amount of time."

"We aim to please. The search for the old butler continues but I cannot promise that we will be able to locate him. Would you like the doctor's name and address?"

"Yes, please. I will phone you with what I find out."

"Considerate of you. By the way, there is another interpretation of the events that you seem to be overlooking."

Gavin closed the file in front of him with a thud. "I haven't overlooked it."

McKewen's eyebrows rose a meticulous quarter of an inch. He stared at Gavin with that old Scotland Yard interrogation stare, the one that probably had criminals shaking in their shoes before two minutes had elapsed beneath the piercing blue spotlight. Noah had eyes like that, eyes that seemed to look right through you to the bones beneath.

"I have seen him on stage," McKewen said after an uncomfortable silence had passed between them. "He plays with great passion. Passion can lead to dangerous things and you know what they say, a fine line between genius and madness."

"Noah could not hurt a fly," Gavin defended with only a slight rise in his voice. "Besides, he was with me in Tokyo when his father died."

"We were talking about a *twelve-year-old accident*, were we not?

The facts could also fit those circumstances, another more compelling reason for the father to distance himself from his son."

Gavin stared at him. There it was, stated out loud and looking back at him with naked possibility. He forced himself to swallow even though his mouth was suddenly dry with fear. The reaction to those family photographs came back to him with a dreadful premonition. What if Noah had suppressed his childhood memories on purpose, unable to live with a terrible truth? If he went forward he might uncover knowledge that Noah truly could not live with. Gavin shivered.

"I say this only to warn you," McKewen continued softly. "Sometimes what we find is not what we expect. If I had doubted your…dedication to your employer, I would never have taken you in as a client. Are you certain you wish to proceed?"

Gavin put his elbows on the table and placed his hands over his face for a moment, blocking out the awareness of those piercing blue eyes. What should he do? He had to know the truth, whether or not he told it to Noah. He had to know what had happened that destroyed the happy family in those photographs and condemned Noah to a half-life of distrust and nightmares. That the truth might tear him apart as well as Noah was something Gavin was willing to risk.

He lowered his hands to see that McKewen had gone and the young receptionist was standing beside the table. The man handed Gavin a small glass of brandy. Without a word he dialed a number on his cellular phone and stood looking at Gavin while the call connected.

"Is this Doctor Lachlan Stuart?" the young man asked. "Mr. Gavin Moore would like to speak to you if you have a moment, Doctor."

The man handed the phone over to Gavin and then turned and left the room. Gavin took a deep breath and put the phone to his ear. It seemed that McKewen had known all along what his answer would be.

❧ ❧ ❧

Of course sunny Rome was out of the question.

The best Noah could do under the circumstances was to retreat to his room while the sounds of the circus resumed on the floor below. Crashes and hammering followed by shouting male and female voices continued to wreck havoc on the nerves. Outside the rain pelted down with its own distracting rhythm, as if it were trying to drown out the taped opera music wavering up through the old house in spurts and starts, interspersed with cursing and more crashes.

Noah sat in the middle of the bed going through sheet music in an effort to select something to play. He tossed aside some of the longer pieces thinking that he might not be able to handle them, and disregarded others because he thought the crowd might not be able to sit quietly after having suffered…endured the *Aida* performance.

They were probably more accustomed to Barry's style of music in any case. In the end he chose the *Canzonetta from Violin Concerto in D* by Tchaikovsky for the pleasure it gave him, and *Autumn from the Four Seasons* by Vivaldi because of its variety and obvious tie in with an autumn festival. He could play each piece from memory and practically everyone knew Vivaldi and Tchaikovsky.

With that chore accomplished, Noah decided against practicing while the house was filled with noise and music. He considered going for a walk but he really did not want to ruin his new boots mucking through the bog left by the rains. All that was left was for him to go down and join in the fray.

Upon exiting his room, Noah heard Dora's voice booming over the music below and he chose the rear stairs out of sheer cowardice. He cut through the kitchen, finding Mary Katherine sitting in a rocking chair near a small fire in the huge hearth, her knitting needles clicking at a rapid clip. Rose Marie was there too, sipping from a tea cup and flipping through a fashion magazine at the old table. Neither woman noticed him until he was well into the room, no doubt because they could not hear him over the noise, even though it was far quieter in the rear of the house than the front.

"Goodness, you startled me," Rose Marie said with a start that almost spilled her tea. "I thought you were out front with the others."

"Got better sense, I should think," Mary Katherine said with a smile. Her needles kept up their pace without her looking at them. "After this lot, Mr. Bainbridge's music will seem like a heavenly choir."

"What can we get for you, dear?" Rose asked. She seemed to have taken a liking to Noah after the incident with Ester. "Some tea perhaps? I would offer earplugs, but alas you must suffer with the lot of us as there are none."

Noah smiled and sat down in a chair across the table from Rose. "Some tea would be nice. Can I sit here with you for a bit?"

"Surely, if you don't mind sitting with two old ladies," Mary Katherine said, now looking down at her knitting. "It's a cold and dreary day. Might as well have all this activity to keep us occupied. Me, I prefer knitting to pass the time." She indicated the pile of yarn folded around her feet. "This will be a lovely blanket for Colin and Lizzie's newest; I'm hoping to have it finished before he comes into the world."

Rose set a cup down in front of Noah and poured tea into it. She also brought over a tray with biscuits and cakes, surreptitiously pushing it near his elbow.

"She just thinks it's a boy," Rose told him sotto voice. "We will not know for sure until it comes in a couple of weeks."

"Oh, you are insulting me now?" Mary Katherine asked without looking up, apparently able to hear Rose's near whisper from across the space and the noise. "When am I ever wrong about such things, Rose Marie Lundford? It will be a boy, I tell you. If not…well, I've gone and used the wrong color haven't I?"

The color of the yarn was shades of blue. Rose laughed and Noah joined in. They sat sipping tea and eating cakes as the knitting needles clacked away. Noah felt comfortable sitting with the women. The kitchen was one of the most cozy and comfortable rooms of the old house. It made him realize that not even his bedroom had the same feeling.

"Has that harpy been at you now?" Mary questioned, stopping her knitting long enough to look Noah over with a motherly eye. "You seem a bit piqued."

"Mary Katherine!" said Rose Marie, sitting her cup down into its saucer with a disapproving clink of china.

Noah felt Rose's embarrassment as he turned to Mary. She was waiting for a reply with her needles posed in her fingers.

"Dora?" he asked in total confusion.

Both women then made similar sounds, like a gentle snort of breath. Rose simply picked up her tea cup. Mary Katherine started knitting again.

"Well, she would be at you, but for other reasons of course. Dora is harmless in her own way. No, I mean the *other* one, cousin *Claire.*"

The way she said the name simply dripped with poison. Apparently Rose was of the same opinion as Mary Katherine when it came to the fashionable cousin from across the way. Quite frankly Noah was astonished at the two and their equal expressions of distaste. Then he recalled the argument that Claire and Rose were having earlier and lifted his eyebrows in surprise.

"Claire? She barely said two words to me."

"Ah really? Well, maybe you are not her type after all," Rose said quietly.

Mary Katherine snorted. "Any man with money is her type," she said sharply. "But since it is a *title* she is wanting, I suppose you are safe enough. It'll be his Lairdship she is setting her sights for now. Father or son, no matter to her. Nothing but *Lady* Claire will do for that one."

"You mean she and father…? Now Andrew…?"

Noah recalled Claire hanging all over Andrew at dinner as if they were an *item* and she wanted everyone else to know it. She had done nothing but insult him. Was that her way of telling him that the Hall was her territory now and that he should get out and leave Andrew to her? Noah blinked. He had certainly never thought that sweet, innocent looking Mary Katherine had a tongue like an adder.

"His Lordship, God rest his soul, was having none of it," Mary Katherine continued with a sniff. "Almost thirty years between them, I should think so. He put up with her for awhile there until he caught her with Andrew that one time. What a shouting match that was."

"You should not be saying such things to Mr. Bainbridge," Rose said, her stiff dignity recovered.

"And why not? He should know how it is. That woman was banned from the Hall. His Lordship is not in the grave for a week and there she is, back to have another crack at the title. I'll be in my grave too before I will call that one her *Ladyship*."

Noah did not know what to say to that. If Claire's aspirations had been a bone of contention between father and Andrew, he would hope that Andrew had better sense than to fall for a gold digger. On the other hand, Andrew might still marry her just to spite their dead father. Whatever, it was none of Noah's concern. Andrew was free to lead his own life now, as Noah had been more or less free for the last few years.

"I am sure Andrew can make up his own mind," Noah said sympathetically. "Of the two, I prefer Dora."

Both women laughed heartily, Rose almost spitting her tea. Mary Katherine wiped tears from her eyes. Duncan came in at that moment, looking at all of them quizzically.

"Better be careful there," Mary said with a wink. "That one eats little boys like you."

Noah blushed a becoming shade of pink. Rose actually reached over and patted his hand. Duncan cleared his throat to interrupt their secret joke.

"Master Noah, the haberdasher is here with your new things.

He is waiting in the men's parlor if you would permit him to fit you properly."

"Certainly, Duncan. Ladies, thank you for the tea. It has been a pleasure to be in your company. If you will excuse me?"

They both nodded, still smiling. Noah gave them a little bow and followed Duncan down the corridor to the parlor connected to the study. The sounds of *Aida* had stopped for the moment, no doubt for a choreography session before the next full blown rehearsal. The sounds of scrapping and thudding continued below the talking voices. Inside the parlor Mr. MacDaughtery was waiting nervously, the items of plastic covered clothing lying across a small desk. Duncan left them alone.

"Mr. Bainbridge," the old man acknowledged with an inclination of his head. "I hope your other purchases have been to your liking?"

"Very much so," Noah was happy to tell him. "The boots were definitely what I needed out here. Thank you. Shall I put these on?"

MacDaughtery removed the black velvet jacket from the plastic and held it for Noah to slide into. It was chilly from the outside weather but the velvet was plush as fur and the jacket fit him with snug precision only a master tailor could create. Noah stood still while the man checked the lapels, the hem, and the length of the cuffs.

"Very good."

While changing jackets, Noah noticed the man's hands were shaking. He said nothing while he buttoned the plaid jacket, waiting until MacDaughtery's hands had smoothed across the fabric of his back and arms checking on the fit. The lapels were trimmed in black piping and the waist was fitted to the small of his back with a buttoned cloth tab. Like the other one, this one fit him like a second skin.

"You are a very skilled tailor," Noah complemented the man. "I have a hard time finding this level of workmanship even in Paris or Hong Kong. Thank you."

The man smiled slightly, somewhat pleased with the statement. "It is my pleasure to serve the brother of his Lairdship."

"Which one shall I wear at the gathering tomorrow night?" Noah asked as he looked down at the tartan jacket he was wearing. "This or the velvet one?"

For a moment Noah thought he had given the man a heart attack. MacDaughtery actually turned white, taking a step back and clutching his fist to his chest.

"A gathering?" MacDaughtery stammered out.

"Dora's group will be performing here tomorrow night and I am going to give a small concert as part of the evening's events. You saw them rehearsing when you came in."

Some color returned to the man's face but he was clearly upset. Noah could not believe what he was sensing from the man. MacDaughtery was afraid. He would not look Noah in the eye and he was shaking like a leaf in the wind. Noah regretted shaking him up so badly with his choice of words but not enough to ignore the reaction.

"What's wrong? Why does my being here seem to upset so many people?"

The man was shaking his head. "You must be mistaken. We are finished. I will take my leave."

"I am not mistaken. I saw you in the window the day we left your shop. You motioned the sign of the cross."

MacDaughtery cringed. "I meant no harm to you. Please forgive me."

"I simply wish to understand," Noah tried to explain.

"Why did you come back here?" the man asked, backing away when Noah reached out toward him. "You dare talk of gatherings on the eve of festival with yer father barely in the ground?"

"What has my father to do with it?"

MacDaughtery shook his head with such ferocity that his entire body shivered. "He was a fool. Leave this place, leave now.

Why did you come back here?"

MacDaughtery bolted for the door and Noah followed as far as to the end of the corridor when it became obvious that MacDaughtery was running for cover like a pack of hounds were trailing him. The little man grabbed his coat from Duncan and was out the door before the butler had a chance to open it for him. The muttered dialogue was too low for Noah to make out the words before the door slammed shut.

Looking as confused as he was, Duncan made his way over. "Is everything all right, Master Noah?"

Noah shook his head. "I wish I knew. What did he say just then?"

Duncan frowned. "Something in Gaelic. It's a saying I have heard a few times from the old timers. It is a charm, I believe, intended as words of protection."

"Against what?"

Duncan shrugged, a slightly uncomfortable gesture for him. "These people are still very superstitious, stuck in the old ways. You must forgive them for their little oddities."

Noah sighed. He was getting tired of their little oddities.

"You look quite the part in that jacket if I do say so, sir," Duncan said amiably. "MacDaughtery does excellent work. Shall I take the items upstairs for you?"

"That's okay, I will take them up."

Duncan nodded and walked back to the front of the hall where someone was bellowing his name at the top of their lungs.

Noah retreated back to the parlor. He removed the jacket and slipped it back onto its wooden hanger. MacDaughtery had fled before they got to the trousers but Noah was sure they would fit as perfectly as everything else. He picked up the clothing and carried it up the back stairs to his room and put it away. With nothing else to do he decided to brave the chaos in the main Hall.

The sounds of *Aida* were once again wafting through the corridors, the soprano and alto voices blending in the music he knew well. They had gotten quite a bit done since hauling the stuff in that morning. The furniture of the open drawing room had been pushed back and rearranged in a smaller space, since the seating and staging for the event took up most of the open space of the entrance hall. The chairs were already set up in rows of ten facing the open floor and staircase. The "scenery" consisted of white linen cloths draped along the lower part of the staircase for dramatic effect.

The hammering had been for the construction of a framework that would serve as a wall and doorway to block off the opposite side of the open space and provide a "stage" setting for the actors to move through and around. The simple framework too was draped with cloth that had been painted with Egyptian looking symbols and golden tassels. The green velvet fainting couch from the small drawing room was now an Egyptian lounge, and the heavy old chair from the front room was the throne. It made for a sparse but easily workable setting.

Noah sat in a chair in the last row and watched Dora put everyone through their paces. She was a better director than everyone seemed to give her credit, paring down the actors movements to the essentials and mouthing the words in Italian perfectly. She was hardly the ideal *Aida*, but then again it was not intended to be serious.

That was perfectly obvious when her stage lover, the young man from Barry's pub, joined her in a song pleading their love and lament; when he clasped her to his manly bosom he was standing and she was sitting down. He was also clad in a toga-style cloth over a kilt, his naked knees in her easy embrace.

Noah smiled into his hand. A lesser woman than Dora might have been tempted to cop a feel in such a situation. Neither one of them seemed too worked up over it, in fact, the young man seemed to be having a blast of a time; at last someone to equal Dora in the ham department. Noah imagined her in horned helmet and chestplate; she might indeed make a very intimidating Valkyrie. She caught Noah's eye and winked.

Across the space Andrew and Claire were in a deep discussion about something. Jamis was nowhere in sight; he had probably taken the truck back to Barry. Moira had gone out earlier to meet with Barry's wife. Everything seemed to be moving along smoothly. Duncan was nowhere to be seen but it would be tea time soon and he was probably busy getting the dining room prepared for the onslaught. Noah almost jumped out of his skin when hands came down on his shoulders.

"Whoa there," Seth told him, moving his hands to come around and sit in the chair in front of Noah, turning to speak to him. "Didn't mean to interrupt your viewing pleasure. Made yourself scarce this morning."

Noah shrugged. "The set looks pretty good. Where is your helper?"

"Gone back to the village with Jamis. Thought I'd ask you for some help if you don't mind getting a little wet."

"With what?" Noah asked cautiously.

"Your idea in the first place. Thought you might help me mark off the parking space on the lawn out front. I have everything we need waiting out on the drive. You look like you could stand to get out of here for awhile."

Noah looked at him, trying to judge the depth of the guileless green eyes. He could use a breath of fresh air. The confrontation with MacDaughtery had bothered him more than he thought.

"Sure. Let me get my jacket."

"Andrew's is just there by the door. Come on then."

Noah followed him and donned Andrew's damp jacket. He had to roll the sleeves up a couple of inches but it would do to keep the rain off. The rain had actually slackened to a mist by then so it was no problem to be hatless. Seth had already piled a grouping of things for their use next to the hideous fountain; a stack of three-foot long wooden pegs, a couple of rubber mallets, a large roll of yellow tape, and some orange and white road cones. Noah picked up the tape roll, surprised to find it police ribbon for marking off crime scenes.

"Where did you get this?" he asked as Seth bent to pick up several stakes.

"Local Constable hardly ever uses the stuff. I figured it would do the job for us. We can mark off the space we need with stakes and tie the ribbon between. I'll use the cones to block off the drive to the garage area so everyone will have to park where we tell 'em."

Noah nodded. For the next forty minutes he helped Seth decide where to place the stakes and how much space they needed to mark off for the expected traffic. The pegs went into the damp ground with hardly a thump and they strung the yellow tape between them without much bother. When they were finished, they surveyed their handiwork.

"That should do it," Seth said. "Even old man MacPhearson cannot miss seeing that in the rain. We will have the exterior lights on I expect."

"At least you weren't in town, having to set up all those big tents in the earlier downpour."

Seth laughed amiably. "I'm thankful for that, mind you. I imagine Jamis will be helping them finish that right about now. Poor fellow. That sister of his pretty much tells him what to do all the time."

"Really," Noah replied thoughtfully.

He absentmindedly followed Seth, walking down the path that led to the rear of the house. Seth was carrying the tool tray and Noah had what was left of the tape. It was probably going to be another foggy, chilly night and Noah could hear the soft sounds of cattle lowing in the distance.

"Claire seems to have a thing for Drew, doesn't she?" he asked innocently.

For a moment Seth did not reply and Noah wondered if he had again tread on dangerous ground. He never knew how any of these people were going to react at any given moment, least of all Seth. For the first time he realized they were alone, far from anyone's sight or hearing, at the collection of garages and storage buildings for yard and garden implements.

"Claire has aspirations that do not become her," Seth said with a hint of sarcasm. He placed the tray on a shelf and turned.

"That's what your mother said," Noah replied, holding out the roll of tape.

Seth's dark eyebrows rose as he took the tape and put it on the same shelf. "Really? Well, not much gets by her I guess. I wouldn't worry about it if I were you. Andrew might play along but he has no intentions of marrying the likes of Claire."

"How do you know? Seems like they might be a good match."

Something like anger sparked in the green gaze for a moment but then it was gone so quickly that Noah wondered if he had truly seen it.

Seth shrugged. "I know Andrew."

"I don't doubt that you do," Noah admitted sadly. "Everyone seems to know him much better than I ever will."

Seth was very close. His dark eyelashes were long, hiding his expression as he leaned in even closer.

Noah could see the pulse beating in the hollow of his throat and the drops of rain on his hair and skin. He could also feel the heat rising along his neck, the awareness of Seth's sexually charged presence touching him even though they were physically separated by more than a foot.

"Andrew is amusing himself," Seth said, moving his gaze over Noah's face. "He dresses you up, shows you off to his friends. You are an oddity, like a beautiful doll, a momentary fascination."

Noah felt the blood rush to his face. He should be used to cutting words, he had certainly had enough of them aimed his way over his life, but Seth's ability to wound seemed personal. Seth chose each word to hit its mark for the deepest cut. His young, handsome face hid a heart filled with shadows.

"I understand you turned down the money to come back," Seth said quietly. "After all these years, what were you expecting?"

Noah swallowed the lump in his throat. "Nothing. I don't fit in here. I'm the one father did not want."

Seth looked at him with a steady penetrating gaze. His eyes were mesmerizing, like the eyes of a cat. Seth slowly lifted one arm and placed his hand against the wall beside Noah's head.

"Don't be so sure about that," Seth purred.

Noah ducked beneath the arm and fled.

He slowed his rapid retreat once he reached the edge of the garden, looking back to see Seth standing at the garage door, silently watching. Disappearing behind the back of the house, Noah leaned against the wall and looked out across the rain-soaked gardens in misery. His heart was thumping so hard it shook the collar of his jacket and it took a good long minute before it slowed to normal.

Noah put his hands to his face. The worst thing was he had no idea why he was crying. The people in the house seemed to be having a good enough time and the concert and festival would probably be fun. They were trying to include him and make him feel welcome…well, most of them were. Then why did he feel like this?

Noah lowered his hands and looked out at the partially forested crags beyond. The landscape was blue and gray and the forest seemed like it was drawn in with heavy black marker. It was an alien landscape to his eyes and it filled him with loneliness. He was homesick. He was homesick and he had just realized that no matter what he did, this was not his home. It never was and it never would be.

And he missed Gavin.

He missed Gavin's endless supply of energy and the invisible connection they seemed to share. Noah had taken that for granted, he saw that now. He would have to make amends to Gavin for the fight that had left them both licking their wounds. He should never have come to Scotland. Gavin had been right about that too, as usual.

It was probably tea time by now. Everyone would be sitting

down in the horrible dining room for tea and artistic discussions on how the operetta was going. He didn't think he could stand that room again, even filled with noisy people. The house seemed to be draining the energy straight out of him, leaving him unfocused and making it hard to concentrate.

Noah had not forgotten the reason he came in the first place, but he had made no headway along those lines. People were not forthcoming, not even Andrew. His brother was still like a stranger. Noah sighed and wiped at his eyes. He was wet and miserable, but he did not think anyone would notice he had been crying. At least, he hoped not.

As it was he avoided seeing anyone but Rose. He went up the back stairs to his room to lie down for awhile, pleading a headache, perfectly understandable to her. He felt her gaze on his back all the way up the stairs. He had scarcely lain down for five minutes when there was a knock on his door and he bade the knocker to enter without rising from his bed. It was Duncan carrying a tray and looking stern.

"It has indeed been a trying day," the butler said, carrying the tray to the table where he set it down. "Rose Marie said that you need a doctor." He turned to look at Noah who had sat up in bed. "I believe she is correct."

"I'm fine," Noah protested, although feebly. "Just a headache."

Duncan approached and placed his hand on Noah's forehead, checking for a temperature. Accustomed to this type of activity from Gavin, Noah accepted it in silence. Duncan removed his hand and fluffed up the pillows at Noah's back, motioning for him to recline again.

"I do not believe you have a fever but you look less than acceptable. I have brought a tea tray and believe you should eat something. Would you prefer that I fetch the doctor?"

"No," Noah grumbled again. "It's just…I'm kind of homesick, I guess."

Duncan nodded and fetched a mug from the tray, bringing it over to the bed. "I can understand that. It must be a huge change for you coming from London. Not everyone is suited for country life. Of course Madame Finsterwall's bunch could make anyone wish to abdicate. If you refuse the doctor then please drink this."

Taking the warm mug, Noah could smell the liquor before he brought it to his lips. "What is it?"

"Rose Marie's idea of medicine. If you are trying to catch a bug, this should cure you straight away. At any rate, it will help you sleep during the resumption of Act II."

Noah took a swallow of hot lemon tea mixed with whiskey, honey, and some other herbal tasting things that he did not recognize. If Rose was mixing a knock out brew, he was more than happy to drink it. The heat and the honey made the liquor more palatable. Gavin would be shaking his head to see how much alcohol he had been drinking since coming to his brother's house. Maybe that was telling in its own way.

"You should try and eat something before you go to sleep. If not, the tray will be here when you awaken. Would you like a fire to warm the room?"

Noah shook his head, feeling the hot smoky drink hit his stomach. "I'll be fine, really. Thank Rose for the drink. If I am not up in a couple of hours, please wake me. I need to practice tonight."

Duncan looked dubious. "I will make your excuses to everyone. Sleep well, sir."

Noah watched the man leave thinking that Andrew was lucky to have someone like Duncan to take care of the place. He eyed the tray of sandwiches and cakes but he was not hungry. Whatever Rose had brewed up in the mug was already making his eyes heavy and he was only halfway through the stuff. He would have to get her recipe for Gavin to add to his concoctions.

Sitting the mug aside, he lay down again and pulled the blanket up to his chin. The rain outside made the room seem colder than it was. Duncan had switched on the bedside lamp as he left, knowing it would be dark soon, and Noah had no doubt that someone would be checking on him periodically. Safe in that thought, he drifted swiftly to sleep, blessedly unaware of the Queen's return to the stage or Andrew peering in through a crack in the door to watch him with a dark, curious gaze.

❦ ❦ ❦

The home of Dr. Lachlan Stuart was in a well-to-do condominium just to the north of Hyde Park. He apparently preferred city life and the location was convenient to his many pursuits in a busy retirement; on the board of several hospitals, medical advisor to several companies, patron of the arts, all-around philanthropist. The doctor's wife was equally occupied with the pursuits of the rich and unfettered; at the moment she was into dogs and dog shows, which accounted for the tiny army of Welsh terriers that besieged Gavin's ankles as soon as he was admitted into the spacious flat.

The two men introduced themselves with a handshake and then Dr. Stuart apologized and went about rounding up the herd of small canines, closing them securely behind a bedroom door. Cut off from the sight of the stranger, they quieted down almost immediately. Dr. Stuart returned to usher his visitor into the living room and politely offer him a drink. Gavin politely declined and sank down on the paisley gold sofa with the dread of a man sinking in quicksand. It hardly mattered; his trousers were already covered with dog hair.

"I'd like to apologize for the intrusion and thank you for seeing me so quickly," Gavin began the conversation. "I understand you are still a busy man, even if currently retired from medicine."

"Let me give you some advice, young man, even though you are far from my age," Dr. Stuart responded, sitting down in the chair opposite. "Never retire. I was out of my mind within two weeks. Keeping busy keeps you young. I still teach once in a while and write articles for the medical journals, but board meetings are just as boring as they sound and unless you are knitting while sitting in one, a complete waste of time."

Gavin smiled, more at ease than he expected to be with the man. Doctor Stuart was in his late sixties, still handsome and in good shape. He had all his hair, as beautifully silver gray as Noah's hair was silver blond, and his long slender fingers could have belonged to a musician instead of a brain surgeon.

"Now that the pleasantries are over," said Dr. Stuart, "I am very curious as to why an investigative agency is looking into a minor, twelve-year-old medical case."

Gavin's smile remained fixed on his face. "I assure you that there is nothing but the best of intentions involved with this inquiry."

"Best intentions can often be personally misleading."

Gavin blinked. The man knew something more than the hospitalization of an unknown child. Was he about to discover the truth face to face?

"Just who are you, exactly?" the man asked point blank.

Gavin sighed. He would never make a good spy or a good detective. "I am private assistant to Noah Westerhaven, the boy I believe you knew then as William Gordon."

Doctor Stuart's expression told him nothing. Stuart took a sip from his glass while Gavin studied him in silence. The man was a patron of the symphony so he had to know who Noah was, at least in that context. Which one of them was going to blink first? Gavin finally figured that it had to be him if he was going to get anywhere.

"His real name is Noah William Westerhaven…Bainbridge."

Gavin had the satisfaction of watching the man connect the dots; the gray eyes seemed to blur as he went back in time in search of a face and then sharpen as he understood what he had only partially suspected. That sharp gaze returned to Gavin's face.

"Right under my nose all these years," Stuart said half musing. "I should have recognized him. Guess I'm not a very good detective."

Gavin smiled, having thought the same thing of himself. "Very few people know that his name is Bainbridge."

"I read about the death of Lord Bainbridge…what, few weeks ago? He was still fairly young. What a shame."

"It has been a most trying time for Noah. He and his father never had much of a relationship all these years."

"And now that his father is dead, he is looking into his past?"

"Something like that," Gavin admitted. "In particular he is interested in what happened the night that he ended up in your care. Noah has no memory of that time, in fact, very few memories of that part of his childhood."

Stuart nodded. "I am sorry but not surprised to hear it. He was in bad shape when they came to the infirmary."

"Was it a head injury?"

Stuart shook his silver head, his expression serious. "He was admitted in what we call a fugue state, a type of coma."

"A coma? With no head injury?"

"There was no physical head trauma other than a slight cut on his chin. He had a couple of broken fingers and some scraps and bruises but nothing that could account for his emotional condition."

Gavin had seen that small crescent shaped scar on Noah's chin. "What happened to him?"

"They said he had been missing all night. It was the middle of winter, near the holidays and had been very cold at night. He had a slightly lower than average body temperature, hypothermia from exposure, and I assumed the injuries were from some misadventure. Little boys get lost while playing or run off frequently."

"And you believed that?"

Stuart looked annoyed. "Why shouldn't I? I recognized Lord Bainbridge, of course."

"Did it occur to you that he might be lying?"

"No. The man was openly devastated. He could barely speak."

"He gave no other reason for Noah's condition?"

"I treated the both of them. Noah was in a highly traumatized state, something usually brought on by a shock of some kind. He was unresponsive to anyone although his nerves responded to outside stimuli; for instance, he would curl his foot when we tickled it or his arm would remain elevated if we lifted it, yet his gaze remained fixed and unresponsive. This is not an uncommon response to shock in children."

Gavin felt his mouth press into a grim line. He had seen Noah in a similar condition many times, a sort of trance. Apparently it was something that had manifested in his early childhood. Only recently had it turned into something more than either of them considered normal for Noah. He did not like what he was hearing.

"He also had the other minor injuries I stated earlier," Stuart continued. "Lord Bainbridge was emotionally distraught to the point of near hysteria. I had to tranquilize him and keep him at the hospital that night."

"Near hysteria? What was he saying?"

Stuart shook his head. "After handing over his son? Nothing that made any sense."

"Were you aware that Noah's mother, Lord Bainbridge's wife, died that same night?"

Stuart looked startled. The news was an obvious surprise to him. "I had no idea. I suppose anyone would be in a similar condition if his wife had just died and his son had reacted with such an emotional upheaval that it put his young life in danger as well."

Gavin had not thought of that. "You are saying that Noah, when told of his mother's death, was so upset that he ran off, hid from his father all night, and purposefully blanked out his own mind so that he would not have to believe that his mother was dead?"

"It has happened, not with conscious purpose you understand. The mind is a complicated organ. When the shock of something is too great, sometimes people are willing to block out the memory completely instead of living with the pain. It happens quite often with children, victims of violent crime, and even soldiers on the battlefield. Sometimes people also just kill themselves rather than face the unbearable."

Gavin groaned out loud. He had allowed Noah to go back to those hidden memories alone. He knew now that whatever the reason for the blank in memory, sending Noah back to face his past alone had been a terrible mistake.

"How long was Noah in that condition?" he asked fearfully.

"It was almost two weeks before he slowly started coming out of it. When he was fully recovered he had no memory of the events leading up to his hospitalization, but functioned normally in every other way. I had hoped he would regain his memory with time but I see that has not occurred."

"No, it hasn't."

"Are you certain you want him to remember?"

Gavin sighed with frustration. "I am no longer certain of anything. Thank you for speaking with me, Doctor."

"I see that I have been of little help in whatever it is you are looking for."

They both got to their feet, the interview concluded. Gavin yanked on his coat, preparing to leave. He shook the man's hand again and said goodbye, walking through the opened door. He had just stepped out into the corridor when Stuart stopped him by calling his name. Gavin turned around.

"Just one more thing—two really—that you might want to know," Stuart said with a frown. "Once William…Noah had awakened from the coma, his father stopped coming to see him. He would call every day but I never saw the man again."

"He didn't come to pick Noah up?"

Stuart shook his head. "No, a woman came to pick the boy up when it was time for him to leave. By the way, Noah asked for him a couple of times before he seemed to understand that his father was never coming back. He never did ask for his mother. Not even once."

"Again, thank you, Doctor Stuart."

"Goodbye, Mr. Moore. Please give Mr. Bainbridge my condolences."

Gavin muttered to himself all the way to the lift. What on earth had possessed him to go on this wild goose chase? It was looking more and more like whatever he found out was going to hurt Noah more than it could ever help him. He really had no idea where this was going to end. Gavin rode the lift down with two giggling young women who did nothing to lighten his mood and got off to walk out into a downpour.

He hated London in winter, which was fast approaching. Maybe he could talk Noah into going off somewhere sunny and warm for awhile after this. He sighed and flagged down a taxi. First he had to face the ghost of the wolf in his den.

Gavin was certain that Noah would not be happy to see him. Noah would be even less happy once Gavin explained everything he had discovered in his snooping—or maybe less happy at what Gavin had not discovered. Regardless, Scotland was not somewhere Gavin particularly wanted to be, with cold winds blowing over the sea and Noah's dead yet unsettled relatives lurking around every corner. Then there would be Andrew to deal with; rich, patronizing new *Laird of the Hall* brother Andrew.

Gavin glowered at his reflection in the taxi window. Maybe it was more like facing the *sons* of the wolf in their ancestral den. He hoped the place was easy enough to find. If he had to stop and ask for directions, he would be lost for sure, like the guy in Brigadoon.

Be damned if they were going to get him to stay in Scotland for a hundred years.

TEN

When you look into an abyss, the abyss also looks into you.
—Friedrich Nietzsche

Noah came to awareness slowly, like floating up from the bottom of a pool. His entire body felt heavy and cumbersome, his mouth dry as dust. He lay there in the tumbled blankets until it registered to his eyes that it was dark in the room and a fire had been banked in the fireplace. He turned his head to stare at the clock on the dark bedside table. Its green glowing face told him it was 12:37, just past midnight.

He groaned quietly. No one had awakened him and Rose Marie's concoction had kept him asleep for hours, through whatever had been occurring downstairs and into the night. The house was silent but wind rattled the window panes and a distant rumble of thunder echoed off the hills. Maybe it had been the thunder that awakened him. Lost electricity would explain the darkness of the bedside lamp; he reached over to turn its toggle switch and it clicked twice with no comforting glow.

Noah sat up slowly. The cotton pajama bottoms and T-shirt he had worn to bed were a hopeless mass of wrinkles and soaked with sweat. His stomach grumbled with hunger. He got out of bed and put on his robe and slippers, padding to the fireplace to stoke the fire for warmth and light. It responded to his halfhearted prodding and when he tossed a couple of logs onto the embers, they caught quickly.

The sight of the tea tray reminded him that he had not eaten since the few bites at lunch, and his stomach rumbled again at the thought of cold tea and stale sandwiches. He decided against the hours-old chicken salad, but figured that the cheese was safe enough. He stood looking out the window. The storm was winding down, the flashes of lightning far off in the distance and the corresponding claps of thunder a long space between.

As he stood there Noah noticed a figure walking along the path that led from the rear of the house toward the stable area. He would never have seen it except for the flashlight scouring the ground in the darkness ahead of the walker. Curious as to who would be out at that time of night during a storm, Noah watched the light disappear behind the buildings, clearly headed for the stable. He finished his sandwich while waiting for the light to reappear. It did not.

Now extremely curious and awake, Noah decided he might just as well go see for himself. If it was someone out for mischief, he was curious to what they would be doing. Were there still horse thieves in the country? The idea struck him as ludicrous. Maybe one of the animals was sick. Noah quickly changed his damp pajamas for dry clothing and grabbed the small flashlight from the drawer, stuffing it into the pocket of his jacket. He quietly descended the rear stairs.

The night was blacker than black. If there was a moon it was heavily obscured by storm clouds that were still dropping rain in a chilly mist. The echo of thunder sounded more ominous now that he was outside. He shivered with a sudden premonition of dread, the small dot of light from the flashlight swallowed up by the darkness. With his jacket closed against the chill and his hand in his pocket, Noah quickly and quietly walked down the path he had seen the figure take.

A flash of lightning illuminated the ruins in the far meadow; he was close enough to see them in the distance. They looked even more eerie in the stark white light before they disappeared again, veiled by the blackness of night. He had never liked storms, and out in the country he could understand why peoples in ancient times considered bad storms portents of doom. A sudden gust of cold wind whipped his hair around his head, sending him into a short spasm of shivering.

The buildings of the stables and attached storage barn loomed before him. Noah was not surprised to see a faint light; if someone was out there they would have to have some kind of light to see by. He could hear the rustling sounds of the nearby trees, the scrapes and moans sounding like living things in the darkness, enough to make his skin crawl. There were no animals out in the paddock.

Noah crept silently to the edge of the building, trying to be stealthy in case something criminal was occurring. He was unarmed and for the first time it occurred to him how foolish it was for him to be out there alone if he thought something untoward was really going on. He switched off his flashlight but kept it in his hand.

The light was coming from several unshuttered stall windows, the flickering yellow glow telling him that it was from a lantern somewhere inside the far end of the stable. He edged along the fence until he came to the far window, holding his breath as he moved to peek inside. The smell and sounds of the animals was the first thing he perceived, his eyes unsure at first what he was looking at through the bars.

A horse was standing in the stall right in front of him, its sleeping form a dark shape against the lighter colored wall. He could hear other animals moving restlessly and the sound of snorting made him jump slightly, bumping his knee against the wall. Noah cringed but the noise was just another sound mixed with the wind and the restless animals. He once again applied his eye to the window.

Voices became audible, whispered quick words that he could not make out beneath the other noises. The sounds came from the stall across from the one he was standing beside, the dimly lighted space just visible through the mesh screen of the interior stall door. Through the mesh Noah could see movement and he blinked in disbelief, his brain slow to comprehend what he was seeing in the shadows. He should have recognized the sounds for what they were, not just horses moving about, but two people in the throes of passion.

Noah felt his eyes widen in disbelief. He could see Seth fairly well, his dark head and lithe muscled body unmistakable even in shadow. What Noah did not understand at first was that Seth had been bound to the wall, one hand tied over his head by leather straps, holding him upright with his back against the wall. Only when the other figure rose from the shadows did Noah recognize his brother with a shock that brought his hand to his mouth to cover his gasp of surprise.

The two involved lovers never heard him. Noah stared in shock when his brother tore Seth's shirt from his body in a single violent motion, the ripping of cloth mixed with Seth's groan of pain and pleasure. The riding crop in Andrew's hand struck his lover's body with three quick slashes, and Andrew wrapped his fingers in Seth's dark curls, twisting his neck to kiss him roughly. Noah felt his face burn with some emotion that he barely recognized in his shock.

Seth made another sound of pain and Noah heard Andrew's low voice answer, although he still could not make out the words. Andrew's hands were sliding over Seth's naked body, claiming ownership with passion-darkened words, promising what was to come. Noah watched his brother's head move lower and the fingers of Seth's free hand twine in the dark brown hair. Seth moaned and the dark lashes closed over his blazing green eyes, lips quivering with passion.

Noah turned away and sank down on his heels, his back against the wall holding him upright. The blackness of the night failed to remove the image from his eyes and he held his cold hand to his mouth with trembling emotion. The sexual tension between the two men was beginning to affect the horses, even the one in the stall beside Noah, now awake and moving around restlessly. It came to the window to snuff at Noah's scent, its warm breath touching the top of his head.

Getting shakily to his feet, Noah avoided its curious nose to peer one last time through the window. His shock at finding Seth looking straight at him almost made him lose it, before he realized that there was no way Seth could possibly see him in the dark with the horse between them. Seth threw his head back with a moan of rapture in response to Andrew's actions, breaking the spell of his terrible gaze, and Noah turned and staggered from the window.

He felt sick and disoriented, struggling to find the path in the dark. The blacker shape of the house loomed in the distance, its massive form without welcome or light. Behind him a horse whinnied, the sound making him stop for a moment of sheer terror that he had been discovered. Nothing moved in the darkness but the trees and the grass. The rain had ceased and the breeze lightly touched Noah's hair. Its touch sent him to shivering violently and he forced his feet to move.

Only when he was inside the dark hollow space of the empty kitchen did Noah stop long enough to catch his breath. He was cold and shaking...and afraid. That came as another shock; that what he was feeling was fear. His blood was practically congealed with it. When he let his breath out in an explosive gasp, he could see it fog in the air in front of him. He turned and went up the rear staircase, back to his warm room where he shut the door and locked it.

Shivering, Noah stripped off his damp jacket and clothing, wrapping himself in his robe. He took a towel to dry his hair while he sat beside the fire, trying to get his blood flowing again. Even after his skin felt warm to the touch, he sat shivering in the robe, watching the flames flicker in the hearth.

So that was how it was between them.

It was not seeing his brother and Seth having sex that caused such a strong reaction in him, he realized that now. It was the violence. He had seen the blood on Seth's skin. Even though Seth seemed to be enjoying it, Noah had no idea that Andrew was capable of such violence. It made him wonder how long it had been going on and how violent Andrew could become.

Had they chosen to meet in the stables because it was a "safe" place for them, away from prying eyes? Seth lived in the cottage with his mother and sister, hardly a private environment. Perhaps they had been meeting in Andrew's room until Noah had arrived at the Hall and been placed in a room almost directly across the hall from his brother. Then again, if they wished to keep their trysts secret they probably avoided any place where the maids or Duncan might accidentally discover them. It certainly seemed to him that they had managed to keep the secret.

Noah bit down on his fingers. He was still trembling. Something else occurred to him as he sat there with his legs pulled beneath him and the fire warming the side of his face. His first reaction had been shock, followed by shame at being a voyeur to their secret passion. The final reaction was fear but only when he shook off the fear did he understand from whence it came.

It was Seth he was afraid of. Not the partial humiliation he had faced at Seth's hands earlier, or even the sense of cold sneering arrogance with which Seth seemed to regard him. It was the man's seemingly magical ability to render him almost speechless and thoughtless by his mere presence. He had felt that sensual resonance while he watched them from a distance with his heart hammering in his chest. It was almost as if Seth had known he was there, perhaps had arranged the entire thing for his benefit.

Noah shook his head. He was imagining things. He was projecting his fears of abandonment on Seth as the object of his brother's affection. Their attraction clearly went both ways. No wonder Seth said the things about Claire with conviction and malice; he was in a position to know where Andrew's passions lay.

Had Seth seduced Andrew or had it been the other way around? Even though Andrew was clearly the aggressor in the stable, Noah doubted that he was the one in control of the affair. Seth had a cunning nature and a palpable aura about him that Andrew seemed to lack even with his title and money. That burning green gaze wielded a terrible power.

Noah sat twirling a strand of his hair. Their affair would go a long way to explaining Seth's arrogant attitude toward the rest of the staff, and even toward him. As the Laird's lover, Seth would consider himself above their level, perhaps even be resentful of Noah's sudden reappearance in Andrew's life. Seth had been sneering and laughing in his face since he had arrived at the Hall. What better way to consolidate his dominance and his need for superiority than to seduce Andrew's younger brother as well?

Noah got up and poked the fire viciously, feeding another log to the flames. Even attributing Seth with the ability to be a master manipulator, Noah was aware that Andrew was the one with the power in their relationship. A few years earlier Seth would have been a young boy, an inexperienced son of a staff member. Seth might have been an easy target for the older, bored son of the Laird. Noah thought about the long cold winter nights and Seth's smooth white skin.

Had their father discovered the affair? Had that been the reason he had changed his will? Noah doubted it. It would have been too easy for their father to simply cut Andrew totally out of the will or throw Seth and his entire family off the estate. That clearly had not happened.

The sound of footsteps caused Noah to look toward the door. Andrew had come back to the house and was walking quietly up the hallway. Noah stared at the doorknob, almost expecting it to turn, but the door that opened and closed was the one to Andrew's bedroom, not his. He let out the breath he had been holding with a hiss.

It was all an exercise in futility. Andrew's love life was none of his business. Seth was an extremely handsome youth, an adult who knew his own mind. If they wanted to have sex in the stable or frolic naked out on the lawn, it was their choice to do so. Now he would have to guiltily hide his knowledge of the secret affair, something that might be hard to do around Seth. The fact that he was slightly hurt by Andrew's lack of candor, and that Seth obviously meant more to his brother than he did, was just one more thing Noah was going to have to deal with.

He sighed. He was not sleepy. In fact, he was miserable. He regretted coming back to Scotland. The house and the countryside seemed to fill him with despair. He wondered how so many generations of the family had managed to exist in such a place without going stark raving mad. Maybe some of them had. With the history, the superstitions, and the odd collection of villagers, who would notice?

Noah crawled back into bed and lay there huddled in the blankets for a long time before he managed to fall into a light, troubled sleep. In his dreams he staggered, lost in the dark, running from something or searching for something he could never see. The wind tore at his hair and clothing like fingers while his feet sank into mud so thick it threatened to drag him down with every step. Somewhere in the darkness he could hear the sounds of horses whinnying in fear while he shivered in the cold.

Never in the terror of his dreams did he see what it was that was searching for him, yet he could feel it. It filled him with horror and the knowledge that it was ancient and evil, a cold numbing presence that robbed him of thought and motion and breath. In his dreams he saw the shadowy figures of Seth and Andrew mating like two animals out on the open heath, their eyes and teeth shining wetly in the moonlight as they transfixed him with their mesmerizing gaze. The figures melted away, leaving Noah shivering alone in the dark with the howl of a wolf echoing in the distance.

When Noah opened his eyes in the first faint light of dawn he was again soaked in sweat and exhausted. The shadowy images of his nightmares faded from his memory like smoke. The room was freezing, the fire long turned to cold ashes, and the rising dawn draped in heavy clouds. Noah lay there with no intention of rising until someone arrived with hot coffee or tea, not even remembering that it was the morning of the day he was expected to give a performance.

ELEVEN

By the pricking of my thumbs, something wicked this way comes.
—W. Shakespeare

That morning certainly did not start off with the glitter of the stage. Noah finally dragged himself down for breakfast only to find he was alone again. Andrew had gone for an early morning ride with Seth out across the fog laden property before the house filled with interlopers. That made Noah even more depressed and he morosely picked at his food until Rose threatened to hand feed him.

He knew he looked terrible. The circles beneath his eyes were like purple bruises in spite of the hours of sleep, and instead of gaining weight on Mary Katherine's abundantly decadent faire, he had lost a few pounds. The fact that Andrew had rather spend time with Seth than with him only irritated him more; he refused to accept the notion that he was simply jealous of Andrew's time.

After breakfast he managed to get in an hour of practice in his room. It would take far more than a week off to make him rusty, yet his mind was unable to concentrate to its usual degree and it wandered off without much provocation. He came to himself once standing in the middle of his room staring at the door of the armoire, just staring off into space; for how long he had no idea.

Then Claire had arrived with Moira in tow and the siege of the villagers began. Noah was looking out the window when she came from the rear of the house to meet Andrew and Seth, trotting up from their ride across the meadow. They looked red-cheeked and windblown astride their powerful horses, greeting her just outside the topiary gardens. Noah could not hear what was being said, but Seth reacted with anger. His change of posture, a stiffening of back and shoulders, gave him away, even though his expression was tightly controlled.

Andrew dismounted and had a short conversation with Claire, who then turned and disappeared, apparently entering the house. Andrew placed his hand on Seth's knee, looking up at his lover still on horseback. Whatever words spoken between them had little effect to mollify Seth's temper. Seth shook the hand off, reached down to grab the trailing reins of Andrew's mount, and then stalked off toward the stables alone with the horses.

Whatever had transpired between them, Noah knew from experience that Claire was not all butter and cream and Seth was more like red hot charcoal. Andrew was no doubt treading a dangerous path between the two. After a moment Noah heard Andrew's heavy booted feet stomp down the corridor and slam the door to his room.

Feeling restless, Noah left his room and navigated the now cloth-draped staircase. He went into the study to call Gavin, only to get no answer. He left a message, hoping he did not sound as depressed as he felt. He sat there in the silence twirling a strand of his hair.

He was still sitting there staring off into space when Duncan rescued him for a late luncheon. By then the house was filled with noise and people and Dora was present in all her glory. She promptly seized upon Noah and asked his thoughts on her staging and design, while not letting him get a word in edgewise.

She kept supplying him with sandwiches and tea while eating half of what she put on his plate, and when she hauled him back out to watch the final run through, Noah actually felt alive again for the first time since the day before. He realized he had Dora to thank for that.

❦   ❦   ❦

The chaos of opening night was little different for the small local production than for the London stage as far as Noah could tell. People ran about issuing orders and bumping into each other. The scenery was suddenly not good enough. The actors had to be talked down from a case of nerves and the musicians were in a knot in a corner trying to get their cues right and their instruments tuned. Due to the size of the Hall it looked and sounded like a busy bus terminal in the throws of rush hour.

Seth and a couple of other men were ready to deal with the arriving vehicles out front. Madeline Fitzgerald, Moira, and several other young women who were ushers for the night were dressed in long gray skirts and black blouses with sashes of the blue/black tartan across their chests. Barry and his fellow musicians wore ordinary clothing, some in kilts and some in tweed; the flute player wore a cap and the guy with the mandolin wore a kilt with a cable knit sweater.

Andrew had wanted his brother to come down the main staircase, what he thought a proper entrance, when it was his turn to perform, but Noah had thought it too pretentious. He planned to come up quietly from the back of the room and join Barry and the others, who would already be up front after the operetta. Along those lines Noah had finally dressed and come down with his violin.

Apparently the costumes for the operetta had been finished at the last minute. The dressers were winding, tying, and pinning their charges into the various robes, caftans, and togas while others were doing hair and makeup. The young man from the pub tugged at the angled hem of his wrapped leopard-print skirt, seeming a bit concerned over the amount of thigh he was showing on one side. His chest was bare, partially hidden beneath a lode green cloth that draped over one shoulder, secured by a steel hatpin that looked deadly enough to cause damage. A thin band of gold foil intended to suggest a crown was perched on his brow and his golden sandals were tied with golden cords around his shapely calves.

Dora had her hair up in the braided beehive from the night of the dinner party, but the color was blue instead of purple. It was a lighter shade than the heavy blue eye shadow she wore over her black-lined eyelids with their artificial lashes. Her lipstick, already smeared, was bright blood red. Two women were binding her middle with a tight golden corset that would have precluded any chance of her singing, so it was a good thing she wasn't. From the pained expression on her face, she would be lucky to breathe.

Noah walked through all the insanity and found a place in the rear of the main drawing room where he could sit undisturbed for a moment. The furniture of the main salon had been compressed inward to allow for the chair placement, but it was still suitable for the household staff and usherettes to use once the performance had begun. Both of the immense fire places were in use to heat the space, and the entire front of the house was blazing with light.

For Noah it was less like a concert and more like some of the school plays he had attended in his youth. He watched the barely controlled chaos with a sense of nostalgia, thinking that even though it was not the grand stages of Europe, the excitement seemed genuine. All the energy and sound would not be over until the fat lady sang. Of course she was not really fat and she would not really be singing, but there it was.

The guests began to arrive. Though the evening had somehow turned out not to be windy or foggy, the exterior lighting was blazing away, casting a beacon out through the darkness. One by one the headlights of cars or trucks could be seen making their way down the lonely dark road from the village, to the manor house that few of them had ever set foot in, at least in the last fifteen or so years.

Some of them came in holding their caps in their hands in awe and quietly took their seats. Others came over to the fires burning in the giant hearths and stood warming their backsides while talking amongst themselves. Yet others shook hands with Barry or Andrew and laughed in muted tones while the hall began to fill. Rose Marie appeared with Mary Katherine in tow from around the sheet hung to portion off the hallway. Both women looked Noah over and made small sounds of approval.

"You look mighty nice in the family colors," Mary Katherine complemented, taking a seat. "It's a shame you dinna choose to wear a kilt."

Rose chuckled softly. "You have plenty of knees to look at, Mary Kate. Did you see poor Basil? If he doesn't catch a cold in that get up, I will be surprised."

"You could always be curing him with that potion of yours," Noah said off hand.

"If I were only twenty years younger I'd be happy to cure anything that ails him."

"Thirty a bit more like it," Mary Katherine giggled.

Noah hid his smile behind his hand. Comfortable in his presence, the two women continued to gossip about various folks and what people were wearing. Duncan appeared and collapsed in a chair at the end of Noah's sofa. He took out a handkerchief and mopped his face with it.

"I believe I am not cut out for show business," the butler said grimly. "I applaud your constitution, Master Noah."

"Behind the scene stuff is a lot harder," Noah confided. "That's why I prefer being out front."

"You are looking very smart. Oh, what are they up to now? I do hope the scenery does not fall over and crush anyone."

"It looked pretty sturdy to me. I am sure Dora personally watched Andrew hammer every nail."

"I am certain she did. Excuse me, I am being directed to lower the lighting."

Sure enough, Claire was waving frantically from the edge of the Chinese screen placed at the end of the Egyptian wall to keep people from meandering through to the staging areas. It seemed that everyone was present and the production was about to begin. Seth came in the front door and walked past the waiting audience, barely giving Noah or the others a glance, disappearing beneath the sheet on his way to the kitchen for whatever he had to do next.

Duncan turned off the lights of the drawing room area, leaving only the main hall chandeliers to light the space and the stage. There was one light burning on the upper landing and a few muted lights behind the stage. The glowing fireplaces seemed even more dramatic, lending an old world ambiance to the production. Andrew stepped around the screen and out front to get things started. He wore a black jacket and formal kilt, looking every inch a Highlander with the folds of a snowy cravat at his throat.

"Friends and family, I welcome you to Bainbridge Hall for the kick off of this year's harvest festival with an operetta and concert. As you all know, this year's offering from the local drama group is a selection from *Aida*, complete with costume and stage direction. As it will be sung in Italian you will no doubt find the translation provided in the evening's programs as helpful as I did."

Some laughter circled the room along with the rattling of programs. The programs, like the costumes, had arrived at the last minute via Jamis and had quickly been laid out on each chair by Caroline and Ester.

"Upon the completion of the operetta we will be treated to music from Barry Fitzgerald and his fellow musicians with a special appearance by a famous violinist from the classical stage of the London Symphony. Please do not leave your seats during the performances. I hope you all enjoy your evening here with us at the Hall and I hope we might all do this again next year. Now…onward unto Egypt!"

❦ ❦ ❦

Stands Scotland where it did? The line from Shakespeare popped into Gavin's head unwanted, much like the foul tasting coffee he was attempting to drink. Apparently it was still there, too far north and too filled with foreboding for his liking; the dark gray sky heralded unpleasant things to come. There he was in a rental car heading out through the Scottish countryside with no sense of direction on the curvy roads in the dark.

Gavin had a knot in his stomach that had not abated since departing London, and the stale sandwich and bitter coffee he consumed after leaving the rental agency only made it worse. He knew the feeling for what it was; dread. He was dreading the look in Noah's eyes when he showed up unannounced and tried to haul him out of there using the history of his uniquely dysfunctional family as a battering ram.

He groaned out loud at the thought of the battle they'd had before Noah left for the wilds of the north. Would Noah have come to his senses since being exposed to his brother's good graces at the house of his childhood, or would he be even more stubborn and despondent? Gavin had no idea. The last phone call had told him nothing, but left him with a nagging sense of unease.

In any case, it was Andrew that Gavin surreptitiously wanted to meet; Noah's older richer brother, now the new Laird of the Hall. Would he be just as messed up as Noah from a childhood of privilege and tragedy? If so then nothing good could possibly come from the two of them together in what Gavin suspected would be an empty rambling old house obviously out in the middle of nowhere.

If their father had kept them apart for a reason, then his death had brought them together again by accident. Whether the reason for that forced separation had also disappeared with Lord James's death was another matter altogether, and one Gavin was not so sure of. Things of such gravity did not happen without a reason. Not even in privileged, mixed up families like Noah's. There was always a reason.

Gavin sighed at his reflection in the dark wind screen, another quote about Scotland popping into his head from a more irreverent source. *Who would want to be a Scotsman?* He could almost see the Monty Python sketch in his mind's eye, the unsuspected English gentlemen turning into kilt-wearing Scotsmen one by one to go trotting off to the Highlands, one arm raised in a fist to the sounds of bagpipes in the distance. It had been funny at the time, that forced march to the moors.

Gavin raised his left fist to the darkness in a silent salute to the absurd just as the first glimpse of what had to be Bainbridge Hall blazed to life in the distance, then disappeared suddenly behind the wall of dark forested hills. Gavin felt his mouth settle into a grim line and put his hand back on the wheel. With that one point of light in the utter blackness of the night, it seemed like the magical Brigadoon stepping out of the mists of time. Somehow Gavin did not believe this was going to change his opinion of Scotland either, not one bit.

His first shock was the impressive look and size of the place, awe inspiring even in the unnatural glare of the exterior floodlights. It wasn't exactly a castle, but it was considerably larger than Gavin had been expecting. The number of automobiles stacked neatly along the drive led him to guess that a party was going on inside, although he had no idea where one would round up enough people from the encircling countryside to invite to a bash. He parked the rental at the end of the line of vehicles, slipped on his jacket, and walked down the drive into the house.

Chaos greeted him, enfolding his startled senses in a heated explosion of unintelligible sound, bright light, and crowded movement in which he was just another anonymous bystander in the commotion. For a moment Gavin was caught like a deer in the headlamps while he squinted in the light. Someone brushed past him out the door, jostling his elbow and moving him farther into the room.

Confused, Gavin looked around at the unfamiliar faces and then at the overall scene. The huge expanse of great hall had been refashioned as an obvious set with a stage area and audience. The blazing chandeliers were huge cut crystal monstrosities that in no way covered the expanse of room. Twin fireplaces fed the space with warmth but the energy he felt was unsettled in spite of the light and heat. The juxtaposition of old world elegance and the oddly situated Egyptian motif mixed with the sea of faces made for a jumbled message to his befuddled brain.

When the same man nearly ran him over coming back into the house, Gavin simply followed in his wake. The hurried path led him around an expensive multi-paneled Chinese screen and into a smaller, less crowded drawing room where several men stood over a figure on the sofa below the curtained windows. Only when Gavin caught a glimpse of pale silver hair and a motionless white hand did his eyes widen in comprehension.

TWELVE

Chaos is come again.
—W. Shakespeare

As operas go, the local production of *Aida*, the abridged version, was nothing short of amazing. It was the *audience* participation that caught Noah off guard. A child of classical stage, he was accustomed to awed silence during a performance; the audience was often felt but never heard. Apparently it was a little different in a small Scottish town.

They sang bits they knew along with the actors. They called out *suggestions* during the performance, some of it actually followed by the lip-sinking actors on stage. They laughed out loud—practically no parts of *Aida* were funny—and some even tried to join in the action. It certainly presented the lamented, woe-filled opera that Noah knew in an entirely new light. Whether it was by intention or accident, it lived up to Dora's reputation as an innovator…or had the word been *instigator*?

At the break between scenes while a few people were shoving things around in a new configuration for the stage and others were changing or reapplying makeup, Dora actually came out and sat down with several women in the front row, their heads in a conspiratorial huddle that could only bode trouble for young Basil Forsyth. The man with the mandolin played to cover the gap in action while people talked in normal voices. When Dora rose to rejoin her troop behind the curtain, the audience attempted to quiet themselves for the next act.

It did not disappoint. The actors moved up and down the lower staircase steps with grace while the farce played out on the center stage below them. At least Mr. Forsyth had a sense of humor. When Dora dragged him down across the chaise where she was seated and tugged his toga from his shoulder to bare his chest, he looked as if he had been expecting it. He leered at the crowd, swooning in Dora's arms with his leopard print skirt hiked up to frightening heights.

Noah laughed until he cried. He would never be able to watch or play *Aida* again without grinning like an idiot. The audience roared with delight. The music ended in sweeping grandiose melancholy appropriate for a lover's final on-stage death. Totally in sync with the audience, if not the Italian wording of the dramatic music, Mr. Forsyth cried out in English.

"For you and Egypt! Kiss me, my darling!"

Dora was happy to oblige. The audience whistled and cat called until Dora had to finally release her captive so he could breathe. She partially pushed him to his feet, letting her hand linger on his firm backside.

They bowed with exaggerated decorum, still laughing. Her bright red lipstick was smeared over his face and she took his head between her hands, rubbing her nose against his. To the delight of the audience Basil grabbed her and bent her over backwards to kiss her again, no easy feat; Dora was three inches taller than he and at least thirty pounds heavier. When he set her back on her feet, it was Dora who was slightly flustered.

Taking the last of their bows, they left the stage. Barry and his musicians repositioned their chairs forward on one side and made ready to play, while some of the audience got up to stretch or find the facilities. Rose Marie hopped to her feet to guard her side of the hallway. The sound of Barry's fiddle began a small tune and then stopped for Andrew to introduce the next performance.

A group of six young girls in Celtic costume took the stage for their two dance numbers, cute as fairies in green and blue velvet dresses with their long hair up in ponytails and ribbons. While they danced and the musicians played, the actors changed into street clothes and drifted out around the edge of the stage to take seats in the audience. Andrew was sitting beside Claire somewhere near the front. Dora made her way to a chair beside Father Perrine and Jamis Selkirk. Young Mr. Forsyth, now totally covered in jeans and a cable knit sweater, was still grinning.

Barry played an excellent fiddle. Noah tapped his foot in rhythm to the ancestral tunes, his face flushed with the excitement spilling over from the crowd. The villagers enjoyed their pleasures wholeheartedly, with laughter and tears. When the girls dispersed and Barry motioned for quiet, Noah reached for the violin sitting in the chair next to him and got to his feet.

"Ladies and gentlemen," Barry said with a smile. "We have with us tonight a rare talent from the London symphony." He motioned for Noah to come forward. "Lord Andrew has been gracious enough to host this evening's performances and his brother has been gracious enough to allow us a sample of his musical genius, known world wide. It is with great pleasure that I introduce to you—Noah Bainbridge."

Noah gave a little bow to Barry and the audience. They clapped and tried to resettle themselves for a more reserved performance. Their faces turned up with rapt expectation and Noah felt the same wave of terror that he always felt right before he played for an audience, no matter how large or small. They would take some part of him away with them, some piece of his soul that he would never get back. Noah tucked his violin beneath his chin and began to play.

The *Canzonetta from Violin Concerto in D* by Tchaikovsky was a typical violin piece, but the moment Noah began to play he wondered why he had chosen it. It was filled with melancholy in its long drawn out notes, a sad and disquieting piece that spoke of the mood he must have been in when he selected it. He played with his eyes closed, every ounce of his homesick sadness projected into the touch of the bow on the strings. The eerie sound of it filled the Great Hall, reaching into the darkest corners of the ancient brooding house like a sigh.

The audience was utterly silent. They had forgotten the riotous laughter of moments before. They were trapped in Noah's spell, their emotions ensnared by the music, but even more so by the musician himself. They felt his despair, carried on the notes to their hearts, reminding them where they were and that the house and the musician had recently dealt with sorrow. When the last note melted away with the slow draw of the bow, there was only silence and the sound of the crackling fire.

Noah dared not look at them. He took a breath and began to play his own solo version of *Autumn* from the *Four Seasons*, by far a more energized and up-beat piece. When he heard them begin to respond to the change in energy, Noah opened his eyes and glanced out among them. Some of the women were still wiping their eyes. Dora had simply allowed the tears to flow unheeded and her damp face was streaked with black mascara. Andrew looked…angry.

The mood shifted back to excitement, the music rising and falling to hint at autumn's changing colors and brisk chilling breeze. Noah lost himself in the trills, tossing his head with emphasis on the quick, hard sections. The audience breathed with him, following every shift. When he finished with a lifting of his bow and violin, they clapped in loud applause and he bowed for a long moment before lifting his head and turning in the direction of Barry just beside the stage area.

Noah grinned at him. "How about a little contest, Barry?"

Barry's eyebrows shot up in surprise. He motioned at himself with one hand in question. The crowd clapped again and made sounds of agreement. Barry grinned and stepped out onto the stage area next to Noah.

"What do you have in mind?"

Noah twirled his bow in his fingers like a baton. "Can you keep up with me? Your fingers are pretty fast. Say let's find out."

Noah started with a recognizable piece, just a quick burst of a tune Barry had been playing earlier. Barry nodded in understanding, taking up the music where Noah had left off and completing the next few bars with a flourish. They were both skilled at the violin, a seemingly matched contest while the music flew in energetic spurts that got the audience clapping and whistling in response. Noah laughed in sheer delight at the fun he was having, an expression mirrored on Barry's perspiring face.

When Noah started off down the path of a gypsy sounding

piece and kept going, Barry finally had to admit defeat. His fingers were not as fast or agile and the malicious glint in Noah's blue eyes told Barry what he already knew; the boy could play circles around him without breaking a sweat. He stepped back with a grin and was content to watch as Noah's slender form dipped and swayed to the wild frenzy of the music, a complete blending of talent, soul, and passion that few artists possessed.

Barry was still watching when the odd string of events happened, although he did not understand at the time what he was seeing. It came from the staircase behind him, a sudden sense of movement that brushed just past him like a gust of wind. Barry remembered only later that it had touched his skin, a blast of icy cold that made his hair stand on end and his eyes widen in surprise.

The surprise had been Noah toppling over backwards, his face an expression of sheer terror. The music stopped abruptly. Barry watched Noah's arms fly out in front of him, still clutching the bow and violin. He heard the boy's breath leave his lungs in a hard gasp as if something had struck him in the chest, and then Noah's head flew back in a cloud of silver hair, taking his body with him.

It all seemed to happen in slow motion that then sped up all at once. Noah crashed to the hard stone floor, saved from bashing his head in by the barest fraction of inches, landing backward on some of the material trailing from the Egyptian scenery. The violin did not fair as well, taking the full brunt of the fall with a splintering crash that sent pieces of wood flying out across the floor to the feet of the people sitting in the first row of chairs.

Someone in the middle of the room screamed. People jumped to their feet amid gasps of shock. In the near silence of the startled crowd, Barry recovered his senses enough to leap to Noah's side. To his horror there was blood on the boy's pale face, flowing freely from a cut to his cheek. Noah did not move.

"Reggie!" Barry called out, glancing at the crowd of shocked faces behind him. "Get up here quick!"

His face expressionless, Andrew knelt beside his unconscious brother. The crowd came to life, their whispering words an unintelligible murmur like water rushing over a rocky stream. Reggie was making his way up through the crowd. Barry saw another small group gathering around someone else who must have fainted from the shock. He turned his gaze back to Noah.

Where had the cut come from? The snapping of a string might have caused the injury but Barry doubted it; such things rarely happened. The violin was smashed to bits, the neck of it still clutched tightly in Noah's cold white fingers. The bow had flown off in the other direction, out of Barry's line of sight. Barry reached down to pry the shattered violin from Noah's grip when Reggie nudged him aside.

Barry got to his feet and Andrew did the same, still silent. Several more men were pressing close and Andrew's butler tried to block their view of the fallen musician. Andrew himself seemed oddly subdued, looking down at Noah's feet without moving. Barry shook his friend's arm.

"I don't know what happened, Andrew, but I think we should call it a night. I'll get everyone's attention." When Andrew only nodded, Barry turned to the crowd. "Give me your attention, everyone! Calm down please. Quiet."

Slowly they quieted down to a gentle murmur. Most of them were on their feet, some women wringing their hands and crying. Barry noticed only then that it was Dora who was being seen to by Father Perrine and Claire, among others. Some of the ushers were turning on lamps in the drawing room area.

"Thank you for your patience," Barry told everyone. Their faces turned to look at him. "It would appear that our evening is at an end. I'd like to thank you for coming and for your concern but I believe Mr. Bainbridge will be all right. Just too much excitement for someone who was already recovering from an illness. Please gather your belongings and make your way home in a quiet and orderly fashion. I will see most of you tomorrow at the festival. Good night."

Barry ignored the smattering of questions and turned to look down at Reggie. Noah was still unconscious, his papery thin eyelids closed in sunken eye sockets. Reggie had placed his folded handkerchief over the bleeding cut.

"Barry, you and Jamis help me get him into the drawing room. Be careful and I will try to keep his head and neck level, just in case."

"He just fainted, didn't he?" Jamis asked, coming up to help lift Noah.

Reggie shook his head. "He would be awake by now. I don't know how hard he might have struck his head. Please be careful."

They managed to lift and carry him to the sofa in the small drawing room, where they stretched him out on its cushioned length. Noah's pale slender hand dropped to the floor and Doctor Fox-Pitt grasped it and felt for his pulse. The young man's lips were as white as his skin and the eyes were motionless in their blue tinted sockets. The doctor placed Noah's arm across his waist and turned to look Andrew in the eye.

"What illness is he suffering, Andrew?" Reggie asked with a frown. "Is this part of it or something else I should be worried about?"

Andrew shrugged, a motion that Barry witnessed with disbelief. It was Duncan who answered from a few steps away, lingering at the door to keep anyone else from entering the room. He came forward with a glance at Andrew that seemed as mystified as Barry's stare.

"Noah was diagnosed with mental exhaustion while on his latest tour of Asia," Duncan explained. "He has been suffering fainting spells and headaches since his arrival. Although we had hoped for a quick recovery, I am afraid he is still very much unwell."

"That does not account for the cut on his face. Barry?"

Barry shook his head. "I don't know. I don't think a string snapped but it all happened so fast. I suppose he could have struck himself with the end of his bow when he fell."

"Hmmm," Reggie said thoughtfully. "Jamis, go out to my car

and fetch my medical bag."

Jamis turned and left without a word. Andrew still said nothing.

"Duncan," Reggie added. "Make sure the crowd is dispersing. I want that door closed so Noah can have a little privacy."

The look Reggie gave Andrew spoke volumes. Barry wasn't sure what was going on but he could feel himself trembling with shock. He was just as much to blame as Andrew. What he could not understand was why Andrew remained silent.

Jamis returned quickly, handing over the medical bag. He had not come alone, another man following him to the edge of the doorway. As Reggie sat the bag down on the coffee table and opened it, the unknown man in the doorway stopped Duncan from closing the doors by putting out his arms like Superman shoving open the steel side of a train car.

"What the bloody hell is going on around here!" Gavin thundered at the top of his lungs.

Every face turned to look at him with a sort of blank stare.

Other than Noah, Andrew was the only face Gavin recognized, having seen his likeness in the family photographs and again in McKewen's report. The others stared at him like he had grown two heads or materialized out of thin air. Gavin stalked into the room, allowing his gaze to fall upon the lower half of Noah's body where it lay stretched unmoving on the sofa. The man with the doctor's bag—did doctors still make house calls?—seemed to be the man in charge.

"Who are you?" asked Reggie, having come up from the bag with a vial of smelling salts.

"Gavin Moore," he introduced himself with a snarl. "Noah's personal assistant and manager. Who are you and what are you doing to him?"

That elicited a chorus of denials and a glare of annoyed impatience from the doctor. Gavin continued forward around the small table, sliding neatly past Andrew to sink to his knee beside the sofa. He reached out and took Noah's thin, cold hand and at the same moment noticed the blood on his face.

"He collapsed during the performance," Andrew stammered, seeing the rage set the muscles of Gavin's face; he had recognized his name of course. "We've just now carried him here. This is Reggie, I mean, Doctor Fox-Pitt."

"I was about to administer the smelling salts," Reggie said, holding the small ampoule out for Gavin to see. "If it's just a faint, this should do the trick."

Gavin shot a glare at Andrew, who glared back. At least Noah's eyes were closed; his trances unusually left him with his eyes open so there was the off-hand chance that it was just a faint. If not...

"Go ahead then," Gavin finally said through clenched teeth.

Reggie broke the vial and waved it under Noah's nose. Gavin could smell the ammonia and taste the bitterness on the back of his tongue. He felt the tremor of reaction through Noah's hand.

Then the blue eyes flew open and the hand jerked out of Gavin's grasp. Noah sucked in his breath and began to flail about like something was attacking him. He knocked the smelling salts from Reggie's fingers and struck Gavin in the chin hard enough to bring stars to his eyes for a second.

"Get a hold on him," Reggie stated with calm detachment.

Gavin was trying to do just that, grabbing for Noah's arms while avoiding taking another punch to the face. The blue eyes were staring up into space with widely dilated pupils in a face frozen in terror. Gavin could feel the terror in the stiff muscles of Noah's body and see it in his mouth, open in a silent scream. He managed to corral the swinging arms, holding them down with his upper body across Noah's chest.

"Noah, stop it!" he ordered, hoping the sound of his familiar voice would reach through Noah's terror. "It's me, it's Gavin. You are all right. Do you hear me? I've got you now." He saw the hypodermic out of the corner of his eye and turned on the doctor with a snarl. "No drugs!"

Reggie withdrew his hand. "He's having some kind of psychotic episode. He could injure himself or you."

"What right do you have to tell him what to do?" Andrew demanded, suddenly interested in his brother's welfare.

"No drugs," Gavin repeated. He could feel Noah's body ceasing its struggle and then heard the slow torturous release of breath. Noah's eyes blinked slowly and then rolled down to look at him. There was no recognition there but there was no blank terror either. "Noah, can you hear me? Noah?"

Noah was utterly still, barely breathing. The cut on his face was still bleeding, a trickle of red sliding into the hair near his ear. When Gavin sat up, Noah blinked again and then looked straight at him.

"Gav?"

Gavin gave a silent sigh of relief. "Yeah, it's me. You're going to be all right, Noah. Don't try to move just yet."

Noah closed his eyes. Gavin turned on the select group of those he considered responsible for the state Noah was in. At least someone had the good sense to have closed the doors. Andrew had the unfortunate distinction of being the one face that Gavin recognized.

"*You*," Gavin stated in a single word that cut like a sword. "I thought we agreed he was coming here to rest. What the hell is all this about?" He waved with his arms to incorporate the general area of the front rooms and all of them. "Is everyone in Scotland insane or is it strictly this family?"

"How dare you!" Andrew roared with his lip quivering in anger. "What gives you the right to come in here and talk to me like that?"

Gavin pointed to Noah. "This gives me the right. If you don't give a damn about Noah then just tell him that and he'll be out of your hair, but I'll be damned if I am going to sit back and let you do this to him."

Andrew blanched bone white. "I didn't make him do

anything."

"You didn't try to stop him either." Gavin turned on Reggie. "If you are a doctor then put a bandage on the cut on his face. If you ever come near him again with that needle or repeat the words you used to anyone else I will have more attorneys breathing down your neck than there are trees in the forest. Do we understand one another?"

Reggie flushed red. "We do, Mr. Moore. I take my medical oath seriously. I would never harm a patient or spread a rumor regarding a private and highly personal matter. I understand your concern over your employer so I will overlook your heated comments. We are all concerned over Mr. Bainbridge's welfare and would do nothing to hinder it. I hope you understand that as well."

Gavin lowered his chin slightly. Perhaps he had overreacted. "I apologize, Doctor. If you would please continue…"

Reggie turned back to his patient. Gavin faced the others still standing rooted to their respective squares of floor. Duncan was guarding the door, his face set in stone. Barry stood with his head down and arms crossed over his chest. Jamis sat in a chair with his legs crossed at the ankles and his arms dangling over the chair arms, where he had watched the entire proceedings with open curiosity.

Andrew had recovered some of his color and his composure. He was eying Gavin with a measured gaze and his once again unmoving brother with silence.

"I should make sure everyone is leaving," Andrew muttered. "Duncan, help me restore some kind of order for the night. Jamis, I'm sure Claire is looking for both of us."

The three of them left the room, Duncan hesitating only a moment before closing the doors behind them. Gavin silently watched Barry walk toward him. With Andrew gone the tension in the room had quickly deflated.

"I think some of this is probably my fault," Barry started explaining, unable to look Gavin in the eye. Gavin did not make it easy for him, standing in commanding silence. "I sort of suggested that Noah play something for our little get together. I had no idea, really, that he was so ill."

Gavin met the man's troubled dark gaze. "I blame Andrew," Gavin admitted with sulky stubbornness. "But I'm also certain that Noah did exactly what he wanted to do. Don't worry about it, Mister…?"

"Fitzgerald, but call me Barry. I own a pub in the village and play a little fiddle on the side. That's what we were doing here tonight, playing I mean. We open up festival weekend every year with a night of music, dancing, and a play or something. Andrew was nice enough this year to let us hold it here. I guess that was a mistake."

"Which part?" Gavin asked with a flat smile.

Barry smiled grimly back. "All of it, I guess."

"Noah did tell me something about a festival, but of course mentioned nothing about trying to play. I suppose he knew what I would say about it. Seems to run in the family, this stubborn streak of selective hearing."

Barry nodded. "Sorry about all this. I hope everything will be all right tomorrow. Come see us at the pub and I'll give you a pint of my best, on the house."

They shook hands with no hard feelings and Barry took his leave. The doctor alone remained, putting away his stethoscope. A square white bandage now covered Noah's left cheekbone, but his eyes were still closed.

"Is he okay?" Gavin asked cautiously.

"You tell me," Reggie stated flatly. When Gavin remained silent, Reggie continued. "He appears to be unconscious again but it seems more like natural exhaustion this time. Has he been suffering these attacks for long?"

"Off and on lately," Gavin grudgingly admitted. "I cancelled his last tour because of it. I thought he was coming here to get some rest in the quiet."

"I assume, knowing who he is, that you have had him examined by experts?"

Gavin made a sound of derision that pretty much covered his opinion of doctors in general. While he might trust them to bandage a cut, poking around in Noah's head was another matter entirely. Reggie clearly saw the contempt on his face.

"His father suffered from severe migraine type headaches," the doctor said. "They sometimes manifest in odd ways."

Gavin raised his eyebrows. "You treated Noah's father? Was that your signature on the Certificate of Death?"

"Yes, it was."

"Are you certain that his death was natural? I mean, you *did* run blood work."

Reggie frowned. "Are you saying you have reason to believe it was not?"

Gavin glanced at Noah, wishing he had not blurted it out in quite that way. "No, at least nothing I can prove. Why did you run that blood work?"

Reggie looked at him for a long moment before he answered. "I had prescribed several drugs for treatment of his headaches and nervous condition. I had to see if there was the possibility of an overdose. There was no sign of those drugs or any other in his blood at the time of his death."

Gavin nodded slowly.

Reggie looked down at Noah, still lying on the sofa. "I had no idea that James had another son," he said thoughtfully. "I've been here only five years or so, you understand, but no one around here ever spoke of him, including James. I image it was a shock for a lot of other people to find out Noah was his son."

"I imagine it was," Gavin said grimly. "It was certainly a shock to Noah."

It was Reggie's turn to raise an eyebrow. "You mean he never knew?"

"He always thought he was a stepson, no true relation to the family. Only when the will was read did Noah find out otherwise. For whatever reason, his father chose to reveal the truth only after his death."

"Strange," Reggie said. "Why hide that? Andrew seems to be all right with it. You did kind of come down on him a bit harshly."

"I show up to a mad house and find Noah injured while he is supposed to be under his brother's care." Gavin sighed. "Maybe I did react a little too quickly."

"It really was a simple accident as far as it looked," Reggie explained. "Perhaps his foot slipped on that stone flooring while he was playing. They used that space for a small musical staging earlier and it was still draped with cloth and such. The cut could have come from his violin when it shattered."

Gavin groaned out loud, seeing dollar signs. "Not the Stradivarius."

"Was it? Oh, I am sorry for that as well. In pieces I am afraid, no chance of repair."

Gavin sighed. "That will be punishment enough for Noah's hardheadedness. In any case, I thank you for your candor and take you at your word that what was said here will not leave this room."

Reggie nodded. "I will remain until we can move Noah up to his room. I take it you wish to wait until the front of the house has been cleared from onlookers?"

"Could you go out and make sure? It's not that I don't trust Andrew but…"

"Certainly."

Reggie left the room to find only a few straggling groups of people still sitting in chairs or standing near the fires. The lights on the upper level were on and the main chandeliers were now dark, leaving the Great Hall bathed in soft shadowy light. He crossed the echoing emptiness to find Andrew speaking with Dora and Father Perrine, sitting on a sofa against the far drawing room wall. Dora looked ashen faced and two sizes smaller, sitting with her shoulders hunched in and her head lowered.

Jamis and Claire were talking separately, their heads together in a corner. Duncan was nowhere to be seen, no doubt seeing to a room for Mr. Moore or some other duty he would have yet to perform for the night. Barry and his wife had gone.

The aftermath of the big evening was a mess; the scattering of chairs and the rigged stage setup would no doubt be left untouched until tomorrow. The bits of broken violin had been swept into a small sad pile of wood chips at the edge of the staircase. It would take as long to reorder the Hall as it did to disrupt it, not the first hit-and-run it had experienced in its storied existence.

"I say, Dora, are you all right?"

She looked up at him with mascara smeared eyes and a bleary expression. "I'll be fine. Andrew says that Noah was not badly injured."

Reggie nodded to alleviate her worry. "He is resting now. Everything is fine. May I offer you a ride home? I think we have all had a trying evening."

"I will take her home," Father Perrine said. "We simply wanted to wait and know for sure that Mr. Bainbridge was uninjured. Since he is in your capable hands, Reggie, we will be leaving. Andrew, you and your brother have my prayers. If there is anything I can do for you, please call me. Good night. Come along, Dora."

Reggie watched the odd couple take their leave. Dora moved in a shambling gait as if she were drunk or exhausted, leaning heavily on her companion for support. She seemed to have aged a decade overnight. Looking back at Andrew the comparison was similar. The young Laird of the Hall was frayed around the edges and more than slightly subdued, not usual for him. It had been a trying night and the dressing down he received from Mr. Moore had obviously stung.

Out in the car in the dark, Father Perrine took a long deep

breath. "I've never heard anything like that in all my life. I could believe it possible that the boy's illness is the price he pays to possess the soul of an angel."

Dora gave a small uncomfortable laugh. "There are no angels in that house, Ian."

"What do you mean?"

"Didn't you feel it?" Dora asked, her hands moving restlessly along the hem of her shawl. "It answered him, Ian. Whatever it was, it came straight down that staircase and crashed into that boy with enough force to knock him down and knock me senseless half a room away. I still can't stop shaking. You know, for a second there I thought I saw... Never mind. I can't think straight."

Father Ian Perrine started the engine and pulled the sedan out of the drive. "You think something attacked him, tonight, with all of us around? That's hard to believe, Dora. Even if it's true, what would you have me do?"

She shook her head. "I don't know. I only know that nothing good will come in that house...not for him."

Perrine frowned at her. "His manager is here now. Maybe that will help."

"Maybe. At least he will be another pair of eyes watching in that house." *Along with all the others*, she thought grimly. Whatever it was, tonight it had zeroed in on its prey with both barrels. It was only a matter of time.

Back in the house Gavin sat watching Noah, wondering what the hell had been going on over the last few days to get him into this state. The white bandage on Noah's face only accentuated the paleness of his skin and the sunken bruises around his eyes. As Gavin watched, the lips twitched and slowly Noah opened his eyes.

"Noah, how are you feeling?" Gavin asked gently.

Noah stared at him. He thought he had been dreaming. In his dreams Noah had been lost in the darkness, running from something that was close on his heels. If he turned his head to look at it, it would have him. Worse, he would see what it was and some part of him knew without understanding that such knowledge would kill him. In his terror, Noah had seen Gavin's face and felt Gavin's hand squeezing his until he thought his fingers might break.

Noah opened his eyes wider. It *was* Gavin looking down at him. Gavin's dark questioning eyes and serious frown. He sat up quickly, too quickly, blurring Gavin's face out of focus. He felt Gavin's hands touching him but the blackness was stronger. Knowing he was safe in Gavin's presence, Noah let the darkness take him.

Easing Noah's limp form back down into the cushions, Gavin cursed silently. Whatever had happened, it had clearly robbed Noah of all of his energy. Even his skin was cold to the touch, dry and papery. The bones of his slender hand seemed far too fragile and trembled between Gavin's palms like a small shivering bird. Maybe he had been too quick to dismiss the doctor's assistance.

On cue, Reggie opened the doors and came back into the room with Andrew in tow. Gavin stood up to face them.

"It's all right to move him now," Reggie stated. "I'll check him again once we get him situated for the night."

"I had the room next to Noah's made ready for you," Andrew said, and then added with unnecessary petulance, "Since we had no prior notice of your arrival it will be cold and stale but the girls can air it tomorrow. Rose Marie is making up a tray for you and Noah to share; I thought perhaps you might not have eaten since you drove in late."

Gavin gave him a grudging thank you. He would be grateful for the food but he doubted he would sleep in the bed tonight, any bed; a chair in Noah's room would be more likely. At least Andrew was not going to assign him to servant's quarters just to make a point. Gavin wouldn't have put it past him.

"That's not necessary," Gavin said, moving to block Andrew's way around the coffee table. "I can carry him."

They looked at each other in a protracted moment of silence until Andrew shrugged and stepped back. Gavin leaned down and slipped his arms beneath Noah's body, lifting him easily. He followed in Andrew's wake with the doctor grabbing his medical bag and silently bringing up the rear.

The house was eerily silent, a shock after coming in the way Gavin had earlier. It was also dimly lit and astonishingly large. The cloth draped staircase was wide enough to handle an entire marching band and long enough that Gavin was slightly winded when he reached the landing with his burden. They turned to the left, where a long corridor of bedroom doors disappeared into the shadows, and Gavin knew that a similar corridor was on the right, a wing probably reserved for guests.

The door to Noah's room was already open and the bed turned down. A fire in the hearth was doing its best to heat the space. The doctor pulled the blankets further back and Gavin placed Noah carefully down on the sheets, easing his head onto the pillow. Reggie thumbed Noah's eyelids back then checked his pulse.

"I'm in the village," Reggie said. "If you need me at any time, do not hesitate to give me a call. Duncan has my number."

Gavin nodded and Reggie left the room. Andrew followed him out without a word, the two men passing a third in the hallway. It was Duncan, who came into the room with a large tea tray.

"If you would give me your keys, sir, I will bring up your luggage. Your room is right next door, accessible through the adjoining bath."

Gavin fished the keys out of his pocket and handed them over. "Thank you."

"My name is Duncan, the butler of the house. Do you require assistance with Master Noah?"

Master Noah? It took Gavin a moment to understand that the butler was offering to help with preparing the unconscious man for bed. Gavin figured he could manage that on his own without too much trouble.

"I can handle it, thank you."

"Very well, sir. I will bring up your things and place them in the room next door. If there is anything you need, the bell pull is just there. I will bring your coffee in the morning and you can tell me then if you wish breakfast in your room or downstairs. I bid you good evening."

Gavin nodded and watched the man leave, closing the door behind him. *Bell pull?* What kind of place was Bainbridge Hall? Apparently stuck in another century. The rooms were heated by fireplaces and you still summoned servants by means of a bell pull. He shook his head. Perhaps he should consider Noah lucky that such a backward place even had a doctor. Just to ease his curiosity, Gavin glanced into the bathroom; at least it was modern and up to date.

Noah was still lying where he had been half propped up on the pillows. Gavin set about removing Noah's shoes and socks, turning then to the more complicated task of getting him out of the tartan jacket.

For the first time Gavin actually noticed the material, a blue and grey/black tartan, the same as the kilt Andrew had been wearing. He eased Noah into a sitting position and held him while he slipped the jacket off. One at a time he pulled Noah's arms out of the turtleneck shirt before pulling it carefully off over the blond head, easing Noah back down onto the pillows.

Gavin brushed the blond hair back into place. Shadows pooled in the hollows of Noah's collarbones and Gavin could count every rib. He tugged off the new dark gray trousers and pulled the bed covers up to Noah's sharp chin, tucking them in around his body. With a sigh Gavin draped the clothing over the upholstered arm chair in the corner beside the bed and turned off the small lamp; with the light from the open bathroom door and the fire light he could see well enough.

He simply stood there, looking down at Noah. The longer he stood there in the silence, the more guilty and angry he became.

When Gavin heard the door to his connecting room close, he went through the bathroom into the darker room beyond.

The room they had put him in was spacious and ancient, much like Noah's. The bed was a huge, heavily carved monstrosity that should have been in a museum somewhere, or perhaps one of the Queen's abodes. A fire was burning in the hearth but the room was as cold and stale smelling as Andrew had said, clearly a room unused for a long time. The butler had brought up his bags and simply left them at the foot of the bed. The keys were on the side table and his coat was draped over the chair by the fireplace.

Seeing his briefcase sitting there with McKewen's file inside made Gavin glad the man had not unpacked for him. He slid the briefcase under the bed. The bed was turned down and they had provided extra blankets and towels neatly folded beside his luggage. A carafe filled with water sat on the bedside table, along with a glass and a small basket of snack items, much like what you would find in a fine hotel. Gavin shook his head and left everything as it was.

Noah still had not moved. Gavin removed his jacket and sat down in a chair by the fire to chase away the chill. He was tired from the trip, but mostly he was worried about Noah. The entire mess was not what he had been expecting and he admonished himself for having gotten off on the wrong foot with Andrew. There was really no reason for the animosity he felt toward the man...yet there it was.

He removed the cozy from the teapot and poured himself a cup, adding sugar. The sweet hot liquid helped him relax almost immediately. What was it about a cup of hot tea and the English? Gavin sighed and looked over the heaping tray of food that the tea accompanied; thick slabs of homemade bread stuffed with roast beef or country ham sat alongside some kind of vegetable puffs and a silver topped jar of raspberry jam. The cakes and biscuits were stacked high with not one, but three types of small bite size tartlets. Chunks of cheese and an entire bunch of grapes filled out the space.

The sight and smell of it set Gavin's mouth to watering. With fare like that how on earth could Noah be losing weight? Did he walk five miles a day through the woods? Gavin took a sandwich and proceeded to eat, looking around the room while he chewed the best roast beef he had ever tasted. When he saw the empty violin case on the dresser he groaned inwardly.

Then he saw the tartan hanging at the end of the armoire. Noah said that Andrew had given him a tartan, although Gavin could not imagine him wearing it. Thinking about it, he finished eating and got up to look at the jacket Noah had been wearing. It was clearly new, tailored specifically for Noah's slender frame, but the front left side panel was damaged; narrowly spaced parallel cuts about five inches long had rent the sturdy material all the way through to the silk interior beneath. To Gavin they looked oddly like claw marks.

Beside him Noah made a sound and moved slightly. Gavin tossed down the jacket and went to sit on the edge of the bed. After another moment, Noah opened his eyes. They were dull flat gray in the dim light, the eyes of someone on their death bed. The voice that spoke Gavin's name was just as weary and frightening, a grating whisper that could have come from the throat of an old man who had smoked all his life.

"Gavin, is that really you?"

"You were expecting maybe the King of Siam, with what must have been going on before I got here tonight."

The corners of Noah's mouth curled upward. "Egypt, not Asia." He tried to clear his throat. "I am actually glad to see you, Gavin."

"Are you thirsty? How about some tea?"

Noah nodded. Gavin really was there, he had not dreamt it. He was lying in his bed, upstairs in his brother's house, and Gavin was there. And then Noah remembered what had happened. His entire body contracted at the thought and sent his teeth chattering with cold.

"Drink this," Gavin ordered, holding the cup to Noah's lips.

The hot tea helped a little, curling warmth into his stomach and beyond. Beneath the covers Noah slid his hand across his naked chest. His ribs hurt. The simple act of moving his hand exhausted him and he lay against the pillows looking into Gavin's worried eyes.

"I'll be all right, Gavin."

"Noah, what the hell is going on around here? What happened down there tonight?"

Noah met the worried, angry gaze in silence. What could he say? *Oh, I think something in the house tried to kill me tonight, Gavin. Don't worry about it.* Gavin would drag him out by his aching wrist and put him in a lead-lined room…or a padded one. In his current condition, he might just agree with the action.

"It was a harmless evening of entertainment," Noah lied. "I overdid it, I guess."

"Harmless," Gavin echoed tonelessly.

Noah had no doubt Gavin knew he was lying; the unspoken words sat in the air between them like balloons, ready to pop. Gavin, always perfectly capable of yelling, kept silent. The silent stare made Noah squirm.

"I hope I didn't scare anyone," Noah sighed. Gavin's eyebrows went up as if to say, *what about scaring me?* "I guess I kind of ruined the ending, huh?" More silence. Noah groaned, shifting his position in the bed. "Why *are* you here, Gav?" he then asked innocently.

Gavin frowned and the balloon popped. "Excuse me for worrying about you. You obviously haven't seen yourself in the mirror, Noah. You look like death warmed over. I have half a mind right now to drag you to the nearest hospital. Somehow I don't think you could stop me."

Noah sighed. His head hurt. Everything hurt. "I'm sure you came with loads to say, but I'm just too tired to listen and too tired to think."

The anger evaporated from Gavin like steam. "I'm sorry. I shouldn't be yelling at you. You need to sleep. I will shut up."

"I worry more about you when you are quiet than when you are yelling. You can yell at me in the morning. I'll even listen."

"*You* worry about *me*? You'll listen? It must be worse than I thought."

"Gavin…"

"I'll shut up. There is a ton of food here. Would you like some?"

Noah shook his head. The lure of Mary Katherine's sumptuous fare was losing its appeal in the growing necessity of sleep. He had been sleeping a lot lately yet somehow he never seemed to have any energy. Maybe Gavin's presence would change that. With Gavin around, things were probably going to liven up, one way or another.

"Good night, Noah," Gavin said.

Gavin lifted the tray and headed off to his room. The calling of his name made him pause at the door to the bathroom. He looked back at Noah lying in the bed with the covers up to his chin.

"Gavin, I really am glad you are here."

Gavin smiled. "So am I. Pleasant dreams."

Gavin finished his tea and a cake or two in his barely warmed room.

He unpacked and changed into pajamas and a robe before brushing his teeth. With his feet in slippers and a blanket from his bed, he snuck quietly into Noah's room and made himself comfortable in the overstuffed chair by the fire, quieting down for the night. It would get cold before morning but he never moved, not even when Noah got out of bed at 3:00 a.m. and covered him with a second blanket.

THIRTEEN

Those days are passed now and in the past they must remain...
   —old Scottish ballad

The morning of festival day dawned bright with promise that barely extended to the foot of Noah's bed. Noah rolled over to the sound of a running shower and blinked at the hint of golden sunlight touching the undraped window. His brain slow to resume its necessary functions, he lay there like a lump. There was a fire burning in the grate. Someone had thrown back the drapes. His robe was lying across the bed. Was that coffee he smelled?

As his brain registered the smell, his stomach did a nauseous flip that signified near starvation. With a groan of discontent, he sat up. The flipping in his stomach moved to his head, making him put a hand up to his face to stop it. When his fingers touched the bandage on his cheek, Noah traced its shape with curiosity, trying to remember how it had gotten there. The sound of a hair dryer brought him fully awake.

Not that he wanted to be. He felt absolutely awful and he remembered why. He crawled out of bed and into his robe at the allure of the coffee pot, thinking that he had better get himself into some semblance of normalcy before Gavin appeared and began the third degree. Coffee would be a good start; he would never get used to rising with the dawn. It seemed to him a time best left to birds and commuters.

The coffee helped, but the five sugar cubes he put in it helped more. Noah wrapped the blanket that Gavin had left on the chair around his shoulders and stood in the square of sunlight coming through the window while he drank a second cup of sugar and caffeine. His stomach still hated him, but at least it hated him no more than the rest of his stiff, abused body. Outside the window, morning was getting underway without hindrance from fog, clouds, or rain; a beautiful day in the country.

Country. He was sick of it already. Noah hobbled over to the chair beside the fire and sat down with a thud and a sigh. He wasn't ready to face the day or Gavin's inquisition. The fact that Gavin had shown up unannounced in the middle of last evening's…developments was not going to help strengthen Noah's argument. If he actually had an argument. After what had happened last night, he wondered if maybe he was just plain crazy after all.

Gavin came into the room through the door of the connecting bath. He really was a sight for sore eyes, a steady dose of reality in a world that was becoming increasingly out of focus. Noah was very much aware that his friend had chosen to spend the night in the uncomfortable chair instead of a nice soft bed. Noah smiled without realizing he was doing so; he really was glad to see Gavin.

Gavin smiled back. He had showered and dressed for the day, ready to beard the lion in his den, so to speak. Looking at Noah's bleary eyes and sleep tousled hair made him reconsider his planned attack, feeling somewhat like a heel that he had been ready to broadside his employer before breakfast.

"How are you this morning, Noah?" he asked, making an effort to keep the guilt out of his voice. "I see you found the coffee."

Gavin poured the last of the dark brew for himself, having already taken a cupful earlier. He sat back and looked at Noah with a dark, appraising gaze.

"I'm tired," Noah admitted, pulling the blanket tighter. "Did you sleep all right?"

Gavin nodded. He had spent worse nights in chairs, not all that long ago. "I told the butler we would be taking breakfast in your room. Would you like to shower before it gets here?"

"I suppose I should. You know this is festival day, don't you?"

"Festival day?" Gavin asked and then recalled something said about it from last night. "Great. I suppose you expect to go watch a bunch of Scotsmen doing something Scottish. Are you up for that sort of thing after last night?"

Noah shrugged. "It could be nice to get out in the sun for a while—out of the house."

Gavin had no doubt about that. "I don't think this place is doing you any good, Noah."

Noah dropped the blanket and stretched. "Don't start yelling until after breakfast, will you Gav? I don't yet have the energy to fight back."

"Go shower. I won't yell, before or after breakfast."

Noah raised an eyebrow at the unusually conciliatory tone but stalked off to the bathroom for the necessary ablutions. One glance at himself in the mirror and he understood Gavin's sympathetic behavior.

His eyes were flat, opaque grey set in purple-bluish circles, and his lips were almost indistinguishable from the white of his face. He reached up and peeled the gauze bandage from his cheekbone, exposing the three inch long cut. It was still a bright red mark but seeing it did not explain its reason for being there so he ignored it and went about his business.

The heat of the shower felt wonderful and he basked in its caressing warmth until he had totally steamed the large bathroom. After drying his hair he yanked on jeans and a black zip-neck shirt, pausing to dab some ointment on the facial cut as an afterthought. He stuck his feet back into slippers and opened the door.

Duncan was there, having just arrived with the breakfast tray. Gavin cleared the small table by moving the earlier coffee service to the foot of the bed. The extra blanket was there too, folded neatly.

"Master Noah, I am very glad to see you are up and well."

"Good morning, Duncan," Noah replied with a smile. "I hope I was not too much trouble last night. You have met Gavin?"

Duncan actually smiled. "We have indeed *met*, sir. Your brother will be glad to hear you are feeling better. He has held off with the tear down until he knew you were awake."

"That was nice of him," Gavin snipped.

"Ah, the stage," Noah said quickly to cover Gavin's comment. "They are taking it down this morning, on festival day?"

"The activities do not really start until ten o'clock when the games begin. That is ample time for the dismantling and cleaning required. To leave it over the weekend would simply be too dangerous and they require the chairs at the school in time for the children's choral activities."

"When will Andrew be leaving?"

"Not until the Hall has been reordered. You are planning on attending the games, are you not?"

Noah smiled. "Would not miss it for the world. I suppose everyone will be there."

"Everyone in the county, I should think. The house will be mostly deserted this weekend as it is a holiday of sorts. Mary Katherine will not be cooking so if you wish to eat something hot other than breakfast today and tomorrow I would suggest you find a bite in town or with the festival's many vendors. Otherwise there are always cold cuts and the like available in the kitchen at your convenience."

"The house shuts down?" Noah supposed even a place like the Hall had to give staff days off. Under staffed as it was already, that would mean fend for yourself.

"Rose Marie and I will be here in the evenings," Duncan assured him. "Tonight it will be later, after the torchlight ceremony. She has already gone for the day—to meet her niece—and I am a judge at some of the games this afternoon."

"You are a judge?" Noah asked in surprise.

"What is the torchlight ceremony?" Gavin inquired at the same time.

Duncan picked up the smaller round tray that had held their morning coffee. "Like so many things here, it is an ancient tradition whose meaning has been lost in time. Laird Bainbridge is the Master of Ceremonies for the bonfire and torch lighting this evening, an honor that the last Laird refused every year. In many ways the entire village will view this evening as a historic occasion, even a rite of passage for the new Laird of the Clan."

"Sacrificing any virgins?" Gavin asked with a straight face.

"Gavin!" Noah exclaimed.

Duncan smiled slightly. "I do not believe so, but in older times that was entirely possible. Of course the church put a stop to that kind of heathenism long ago. Now the main purpose is visiting with far flung relations and, of course, the consuming of *beer*."

"Ah then," Gavin said with a grin. "We shall get along fine."

"I am sure you will enjoy it, sir. Now if you will excuse me, I must see to the dismantling and you may eat your breakfast in peace. Good day, gentlemen."

When he was gone, Gavin shook his head. "What planet are we on? I knew I was sending you to Scotland, but I had no idea that meant back in time as well."

Noah sat down. "For my sake, Gavin, could you try and get through the day without being too rude to my relatives."

"*Relatives*? The plural? Who else is hidden away in this mausoleum?"

Noah frowned at the way Gavin phrased it. Too many things might indeed be walking about in the darkened and silent halls of the manor house. Whether or not they were his *relatives* was yet to be discovered.

"It seems I have some cousins who actually live nearby. I think half the people in the county may have Bainbridge blood in their veins."

"Reeeaaallyy," Gavin drawled and looked thoughtful. "Eat your food while it's still hot."

The plates were filled over with scrambled eggs, bacon, sausage, and potatoes. Noah ate like he had never tasted food, shoveling mouthfuls without pausing to breathe or speak. Gavin ate with more decorum but was pleased to see that Noah had an appetite. The scones were fluffy and delicious and he was stuffing the crumbs from the third one into his mouth before he came up for air.

"You need to get Mary Katherine's oat cake recipe," Noah mumbled.

"Maybe we can just steal Mary Katherine," Gavin agreed. The scones were better than he could make. "She must have a secret ingredient."

"I wouldn't be surprised. Everyone here seems to have a secret."

Gavin lifted his eyebrow at Noah's expressionless face. "What happened last night, Noah? What's going on in this place?"

"You first," Noah said, dropping his napkin to pick up his tea cup. "I know you came with ammunition. You're dying to tell me how all my ancestors were werewolves or crazed Viking marauders who ran around covered in blue paint."

"Werewolves? What made you say that?" Gavin exclaimed with suspicion.

"No reason. It's just that the whole village seems to have wolves on the brain."

"Really," Gavin said again. "All right. Remove the tray and I'll be right back."

Perplexed, Noah watched him get up and disappear through the bathroom. He removed the large tray with the empty dishes to the foot of the bed, taking the last piece of toast and stuffing it in his mouth. As an afterthought he went and locked the door. When he turned, Gavin had entered the room with a leather binder in his hands. Noah swallowed his toast and resettled himself in the chair by the fire.

"You knew I was going to do it anyway, didn't you?" Gavin asked guiltily.

Noah made an expression of patience long suffering. "Duh. I know you Gavin. You are curious, nosey, over protective, nosey, bossy, nosey—"

"Yeah, yeah, I get it. If you don't want to know any of it, I'll just take this back."

"Open your bloody file, Gavin. I'm sure it cost enough money to find out that my brother really does hate me and my father was totally nuts."

"Does he? Hate you, I mean."

Noah shrugged. "I honestly do not know. Do you find that strange?"

Gavin shook his head. "Not in any family, much less this one. You mentioned secrets. Perhaps your father had the biggest secret of all. Unfortunately it looks like he took it with him to his grave."

Of that, Noah had no doubt. He sighed, feeling a strange combination of curiosity and dread. Gavin's dark eyes were watching him, waiting for permission to proceed.

"What did you find out, Gavin?" he finally asked.

Gavin told him. They went over Noah's short life from his time at York up to the point he came to the Hall as the son of a Lord. They traced through the last hundred years of the Bainbridge Clan, the odd coincidences, and Andrew's recent history. They looked at certificates of birth, marriage, and death. Gavin explained the theories and connections as he and McKewen had discussed them, without holding anything back.

Gavin talked and Noah listened, quietly, without any hint of emotion. His life unfolded before his eyes in ways he never understood, might never understand. It was all too pointless and cruel. It made him tired and it filled him with bitterness. Gavin stopped, removing his glasses, when he saw the dejected droop of Noah's thin shoulders. They were looking at the family crest in all its terrible glory.

"So, even you could not find out how mother died," Noah said softly.

Gavin winced at the flat sadness in his voice. He kept forgetting that the history on the printed pages was more than words to Noah; he had lived it, was still living it.

"Andrew has really told you nothing?"

Noah shook his head slowly.

"You still remember nothing, not of the hospital, not anything?"

"I get flashes of things," Noah explained. "But not of that night. I want to show you something, Gavin."

Noah opened the door and led Gavin across the hall to his father's room. The door remained unlocked since that night, no longer hiding any secrets. Once inside with the door shut, Noah directed Gavin through the sitting room and into the bedroom beyond. In the cold light of day it was just another room, but the painted eyes of his mother seemed to flare with life as he stepped into her view.

Beside him, Gavin made a small wordless noise of surprise. Noah merely stood there in silence while Gavin looked at the painting and the items on the narrow desk. When he had absorbed the nuance of the atmosphere, Gavin turned and looked at him.

"It's a shrine," Gavin stated. He felt as uncomfortable as Noah looked with the eyes of his dead mother watching them. "Not the actions of a man who hated his son."

"I don't know what to make of it," Noah said with a slight shiver. "He followed my career over these last years. He was paying my way. He obviously adored my mother, lived with memories of her, here in this room."

Gavin shivered. The place gave him the creeps. "Can we get out of here now?"

Noah nodded and Gavin followed him back across the hall. Noah's room was markedly warmer but cozy was not a word Gavin would have used to describe it. The lumbering antiquity of the entire house made for odd impressions and sinister shadows. While he went directly to the fire to warm his bones, Noah stood looking out the window.

"Gavin, you have known me for some time now. Do you

think I am crazy?"

Gavin frowned, unsure where the conversation was headed. When he did not immediately answer, Noah turned and looked at him. The solemn expression in the tired blue eyes made Gavin's heart ache.

"No, I do not think you are crazy. I cannot vouch for your father, though. Staying in this place for any length of time might well make anyone a little nuts."

"My father wasn't crazy." Noah sighed; the yelling was about to start. "There is something in the house, Gavin. I think it might be my mother."

Gavin felt his jaw drop open. When nothing came out, he closed it again. This was an outcome he had not foreseen and it sent a chill over his skin. Noah stood watching him like the eyes in the portrait, calm and penetrating. He felt, not for the first time, that those eyes could see into his soul.

"Noah," Gavin finally said into the silence. "I want you to leave this place and come home with me. There is nothing good for you here."

Noah smiled thinly. "That is another way of saying you think I am crazy."

"I don't think you are crazy. These...trances you go into...I don't know what they are but I have seen them often enough to understand that they hurt you, that you might be in danger because of them. You look terrible, Noah. I don't want... I can't protect you from these things, especially not here, in this house. The night your father died almost killed you and you were an ocean away. I don't understand how you knew it, but I believe it. What did you see? What *happened* last night?"

Noah watched the fear grow in Gavin's dark eyes, his voice more desperate with each sentence. How could he make Gavin understand? There were things at work in the house that only he seemed to be aware of, a building energy that threatened to explode like a cork from a bottle. He had felt it since the first day of his arrival, an expanding need that was draining the life out of him to accomplish its dark task.

He had told Gavin that he thought it was his mother but Noah knew that it was not. It was something else, something far more ancient and sinister. It had taken his father's life and for all he knew it was Andrew who would be next. His father had not been crazy. He had been afraid, yet his caution and his fear had not saved him. If Noah told Gavin that something was trying to kill the last of the Bainbridge line, Gavin would haul him out of there so fast he would be in a London hospital before he could blink.

"Do you trust me, Gavin?" Noah asked quietly.

There it was, the next test of that hard won trust. Gavin took a deep breath and let it out slowly. "I *believe* you. I am not sure, in these circumstances, if I can trust your instincts."

Those words stung Noah, but only for a moment. "I understand. You think I have lost my objectivity."

"There are layers and layers going on here. Something in your past obviously traumatized you so much that you still have no memory of it. Maybe these flashes you are getting are warnings from your subconscious. It all seems centered on you, Noah. That pretty much demolishes any objectivity. I know you are desperately looking for something, some connection to your past. Even if you manage to find this truth you seek, what if you are wrong?"

That hurt. Trust Gavin to pull no punches. And he was right, it did all seem to be centering on him. His arrival had awakened something in the house, something that was tuned in to his presence. Noah's father had tried to warn him, even through his death; that mind shattering connection that had all but flattened him on stage. What if the *thing* he felt in the house had simply recognized him from that momentary psychic link?

Noah could not forget the thing on the stairs. It had come straight down and crashed into him like a ton of bricks. Perhaps it had killed his father in the same way. What might happen the next time if he was a little weaker or caught totally off guard? He shuddered, aware of Gavin's eyes watching him.

"Then I will deal with it," he said quietly. "I trust you, Gavin. Since you are here now, can you not give me just a little more time?"

Gavin was not happy about being kept in the dark. He understood now what Noah had meant with his earlier comment about *family ghosts*; that bedroom across the hall was certainly filled with them. Well, they were Noah's family ghosts, and if he could uncover enough of them over the weekend then perhaps they would never have to come back for a second visit.

"I am under protest, but as I seem to currently have no other option…"

Noah gave a small, uneasy laugh. "Protest noted. You don't have to come to the games today if you had rather not. It's kind of a family obligation, to Andrew."

"Are you kidding? Food and beer is always a good distraction. The sun is shining and I will be able to observe the locals in their natural habitat. You look like you could use some sun. Are you wearing that thing?"

Noah turned his head to see the indicated tartan hanging on the wardrobe. "I suppose I should, at least for a little while."

"I don't know about kilts or werewolves," Gavin said, closing the folder. "But I think you might look good painted blue. You *aren't* a virgin, are you?"

Noah blushed, the action bringing some color to his pale lips. "Get out of here and let me get dressed."

Gavin laughed as he picked up the leather folder and headed back to his room. Behind him Noah slammed the bathroom door. Well, that was more like it. Putting the folder away, it occurred to Gavin that they had managed to get through the discussion that morning without shouting at each other. The day was young. He grinned to himself. Virgin or not, he was sure quite a few of the village ladies would be lighting torches for Noah. He would light one himself…if only he had the nerve.

In his room, Noah tossed things around, changing clothes. The black velvet jacket and heavy tartan would be hot standing around in the sunshine. He stood eyeing himself in the small wardrobe mirror, chewing his lip in dismay at the tarnished reflection. He looked like little Lord Fauntleroy or the young arrogant aristocrat in that famous blue boy painting. Both images nauseated him, especially after Gavin's comment.

He turned to look for his tartan jacket, seeing it crumpled and tossed on the chair by the bed. Knowing how much it cost, he cringed when he saw the condition it was in and then sobered when he found the long slash marks. Noah put his fingers through the rents in the cloth, directly over the corresponding spot where his ribcage hurt. Even if he had believed the incident a figment of his imagination, the cut on his cheek and the slashes in the jacket said otherwise.

Noah folded the damaged item and hid it in the bottom of the wardrobe. Donning the velvet jacket and managing to correctly drape and secure the tartan, Noah remembered to take the hat out of its hiding place and set it on the bed. When a knock came at the door, he was ready.

"Come in."

It was Andrew. Noah smiled at his brother, seeing the painted image of their father in Andrew's kilted and tartan-clad figure. He gave a little bow, which Andrew returned stiffly.

"I wanted to make sure you were all right before I left," Andrew said cautiously. "You look very authentic but you don't have to come to the village games on my account. I think you should stay at the house and rest."

Noah made a face. "You don't have to worry about me. I have been looking forward to this for days. It is a nice sunny day for a festival."

Andrew seemed to relax a degree. "Yes, I don't know how we got that lucky. It usually is foggy or raining."

"I'm sick of rain and, sorry to say it Drew, of this house. A day in the sun with laughing people and the smell of food sounds good to me."

"So it does. I suppose I can trust your *assistant* to look after you today. I have to open the start of the games in an hour. Duncan explained to you about the lack of staff over the weekend?" Noah nodded. "I suppose it's a good thing your man showed up just now. He can take up the slack. Why did he arrive unannounced?"

"I knew he was coming," Noah lied, somewhat surprised at Andrew's tone. "I forgot to tell you. He was delayed so he missed the concert anyway. I apologize if his arrival inconvenienced anyone."

"With the games going on and the lack of staffing in the house, I'm afraid the inconvenience will be his. No matter. I am glad to see you looking better. Reggie has already called this morning to check up on you. You are probably the most excitement he has had since old man Gillespie's kidney stones."

Noah smiled sheepishly. "I guess I should be apologizing to him too."

Andrew snorted. "Don't be silly. A fainting spell is hardly a bother for Reggie. If you could come down with a nice case of malaria or maybe bubonic plague, that would really entertain him."

They laughed for a moment, lightening the mood. Something had shifted between them over the last day and night, a return to a more formal relationship of two strangers. Maybe Gavin's presence had something to do with it. Maybe it was Noah's secret knowledge of Andrew and Seth that was creating that invisible wall. Whatever it was, they now regarded each other with coolly exaggerated politeness.

"I'll see what I can do," Noah said. "Don't worry about me, Drew. You have enough going on today. You look well enough like a presiding Scottish Laird. Where's the sword?"

"Too heavy to lug around all day with this getup. Truly, I don't know how anyone ever fought with those things. I believe they just held them over their heads and waited to see which one's arms gave out first."

"Maybe they were just for show," the familiar voice drawled. "See, mine is bigger than yours."

They both turned their heads to see Gavin standing in the doorway to the connecting bath. He was not smiling. He and Andrew considered each other with wary dislike, making Noah wonder yet again what level of verbal or physical fisticuffs had likely occurred between the two the previous night. The animosity clearly went both ways.

"Good morning, your Lairdship," Gavin then said, giving a slight dip of his head in deference to Andrew's title. "I should thank you for providing such a lovely room on short notice. Really, it is not often that I have had the pleasure of staying in a place with museum quality appointments. It's so…quaint."

"I take it you have not seen Balmoral then," Andrew countered, taking the slight insult with the shrug of his lip that only a true aristocrat could manage. "I could arrange an introduction to the Queen and family but I'm afraid she will not be in residence for another month."

Gavin smiled, about to say that he and Noah had already met the Queen, but a look from Noah's flashing blue eyes kept the words stuck in his throat. He had made that inane promise about not irritating the relatives. Clearly he was going to regret that decision.

"Perhaps on another visit then," Noah interjected before Gavin could speak. "You should be going if you are to start the proceedings, Drew. Don't worry about us. We will be all right on our own."

Andrew looked down his nose at Gavin before returning his gaze to his brother. "It will be a long day. Do not push yourself too hard, Noah. I will see you at the festival then."

"See you later, Drew."

Gavin came farther into the room as Andrew departed. He had not believed his eyes at first, stepping through the door to find both brothers facing each other in full Scottish regalia. It had been like walking into a scene from a history book. Something about seeing them like that, figures of the past facing off with each other, gave Gavin a jolt of uneasy awareness. The past was too near the surface in Bainbridge Hall for his liking; a shadowy heaviness in the house that could too easily enfold the observer like a fly trapped in amber.

"Gavin, what did you *do* last night?" Noah asked straight out.

Gavin's expression was inscrutable. "I didn't do anything. I was upset. Maybe I upset a few other people."

Noah groaned softly. "Please don't go out of your way to insult Andrew. What happened last night was not his fault. He is doing the best he can to make me feel at home here. I don't want to return his good will with slightly couched insults or animosity."

"I'll do my best to be civil."

Noah viewed the statement with doubt. "Fine. You came in under fire last night so you probably didn't get to see much of the house. Would you like a tour before we head out to the village?"

"I suppose it couldn't hurt to get a more sympathetic view of the place."

Noah grabbed the hat and put it on, giving the crest a rakish tilt. He managed to wear the outfit with the same sartorial elegance he gave to everything from King's Row silk suits to basic cotton pajamas; an authentic ease that came from within. The tartan would no doubt get uncomfortable as the day wore on, but for now he wore it well.

The ancient house wore sunlight with grudgingly less ease. It poured in through the large windows of the Main Hall like golden honey, giving the autumn colored tiled floor burnished light without warmth. No fires burned in the automobile sized hearths; heating a space the size of the main hall alone would be near impossible and excessively expensive even with modern forced heat. The house was a white elephant, like many such places yet standing in the Isles, a uselessly extravagant statement of bygone wealth and self importance.

The scenery of the night before had been removed, the

boards and cloth neatly stacked in a space beside the main door. The chairs were gone, hauled away earlier to be set up again elsewhere. The rest of the front hall had been swept clean but the furniture of the drawing room was still shoved into the far corner of the space, leaving a vast empty floor between. Other things had been whisked away to their appropriate places.

Gavin viewed the house with far more distaste than sympathy. The sunlight did it no favors, exposing the flaws in the woodwork and the threadbare patches in the tapestries and drapery. Parts of the house seemed to expel warmth and sunlight like anathema, clinging to the shadows. The dining room was one such place, the heavy dark table and immovable doors countering the feeble sunlight as it tried unsuccessfully to penetrate the gloom; the many staring eyes of the dead held sway in the shadows.

Noah clearly hated that room. Gavin watched him shiver in a cold puddle of sunlight while he explained about the dinner party. The only thing worse than that room was the full sunlit view of the stained glass window at the top of the stairs. The rain of color through the scene of violent death struck Gavin as obscene. The crest and motto bothered him in ways that he could not quite explain easily. Noah spared him the walk through the *hall of the dead*, as he put it. Simply looking into the long dark corridor populated by painted men and motionless suits of armor gave him the creeps.

Once the tour was over, Gavin found that his sympathy lay with Andrew instead of the house. How anyone could turn out even partially normal growing up in that ancient monstrosity was a miracle in itself. Seeing Noah's clearly negative reaction to it made Gavin all the more determined to get him out of there. He hurried them out into the sunlight of a clear autumn day and into his rented Land Rover with the intention of driving away and never coming back.

Of course, intentions without action are lost. When Noah pointed in the direction of the village, Gavin simply turned that way. They were going to a gathering, whether he liked it or not. As it turned out, he would regret this decision later. He would regret a lot of things.

❦ ❦ ❦

No one could remember a warmer day for festival time. Wool, velvet, and heavy tweeds were wrecking havoc on the party goers, lining them up in a steady stream for pints of beer and refreshing cold sodas. Those who had no choice sweltered, and those who could stripped down to levels still considered decent. The vendors were doing a brisk business, their tents and canopies affording some respite from the broiling sun. Others just gave up the fight and lay tanning on blankets scattered about the open lawn between sales tents and staging areas.

Noah gave up his tartan within the first hour. The second hour saw him divesting himself of the hat and velvet jacket. Even with the heat, he would not have missed it for the world. The festival was colorful, noisy, and filled with motion.

There were men in kilts and all manner of tweeds and tartans. The women wore the female equivalent; long skirts of muslin with tartan sashes over their shoulder, tied in bows at the hip. Some men were dressed like knights in tunics and chain mail, demonstrating the use of hand axe and claymore. Noah felt like a kid lost in the pages of a history book come to life; a strange combination of costumed locals and short-wearing tourists creating the effect of the surreal.

They discovered Duncan judging the caber toss competition, a game of some skill as well as muscle. The contestant had to hold a large heavy log upright against the body, take a few steps, and pitch it forward so that it hopefully tipped head-over-heel some distance away from the thrower. As near as Noah could figure, you were lucky if it did not give you a hernia much less smash your toes. The competitors were a burly lot, more than half sporting a frightful amount of hair in the form of beards and ponytails.

Duncan looked official enough in his tweed jacket and kilt, the first time they had seen him in anything other than a butler's dark suit; he wore his red judge's sash proudly. Other games included shot fling, target archery, axe throwing, and foot races for the children. Seth was playing in the hurling match, running up and down the field like a deer, waving in their direction when he caught sight of them. Rose Marie and her niece paraded by with a clutch of other females on the way to the school, stopping long enough to introduce themselves.

A piping competition—bagpipes, the ubiquitous Scottish sound—was underway just across from the hurling field, and the school was hosting a choral event. The serious music and dancing was due to begin somewhat later, followed by the torchlight ceremony after dark. Some clouds were beginning to form to the west, a sign that the night might bring retribution for the too-perfect day.

To Noah's surprise several people came up to him expressing concern for his health and appreciation for his music, chatting happily as if they had known him all his life. Others walking by actually acknowledged him with silent nods and serious expressions, something that amused Gavin no end. At least Gavin refrained from calling him *Master* Noah.

All of the village shop doors were flung wide open and food and drink flowed freely from the vendor tents. There were vendors selling every imaginable object from ashtrays to tartan neckties, and other areas designated for children's activities like face painting and bead stringing.

Barry's pub was piling them in and he alternated working the pub and vendor tent with his wife and employees. When Noah and Gavin arrived at the pub's large canvas tent for some refreshments, Barry was in service. Seeing them he broke into a wide grin and waved them through the throng of revelers.

"How are you feeling? Enjoying the festival?"

"It's great," Noah said with enthusiasm. "I haven't had this much fun in a while."

Barry studied his face. "Looks like you are recovered from… what happened, except for the cut on your face. Sorry about your violin though."

Noah's face paled. "My violin?" He had not even thought about his violin with all the commotion and Gavin's surprise arrival.

"It broke when you fell. You are lucky, could have been your head I guess."

Noah felt sick. That violin had been part of him, a piece of his soul. "Is it…?"

"Smashed to bits," Gavin told him. "Sawdust."

A musician himself, Barry understood the misery in Noah's face. He shook his head at Gavin's comment. "You are a cruel man, Gavin Moore. Cruel and heartless."

"Serves him right," Gavin added. "Children who don't take care of their toys—"

"He's just mad we aren't headed back to London right now," Noah said sourly.

"Who needs London when you have Barry's special stout? Come with me to the break area and I'll fix you up. Least I could do for a fellow musician."

Barry swept them past his servers and into a back area of canvas, where a few cots and a couple of small tables and chairs were set up amid the boxes and barrels. The space was currently empty except for an older gentleman asleep on one of the cots.

"Make yourself at home and I'll be right back with some food and drink."

Noah sat down with a sigh. "Is it really smashed?"

"The violin?" Gavin replied as they sat down. "Obliterated would be more like it. You didn't look much better last night. Ready to tell me what really happened?"

Noah stared at him. Gavin stared back. Barry returned, bringing the mouth watering aroma of food, stopping their contest of wills.

"Here you go," Barry said, offering the plates. "I know you are finicky but I thought fish and chips would be fine."

Finicky? Noah thought, taking the hot plate and cold can of soda.

Gavin took a long deep drink from his glass of beer and complimented Barry on his brewing skills. The two strangers seemed very much at ease with each other, making Noah wonder what they had been discussing while he was lying unconscious the night before. The fish and chips were indeed hot and delicious.

"Who's that?" Noah asked, indicating the sleeping man with a tilt of his head.

Barry looked at the man, who rolled over with a snore. "That's old man Gillespie. He pretty much starts the day in that condition. Believe it or not he won the axe throwing competition this morning. I didn't ask if he actually hit the target or they gave him the prize to keep him away from an axe."

"I thought old man MacPhearson was the town alcoholic."

"MacPhearson? Well, he's more of a problem. He's blind as a stone and deaf as a post but he insists on driving that ancient car of his everywhere. Keeps the walkers on their toes and the fences new. He's only managed to hit one sheep, but it recovered quickly enough. Poor thing had tire tracks on its backside for a month."

Gavin almost choked on his beer, he was laughing so hard. Noah smiled and shook his head. Small town people seemed a lot more forgiving of small personal sins than the people he knew. Perhaps it was because they knew each other so well.

"I am glad you are enjoying yourselves," Barry continued on another line. "Let me tell you, I was worried sick last night. I guess I wasn't the only one. Dora was around here earlier asking if I had seen you. I'm surprised you have managed to miss her so far."

"Dora?" Noah asked curiously.

"I think she was sort of shook up about it. Kind of shook me up too, I guess. I never felt anything like that before. Still can't explain it."

"Felt what?" Gavin asked, suddenly on the scent of last

night's secret. "What are you talking about?"

Barry shook his head. "Weirdest thing. It felt like a wind rushing down the staircase behind me. Then Noah just...fell over backwards. I remember watching his head fly back and his feet actually lift off the ground. Weirdest thing. I have goose flesh just thinking about it." He shivered slightly. "Totally nuts, right?"

Neither of his companions said anything.

"Well, looks like everything is all right anyway. I'd like to thank you for the chance of playing together last night. You really are in another league."

"Maybe we can do it again sometime," Noah said with a smile. "On a real stage."

"That would be great. Well, I will leave you to eat and recover for a minute. Enjoy the rest of the day."

"Hey," Gavin called to stop him. "If we go looking for this Dora person, where can we find her?"

"She's probably working at the far end of the vendor area. Noah knows her."

"I suppose she's dressed like Flora MacDonald today," Noah commented with a grin. Flora MacDonald was a popular and well known romantic figure from Scottish history.

Barry laughed. "That would be too obvious. I think there are about a dozen Floras running around here today but Dora is not one of them. Be seeing you."

When he was gone, Gavin turned his dark gaze to Noah, who looked down at his food and resumed eating. A full thirty seconds of silence went by before Gavin reached over and pulled the plate out from under Noah's hands.

"How *did* you get that cut on your face?" he asked.

Noah sighed, wiping his fingers on a napkin. "I don't know. If I knew, I would tell you. I don't know a lot of what is going on in that house."

Gavin glowered. "This is not acceptable. You said nothing

about a physical attack."

"No one attacked me, Gavin. My God, do you think a whole room of people would have just sat there if they saw someone attack me? You worry too much."

"You don't worry enough." He shoved the plate over. "Eat. I want to find this Dora person."

Noah ate while Gavin went up front to get a second beer. The misery over his lost violin was long gone, overwritten by the curiosity of what Dora could possibly want and by the effort to keep secrets from Gavin. The first could be anything. The second was proving impossible. He could pull rank and send Gavin home, but he had the unsettling suspicion that Gavin's presence had jarred something loose, and it might be a good thing to have someone at his back he could trust.

With various possibilities bouncing around in his head, Noah finished his refreshment break and thanked Barry for his hospitality. Gavin stalking silently at his side, they went in search for Dora. And found her at a tent selling new age—which really meant ancient—charms, crystals, herbs and potions. That she considered herself a white witch should not have come as a surprise; however, her choice of costume was very enlightening.

She was blue. That is to say, half of her face and body was covered in shiny blue paint, one naked arm and shoulder marked with wide streaks of white and black. A dark, ragged-hemmed toga, partially hidden by a leather jerkin and spotted animal skin, came to her knees. A dagger of deer antler was tucked in a braided leather belt at her waist. Bits of shell, beads, and feathers adorned her plaited brown hair and heavy bangles encircled her wrists and ankles. Completing her costume, the one bare, white foot had blue painted toenails.

Noah had to grin in spite of himself at her chutzpa and the look of stunned bewilderment on Gavin's face. Dora was truly one of a kind. Not only did she have the nerve to dress like a high Celtic—or was it Pict?—warrior queen, she actually looked terrific. It seemed to suit her tall sturdy size and enormous personality.

"Boudica, my queen," Noah called to her with a wave. "You look smashing."

Dora preened at the compliment. She finished waiting on a customer and turned to them before they reached the tent. Her coworker was none other than Moira; more sedately dressed as one of the many Flora MacDonalds. Moira nodded to them and went back to assisting a young, hippy-looking couple decide what mystical treasures they should purchase.

"You're hurt!" Dora exclaimed on looking at Noah a little more closely. "They told me you were all right. I'm going to kick your brother when I see him."

"It's nothing," Noah replied to her concern. "I totally enjoyed your performance last night. Guess I ruined an otherwise great success. I'm sorry to have worried you."

She glanced at Gavin, a stranger to her, quickly sizing him up. Taking Noah by the arm, she walked him to one side. Gavin followed within easy earshot but she seemed not to notice.

"Do you have any idea of what is going on in that house?" she whispered.

Looking at her blue painted face, Noah felt his eyes widen.

Why had he not seen it before? He thought about it now and realized he had been a fool. She had watched him that entire first night at dinner, eating less than he, drinking even more. The comments about the atmosphere of the dining room the next day at lunch. The effort she had made to drag him out of his depression. It was all staring at Noah from the depth of her dark eyes. He felt his skin go numb.

"What do you mean?" he asked, hoping he had not given himself away.

She was no fool. Her eyes narrowed. "You aren't as slow as your brother," Dora said with a hiss. "Something in that house came for you last night. It knocked you flat and left that mark on your face. Do you really think you will be so lucky the next time?"

Noah stared at her. If he opened his mouth and admitted the

truth, she and Gavin would be all over him. It was already too late, Noah realized. Gavin had heard her. Noah shivered with the knowledge that everything this woman did, all of her crazy personas, all of her outlandish behaviors, even the costumes she wore, was all an act to hide the true nature of her own insidious secret. Dora had known what he was the moment they met. She was just like him; an aberration of nature.

"You saw it, didn't you?" she asked, already knowing the answer. She shivered. "I saw... Something came down those stairs. Barry said he felt it go past him. Whatever it was, it sucked the air right out of me."

Noah felt Gavin's hands catch his arms from behind. Had he swayed? A surge of energy jumped through his body at the touch and Dora released his wrist as if she too had felt it. She turned toward Gavin.

"Who are you?" she asked.

"I was just about to ask you the same thing," Gavin replied with a frown, releasing his grip on Noah. "What have you to do with any of this?"

She made an expression of annoyed irritation. "I have nothing to do with it. I'm a nosey busybody just like you. Who are you again?"

"Gavin Moore, Noah's assistant. Are you saying that you actually believe there is something unnatural in the house?" Dora looked at the two of them like they were a box of rocks. "Do you think it is Noah's mother?"

Dora seemed shocked for a second. Her blue face shifted, turning to Noah; it was difficult to read her expressions in that two-toned face. She took Noah's hand in hers.

"Is that what you think? Poor child, there is no way that Helen is in that horrible house."

"You are right, there are no such things as ghosts," Gavin said, having decided that the blue woman was just another nut. "If something odd is going on here—and no one has proven anything is going on—it has flesh and blood behind it. I won't have you going around putting these ideas into Noah's head. He has been seriously ill. He doesn't need all of you…"

"Freaks?" Dora provided sweetly.

Noah listened to them arguing, frozen inside of his body. His blood had turned to sludge, rendering him incapable of moving or feeling or thinking. He knew it was shock; shock of hearing someone else casually speaking what he feared was true, shock of finding someone like himself hiding in plain sight behind a blue-painted face. Even Gavin thought them both crazy. Perhaps they were.

The argument was ceased by the arrival of Moira, who had walked up unnoticed during the heated exchange. She placed a necklace of green corded silk holding a small silken pouch over Noah's head before turning to the combatants.

"You two are chasing off customers," she said without a hint of animosity in her voice. "Might I suggest a calming essence of herbs or perhaps a cold drink?"

Gavin and Dora both stared at her in hostility. She smiled and took Noah's hand, leading him off to the tent. The other two simply had to follow. In the cooler shade she turned to look at Noah with an appraising gaze. He had never really been that close to her before and was surprised to notice a becoming splash of freckles across the bridge of her nose. She smiled at him, a smile that was nothing like the haughty sneer of her brother, and he smiled back.

"You really should be careful in the sun," she told him, reaching for a jar on the nearest small table. "Your skin is as pale as milk. I have just the thing for that cut. It will help it heal with barely a mark."

Noah stood still while she gently applied a touch of cream to the cut on his cheek. Her touch was feather light and the cream instantly cooled his hot skin. His gaze travelled down the long white curve of her neck to the swell of her breasts just visible over the curved neckline of her blouse. Only when his eyes met hers again did he realize the effect of her touch; the same sexually mesmerizing ability that she shared with her brother.

"Thank you," he said and stepped away from her raised hand.

Her smile widened. "You are most welcome."

"I should have thought of that," Dora grumbled. "Give him some to take home, Moira."

"What is it?" Gavin asked suspiciously.

Dora sighed and rolled her eyes. "Only some ointment prepared with almond oil, honey, and healing herbs. I don't go around poisoning people, bad for business. In fact, Moira, add some of that lemon balm and lavender oil to the bag. Mr. Moore needs to learn how to relax."

Noah stifled a laugh at the look on Gavin's face. Dora reached for one of the many natural stone bracelets on display, taking one of creamy brown and white agate, which she slipped easily over Gavin's wrist. He held up his arm and looked at it.

"Good for realigning your balance center," Dora explained with a smirk. "It's on the house."

"I don't need your witch doctoring, lady."

"Oooh, I would say you needed a lion tamer. Whips and chains more your style or did you get enough of that?"

Noah watched Gavin's face blanch white as the tent. Whatever mark she hit was deep and it hurt. It made Noah realize that there were still things about Gavin that even he did not know. That Dora could hit the mark so clearly having just met Gavin said a lot about her natural insights.

"I apologize," Dora said, lowering her gaze. "I sometimes forget that words can be effective weapons. We are all what our past has made of us. It takes fire to transform the soul and sometimes the sparks leave scars."

Gavin stared at her like she was a dragon about to devour him. Noah had never seen that look on his face before. It was frightening and astonishing. Slowly it melted into an expression of silent wariness. Gavin did not remove the bracelet.

"I urge you to be very careful," Dora continued, turning again to Noah. "If you are digging into the past, things are never as far from us as they seem."

"So I am finding out," Noah mumbled.

Moira handed him the small paper bag of items. "The music and dancing are about to begin. If you get there early enough you can find a place to sit in the shade."

They walked out of the tent into the sunshine and back down the grassy path between the vendor tents and the game field. Noah glanced at his silent companion. Gavin walked along with his jacket over his shoulder, like nothing had happened, calmly looking around at the people coming and going to various tents. If Noah had not seen that reaction with his own eyes, he would never have known any difference.

They found the spot easily enough and just managed to snag a shady piece of lawn for themselves. The sound of Barry's fiddle was joined by flute and mandolin while the crowd began to arrive and the groups of costumed dancers took their places. When Gavin released a heavy sigh, Noah turned to look at him. The dark eyes did not meet his gaze, but looked out over the crowd.

"What is it about Scotland?" Gavin said wistfully. "Does the land breed this particular brand of insanity or is it just the boredom?"

Noah smiled slightly. "It's the wind and the sea," he replied, quoting what Dora had told him the night of the dinner party. "And the loneliness."

"If that's true then we are all somewhat crazy."

"Exactly."

"Hmmm." Gavin looked at the agates encircling his right wrist. "That woman…"

"Which one?"

Gavin looked at him with a totally blank expression that said he had barely noticed Moira beneath the beating he took at Dora's hands. "The blue one. You have any more friends like that

I need to know about?"

Noah smiled. Gavin was right about that; Dora *was* his friend. "There is no one else like Dora. I am sorry if she upset you. She didn't mean it. She likes you."

Gavin's eyebrows rose. "How do you know? I would hate to find out what she's like when she doesn't like you."

"So would I," Noah agreed. "She did lie to you though. That bracelet isn't for balance. Agates are for protection. She gave you an amulet against evil."

Gavin considered the bracelet for a moment and then took it off and placed it on Noah's wrist. "In that case, maybe you should wear it. I'm going for a beer. Want anything?"

Noah shook his head and watched Gavin trot over to the nearby beverage tent. He looked down at the bracelet now on his arm. He had no doubt that was what Dora intended Gavin to do with it. There was no way he would tell that to Gavin.

It was proving to be a strange and enlightening day among a gathering of strange and enlightened people. Noah looked up at the far darkening clouds and wondered what the night would bring.

FOURTEEN

Foul whisperings are abroad: unnatural deeds do breed unnatural troubles.
  —*Macbeth*, W. Shakespeare

The party was still in full swing when Gavin and Noah wandered into town with the intention of finding an evening meal at the pub. Gavin had been eating nonstop all day but insisted that he was still hungry; the endless flow of meat pies, fish and chips, sausage rolls, fruit cakes, scones, and beer had only whetted his appetite. Finding that hard to believe, Noah followed him to the pub where they were ushered in after only a short wait.

Once inside, the smell of food nauseated him and he picked at his dinner of grilled salmon while Gavin devoured a platter of roast beef and potatoes covered in gravy. They said little, the noise of the busy place not conducive to serious conversation between bouts of chewing. When Noah finally gave up the pretense of eating, Gavin sat his glass down with a thud.

"You aren't eating much. Feeling unwell?"

Noah looked grimly at the piece of bread dripping gravy that Gavin popped into this mouth. "Watching you eat that stuff isn't helping."

"This stuff is great. You do look a bit green at the edges. Too much sun?"

Maybe that was it, Noah thought. He wasn't used to the sun or the food. Gavin seemed a bottomless pit when it came to food or beer, and obviously he had gotten over whatever shock he had felt earlier. Noah felt sluggish and odd.

"I think I should probably go back to the house."

"The torch thing is just an hour or so away."

"No one will miss me. It might be raining by then anyway."

"The gods-that-be would not dare to rain on Lord Andrew's parade," Gavin said with the last swallow of his beer and then looked guiltily at Noah. "Sorry about that. Come on then. I'll take you back to the house. I really don't need to watch the village pay homage to its heathen past anyway."

"What makes you think it's the past?" Noah grumbled.

Gavin tossed down money for their dinner. "What was that?"

Noah did not elucidate. Once they were outside, Noah showed Gavin the wolf shape cut into the stone doorway of the pub and the store next door. He pointed out a few more things as they walked in the direction they had left the Range Rover. The sounds of music and laughter drifted through the air, but clouds were gathering and the breeze from the ocean would soon cool off the land. At the far hill on the edge of town the lights were on in the church.

"I need to talk to Father Perrine," Noah said with a sigh. "I should have done it earlier. Looks like he is open for business."

"He has a short candlelight service quarter past nine, after the bonfire." Gavin shrugged at Noah's expression. "I heard some ladies talking about it. I guess some of the parishioners feel the need to have a spiritual cleansing after taking part in the *heathen fire ritual.*" He shaped quotation marks for the words with his fingers.

"That gives us plenty of time to talk to him tonight. He and Dora are like Siamese twins. I'm sure he knows a lot of what goes on around here."

"The blue witch and a priest? I fear for this town, I really do."

"Remember the crucifix in father's room? Andrew seemed to think that he had been talking to Father Perrine before his death. He was at the house too, at the dinner party and the concert."

Noah stumbled and caught himself against the hood of someone's beat up Cooper. He held on for a moment as his head swam.

"You aren't talking to anybody tonight," Gavin said with a

frown. "Are you sure you are okay? We can find the doctor."

"I do feel a little odd. Maybe I'm just dehydrated. You can talk to Father Perrine, Gavin, after you leave me at the house. Take your *history* book. He might be more open to speaking with you about it than looking me in the eye."

"I'm not leaving you at the house alone."

"Don't be silly. Everyone else will be coming home in a short time. I can't get into any trouble in an hour. Besides, Rose Marie might already be there."

They were at the Rover. Leaning against its sturdy frame, Noah looked out over the ocean. He could see a flash of lightning in the distance. A chilly gust of wind touched his face and then he was looking into Gavin's dark eyes.

"It can wait," Gavin said.

He made no move to open the door or walk around the vehicle. The space between them was heavy with unspoken words.

It was not the first time that Noah had been aware of Gavin's feelings, and yet the moment would pass as all such moments had before, with neither one of them having the courage to act. Noah realized that he would have to be the one to remedy that, but now was not the time or place. He reached out and caught hold of Gavin's wrist, feeling the steady pulse quicken beneath his touch.

"I'd like you to talk to him tonight," Noah said quietly. "He will be leaving early tomorrow on a five day retreat. I know because he was talking about it at the dinner party. He was annoyed that it fell on festival week and because he had to back out of officiating at a wedding ceremony. I'm sure he knows more about my father."

"Like what?"

"Like why he locked himself in his rooms and why he might have been out on that trail the day of his death."

Gavin sighed. "You really think he will talk to me?"

"You have my permission." Noah released his hand. "More

to the point, you have Dora's."

They drove up to the house in silence. It was going to be a stormy night on the heath but the house had stood in its place for centuries, stout grey walls holding back the weather and the passage of time. The large front windows looked out upon the gathering gloom with patience. The lights burning inside did not dispel the shadows, nor did they break the stillness within. When the two men entered its walls, the house watched without emotion. Cold and resolute, the stone kept its secrets.

✤ ✤ ✤

Warm, welcoming light spilled out of the stone church on the hill, but from it Gavin felt no comfort. Had he been in Scotland for only a day? It seemed like a lifetime. He had been reluctant to leave Noah alone in the brooding silence of the empty house, but there was no arguing with him when he was in that mood. So there he was, walking up the long winding steps to the church while the sound of the crashing sea mingled with his footsteps.

The old oak door groaned when Gavin pushed it open and went inside. It was smaller inside than he had expected, a space of darkened flooring and heavy overhead timbers. A narrow aisle between two rows of wooden church pews led to an altar carved from a huge block of stone, the same dark grey stone that colored the hills around the town. Narrow stained-glass windows were dark in the fading exterior light.

"Good evening," said a voice to Gavin's right, the sound amplified somewhat in the acoustical emptiness. "May I help you?"

Father Perrine was much younger than Gavin had expected, probably in his mid-thirties. His dark hair was slightly longish and one unruly lock curled across his smooth forehead, making him habitually raise his right hand to brush it back. His black cassock accentuated his slimness and youth at the same time it gave him the air of authority he required for his position.

"Good evening, Father," Gavin said respectfully. "I hope to borrow a moment of your time. My name is Gavin Moore. I arrived at the Hall last night."

"Ah," the man said, nodding with a slight smile. "You are Mr. Bainbridge's manager. I did not see you come in but I certainly heard you." Gavin pressed his mouth into a grim line. "I believe I glimpsed you both at the festival earlier in the day. I certainly hope Noah is recovered sufficiently?"

"He is recovering," Gavin said, shaking and releasing the man's hand. "Noah is the reason I came to see you. We spoke with Dora earlier today. She has some pretty wild ideas about the house and what she thinks might be going on. I'm afraid that Noah might be having similar ideas."

A barely perceptible glimmer flickered across the priest's dark eyes. "You have spoken to Dora? She can be a little...extreme. I assure you, she has only the best of intentions."

"If Noah is really in danger in that house, I need to know where the danger is coming from. You are probably aware that Noah has been gone from the Hall since his mother died. That has been hard enough for him over the years and then, out of the blue, his father dies under mysterious circumstances and crazy things start happening."

"Crazy things?"

Gavin hesitated for a moment, unsure how to leap into the explanations with a stranger. "Noah never knew that he was related to the Bainbridge family by blood. He had believed himself a stepson all these years. When he found out otherwise, the news devastated him. I cannot begin to explain to you how that must have felt. He grew up alone and unwanted by his own family."

Father Perrine directed them to a pew, slowly nodding his head. "I understand how traumatic that must have been. I was shocked to see him after all this time."

"Did you know that James changed his will?" Gavin inquired, sitting down. "Some months before he died he changed the will to include Noah. He added an incredible clause telling Noah to stay away if he wanted to inherit anything."

"And yet he came back," Perrine said softly.

"Yes, he came back. Part of him is still in that house, locked away from his memory. He will do anything to find the truth, even put himself in harm's way."

"He did collapse at the concert," the priest agreed. "And he fainted here, in the churchyard the other day. Do you think that maybe he is…? Maybe the house and his memory loss are playing tricks on his mind. He does seem fragile."

Gavin lifted his eyebrows at the priest's description of Noah. Stubborn, mule headed, but fragile?

"Noah *was* diagnosed with acute mental exhaustion just before he came here."

"Well, there you are. The death of his father has been hard for him to take. That rambling old house must be full of shadows from his childhood around every corner. If he was suffering from a breakdown before he arrived, then perhaps the Hall was not a good choice for his convalescence."

"Too late now. A team of wild horses could not drag him out of there."

"In that case maybe it is a good thing you are here. You can watch over him and you are not a local, caught up in the history and drama of this place."

"I'd like nothing better than to drag him out of here but he refuses to leave. He needs to know the truth. I'm *asking* you in confidence what you know about Noah's father. Did Lord James confide in you during those final days? You are not bound by the rules of confession if the man is dead."

"That is where you are wrong," Perrine said sadly. "Confession and redemption does not stop at the grave."

"Noah seems to think he came to you for help. Help for what? Saving his soul? Saving his sons? You couldn't help him, could you?"

The priest sighed and fingered his rosary. "Men sometimes regret things they have done. Lord Bainbridge had been a haunted, isolated man for all the years I knew him. He never once set foot in this church, but in the last few months before his death he had turned to religion to ease his conscience. I met with him on several occasions, always in secret. He seemed to be… losing his grip on reality."

"In what way?"

"He imagined all sorts of things. He thought there was something…unnatural in the house but he refused to allow me to even do a blessing. He said he heard voices, saw things. He talked incessantly about a curse and about absolution he could never hope for. He was becoming more and more paranoid. I understand that in the final days he locked himself in his rooms and rarely went out."

"Yes, I have seen that room. Was that what Noah's father believed, that the family curse was coming after Noah?"

"It doesn't matter if he believed it. Family curses…they are just myths."

Gavin shook his head. "You might not say that if you saw the documentation I have seen. First sons always inherited but second or third sons seem never to make out so well. They died young, in fact, every one of them through the generations."

"Is that true?" Father Perrine asked in surprise.

"Written records in black and white," Gavin said, sitting with his hand on the folder he had brought but had yet to open. "Consumption, falls, deaths in infancy, death by accident, cut down on the battlefield, and so on. Did you know that the last Lord Bainbridge had a young brother who died in his infancy?"

The priest said nothing but his eyes gave him away. He knew much more than he was sharing.

"And another thing that is driving me crazy," Gavin continued. "Wolves. There are wolves everywhere. Had you not noticed? The family crest is a scene of wolves. Here in the village there are carvings of wolves on almost every building. Why wolves? I should think a wolf symbol in the middle of sheep country kind of strange."

"It's an ancient symbol of power. The village and the land it sits on were once owned by the Bainbridge family. They built this church and paid for the school."

As Gavin sat there looking at the symbol of the living tree carved into the church altar he suddenly remembered where he had seen it before. It was so different yet so obvious. The parishioners had probably been staring at it for centuries and never understood the significance. He pulled out the copy of the family crest from the folder he had brought and put it down on the bench between them.

"Take a good look at this Father. Does it seem familiar to you?"

Father Perrine looked at the color copy of the crest in all its bloody glory. He cringed at the violence it contained and shook his head.

"I have seen it at the house of course. I don't know what else you mean."

Gavin held it up so that the priest could see the drawing and the altar carving simultaneously. With his other hand he indicated what he wanted the priest to notice. The long curving lines of the stag became the naked branches of the tree, the stag's body its twisted trunk. The tearing wolves became the jutting rocks below, each reaching up toward the solid branching tree. To compare them side by side made the stylization obvious and the intent more sinister.

With some amount of satisfaction, Gavin watched realization and horror move across the priest's features. The man's eyes widened, tracking from the paper to the altar and back again.

"This is wicked, a purely wicked intention!"

Gavin shrugged. "You said it yourself. They owned the village and they built the church. Even they had the sense to know they could hardly put that gory crest on a sacred building so they… improvised something a bit tamer. It was their little secret. Every time they saw it they had a secret laugh at the town's expense. The significance was probably lost with time."

"So you are telling me that you think the Bainbridge family is what? Cursed? Followers of some heretical religion? Genetically predisposed to insanity?"

"I don't know what I'm saying," Gavin said in frustration, running his fingers through his hair. "None of this makes any sense but one thing still bothers me—Andrew. They had not spoken for years yet he is the one who asked Noah to come back. He has volunteered no information and still dodges Noah's direct questions. And he seems to resent my presence."

"Well, that couldn't be because you arrived with preconceived ideas and confrontation on your mind, could it? Andrew has big shoes to fill. You show up unannounced and proceed to tell him that he does not know how to take care of his brother. Even someone whose name is not Bainbridge might resent that."

"I see your point," Gavin admitted guiltily.

Father Perrine sat back, watching Gavin put the drawing away.

"You strike me as someone who believes in facts, not wild theories. Do not allow ancient history to delude your thinking. You cannot really believe there is a family curse so something else must be worrying you. Are you hinting that you believe Lord James's death was unnatural in some way?"

There it was, finally out in the open. *Murder.* Gavin still could not say it out loud even though he was certain that Noah thought it as well. The man died of a stroke. There was no way to prove it anything else. So why did that nagging doubt linger with such force? The time to kill the man surely would have been before he altered his will. Even then there was only one person who had a reason. What if the reason had nothing to do with the money? What else was there? The recently exposed family secret?

"You don't believe Andrew…"

"Is capable of murdering his father?" Perrine shook his head. "He had no reason in any case. The day to day running of the Estate was already in his hands, or rather Duncan's. Andrew handled a great deal of the Lord's business ventures and had plenty of his own money. While they did not necessarily get along, they harbored no visible animosity toward each other. Lord Bainbridge did not necessarily strike anyone as even remotely friendly. He was a complex man, not always easy to deal with, but no one wished him dead."

"I wonder. Maybe I am just paranoid and maybe this really has nothing to do with anyone other than Noah." Gavin sighed, rising to his feet. "Thank you for your time, Father. I still have quite a bit to work through it seems. You are right about the history of this place. It seizes you the moment you set foot on the ground and breathe the rarified air."

The priest also got to his feet. "We are talking about centuries of a land and people that are mostly unchanged from those ancient days. In the bright light of day the tourists see what they want to see, but at night the villagers still huddle around their fires, connected to their ancestors by the flickering flames."

Gavin shivered at the priest's words and the dark warning he thought he could see in the man's eyes. Outside darkness had come. Thunder rumbled across the sea. Along the hillside at the other end of the village Gavin could see the line of torches snaking along through the blackness like a serpent of fire. Somewhere along that burning path the new Laird was presiding over a tradition centuries old while the modern world lay forgotten in silence.

In that Gavin also found no comfort.

The house was so quiet that Noah could hear the thunder even though it was a long way off. He had been lying on the sofa in the drawing room with the two main chandeliers blazing into the darkness and his tartan draped over his body like a blanket. The house was cold but not unbearable, still retaining some heat from the day's sunlight. Once everyone was back for the night, fires would be rekindled, hot tea poured, and tales recounted.

No one had been there when they arrived, at least no one that answered their calls. In a house the size of the Hall one could never be sure. Trudging upstairs had seemed like too much of a hassle since his legs felt like lead and his head was not much better. Noah suspected too much sun as the culprit, his forehead hot to the touch. Feverish, that must be why he felt so odd.

After he finally had Gavin out the door, Noah lay down with the intention of staying put until the others arrived. That was some time ago and now he was thirsty. Still he did not get up until he heard a sound in the direction of the study or the kitchen beyond. He sat up and peered down the dark part of the hallway, expecting to see a light pop on somewhere in the blackness. None did.

"Anyone there?" he called out.

Nothing. No one. He tossed off the tartan. Another sound pricked his ears, making his hair stand on end. He got up and walked to the edge of the dining room, holding on to the wall as he swayed about unsteadily. The strange lightheadedness made sparks of light behind his eyes for a moment. He felt the unnatural coldness of the room reach out. Then he saw only darkness.

When Noah opened his eyes the odd sparks of light were still there. He blinked, trying to get them to go away, wondering why his mouth felt like it was filled with cotton. Slowly it seeped into his brain that he was lying on his back and unable to move. Above his field of vision were the glass eyes of the animal heads looking down at him as he lay on the dining room table. Their dead eyes reflected the sparks of light that moved with eerie slowness across the shadowy ceiling.

Noah felt his eyes widen in disbelief. It was mist he was seeing, or rather some dimly illuminated thing that looked like mist, gathering and floating in the darkness. A wave of dizziness washed over him when again he tried to move and could not. His hands were bound across his waist and he could neither lift them nor roll over. The cloth gagging his mouth was equally tight.

Cold numbing fear shot through his veins, temporarily heightening his awareness. The weight of the atmosphere pressed down on him like a living thing, gaining strength with each passing moment. Noah tried to free himself, managing only to bang his head painfully and quickly lose his breath. Whatever was gathering above him was pulling his energy away to use for itself, draining him like a battery. The ropes were a guarantee that he would not get away this time.

Shaking with fear and the knowledge that what he was seeing was real, Noah watched the forms taking shape. There was nothing he could do to physically escape. He could feel his heart pounding in terror. Whoever had placed him there, in the room of his nightmares, certainly intended to kill him.

Noah closed his eyes, choosing not to see the form of his destroyer or give it more power over his fear. He concentrated all of his ability on strengthening his psychic shield, the only thing he could do to defend himself against such unnatural forces. He didn't have the energy to do it for long. Whether he would be alive or dead by the time Gavin returned was anybody's guess.

❧ ❧ ❧

Gavin considered it odd that the house was dark when he pulled up to park. The main hall had been blazing with light when he had left Noah downstairs not thirty or forty minutes earlier. He got out and slammed the car door. Lightning flashed in the distance and nearby trees were beginning to sway in the wind. They were far out in the country; perhaps the power had gone out. He walked into the main hall and stopped just inside the doorway. It was so dark he could barely see the edge of the staircase.

Had Noah fallen asleep? Surely he would have left a candle burning.

"Noah? Where are you?" he called.

When he got no reply, he began to worry. The bonfire lighting was still going on; apparently no one had come home yet. What was that sound, low and eerie, interspersed with thumps? Gavin turned to the left, toward the sound he could hear faintly. He should have known something was wrong when he had to push open the heavy oaken doors of the dining room, doors supposedly too old and heavy to close. Gavin stood transfixed in the doorway, almost unable to believe his eyes.

Like the rest of the house, the room was pitch black...or it should have been. Instead there was dim flickering light. That feeble light was coming from an eerily luminescent mist, floating and curling in the frigid air like wisps of smoke or fog. The strange mists were alive, dancing and diving and circling around something below them on the long table.

As his gaze fell upon what it was that lay there, Gavin felt his breath catch in his throat and his hair stand on end. It took him a full four seconds of shock before he could get his legs to move and then it was only the sound, a low eerie exhale of terror that galvanized him into action.

Unaware that the gathering mists had reacted to his intrusion with momentary dimming, Gavin raced up the length of the table to where Noah lay on his back in the center of the room of horror. Trying at first to pull him off the surface, it took Gavin another moment to realize that Noah was bound hand and foot, tied to the table in such a way that he could not have rolled off or freed himself. The earlier thumping noises had been the sounds of Noah's head and heels banging off the table top as he fought uselessly against the ropes that held him prisoner.

The...*things* circling his prone body were gathering strength.

Gavin launched himself at the taut rope holding the sacrifice to the table. That word leapt into his head without hesitation, for *sacrifice* was what it looked like to him. The room was freezing cold. He could see his breath as his cold fingers worked the knot in a frenzy of terror.

One of the smoky, luminescent tendrils moved up over Noah's motionless body, hovering not more than two inches above his chest. When the rope released in his hand, Gavin reached out and grabbed the fabric of Noah's shirt, yanking him over to the edge of the table. The mist swirled away at his movement, diffusing into the darkness once more.

Gavin slid his hands beneath the unmoving body and lifted Noah off the table into his arms. Once he had passed the end of the dining table, he noticed that the heavy oak door had closed behind him. The growing atmosphere of the house was becoming too strong. Hoping he could get the both of them out of the house without serious injury, Gavin aimed for the French doors.

Balancing the unconscious man in his arms, Gavin reached one hand out to shove back the bolt on one of the doors. He yanked it open with a vicious twist of his hand and sent it crashing against the wall with a kick of his foot. The cool, dark breeze of the outside garden filled his lungs and chilled the sweat on his face.

Gavin carried Noah away from the terror of the house, not stopping until they were well away from the glass doors of the dining room, out near the rose garden at the edge of the green topiary maze. There, safe among the sheltering branches, he dropped to his knees in the grass. He eased Noah from his shaking embrace down onto the lawn before collapsing himself, onto his back, where he lay for a long moment sucking in his breath.

The night sky was filled with fringes of lightning, running jagged fingers into the black clouds overhead. He almost could not believe what he had seen with his own eyes in that room just now. Almost. When Gavin had himself under some amount of control again, he sat up and looked over at the silent reason for all his terror.

Noah was staring up at him with eyes so huge that they looked like twin moons over the gag covering his mouth. How much had he been aware of before he had passed out from the sheer terror? Why did Noah have to look at him like that?

With a groan and a curse muttered beneath his breath, Gavin reached out and pulled the victim over into his embrace. He set his fingers to working the gag loose. It finally released and he carefully removed it and tossed it aside. Trying not to look into that beautiful, scared face, Gavin turned his attention to the ropes knotted around Noah's cold wrists.

Someone had wanted to make sure his escape would not be

easy, the soft cord twisted and knotted with devilish skill. Noah had not moved or spoken a word, leaning against the hollow of Gavin's shoulder, sheltered in the crook of his arm. Once the hands were free, Gavin made the mistake of looking into Noah's face. The long silver hair was draped over his cheek and his eyes were like mirrors, reflecting Gavin's emotion.

Unable to stop himself, Gavin lowered his head the few inches required to touch his mouth to Noah's silent, trembling lips. That single unguarded second in time left no doubt that Noah was still in a state of confusion. For a brief moment, those trembling lips clung to him, Noah's cold shivering body melded into Gavin's embrace. Then fear and life and coherent thought returned to frozen limbs and Noah pushed him away, rolling out of Gavin's grasp.

For another moment they regarded each other in that screaming silence. Gavin remained where he was sitting, Noah where he had rolled a few feet away, lying on his stomach with his feet still bound at the ankles. Propped on his elbows, the same look of confusion filled his eyes. Maybe that alone would be enough to let Gavin escape the moment unscathed.

Noah's lips still tingled from the kiss. His thoughts did not seem to work properly, crashing about in his skull like drunken fireflies. His wrists hurt and even though the air of the garden was still fairly warm for so late, his skin felt almost frozen, his entire body shivering with uncontrollable tremors. They were outside in the dark, nothing else around them but the scent of the fading rose bushes and the sound of their heavy breathing.

Had it been real and not a dream?

One look at Gavin told Noah everything he needed to know, even if he had been prepared to ignore the ropes, still tight around his ankles. Gavin sat with his legs sprawled out before him, leaning back on his arms. His face was as open as his position; stunned disbelief warring with several other more subtle emotions. There was no other reason for Gavin to have dragged him out of that room and carried him that far from the house.

"You saw them," Noah said with a croak, finally breaking the silence that sat between them like a wall of denial. "They were real."

Gavin's response was to lie down, flat on his back in the grass. Noah rolled up where he could get at the ropes around his legs, taking a minute or two to free himself completely. That accomplished, he crossed his legs beneath him and sat looking back at the dark shadow of the house behind them. What had just happened?

"He tried to kill you," Gavin said in a flat voice; not the first time Gavin seemed to know what he was thinking.

Noah looked back at his rescuer. Gavin was sitting up again, also staring down at the dark empty house. No, that was incorrect—not *empty*.

"That is not possible."

Gavin shook his head. "Who else do you bloody well think did it? He is Laird of the estate. Nothing goes on here without his approval and *direction*. It wasn't an accident that you were brought here after all this time. It wasn't an accident that something attacked you last night. It isn't an accident what happened just now. Unless you conjured up those…*things* yourself, from what God forbidden hell, I don't know!"

Noah refused to believe that his brother could be responsible. He clung desperately to his own interpretations of events. "You are wrong. He would never… Andrew would never hurt me."

Gavin let out a heavy frustrated sigh. "Maybe not. Maybe what he has in mind is a whole lot worse than simply murdering you."

Noah jumped to his feet, a mistake since whatever had dulled his senses seemed to be lingering in his muscles as well. He staggered, dropping to his hands and knees. Gavin was beside him in an instant, pulling him to his feet, wrapping warm solid arms around him to hold him up. In a moment of weakness Noah sagged against that strength, so exhausted that he felt he might just lie down where he was and fade into the earth.

Gavin ruined the moment by shaking him. "Do you need a doctor?"

Noah shoved at the solid chest with his elbow and Gavin released him instantly. He wobbled only slightly, turning around to aim his uncooperative feet down the path back to the house. There were lights on again, but somehow that did not make it look any more inviting. Closer now, the thunder rumbled.

"Don't tell me you are going back in there?" Gavin asked with disbelief.

"Where else would I go?" Noah replied.

Gavin caught up with him, stopping him with a hand on his arm. Noah did not turn around but stood there silently. His long hair moved in a cold gust of wind.

"You should go to the police," Gavin said quietly.

In answer Noah merely looked up at Gavin in silence.

Noah did not have to explain that no policeman would believe their story, even with rope marks to back them up and those were already fading away. Noah had a history of psychological instability and it was a given that everyone concerned would have an alibi were there any question. Other than that, Noah had to find out on his own what was really going on within the walls of Bainbridge Hall, and he was not going to leave until he found out, however dangerous or ugly the bitter truth might be.

With that silent steely resolve sitting between them, Gavin moved his hand and watched the slender, silver-haired figure walk alone, straight back into the den of wolves. He really had no choice in the matter. There was simply no way now that Gavin would leave Noah to face that unknown evil alone. After a few moments of arguing with himself over how it might play out, he followed, quietly cursing every step of the way.

FIFTEEN

Whatever our souls are made of, his and mine are of the same.
   —Wuthering Heights

The miracle of the lights was Rose Marie, returning to find the house black as pitch and twice as cold. She had promptly dumped her packages at the door and gone through the lower floor turning on lights one room after another. Noah and Gavin gave her a fright coming in the kitchen doorway, but she recovered enough to berate them for leaving her in the dark before she went to recover her things. They silently walked to the dining room only to find it dark and unprepossessing with no sign of ropes, damaged doors, or lingering mist.

Noah gathered his belongings from the drawing room and disappeared upstairs while Gavin helped Rose Marie with her things. She prepared tea and chatted about the day while he made up a fire to warm her quarters at the back of the house. The festivities had been a qualified success, owing in part to the unusual sunny autumn day. Once the tea was ready, she sent him upstairs with a tray to share with Noah. Reaching the top of the landing, Gavin heard Andrew and Duncan coming in the front door.

When Gavin entered the bedroom, Noah looked up from the kindling he was trying to light in the dark fireplace. Noah had showered and changed; his blond hair was damp and his feet bare. Noah's hand shook so hard that it took three matches to get the fire started, its feeble, flickering flame taking to the wood with a promise of much desired warmth. Gavin placed the tea tray on the table and sat down.

"Where are your slippers?"

"I won't need them in a minute," Noah replied, rising from his crouch before the fire.

Gavin's face was devoid of emotion as he poured the tea, as blank with shock as Noah felt. Noah settled down in the opposite stuffed chair. He shook his head at the offered cup; his hands were shaking too badly. Gavin sat the cup down and then leaned back in his chair without a cup of his own.

They watched the fire crackle and grow instead of looking at each other. The silence expanded until it threatened to swallow them up like a giant black hole. When a crack of thunder rumbled nearby, the uncomfortable paralysis was broken, but not the difficult moment.

"Do you think I am crazy now?" Noah asked quietly.

"Yes," Gavin sighed, "but then you wouldn't be the only one. Drink your tea. It will make me feel better."

Noah obliged with hands somewhat less shaky. The strange disembodied feeling was slowly fading away beneath the comforting warmth of the fire. He had no idea where to start explaining things to Gavin, but he knew he had to make an effort. Something... *someone* had indeed tried to kill him for the second time in as many nights. With a chill he thought about what might have happened if Gavin had not been there in time.

"Are you all right?" Gavin asked, seeing him shiver. "Try to eat something."

Noah shook his head. Food was not what he needed. Thinking perhaps that he required more time to recover, Gavin volunteered to speak first. Normal conversation seemed too much to ask, but any semblance of normality would help erase the horror they both clearly felt from what had just occurred.

Gavin told Noah about the conversation with Father Perrine, about the stylized form of the family crest on the church altar, and about seeing the torches snaking down the hillside in the darkness.

"And then I come back to the house and find you offered up like a sacrifice in that room of horrors."

Noah sat down his empty cup. "I will admit that ropes do not tie themselves."

Gavin's eyebrows shot up. "You are willing to at least entertain the idea that someone wanted to kill you?"

Noah sighed. "Only if you are willing to give Andrew the benefit of the doubt."

Gavin glowered at him. "Doubt? I doubt everything I have seen and heard since I got here. I doubt my own sanity. I doubt anything you have to tell me is going to change the terror I felt downstairs." He sighed at the hard expression in Noah's eyes. "But I do not doubt your loyalty to this brother you hardly know. I do not understand it, but I do not doubt it. At this point, it is the only reason that I can see for you to remain in this house."

Noah was too tired to hold on to the quick flash of anger that fled of its own accord at the last of Gavin's words.

"There are some things I need to show you, Gavin. Try not to explode once you see them, all right?" The dark eyes grew wider, filled with worry and dread. "Your report talked about a family curse and just now you said that Father Perrine mentioned James thought the same thing. What if there really is a curse? I think that may be what killed him."

Noah got to his feet and recovered the thin parchment pages he had hidden in one of his books. He unfolded the crackling sheets and handed them to Gavin without a word of explanation; they spoke volumes on their own. He then went to the wardrobe and took the torn tartan jacket from its hiding place and held it in his hands while Gavin looked at the rubbings and read the odd poem with growing anxiety.

"I lied to you about last night," Noah stated with a slight touch of guilt. "It wasn't a faint from overexertion. I didn't have a spell either. Neither did anyone attack me. Any *one*."

Gavin looked up. Noah held the coat in his hands with the rents clearly visible. Gavin had seen them last night without taking the time to understand what they meant; they were the tangible visible signs that Noah had truly been attacked by something. Noah handed him the coat. Gavin stared into the unblinking blue eyes, clouded with exhaustion, and something in his heart cracked.

"Whatever is in this house, I know it isn't *human*," Noah admitted slowly.

Gavin sighed. "I know you can't accept the fact that Andrew—"

"It isn't Andrew!" Noah exclaimed with irritated annoyance. "Would you shut up and listen to me for five minutes? Did you look at that poem, at those rubbings?"

"Yes, I did. *The youngest forfeit life to give, in order that the Clan shall live.* That is a clear enough threat to me that your life is in danger. Why the hell don't you see that?"

Noah groaned. "I admit my life might be in danger. I am worried *Andrew's* life might be in danger. Don't you understand? Nothing *human* killed my father. Nothing human attacked me last night. I *saw* it, Gavin. I *saw* it that night on stage when my father died. I saw it last night when its *claws* cut into my jacket and left a bruise on my chest. It was a *wolf*, Gavin. It came down the stairs like part of that horrible window had come to life, leaping over Barry's shoulder and *straight at me*. I barely had time to raise my arms to protect myself. It hit me *like a living thing* with weight and power. It was the same thing I saw confronting my father on that pathway where he died. *It was something in the form of a wolf.*"

Gavin stared at Noah, at the cut on his face and the spark of terror in his eyes. He looked back down at the black shadowy figures of wolves on the papers in his hands. Wolves on the family crest prominently displayed all around the house and on every building in the village, including the hapless church. Wolves everywhere but in the one place where the eyes of the trophy dead had looked down upon the intended sacrifice; not a single wolf head or wolf skin among the hunter's prey. Was that perhaps because the wolves walked among the living?

"The Cursed Path," Gavin muttered. "That is what the name Bainbridge used to mean in the old tongue. Where did you find this poem?"

"Stuffed in a book in the study along with the rubbings. I

have no idea why they were there or even where they came from. I have been unable to find anything that resembles the rubs, either in the house or on the grounds. Father was looking into such things before he died. They could be his."

A knock at the door was almost lost in a loud rumble of thunder and they both jumped with surprise. The storm would soon be upon them in full fury, the price paid for too fine a day. Gavin quickly folded the papers and stuck them beneath the jacket on the floor at his feet.

Noah went to the door. It was Andrew and Noah stepped back without a pause to allow him into the room. He came in, hesitating only slightly when he saw Gavin. He smiled, and Gavin smiled back with what he hoped did not come across as a smirk of condescension.

"I see you are both settled in for the evening," Andrew said, stopping at the edge of the sitting area. "Not a bad idea after a long day with a storm in the offing."

"Your torch ceremony looked rather splendid winding its way down the hill in the dark," Gavin complemented.

"Yes, it went rather well. The best day for a festival we have had in years. I hope you enjoyed yourself?"

"Oh yes," Gavin said drily. "I will truly never forget it. It seems almost a shame that we will be leaving tomorrow."

Andrew's countenance fell. Noah managed to keep the shock and anger off of his face as his brother turned toward him.

"We were just discussing the matter," he muttered.

"I do apologize, Noah," Andrew stated with a sorrowful voice. "I'm afraid I have been rather a terrible host. After what happened last night I should have arranged to spend more time with you, see to your needs, and instead I left you to your own devices. I am a poor excuse for a brother and I am sorry."

"It's all right, Drew. The village expects a lot of you."

"Yes, so they do, but that is not an excuse, is it? I mean, spending the day with your *assistant* is hardly the same as spending it with your family."

"Now see here," Gavin sputtered, getting to his feet.

"You got too much sun today," Andrew continued, ignoring Gavin's presence. "Are you all right? Your illness seems much more pronounced than I was led to believe."

"Maybe it's this house that is making it worse," Gavin interjected, much to Noah's irritation.

"The house?" Andrew looked puzzled. "I know we are a bit backwards here in the country but I thought you were getting along all right. Maybe in hindsight I should have engaged a nurse for the duration of your visit or at least added a few more staff."

"It's fine Andrew. I will be fine. We will talk in the morning."

"Very well. You should take your tea and get some sleep, although that might be difficult until the storm has passed. Good night, brother."

"Good night. And I did enjoy the festival today, very much."

"I am glad. Well, then we will sort it out in the morning. Good night."

Noah had barely closed the door when he turned on Gavin, eyes bright with anger. Outside a crash of thunder shook the window and the lights flickered ominously.

"I told you I am not leaving," he said quietly through clenched teeth. "And if anyone is going to speak to Andrew about this it will be me."

"Then you had best get to speaking because I am not going to sit by and allow someone or something to murder you while he stands around insulting me."

That set off the fight that had been brewing all day. They kept their voices in raised whispers as they argued; a testament to the shared awareness of their situation. It was a strange argument, about the problem at hand…and other things. Gavin found it amazing that Noah would argue at all considering someone had tried to murder him, yet understanding why he refused to listen. Outside the violent storm roared its rage where their voices could not.

The lights finally went out, leaving the room lit only by flickering firelight. Unlike other of their disagreements, this time neither one of them was backing down; it was too important. They stood face to face, hands clenched in fists, lungs heaving through a rumble of thunder.

Noah looked more alive than he had since Gavin arrived, his cheeks tinged with anger and his eyes flashing in the dim light. Staring down into his stubborn, beautiful face, Gavin was more afraid than he had ever been in his entire life. He could knock some sense in that stubborn silver head, but short of tying Noah up again and physically hauling him off, there was no other way to get him to agree to leave.

While that might be momentarily gratifying it would accomplish nothing. The glinting blue eyes and upward tilted chin were daring him to try it. They were daring other things too.

"Noah, you are the most—"

"I can't leave, Gavin."

With a groan of desire long held in check, Gavin reached out and caught Noah's arms, pulling him the few inches needed to touch that angry, trembling mouth. To his shock, Noah answered his desire with a low moan of passion that set Gavin's blood racing through his veins.

Noah allowed Gavin's desire to roar into him with that one kiss. He needed the blind, sweeping passion that poured out of Gavin like rain; it could take him out of the horrors of the house, if only for that moment. Their mouths devoured one another, a wild clashing of teeth and lips and tongue. He had no idea where the desperate need came from but he was willing to give himself to it without question.

After only a moment of such dangerous emotion, Gavin put some space between them. He lifted his head long enough to breathe, long enough to push himself away from the hands sliding across his back. A flash of lightning lit the room and then a crash of thunder rumbled through the house. In that eerie blue light, Noah's eyes met his with unflinching awareness.

"Are you sure this is what you want?" Gavin asked in a ragged whisper.

Noah's mouth curled up at the corners. "Don't take this the wrong way, Gav, but...you're fired."

Gavin blinked, not exactly sure what that meant. He couldn't think straight. "I'm sorry, Noah. I sort of forced my way in where I'm not wanted. Just tell me what—"

Noah's reply was to find Gavin's mouth and shut him up. Gavin's confusion lasted only a second or two before his arms rose to lock them together and his breath came out in a sigh against Noah's lips.

Emboldened by desire, Noah allowed his hand to travel over Gavin's flat stomach and down across one hard hipbone, to brush Gavin's erection through the front of his trousers. Gavin moaned into Noah's mouth. The very sound made Noah shiver with anticipation. When he slid his fingers up beneath Gavin's shirt, Gavin reached to assist him with removing the barrier of cloth.

Gavin gasped when Noah's tongue slid warm and wet across his collar bone. He grabbed a handful of the long hair and pulled Noah's head up, taking his sweet hot mouth with passion. Gavin had been prepared to endure his love for Noah from afar. He had only dreamed how it would feel to hold Noah in his arms at last, the soft skin and lithe muscles pressing against him. The thought that Noah might be able to return his love was almost too much to bear.

No hesitation this time. The kissing had a life of its own, melding of flesh and breath and need. Sweat sprang out on their skin, the building heat erupting between them like a volcano. Noah's thin shirt came off over his head. Gavin's hands moved to take its place, his fingers splaying around the hard, slender ribcage, feeling every rib.

This time when Noah's hands went to Gavin's belt, he moaned his permission, his lips sliding from Noah's hot mouth to the curve of his neck and shoulder. Gavin's fingers found one small erect nipple and the flick of his thumb was rewarded by a gasp and a shudder. Gavin smiled when Noah's hands cupped the curve of his butt.

The bed seemed an impossible distance to cover, but they groped their way without letting go of each other. It took only a moment for them to be naked in each other's arms. Noah was quickly lost in Gavin's desire, unable to think, able only to soak up the sensations of his body and answer Gavin's passion with a wild desire that had startled him only a few minutes ago.

It was wonderful; the length of naked skin touching his, Gavin's hot devouring mouth and warm strong hands. Noah gasped when one hand slid down between their bodies to encircle the head of his penis with a gentle squeeze. The very action of Gavin touching him like that made Noah suck in his breath; his entire body tingled with pleasure, very near coming.

Noah really had no idea what to expect. His sexual experience was limited to a collection of memories of young fumbling hands in dark school closets and kisses stolen behind bookshelves. When he got older he was just too busy and by then the offered sexual advances had taken on another meaning. Once Gavin had arrived on the scene, the possibility had occurred to him, but knowing Gavin's definitions of professional boundaries and his own daily terrors, he had simply been too afraid.

Gavin's hands moved with delicate torture across Noah's body, soft and hard, teasing and exploring, driving him insane with pleasure. It was so different from Seth's drugging touch. Noah moaned, the coiling pleasure of his body rising to answer the pressure of Gavin's lips and tongue and hands. No matter what came next he would always have this night of passion, locked in his heart forever.

Gavin wound his way down the enticing length of skin and let his hot tongue tease the secret places his fingers had brushed. Noah arched his back and moaned, twisting the sheets in his passion, his lithe slender body taut as a bow string. Gavin loved the way Noah moaned his need, the way he gave himself over completely to his desire. Gavin lifted his head for a moment, meeting Noah's electric blue gaze.

"I love you," Noah panted, reaching to slide his fingers into Gavin's dark hair.

Gavin again lowered his mouth over Noah's erection and swallowed, pressing with lips and tongue. It was too fast and too much for Noah to take. He came with a gasp of breath, his body arching beneath Gavin's hands, pouring his energy into Gavin in waves. When Noah was trembling and panting with his release, Gavin slid up the length of his body, taking his lover in his arms.

Noah wrapped his sweat slicked limbs around Gavin's hot body. Gavin was trembling in his embrace, melting against him, his erection pushing against the hollow of Noah's hipbone. He reached down and took the silken hardness in his fingers. Gavin let his breath out in a moan and thrust his hips forward, sliding his erection against the palm of Noah's hand.

Noah felt the wave of Gavin's sexual release. He clutched Gavin's shaking body against his, fingers tight around the pulsing smoothness, his legs locked around Gavin's legs. His lover's weight on top of him was nothing, part of his own flesh, light as the feeling that almost burst Noah's heart.

"I love you," Noah said again, taking Gavin's panting mouth with his own.

The sound of the storm was passing into the distance, taking along with it their wild energy, the passion spent. Gavin's hand rose to stroke Noah's silken hair, shifting their bodies so they lay side by side, arms and legs entwined. The silence of the house began to settle down around them. It was late and they were exhausted by a long day and so much emotion.

Noah curled into the warmth of his lover's body. Gavin's solid chest and strong thighs seemed familiar, as if they had always been together, naked and entwined in an intimate embrace. He ran his fingertips along the smooth breastbone and Gavin caught his hand and brought it up to his lips. The touch of soft tongue and hard teeth made Noah shiver with desire.

Gavin placed Noah's captured hand over his heart and held it there. "You've known all this time," he said quietly. "I am such a fool. A coward and a fool."

"Then we are both cowards," Noah replied with a sigh. "You waited for four years for me to make the first move. Four *years*. All that time I was wondering what it would be like to kiss you."

Gavin laughed gently. "So we were both prisoners of our emotional scars, even though I loved you from the moment I met you. Back then you were not yet eighteen, looking more like fourteen. I was too disillusioned to trust my feelings…and I was in awe of you."

"I knew that barrier had fallen that time in Milan when you threatened to put me over your knee."

Gavin chuckled. "You were being particularly pig-headed as I recall. Not your most charming trait."

"Oh really? And what is?" Noah teased.

Dark brown eyes filled with emotion, Gavin looked at him.

"Your empathy. You feel things deeply. You think it is a weakness so you try to hide it, but it comes out in your music. It is what draws people to you and makes you the best at what you do. You see into your own soul and the souls of others. I will admit that sometimes it frightens me, and yet it is the reason why I love you."

He had said it again. *I love you.* Gavin had sworn never to say those words to another person, yet they tumbled out of his mouth so easily. He could see them reflected in the soft blue eyes, the color of the sea and sky, his entire world held in Noah's gentle gaze. His heart felt open again and at peace for the first time in a long time.

"I love you too," Noah replied, leaning to touch his mouth to Gavin's soft lips.

Kissing Gavin was everything Noah could have imagined and more. There was a calm understanding between them that went beyond love or desire or trust. It was a connection as old as time, a meeting of souls that had nothing to do with the lives they lived now or the bodies they inhabited in those lives.

Gavin's arms went around him, rolling Noah over into the mattress. Their eyes met for a long unflinching gaze. Noah felt his penis stir to life against the press of Gavin's abdomen and his lips stretched into a sexy smile.

"Have you ever…?" Gavin asked softly.

"No," Noah admitted with a blush. "I've never been with anyone before, not like that. It feels…right with you."

Gavin shook his head. "I suspected you were a virgin. And here I was worrying that you and Takamura… Forgive me. I am an idiot."

Noah laughed silently. He knew Gavin was jealous and had teased him during the phone call about Takamura. While it had irritated him before that Gavin thought he might sleep around with anybody, now he found it funny.

"Takamura doesn't want my body, Gav. His youngest daughter is getting married in March and he wants me to compose something special for her wedding. The book of poetry is her favorite, sent for inspiration. You were jealous."

Gavin growled deep in his throat. "Of course I was jealous. Every time someone went off in a corner with you it drove me crazy. I couldn't believe that you would turn down all of those rich men and women who looked at you…the way I looked at you."

"No one looks at me the way you do, Gavin," Noah whispered. "I want you."

"We can take it slow," Gavin suggested gently.

"Four years not long enough for you?"

Noah's fingers moved lightly across Gavin's lips and cheek. Gavin nodded, unable to speak at the lump of emotion in his throat. He reached to catch Noah's hand.

"Then kiss me, Gavin."

Their lips found each other in the darkness. This was as it was meant to be, warm gentle kisses in the firelight. Noah loved being in Gavin's embrace. His long fingers roamed Gavin's naked skin. His body felt like it was on fire, every nerve heightened to take in the sensations that Gavin was creating. More than willing, Noah gave himself to that passion, letting his body answer the touch of Gavin's hands, surrendering his mouth to Gavin's searching tongue.

Breathing in harsh panting gasps, he reeled in ecstasy as Gavin showed him the wonders that fingers and tongues could bring. He licked the sweat from Gavin's glistening skin, reveling in the hardness of straining muscles, moaning his desire against Gavin's magical mouth. Gavin's naked skin was hot and familiar, his embrace a safe haven unlike any that Noah had ever known.

When Gavin stopped what he was doing, Noah locked his gaze with that of his lover.

"What's wrong?"

Gavin groaned. "Nothing. I need to grab the condom out of my wallet and I don't want to step out on the cold floor."

Noah laughed in a low sexy purr. "You carry condoms everywhere you go?"

Gavin ducked his head to avoid Noah's gaze. "The same one has been in my wallet for years now. I kept it in there…you know…thinking that maybe…"

"Maybe you would find some sex starved maniac and need it? Well, you have."

Gavin lifted his head. He still could not believe that this was real, that Noah was in his arms at last. Love and desire was shining in Noah's half closed eyes, his sensual lips soft and swollen from kissing. The love and trust that Noah had given him almost broke Gavin's heart.

He rolled out of bed and sifted through the piles of clothing until he found what he was searching for. Noah's long arms reached to pull him back down into the warm sheets. They kissed, the passion again building between them until they were panting for relief. Noah broke the kiss, running his hands down Gavin's strong back.

"I'm not afraid," he whispered.

Very gently Gavin moved to roll them over. Noah's strong arms held him in place, his tongue darting out to lick Gavin's chin.

"I want to look into your face," Noah told him.

With a groan, Gavin opened the small packet. The condom inside was still slippery with lubricant and he managed to slide it over his erection fairly easily in spite of the fact that his hands were shaking. He held his breath when Noah's legs lifted to allow him access. Slowly Gavin eased himself inside his lover's body.

Sweat broke out on his skin. He tried not to move too abruptly, giving Noah time to adjust to the invasion. With an exhale of breath, Noah arched his back, exposing the long line of his neck. Gavin dipped his head to lick the sweat from the hollow of Noah's throat, wanting to know every inch of him.

Noah wrapped his arms and legs around Gavin's back and closed his eyes with a moan. When Gavin pushed deeper inside of him it was like nothing he had thought it would be. The sensations it created made his body tingle like an electric charge. Trapped between their bodies, his erection felt like raw nerves, every move that Gavin made bringing a shock that had Noah gasping in response.

A wave of love washed over him, so deep and strong that it was almost like pain. When his body exploded, Noah drew a breath with a sob and released it with a cry of Gavin's name. He heard Gavin's answering moan of pleasure and Noah opened his eyes again to watch Gavin's face as he lost control. Gavin came the instant their eyes met, pulsing inside Noah's hot tight body, barely aware of time and place. All Noah knew was that they were finally one, body and soul, forever.

They held on while their bodies trembled and shook, their hearts thundering in unison through sweat slicked skin, their breathing matched in a single gasp. In a few moments when he found he could move a little, Gavin eased out of his lover's body. He rolled over, bringing Noah with him.

Noah panted for breath, his body half over Gavin's, his head cradled in the hollow of Gavin's shoulder. With no words, they kissed gently. In that craving, desperate desire they had found a place where they resided alone, far from the reaches of whatever lay in wait in the cold, desolate house on the moors.

Gavin watched Noah's expression change, tears flooding his blue eyes and running silently down his face.

"Why are you crying?"

"No reason," Noah whispered. He sighed and all of the doubts and fears escaped from his body with that one breath. "I'm sorry I made you wait for so long."

"Noah," Gavin sighed and kissed him gently. He reached to brush Noah's hair back from his face. "Are you sure you are all right?"

Noah nodded.

"I'll be right back," Gavin told him. "Keep my place warm."

He rolled out of bed and disappeared into the bathroom. A minute later he returned, sliding beneath the sheets that Noah had pulled up over their bed. He put his arms around Noah's warm slender body that seemed to fit so well against his own.

Gavin kissed him, a warm deep kiss filled with love and promise. When they broke the kiss, Noah sighed and rested his head on Gavin's arm. Gavin watched him drift to sleep, content just to hold him and gaze into his face. He held Noah long into the night, wondering how a soul so innocent could have possibly belonged to that horrible, evil house.

Only much later, when the sound of thunder once again started to rumble through the darkness, did Gavin rise from the bed to rekindle the fire. Noah had been restless in his exhausted sleep, tossing and turning in the sheets. Gavin thought it best if he returned to his own bed for the remainder of the night. Noah needed to rest and he might sleep more comfortably alone.

Besides, Gavin did not want to compromise Noah in the morning…not in his brother's house. Once he had the fire going and the scattered clothing picked up and dropped at the foot of the bed, Gavin spread another blanket over Noah's sleeping form and quietly retreated from the room.

His connecting room was freezing cold and the icy sheets now seemed unbearably empty without Noah's warm slender body next to his. Gavin gritted his teeth and shivered in the darkness until his body heat warmed the space where he lay. After a short while he drifted to sleep with a smile on his face and the distant sound of thunder fading into his heartbeat.

SIXTEEN

Though this be madness, yet there's method in it.
   —W. Shakespeare

At first Noah did not know what had awakened him. The fire had burned down to coals but the room was still fairly warm for what had to be the dead of night. He was alone in his bed, which made him wonder if he had been dreaming about making love with Gavin, but the moment he stretched, his body told him that part of it had been real. It was in that moment of contented lassitude that he heard the sound again, a voice calling his name in the distance followed by a low rumble of thunder.

More awake, Noah sat up in bed. There was just enough light for him to see that he was alone. The door to the bath was closed and the drapes at the window wide open so that he could see the spidery tendrils of lightning run across the black sky beyond, followed by slow tumbled thunder. He shivered, crossing his arms over his naked chest. The voice called again, closer this time but still an eerie echo that might have been Gavin's voice.

Noah slipped from between the sheets and sorted his sweat pants from the pile of clothing at the foot of the bed. Stepping into them he noticed the door to the hallway was open. Gavin must have stepped out into the corridor for some reason. Maybe he had gone across the hall to James's room to check something out beneath the cover of darkness. Noah rubbed his eyes and walked through the doorway without thinking much about it.

It was immediately darker in the corridor but there was no one he could see. As far as he could tell all the doors were sensibly shut. Again the voice called, clearly his name coming from somewhere on the landing or below in the main hall. He was going to strangle Gavin for waking him up to go ghost hunting at that hour. He did not relish going down those stairs in the dark.

A flash of lightning startled him. Noah had always hated

storms, even in the city. The hollow expanse of the isolated house made it worse. He stumbled and bumped into something in the dark. Instinct—and fear—made him lash out, striking something solid. A soft grunt of pain reached Noah's ears, stopping his next blow from landing as he recognized the sound. They staggered, somewhat out of balance, until the wall near the large stained-glass window at the top of the landing stopped their odd little dance.

It was Andrew who had scared him half to death. Even as his muscles relaxed, Noah realized that something was wrong. Andrew's fingers, raised to catch Noah's flying fist out of self protection, remained hard against his wrists. Noah was held there against the wall, his brother's larger body pressing into his. In another flash of lightning he saw Andrew's face, an alien mask washed red and white in the quick blinding light passing through the window, the dark eyes like glittering glass.

"Andrew?"

Cold terror squeezed the air from Noah's lungs, freezing the blood in his veins. It was an expression he had seen once before, in his nightmares. He tried to pull his hands free of the numbing grip, managing only to twist into a painful contortion with one shoulder pressing hard against the sharp metal corner of the window, the freezing cold of the heavy paned glass burning into his naked back. His breath whooshed out of his lungs at the icy touch.

In that moment Andrew's hands released him only to rise toward his throat. For a moment Noah was struck dumb. As his brain sparked back to life, Noah pulled his hands up between their bodies and pushed, hard. The connection broke, long enough to give him the space to breathe and to wedge his elbow against Andrew's chest to keep the space there. A hard tug on his hair made Noah wince. Andrew moved to recapture his arms, pressing with all his weight.

"Stop," Noah said in a ragged breathless plea. "Andrew, stop."

The two brothers struggled in silence while the thunder rolled through the dark house. It seemed to Noah that the storm gave Andrew limitless strength, while the house drained his away with each dreadful second. The silent, unfaltering attack terrified him with its intensity and his inability to break free, an all encompassing horror made greater by the realization that such an attack had happened once before.

With a shuddering moan of fear it all came back to Noah when he was least prepared to face it, the sweeping black memory broken free from its prison at last. For an instant they overlapped, past and present, two forms struggling against the current of time…

✤ ✤ ✤

…There had been a storm that night too, an unusually fierce winter storm eight days before Christmas. The Hall had been festooned with wreaths and garlands in keeping with holiday tradition that went back beyond the coming of a Christian King, a minor deference for a family yet paying homage to a pagan god.

Only one person there had ever dared imagine such a terrible thing and yet James had feared it as a possibility long before he had relented to bringing his young son to the family home. It had been silent for so long—the house—that his wife had thought his precautions foolish and the story he had told her merely a tale to frighten children. So he had relented.

For three years he believed she might have been right. For three years James Bainbridge enjoyed a life he had never thought possible, filled with love and laughter. He had almost forgotten the reasons for his silent prayers in the shining eyes of his wife and new son. They had been to him like air to a drowning man, the promise of a hope realized at last.

But even before that terrible night James had known it was not to be. When had he seen it in his youngest son's eyes, that shattering knowledge that they were different somehow? It was simply staring back at him one day, that innocence gone. James had felt the house coming to life little by little and had chosen to ignore it at the cost of his sons. When that night came at last, it was his wife who had dared to come between her son and the *house*, the powerful instrument of their family...obligation. It had cost her life and his sanity.

Worse than that, it had cost James both his sons. The *house*—for that was how James viewed it, not as the family curse or the price paid for past allegiance...no, he could not accept the terrible truth in that—but the *house* always got what it wanted, sooner or later. With that knowledge James had done the last thing possible, although it had nearly destroyed him. He had sent Noah far away from the inheritance that would claim him, a living, breathing horror that would always be waiting, waiting for the ancient pact to be fulfilled with another offering of blood.

It had tried that stormy December night, to fulfill the contract. Unknown to James, it had already tried on more than one occasion, only to discover that Noah, like his father, was better equipped than most to defend himself against such intrusions. That night it had taken a more direct approach, actually pitting brother against brother while the wild energy of the gathering storm had raged around them.

It had not simply been his brother that Noah had struggled against, but some unknown nameless entity that demanded its sovereignty, its possession of the promised soul long denied. As a child then, facing a much older boy, Noah had done the only thing in his power that night; he had run, run for his life through the dark old house of terror. His shrill screams still reverberated through his bones, the sound of ultimate panic echoing with the thunder claps into the darkness.

Andrew had been slow at first, the thing in possession of his body momentarily disabled by Noah's initial surge of psychic energy, an instinctual reaction to the thing's presence. By the time Noah had run the length of the hallway and made it to the landing at the top of the staircase, it had caught him.

There, beneath the terrible scene of blood and death that represented their family curse, they had struggled in silent battle at the top of the dark looming stairs. The oldest and youngest sons of the Bainbridge Clan, representing a lineage older than their recorded history, beholding to an ancient oath sealed with blood. The only thing that saved Noah that night had been a mother's unwavering love.

Helen had suddenly appeared out of the darkness, her white hair flowing about her ghostly pale face like a banshee of legend as she flung herself onto Andrew with tooth and claw. She had literally pulled Noah free by the nape of his neck and tossed him to safety the distance of five steps down the staircase before she turned back to meet Andrew's unnatural fury. Noah could hear the sound of her heavy, controlled voice telling him to run.

He had run, half tumbling, half sliding down the stairs and out across the expansive floor of the entrance hall with his heart in his throat. Only at the door had he dared to glance back. He had watched her fall, an oddly silent, slow-motion backwards tumble down the entire length of the staircase, her light blue chiffon nightgown billowing out around her like a cloud.

When she hit the bottom with a sickening thud, Noah had opened the door and fled out into the storm, heedless of his tears mixing with the cold rain, aware only of the staring mask of a face with his brother's glittering eyes at the top of the staircase...

Noah felt the same rage coming from Andrew now that he had felt that night of his shattered childhood. It crashed back into him with sound and fury, that terrible unimaginable memory, stealing the power from his limbs and the sight from his eyes. As it had that night so long ago, his mind simply refused to accept what it knew now with certainty.

It was his brother's eyes looking at him with that cold unblinking stare, not some formless ancient horror that still lurked in the shadows of their ancestral home. It was Andrew, his half brother, the newest Laird of the County MacLearen, Keeper of the Rights and Laws of the Clan of *Those of the Cursed Path*.

The eerie, blood curdling scream was still echoing in Gavin's head when he sat bolt upright in bed amid a tumble of sheets and pillows and stared out into the cold blackness of his empty room. What the hell was that? His heart was pounding so hard that he could feel the bed shaking. Thinking only of Noah, Gavin vaulted out of bed and dashed through the connecting bath; it occurred to him only much later that the bathroom door was closed when he had left it open between both rooms. He stood there with his hand on the doorknob, staring at the empty bed.

Stunned and confused, Gavin shook his head, trying to get his sleep addled brain to function. His gaze travelled around the room, ticking off what he saw while he tried to make sense of it. The fire had burned down. The bed was empty. The hallway door was wide open. Kicking himself for his complacent stupidity, he ran to the door and out into the hallway. Nothing but darkness and silence. He squinted at the illuminated dial of his wristwatch; two-thirty a.m.

Gavin shivered in the chilly air of the corridor. He turned on his heel and ran back to his room long enough to yank on clothing and shoes and dig for a flashlight. He cursed himself for believing it safe enough to sleep. He should have known better. He had forced Andrew's hand with his flippant comment about them leaving and now his heart was frozen with fear and Noah was missing. Turning to leave the room, Gavin gave the servant bell-pull a couple of hard yanks as an afterthought.

The panic he was beginning to feel solidified like a rock in his chest when Gavin found Andrew's room equally dark and empty. He left the door open and flung open the door of the Lord's room next. Dashing inside he found Noah's beseeching eyes reaching out to him from the cold white beam from his flashlight as it moved across the portrait of Helen.

Her eyes remained alive but someone had taken a blade to her likeness; the canvas that could be easily reached at arm's length was hanging in long tattered rents. The narrow desk below her had suffered a similar fate; the objects swept off onto the floor and broken into bits, the drawers ripped out and their contents overturned in a tirade of rage.

Gavin's heart plummeted to his stomach and rolled with cold

nausea, making him lean against the foot of the bed for support while his head spun. He staggered to the door and clung to the doorframe. A bright flash of lightning visible through the front windows illuminated the long hallway for a few seconds, long enough to make Gavin despair of the sheer overwhelming size of the place in the dark. It could take him an hour or longer to completely search the house, an impossibly long time when every second counted, and he was certain that it would.

Plunging head first into the darkness, Gavin almost collided with the butler coming around the corner from the landing. The man had pulled on trousers and a shirt to answer the call of the bell pull that rang in his room at night. With his hair up in tufts, Duncan looked surprised and half asleep.

"Where is Andrew?" Gavin demanded, grabbing the man's arm in a hard grip. "He has Noah and I don't know how long it's been already."

"What are you talking about? What is happening?"

Gavin released him. "Noah's life has been in danger since he came to this house. Someone almost succeeded in murdering him earlier tonight and now he is missing and his father's rooms are all torn up. *Andrew* is missing. Where is he? Where would he take Noah? Are all of you in on it?"

"Oh my God," Duncan exclaimed, emphasizing each word.

Duncan looked stunned, his age suddenly more apparent. Gavin did not have time for explanations. A blazing flash of lightning illuminated the stained glass window in front of them, giving ghastly life to the images of horror in that few seconds in the dark. The following crash of thunder seemed to shake the whole house to its foundations.

"Call for help," Gavin ordered. "I'll start searching downstairs."

He did not wait for Duncan to move but flung himself down the stairs with an almost heedless disregard for his own safety. He turned toward the small front drawing rooms, sliding to a stop when the front door suddenly crashed open and swung madly on its hinges. He stared at the door with fear numbing his blood but his mind was working furiously to latch upon some clue, to make some sense of it all.

And it came to him as clearly as a flash of lightning burning its path across his retinas. In his mind's eye he witnessed the struggle at the top of the stairs, the two silent combatants locked in a deadly embrace. He watched her fall, the final tumbling crash to the bottom of the stairs ending her life, right at the spot where he stood. Noah had run; out the door and into the night, ran without awareness of his surroundings, to hide from the thing at the top of the stairs, the thing that had murdered his mother.

Gavin came back to his senses with a gasp of breath, tears pouring down his face, knowing it had happened before. Although Noah was its target, it had been Helen who had died then. It all made a terrible, horrible sense. And now, on the night of the ancient ritual of fire, with Andrew's help, the unnatural family curse had a second chance to take the victim it wanted; Noah, the youngest son of the clan.

They had to be outside. That was where Noah had run for protection back then, outside to the stables. Gavin went through the open front door. He could have shortened the path by going through the house but then he would have had to pass the dining room in the dark, and anything would be preferable to that, especially on that night, at that moment. No, he followed the footsteps of the invisible young Noah who was leading him, out the front door and into the storm.

It was not raining but the wind whipped through the trees with a frightening roar and thunder boomed like cannon fire cracking across the hills. Gavin ran down the path alongside the house, past the dark hulking shapes of the garages and through the main garden lawn. He stopped at the edge of the roses to get his bearings, having seen the rear of the house only briefly during the daylight hours.

A bright flash lit up the sky, giving the things around him the unnatural color of black and white. The wind seemed to be pushing him forward and he struck out for the stable buildings, the crack of thunder so loud that it set his ears ringing and made his hair stand on end. His flashlight began to fade. Without the lightning to show him the way, the path would have been treacherous in the moonless night. He slid to a stop inside the stable entrance with his heart in his throat.

"Noah! Noah, answer me!"

No reply other than the sounds of nervous horses and banging wind. Gavin began looking into stalls, searching the shadows for a glimpse of silver hair. A big black horse rushed its gate, cracking the wood and pawing at the ground. Gavin looked in every stall. There was nothing, no one. He searched through the tack room where he picked up the only thing he could find that might be useful as a weapon; the tool had a heavy curved blade used to clean the hooves of horses, a pick of sorts.

Again the black horse reared and gave a scream that made Gavin shiver. As he looked at the animal he saw two things that made his eyes widen with astonishment; the head of the animal and the window behind him were outlined with an eerie greenish mist. He blinked hard. It was still there. Beyond the animal, through the window, he could see the faint light moving in the darkness. The ruins of the keep! They were already more than halfway across the meadow.

Gavin's heart constricted in fear; he was going to be too late. Andrew must be totally mad to think he could murder his brother in the dark of night and keep it a secret. Even in places like this remote village there were laws and policemen. But those things did not figure in the thoughts of the truly insane.

With a simultaneous crash of thunder, the black horse smashed through its gate. Gavin leapt back against the wall to avoid its wild passage to freedom but the animal did not bolt; it came over to him with tossing head and nervously prancing feet. He put out his hand to push it away and felt its muscles quaking beneath his touch. It actually turned its head and looked at him, the greenish glow of its large round eyes regarding him steadily.

"Oh my God," Gavin said in a breath that fogged the air.

The horse pushed up against him with enough force to get

his attention. It was telling him to hurry. Although his legs were shaking like tree branches in the wind, Gavin climbed up onto the box used for such things and flung himself up onto the animal's naked back. The moment he thrust his fingers into the creature's thick mane it took off, the sound of its steel-shod feet clattering on the wooden floor like hailstones. They tore off across the flat stable lawn and jumped the small embankment with Gavin holding on for his life.

In a flash of lightning that lit up the meadow like midday, he saw them; three figures outlined against the dark stones of the ruined chapel, the circle of the ancient keep. The words of the poem came back to Gavin with terrifying clarity. *From yea sacred standing stones, o'er blackened sacrificial bones, the eldest knee bowed to seal, ancient power his to wield.* Andrew had taken the words for their literal meaning and he was no longer waiting for the house to do the deed for him. The crash of thunder drowned out the muffled scream that should have reached Gavin's ears.

❧ ❧ ❧

Without the intermittent lightning or their small beams of light moving across the swaying grass, the darkness of the night was absolute. The tall grass of the meadow rattled like old bones in the wind that howled around the stone escarpments with disembodied moans. In front of them the ancient stones waited. Behind them came the unmistakable fall of hoof beats raining down on the earth like a pounding heart.

Noah saw him in the flash of lightning, the dark and terrifying sight of the black horse and crouching rider flying across the grass like a demon loosed from hell. He screamed Gavin's name but the thunder cracked almost on top of them, drowning out his cry. The two men holding him dropped him like a sack of grain when they saw the horse and rider in the distance. Noah took a sharp kick to the stomach to ensure his gasping silence, followed by a curse from Andrew.

He looked up at his brother's face in the dim light, horrified at the wild glittering eyes and wind tossed hair. The tall grass whipped around his face, partially obscuring his sight, but he knew that Seth had gone to face their pursuer and Andrew was almost incapacitated with fury. Noah was numb with cold and the truth of his brother's hatred and betrayal.

Andrew was responsible for the death of their father and Noah's mother. With one thrust of the double-edged dagger Andrew held in his hand, the final deed would be done. Noah's blood would spill out onto the ancestral ground to mingle with countless other youngest sons of the Clan, sacrificed in deference to a nameless deity, in pursuit of eternal power and vain glory.

Noah felt his heart almost freeze in his chest. The most unbearable cut of all was that his own stubborn foolishness had dragged Gavin into the same fate which awaited him on that dark and windswept moor. Gavin would die with him, both of them lost to Andrew's madness.

After Noah's collapse on the landing, they had bound him hand and foot and carried him, suspended between them, from the house. When he regained his senses at the edge of the gardens and began to struggle, Seth had punched him in the head until he blacked out. With one eye swollen almost shut and blood from his cut lip still trickling down his chin, Noah was in no mood to make things easier for Andrew now that he was alone.

"Andrew, please stop. You don't know what you are doing," Noah pleaded desperately, listening for the sound of the horse coming nearer. "You can't—"

His brother turned on him with a snarl of rage. "Do you really think your arrogant lover can change anything, dear brother? You are meant to die tonight and die you shall. Whether he dies before you or after makes no difference to me."

Andrew kicked him hard in the hip and sliced through the ropes holding his ankles prisoner. "Now get on your feet!"

The pain only strengthened Noah's resolve. Whatever was going to happen, it was better for him and for Gavin if it happened there, on the open meadow, instead of whatever Andrew had in mind within the stone walls of the ruin. A streak of lightning outlined his brother's panting form and a crack of thunder covered the cry of rage. When he did not move, a flurry of punches descended upon his body, but Noah closed his eyes and took them in silence.

Frothing at the mouth and seeing the rearing horse find Seth in the darkness, Andrew grabbed his brother's motionless form by the arm and dragged him through the sharp cutting grass. The mossy stones were close now, so close he could see them in the dark and feel the power reaching out for him. Soon it would all be over.

Noah allowed Andrew to drag him like a dead weight, the stones bruising his back, the sharp stalks of grass cutting into his naked skin. He looked back into the darkness where he could hear but not see the altercation going on between Gavin and Seth. The unmistakable scream of the horse cut through the night wind, mixed with a strange growling sound that might have been a voice.

Noah felt the cold slick moss of the chapel stones sliding beneath him, but Andrew was dragging him away from the chapel walls, toward the graveyard. With mounting terror Noah flailed his bare feet, trying to get them beneath him so he could stand, only to be yanked down with every attempt. Andrew dragged him relentlessly forward until they stopped at the edge of one of the larger stone crypts, where Andrew released him, kicking him in the shoulder with a vicious blow that made his vision fade to a pinpoint for a few moments.

The momentary incapacitation was all that Andrew required to move the heavy iron door that would lead into the crypt. Once inside, the grating of stone on stone uncovered another small entrance and a set of steep stone steps leading down to the subterranean level, where the ancient family crypts lay in blackness. The cold musty air fogged Andrew's panting breath as he turned to his victim, the gleam of a nightmare almost fulfilled shining in his terrible gaze.

Andrew pulled Noah to his feet and held him against the edge of the cold stone doorway. Noah stared across into his brother's eyes, unable to look away. The touch of Andrew's hand on his neck made his skin crawl. It simply could not be his brother.

"Andrew…"

"Welcome home, dear brother," Andrew said with a smile.

With no warning Andrew flung his brother, bound and bloodied, headfirst into the stygian depths. He stood listening to Noah crash down the slick stone steps to the debris covered floor below. After a moment of gloating silence, he carefully followed, taking one step at a time with careful precision.

Noah hit the bottom with a sickening thud that knocked the wind out of him and cracked his head hard on the stone floor that was only slightly covered with dirt and moss. In the total blackness of the ancient underground vault he could see nothing, but he could hear things scurrying about. It was the place of his nightmares, a true horror that had awakened to claim him at last. Only when he saw the faint beam from his brother's flashlight descending the slick damp steps did the blackness become absolute.

⚜ ⚜ ⚜

Outside in the gathering storm Gavin had hopes of reaching his quarry without a single idea of what he was going to do once he found them. A few drops of rain were falling on his face in the dark, the threatening downpour only minutes away. The thunder rumbled off the surrounding hills with deafening echoes. He clutched the horse's mane with numb fingers, leaning down along the creature's neck while it took mad flight across the uneven meadow. Without the horse and its speed he would never have made it in time.

Neither he nor the horse was prepared for what confronted them out of the darkness. A black shape flew at them from the tall grass, striking the horse in the shoulder and brushing Gavin's leg with its weight before falling away. The animal swerved from the blow, slamming its haunches down to slide to a stop. The horse screamed in fright and reared with its front hooves slashing at a low darting figure that retreated in the grass.

Gavin tumbled off its back, a handful of black hair still clutched in his fingers. He landed in the tall grass with a gasp of surprise and a dull jab of pain in his knee, half twisted beneath him. For a second he sat motionless. Then the horse took off into the night, its hind feet digging into the earth, flinging small clumps of dirt and stone in all directions. As its solid presence was replaced with open space, Gavin vaulted to his feet in the swaying grass, aware that he was now at the level of whatever had sprang at them.

In the next moment he heard it, a low growling sound that was approaching him almost unseen in the tall grass. He had lost his flashlight but he still had the sharp tool from the stable and he yanked it out of his waistband, glad that it had not sliced a hole into his back when he had fallen. He clutched it now with a steady hand, watching in horrified disbelief as the thing hunting him came out of the grass directly in front of him, its low threatening form caught in a bright crash of lightning.

How could it possibly be a wolf?

There were no wolves in the Isles; too many centuries of sheep herders had seen readily to that. A small bit of warning crept up into his conscious thought; don't stare the animal directly in the eye. Yet he was unable to drag his gaze away from the piercing orbs, wild greenish-yellow discs looming as large and dangerous as the sun. Staring into its glowing eyes turned Gavin's blood into ice and his body into useless goose flesh, leaving no doubt which one of them was the hunter and which the prey.

An eternity seemed to pass, staring at each other across the too-short space between, an eternity of numb realization that the animal was going to attack and that not only could Gavin not move, he had nowhere to run. Time slowed down so that his awareness was magnified in strange proportions.

The wind ruffled the animal's fur, every shaft of its dark gray coat the size of a tree branch to Gavin's eyes. The darkness beyond and the swaying grass at his feet seemed to retreat into the distance, leaving only the empty hollow of himself and the menacing shadow of his approaching death. The creature growled, low and deep in its throat. The sound seemed to vibrate through Gavin's skin and bones, more of a feeling than a sound, triggering some vast, otherwise unknown terror within.

He was unaware that he had been holding his breath until the animal made a sudden move. Gavin sucked in a lungful of air and let it out in a scream of defiance. The sting of cold air in his starved lungs and the sound of his own voice shattered the paralysis, but turning to run was no longer an option, if it ever had been. The animal was fast, so fast that it seemed a blur in Gavin's vision, a dark form propelled in deadly aim straight across the grass like a bullet.

He retained the presence of mind to lift his arms across his head and throat in a feeble effort to protect himself. The space between them vanished and the heavy weight of the creature flew upwards and hit him full in the chest. There was no doubt that he was going down beneath that charge of muscle and teeth. They toppled over to the ground with a thud that took what was left out of his lungs in a gasp of pain.

Sharp teeth tore into his arm inches above his face while the animal's feet scrabbled across his chest in an effort to regain its footing and the advantage. Gavin felt the searing pain of his flesh ripping in its mouth but he was unable to utter even a whimper of sound. Trying to roll over, he kicked up with his knees and shoved the animal off. The move only increased the pain, the teeth refusing to disengage while his arm twisted up and over with the direction of the animal's momentum. He could see its yellow eyes glaring down through a spray of his own blood.

In the distance the sound of a human voice reached Gavin's ears, a scream from Noah. The animal shifted its hold, trying again to rip out his throat. With a sort of dull detachment Gavin remembered he held the curved metal tool in his hand, unfortunately the wolf was holding him by that arm. He shoved at its snout with his other hand, luckily striking one of the yellow eyes, and managed to keep the snapping bloody fangs of the open mouth from his head by inches.

He brought the blade down against the animal's shoulder,

dragging its curved tip through the dark fur. The animal jumped away with a yowl of pain. Fresh air flooded Gavin's heaving lungs. He sat up.

As quickly as it had disappeared into the darkness, it reappeared in a silent leap that carried it straight for Gavin's throat. Gavin fell back at the last moment, raising his weapon to strike the animal. In midair the creature tried to shift direction with his movement. The heavy weight of the wolf hitting his arm caused the both of them to roll, but the blade struck the animal in its vulnerable underside and Gavin held on to the tool with every ounce of his strength.

Sobbing for breath, Gavin lay shivering in a heap. The bloody tool was still in his hand. He did not understand why the wolf had just released him and vanished. He was covered in blood, some of it his, most of it belonging to his attacker. In the darkness he could hear the whimpering of the mortally wounded animal fading away and rain began to pour down from a bottomless sky.

Not knowing how he could, Gavin got to his feet.

His left shirt sleeve was in tatters and the arm was in much the same condition, throbbing with every beat of his heart. He ignored it like he ignored the rain and the blackness, one single purpose driving him forward. His very existence was for that one purpose, led by fate to that place and that moment in time. If he had to die so that Noah would live, that was a price Gavin was willing to pay. If he had to kill Noah's brother to ensure that outcome, he was willing to serve that penance as well, and whatever condemnations came with it.

Clutching the bloody weapon in his right hand, he staggered the remaining yards toward the feeble greenish light coming from the graveyard. He left a bloody smear on the stone doorway as he paused to gather his strength before taking the steps down into the earth, then he walked slowly down into the heavy cold place of the dead. It no longer held any unknown terrors for him. It held only judgment.

❧ ❧ ❧

Noah regained consciousness to the sound of boots scuffling against stone. He blinked in the muted flickering light and turned his head to see Andrew slowly making his way around the circular room, carefully lighting the torches that sat in each heavy iron holder. Their black, acrid smoke rose up to the stone ceiling, the rough hewn rock darkened with the soot from past torches burned in witness to centuries of secret ritual.

So this then was their terrible family secret. The hidden knowledge that had cost his father's life and Andrew's sanity. Noah must have made a sound, voicing his dismay, because Andrew glanced over at him while lighting the last torch.

"Better for you if you had not woke up," Andrew said in a low voice. "No matter. It will all be over soon."

Noah realized he was lying on a stone altar in the center of the room. His feet were once again tied with rope. Even if he managed to roll off the raised slab, he would have little chance of escape as long as Andrew was present. He also had little doubt that Andrew was going to leave him there…alive.

"Listen to me Drew. You don't have to do this. You can fight this thing, like father did all these years. I understand now. He tried to save us Drew, both of us!"

Andrew laughed, walking closer to the altar. His eyes glittered like diamonds and his face was slick with sweat.

"Save us?" he repeated in a mocking tone. "He never did anything for me! He was a coward! He thought he could turn his back on his responsibilities and deny fate. He chose you over the welfare of his own clan, of his first born son, of his God!"

Noah cringed. The words echoed around the hollow room, the torch light flickering in response to the force of Andrew's rage. Something else in the crypt reacted to the emotion. Noah could feel the invisible energy swell and twist around them, pressing down on his psychic awareness with a nauseating pressure that he had never felt anywhere at that level, not even in the house. It was like a living entity, waiting in the shadows for countless years, for another soul to fill its endless, ravenous hunger.

That it had Andrew in its power was no longer in doubt. He had no idea how his father had managed to keep it at bay for as long as he did. His only chance was to try and get through to Andrew, that part of his brother that he prayed was still able to reason, and hope that Gavin could handle Seth alone.

"He tried to stop the cycle of horror," Noah told his brother in a solemn yet quavering voice. "Drew, he did everything he knew how to do to keep you from losing your soul to this evil, from one day having to face the terrible truth and the more terrible choices that he had to face. He did choose you. He chose you over everything else, even after he knew that you were responsible for my mother's death."

Andrew was staring at him, strangely, frighteningly silent. Although the dagger was not in his hand, Noah knew it was nearby. He was now sweating as much as Andrew, the coldness of the stone and the creepy room temporarily forgotten in the struggle for his life. He took a long, deep breath, fearful it might be his last.

"He forgave you Andrew," Noah said quietly. "He did all of this to protect you, not me."

From the grounds above the crypt, a long drawn out sound like the howling of a wolf made Andrew start. To Noah's horror, his brother started to laugh. The laughter rang through the small stone room, drowning out the last hollow note of the animal howl, and freezing Noah's blood in his veins.

"We can stop this now," Noah said in a strong clear voice, knowing it was probably his last chance. "The two of us, together as brothers."

"Too late," his brother said with a hiss. "It was too late the day you were born. Now shut up."

Reaching into his pocket, Andrew walked up to the altar.

"Please Andrew."

Andrew took the cloth from his pocket and stuffed it into Noah's mouth to silence him. With that done, he patted Noah's cheek in a parody of affection.

"That's better," he said with a smile. "Now we won't have to hear you scream."

Andrew looked up at the sound of footsteps on the stone stairway. He seemed surprised to see Gavin, stopping what he was doing to snatch his dagger from where it lay on the altar near Noah's feet.

They were aware of each other at the same instant. Gavin's heart lurched when he saw Noah's bound, half-naked body lying on the stone, clearly helpless in the face of his brother's madness. He gripped his weapon so tightly that his fingers hurt.

"Put down whatever that is you are holding, Moore," Andrew ordered harshly. His gaze was taking in Gavin's bloody shirt and hard, cold eyes. "What have you done to Seth?"

"Seth?" Gavin repeated the name.

Gavin watched Noah's eyes open and lock onto him from across the space between them. Noah's mouth was gagged with a bloody rag, his wrists and ankles bound with rope. One eye was swollen almost shut and his bruised skin looked grey from the dust and cold. Gavin felt his frozen heart fire with rage to see him like that. He walked two paces closer.

Noah stared at him with love and terror. Gavin looked like a warrior of old, advancing with steady deliberation in his tattered, bloody shirt. With the ropes on his body and the oppressive power of the dark pit pressing down on his consciousness, there was little Noah could do other than trust Gavin. He did trust Gavin, implicitly, with his life and his soul.

Andrew brought his dagger down across Noah's neck to assure compliance, pressing its gleaming blade against the delicate skin. Gavin took another step. Andrew grabbed a handful of the silver-blond hair and pressed the blade harder, a thin trickle of blood appearing on Noah's throat.

"I said, put down the weapon, unless you want him dead now."

Gavin realized he could not risk Noah's life without at least a chance of escape. He kept his eyes locked on Noah's wide blue ones, trying to tell him not to be afraid. Very slowly he stepped another pace closer.

"Stop there or I'll cut his throat."

Gavin stopped. With a quick flick of his eyes, he looked around.

The stone room was circular with a large, ancient altar in the center, an altar not unlike the one in Father Perrine's church. This altar was marked with the human-like figures of wolves cut deep in the stone, the same wolves that Noah had shown him on the parchment rubbings only hours before. Similar carvings were on the walls, flickering with life in the changing light from torches burning in iron holders.

Gavin stood there, dripping rainwater and blood onto the unholy ground.

"Good boy," Andrew said.

Before either of them knew what he was doing, Andrew's dagger flashed through the air. Gavin felt his heart leap into his throat at the sudden threatening movement but the blade slashed through Noah's blond hair instead of his neck, sheering off the locks that Andrew had been clutching in his fingers. Noah cried out in terror, the sound muffled by the gag.

Andrew laughed, a loud maniacal sound that echoed off the rock walls around them. Strands of Noah's blond hair floated from his fingers to the floor like gossamer threads.

"You love his hair, don't you?" Andrew asked, bringing a pale lock of hair that he still held in his fingers up to his lips. "He is beautiful, like his bitch of a mother. He will make a fitting sacrifice for the god of our ancestors, won't he?"

"Why are you doing this?" Gavin asked, taking the only course open to him at the moment, trying to reason with an unreasonable man. He still held the curved blade in his hand. "Noah never did anything to you."

Andrew screamed, a ranting angry shriek that made Noah flinch violently.

"He stole everything from me!" Andrew shouted, waving his dagger about. "He made my father deny his duty to the clan! My father, a coward and a traitor! This is his fault and now he has to pay, pay for turning his back on all of us, pay for denying me my birthright. His life must be sacrificed to the ancient one for the fate of the clan. There is no other way. Without his blood we will become lost to oblivion."

Gavin shook his head. "Look around you, Andrew. The dead are dead. They stay dead. Noah can't bring them back. Nothing you do can bring them back or give you what you want."

Andrew's dagger flashed again and Noah screamed in pain, the blade cutting into the skin of his naked chest, leaving a bleeding line across his ribcage. Gavin felt his blood boil with rage but remained where he was, as much a captive as Noah while Andrew wielded the dagger. A trickle of Noah's blood began to seep down the side of the altar.

Gavin ground his teeth while Andrew laughed. Although tears were rolling down Noah's face, his eyes were amazingly steady on Gavin, understanding that he had to remain ready for any opening that Gavin might see to their advantage. The sheer courage and trust that took made Gavin tremble with love and gratitude.

Andrew mistook his trembling for fear.

"It could have all been finished without the blood and the mess if you had just stayed with the good Padre for another ten minutes. Stupid fool. Barging in here, upsetting everything. I should have just let Seth take him like he wanted; no one would have questioned his mangled body found on the moors with his throat ripped out."

Gavin felt his eyes widen with horror. Wolves carved on every surface, wolves in the family crest and in the village. Not just the symbols of wolves, but actual wolves walking among the sheep, pretending to be human. These human wolves were part of Andrew's clan, an ancient family beholding to the dark magic that had created them and the blood that bound them together.

"Who are you waiting for?" Gavin asked, knowing the answer now. It was Seth's blood on his clothing. It had been Seth in the form of a wolf lurking through the grass in the darkness. "Neither one of us can afford to yield. Are we going to stand here like this, at an impasse forever?"

Andrew had the good sense to look worried. He might be mad, but he was smart enough to realize that he could not simply kill Noah as long as Gavin was there to call his hand. Without Seth for backup the play of the cards would be a shaky deal. The sharp curved blade was still in Gavin's bloody hand.

"You can free Noah and we will call it even," Gavin continued to bargain with the devil, watching the thoughts skitter behind Andrew's glittering eyes. "We will just go away like he was never here."

"That will not solve my problem."

"You cannot possibly believe that you can get away with this now. Noah is a famous person. Even if we both conveniently disappear, loads of people will notice. Dora will notice."

"Dora?" Andrew snorted with disdain. "Everyone knows she's crazy. Just like my crazy father and my poor crazy brother who broke down one night and wandered off across the moors to his death."

Gavin cringed inwardly at that comment and the thought that Andrew could so easily have gotten away with it. If Noah had not been strong enough to survive the psychic attack the night of the concert—or the attempt only hours earlier in the horror of the dining room—he might have indeed turned up dead from exposure or from having his throat ripped out by an animal. Andrew's dark plans had been ever changing, building in desperation until his madness lost control.

"Duncan knows."

Andrew shrugged. "I can handle Duncan. He is nothing more than a servant and he will do what I say. It comes back to you. Shall I cut him again? I think you will grow weary of his screams of pain long before I do."

"If you touch him again, I will kill you," Gavin stated in a soft monotone. "Unlike you, I will have nothing more to lose."

Andrew grinned wickedly. "You will not strike me with his life in the balance."

Gavin's expression did not alter, nor did his voice change its deadly serious tone. The flickering light of the burning torches reflected in his dark eyes and it seemed that an iridescent green mist had gathered around him like a strange fog. Noah watched him with a terrible fascination, his entire being focused on Gavin's granite will. No Roman or Viking God could have looked more fearsome or intense.

"I will kill you," Gavin continued steadily. "I will burn your ancestral home to the ground and sow the earth with salt. I will not be finished with you until there is nothing left of your name or your history or your Clan to ever show you existed in this world. You will be the last of your cursed lot; dead, cold, and forgotten."

It was a calculated risk meant to infuriate Andrew to the level that he would forget his hostage entirely and charge directly at his attacker. It might have worked, but they would never know. Seth chose that moment to stagger down the crypt steps. Gavin warily shifted to watch him descend while keeping an eye on Andrew.

Seth took each step with slow deliberation, leaning heavily against the slimy moss covered wall, leaving a trail of dark wet blood behind him. He was naked but so covered in blood and mud that it was not immediately noticeable. One arm hung uselessly at his side and the opposite hand pressed over a gaping wound in his abdomen. Blood pulsed from a cut in his neck and his once bright green eyes were dull flat black.

"Seth!" Andrew cried out in shock.

In silence they watched Seth topple over and fall the last five steps to the floor below. Andrew's expression was frozen in horror, his gaze riveted on his dying lover as Seth rolled onto his back and lay still. For a moment Andrew seemed to forget everything but the dead black eyes staring up into his.

Gavin took a step toward the form lying on the altar. Andrew, his lips drawn back from his teeth in frothing fury, totally ignored his helpless brother, instead turning all his grief and rage on the man who had killed his lover. Andrew darted around the altar with his dagger raised and Gavin moved forward to meet him.

On the slab of stone, Noah quickly flexed his legs at the knee and kicked out with all his strength, catching Andrew off guard and connecting hard enough to almost knock him down. Gavin's curved blade struck the off-balanced Andrew in the neck, ripping through his flesh. The blood seemed to shower into the air like slow motion raindrops, hitting the ground with an audible spatter.

Andrew spun around from the force of the blow, staggering like a drunken man. A strange look spread across his face as he fell with the dagger still raised, a look of stunned disbelief. Blood poured down his clothing from the neck wound, a mortal blow that would kill him in seconds.

He pitched forward and Noah screamed a visceral wail of agony. The blade came down into Noah's thigh, his brother's dead body sprawled across his abdomen. Blood rolled down the side of the stone altar and a strange gust of wind where there should have been no wind sent the torches to wavering wildly. A couple of them guttered out. Gavin wasn't sure if it was his imagination or if he really could hear the groaning and creaking of the stone around them.

He dropped the deadly tool from his stiff fingers and it hit the stone floor with a hollow clang. With a great heave of fear and disgust, Gavin pulled Andrew's body away from Noah, and it slid to the floor, where it fell partially across Seth, close to his feet. He looked down at the two of them for only a moment before he turned his grateful gaze to Noah, who was still very much alive.

Gavin ran his hands across Noah's face and shoulders in a second of sheer relief that left him shaking with more terror than he had felt in long, heart-stopping minutes. The blue eyes looked up at him in pain and anguish, Noah's shivering body cold as ice to the touch. The handle of the dagger was sticking out of his flesh, thrust several inches through the muscle of his upper thigh.

"Oh God, Noah, I'm sorry, I'm so sorry. He's dead, Noah," Gavin reassured him. "He can't hurt you anymore."

Very carefully, Gavin pulled the gag from Noah's mouth. He gently kissed Noah's shivering bruised lips. When he would have rolled Noah over to release his hands, Noah's cry of pain made him stop. The dagger in Noah's leg made moving him impossible.

"You're badly injured. I'll have to leave you here to go for help."

Noah shook his head and licked his swollen lips. He couldn't stand the thought of being left there in the dark with his brother's dead body and whatever else might still be swirling about in the shadow. He was aware of some odd sound in the distance, distorted by the layer of earth and stone above their heads.

"I can walk if you pull the knife out," he told Gavin. "We aren't safe here, Gavin. Please don't leave me here."

Gavin's fine strong hands smoothed over Noah's hair, and for a moment, all the pain that Noah felt faded away. All that mattered was that the two of them were together. Gavin would make certain that they would get out alive.

"I won't leave you," Gavin promised. "But pulling out the knife is too dangerous. What if it nicked an artery?"

"It's in the wrong place for that," Noah said through gritted teeth. "It's barely in the side, where there is mostly muscle, not even near the bone. Pull it out, Gavin. Trust me. We've got to get out of here."

Gavin untied the rope from Noah's ankles. He pulled his ruined shirt off next, heedless of his own injuries, and looked down at the handle of the dagger sticking out from Noah's flesh. Noah was making inarticulate sounds of pain. Gavin ripped the cloth of the bloody sweat pants enough the see the entry point was where Noah had said, high on his outer thigh, barely through the muscle.

"This is going to hurt," Gavin told him. "Take a deep breath."

Noah sucked in his breath. Gavin smoothly pulled the blade from Noah's thigh and slapped the rolled up shirt down over the wound as Noah stiffened against the pain. He took the rope and tied it tight around the makeshift bandage over the stab wound. Gavin gently pulled Noah's upper body into a sitting position and used the bloody dagger to cut the ropes binding his arms.

Free at last, Noah placed his numb, shaking arms around Gavin's naked back and held him that way for a moment or two. They were both weeping, badly injured, but somehow still alive. Slowly Gavin released his grip and looked down at Noah, battered and half frozen, covered with dirt and blood. He kissed Noah's forehead.

"Okay, I'll get you out. Let's get you on your feet first."

Noah proved to have more courage and strength than Gavin thought anyone should have to possess. He managed to walk past the body of his brother; slow painful steps while he leaned heavily on Gavin for support. He cried out with every step up the steep stone stairway as he climbed up from hell. The shallow wound across his chest washed his lower body in red, adding to the larger stain left by Andrew's blood. The makeshift bandage on his thigh was spotted with blood before they made it out into the cold darkness of the meadow.

The rain had stopped, or at least lessened to a barely noticeable drizzle. Thunder rumbled far off in the distance and the moon had broken through the clouds just beyond the hills. The entire landscape seemed surreal, washed in black and white. The long grass still swayed in the wind but the rain had taken away its skeletal sound, leaving only whispers. Noah's hair was as silvery white as the moonlight and Gavin's eyes were as black as the sea.

Noah continued to slowly walk, leaning on Gavin until they were in sight of the torch lights of the rescue party before Gavin decided that was enough and lifted him to carry him the rest of the way. It was still a good two hundred yards across the meadow to the approaching group. It would be over soon. With shouts of alarm raised, help came running from three different directions.

By the time Gavin got to them, he was shaking from the strain of his ordeal, and they were both covered in Noah's blood. Noah fainted quietly away as hands reached to take him from Gavin's hard desperate embrace.

SEVENTEEN

On doit des egard aux vivants; on ne doit aux morts que la verite.
To the living we owe respect; to the dead we owe only the truth.
   —Voltaire

The rescue party had been on the way even before Duncan finished searching the upstairs bedrooms and finding them empty. Seeing the portrait of Lady Helen in shreds rendered him wide awake and coldly terrified of Gavin's rambling speech. He had roused Rose Marie and been about to call for help when the phone rang and Madeline Fitzgerald was on the line telling them that Barry, Dora, and Reggie were heading their way. Should she call the constable?

Not knowing what to tell her, Duncan said no. He really had no idea what was going on and with Dora on the way, anything was possible. If there was anything he could do to keep the family name out of harm's way, he would. They arrived at the front door just as Duncan finished lighting lamps and gathering a collection of flashlights. Of the three of them, Dora looked the worst; her eyes were smudged black pits but her hands were steady and cold as marble.

While Duncan related the emergency, the faces of the other two men looked progressively grimmer. Apparently Dora had called Barry only a half hour earlier, mostly incoherent, babbling about murder and wolves and sins of the fathers. It had taken Barry ten minutes to calm her down enough to understand what she was saying. He then had no choice but to believe her; he too had felt whatever it was that attacked Noah on that staircase. Not knowing what to expect once they got to the Hall, he had called Reggie.

They were an odd choice for a rescue party to be sure, but none of them had blood ties to the village, something that Gavin would understand much later. They went straight back out into the howling maelstrom armed with flashlights and grit. Only when the black horse returned with its eyes wildly rolling and its neck bleeding from a wound did they turn their gaze to the ruins across the blackened plain.

Dora was the first to see them walking out from the darkness. For a moment the odd looking figure seemed to be bathed in a greenish glow, not unlike the strange green light she had seen in the masts of sailing ships when she was a child. Then the glinting of moonlight on silver hair transformed the unlikely shape into what it really was; Gavin Moore holding Noah in his arms as he staggered across the uneven meadow. She shouted to the others and ran toward the man that had indeed been tested by fire.

Both men were half naked and covered in blood. Whether Noah was dead or alive, she did not know. His mangled body was covered in dark shadow that could only be blood and his head hung over Gavin's arm, exposing his long slender neck with no visible signs of life. Gavin looked little better, his eyes unblinking black pits of shadow in the darkness. He walked straight up to her without seeing her.

"Gavin, my dearest," Dora told him gently, touching his arm when he merely stood there like a statue. "It's all right now."

Barry came up beside her, panting from his jog across the meadow. Reggie was following a distance behind him, having shouted back for Duncan. Barry remained silent, taking in the condition of the two men and listening to Dora's gentle voice. The look in Gavin's eyes gave him a shiver.

"You are safe now, dearest," Dora crooned softly. "It's all right. You can let go of him now."

Gavin looked at her, finally really seeing her for the first time. Something crumbled behind his dark scary eyes. He collapsed to his knees on the ground, still holding Noah like a drowning man holds onto a log. He began to sob, a deep soul wrenching anguish that shook his entire body.

With Dora's gentle coaxing they got the story out of an almost incoherent Gavin, who sobbed in exhaustion and despair, refusing for almost five minutes to release his grip on Noah's limp body. The tale was almost unbelievable. Other than the condition they were in and the circumstances of the night, almost no one would have believed it. The silence of the small circle of people attested to the fact that they were horrified by the truth of it.

Finally Gavin relinquished, allowing them to take Noah from his embrace. One look at the blood soaked leg and Reggie sent Barry scurrying to fetch his vehicle; its four-wheel drive could get out into the meadow without much worry of getting stuck in the mud. Dora wrapped her jacket around Gavin's shoulders and Reggie draped his over Noah, holding him until Barry's Rover came bouncing up to them across the grass.

At the dark house, Rose Marie came running out to them as the vehicle stopped to disgorge Duncan and Dora. She took one look inside and wrung her hands. In shock and still covered with Noah's blood, Gavin sat in the backseat holding his injured lover, swathed in a blanket, across his lap. He had lapsed back into the trance-like state of staring silence.

"My God, my God," Rose Marie said in horror. "What happened? Did you hear that strange howling? Where is Lord Andrew?"

Duncan sighed, a deep troubled breath. "He is dead. Killed by his own madness and Seth with him."

A scream shattered the night.

They all turned to see Moira and Mary Katherine standing at the edge of the rear garden pathway. They had been roused earlier by Rose Marie and had dressed and come over to the main house, appearing just in time to see the vehicle drive up from the meadow with its terrible news. It was Mary Katherine who screamed and ran forward to launch herself at Duncan.

"Seth? Dead? Where is my boy? Where is he?"

They tried to tell her but she was in no condition to hear. Near hysteria, she slid down the length of Duncan's body to huddle in a ball of misery on the ground.

Moira walked up to them in a quieter fashion but her

controlled silent weeping was just as heartbreaking. She took her mother by the shoulders and lifted her off the ground, turning her toward the dark empty house. They walked away in a slow shamble, Moira murmuring a steady soft stream of meaningless words. Shocked and horrified, the small group watched them disappear into the doorway before turning to look at each other.

"I must get Noah into surgery right away," Reggie stated from the vehicle. "Duncan, call my nurse, Mrs. Forsyth, and tell her to be at surgery in five minutes. Dora, I'm trusting you here with those two. If you can, have Mary take some sleeping medication and put her to bed."

"I should call Constable Thornton," Duncan said miserably. "This is so…"

"Don't do anything until Barry gets back and we have decided what to do next. Duncan, Andrew was my friend too. We are all his friends. But if he did this terrible thing… This whole thing is just too crazy for the police to believe unless we have some sort of understanding."

"He's right, Duncan," Dora agreed. "This is too big for us."

"It's too dark for the Constable to do anything yet," Reggie continued. "He has no precedent for dealing with this sort of thing in any case. He will have to send for the Yard detectives and that will be another entire set of worries. Just wait until we can get the whole story straight. The dead don't have any more worries. I must care for the living. Barry, get going."

The vehicle drove off into the dark and the three shell shocked people went back into the silent house to do as they were directed.

The village surgery was small but well equipped, and Reggie was more than capable of anything but the most difficult cases. He could set a bone and remove an appendix in his tiny operating room, but patients in need of brain surgery or treatment for cancer had to be sent to Edinburgh. Noah's stab wound was not a problem. Reggie's nurse had been trained for emergencies, but never in her time at the village had she seen the likes of the two patients that came in that night.

They allowed Gavin to watch as they stripped the blood soaked clothing from Noah's abused body and set to work cleaning him up. Gavin stood rooted to the spot in his bloody trousers and blanket. He shook his head when they asked him how badly he was injured and swatted hands away when they tried to find out. They left him alone until Barry pulled him out of the room so the doctor could work on Noah's leg injury.

Noah remained blessedly unconscious throughout the torturous ordeal, for which Gavin was grateful, Noah having suffered enough for one night. They stitched up his many wounds and shot him full of antibiotics and pain killers, squeezing a pint of blood into him just to be on the safe side. Barry watched from the far end of the small room, his heart bleeding for them both. They finally transferred Noah to another room, wheeling him there on a gurney with tubes running in and out of his pale, motionless body.

Only when they knew they had Noah in hand did they turn their professional attention to the silent Gavin, who finally submitted to Reggie's attention without uttering a sound. Luckily there were no broken bones. The doctor swabbed out the puncture wounds to Gavin's arm with alcohol and bandaged it from shoulder to wrist. When they were finished, Reggie led Gavin to Noah's room, where Gavin took hold of Noah's hand and sobbed with open wretchedness.

Reggie watched him for a moment, wondering how the man could possibly still be on his feet, but seeing them together, he understood. He went out to talk with Barry in hushed tones for a few minutes.

When they returned, Gavin was silent again. They sat him down and slowly, quietly got the entire story out of him in a more coherent, if yet wild fashion. Finally exhausted, Gavin did not resist when they steered him to a bed on the opposite side of the small room and gently pushed him down onto the sheets. Against his will but at the end of his endurance, Gavin closed his eyes and slept.

Reggie and Barry looked at each other with grave expressions. They believed his story. That was the worst part. They believed every crazy word of it. Whether they could get anyone else to believe it was another matter. Barry went to wake Constable Thornton. At least they could start there.

Reggie sent his nurse home with none of her questions answered, then went into his tiny office and phoned the Hall to speak with Dora for a few minutes. She added her explanations in a tired flat voice, every bit as wild and yet serious as Gavin's story had been.

When he put the phone down, Reggie let his breath out in a sigh. It was turning out to be one of the stranger nights of his life. He pulled a bottle from his desk drawer and poured himself a large whiskey, neat.

⚜ ⚜ ⚜

When Noah at last opened his eyes, Gavin's grim face was the first thing he saw and Gavin's warm hand holding his was the first thing he felt. He moaned softly at the biting sting of pain coming from his leg, watching a tear trickle from Gavin's dark eyes. More pain followed, stabbing up into his stomach and burning hot in his throat, but Noah knew it had nothing to do with his damaged body. The tears burst hot and wet from his eyes and he caught his breath in a sob.

"Noah, please don't," Gavin pleaded, watching Noah's face crumple in grief and despair. "Please, don't."

Noah wept a flood of silent tears. The wretchedness in his face and the silent weeping was even harder to watch than the anguished sobbing that had taken place in the depths of the crypt. Gavin could not stand it. He sat on the edge of the bed and carefully lifted Noah's upper body into his embrace. After a slight sound of pain and a momentary resistance, Noah clung to him, arms around his waist, face buried in Gavin's clean fresh shirt.

Gavin stroked Noah's ragged hair, murmured to him quietly until his weeping slowed and his breathing was soft and deep.

Gently Gavin eased him back down onto the pillow and pulled the sheet up to his chin, covering the white bandages wound around his chest. Noah's eyes were half closed, sunken in their blue-black bruises. Gavin brushed the soft blond hair away from the bandage on Noah's forehead.

"Are the pain killers working?" he asked.

Noah blinked slowly. "I think so. I don't hurt too much."

"Are you cold?" Noah's head barely moved to nod, yes. Carefully Gavin eased the blanket over the sheet. "Close your eyes and sleep. You are going to be all right."

Noah had to listen very closely to hear the next words coming from Gavin's lips.

"Don't hate me, Noah. Please. I don't think I could stand it."

Noah's eyes flew open and he bit his sore lip hard to keep from screaming. He stared into Gavin's face for a moment until he felt he could speak. He reached and caught Gavin's hand, squeezing it.

"None of this was your fault, Gavin. Don't blame yourself for anything Andrew did to us, for what he forced you to do to him, not ever."

Gavin looked into the fierce blue gaze and managed a halfhearted smile. "I love you," he said simply.

"I love you too," Noah replied. "I will always love you."

"Go to sleep," Gavin said again. "I'll be here."

Noah sighed heavily and closed his eyes.

Gavin held his hand and watched him drift to sleep, letting his gaze scan over the tubes and wires. Oxygen was carried to Noah through a plastic tube in his nose, IV fluids through another tube and a needle in his arm. He had wires running from his body to a machine over the bed that monitored his heart rate, respiration, and oxygen levels. There were dark bruises around his eyes and lips, and other parts of his body covered with the blankets were swathed in bandages. His hair was in disarray from having been whacked off at strange angles by the sharp blade of Andrew's dagger.

But he was alive and his body would heal. And that was all that mattered to Gavin.

He tried to swallow the lump in his throat but it wouldn't go down. Overcome with gratitude and relief, he let the tears come again. There was no shame in weeping over someone you loved more than your own life.

Noah's face looked battered but serene, peaceful and at peace. Gavin knew without a doubt that the curse of the Bainbridge Clan was over. He would never again allow Noah to be hurt by anyone. He would take them away from Bainbridge Hall and never go back. And he would never, ever allow Noah to feel responsible for the terror that the actions of a madman had brought into their lives.

He fell asleep in the chair with his forehead resting on the edge of the bed and Noah's hand clutched tightly in his.

EIGHTEEN

Truth, bitter truth.
—Danton

The last day of the local autumn festival was not nearly so beautiful as the first. Dark grey clouds thickened the sky with the hint of more rain, and the winds of the previous night had torn through several of the tents, leaving their poor rain-sodden shells collapsed in boggy heaps. The tourists romped about with less enthusiasm and the locals went on without knowing what dread happenings had transpired during the terrible hours between dusk and dawn. At least, none of them would admit to knowing.

Constable Thornton *was* a local and perhaps because of that fact he listened to Barry's story in silence and then went with him back out to Bainbridge Hall in the darkest hours before the dawn. The two of them, with Duncan alongside, found the crypt and the bodies much as Gavin Moore had said; bloody and very dead. Duncan broke down and had to be helped outside by Barry, leaving Constable Thornton to survey the scene with grim expertise.

Thornton had been told stories in his childhood about such things; shape-shifting wolves and human sacrifice. Seeing them unfolding as reality in a family as old and revered as the Bainbridge clan gave him pause. The circular room and symbol-carved altar made the truth of it apparent and gave him chills.

Harder to explain was the mutilated naked body lying partially beneath the clothed body of Laird Andrew Bainbridge, who had died exactly like Moore said, with his throat cut. The two weapons lay near each other on the stone floor, the dagger and the curved hoof knife, both bloody and sharp.

It did not take Thornton long to know that the press, not to mention Scotland Yard, would crucify both survivors if the truth were to come out in its gory and unbelievable entirety. The one thing on the side of Moore's story was that Andrew's father had been known for his eccentric ideas and odd behavior. Perhaps that would suffice to explain Andrew's actions as well those of his dead servant. It would have to do. The weapons, blood, and creepy location told their own story.

Thornton walked up out of that pit of death and breathed in the clean country air of approaching dawn. It was not going to be easy, but the best they could do was stick as near the truth as possible. He could see to it that everyone got their stories straight.

It was early yet and would take the Yard some time to get people out that far. He had witnesses to interview and his breakfast to eat; nothing like dealing with foul deeds on an empty stomach. Thornton marched to his vehicle and climbed in with the other two men in silence.

⚜ ⚜ ⚜

When the Constable showed up with Barry in tow early that afternoon, Gavin and Noah were ready for them. Dora had been by earlier, allowed only a moment to check on them before Reggie ran her out. She was pale and unusually subdued but she and Gavin regarded each other with a newfound understanding. Reggie explained to them earlier about the need to alter their story, omitting the more unbelievable parts, but they had trouble deciding which parts those were.

Constable Thornton wanted to hear the entire story, believable or not, straight from the purported victims of the disaster. He had searched the appropriate rooms at the Hall and located McKewen's telltale folder along with the diary of the late Laird James hidden in Andrew's dresser. He had seen with his own eyes the destruction of the late Laird's room and the horror of the crypt. He heard Barry's account of the night's terrors and listened to Duncan's despairing recital that agreed with the early facts as Moore had stated them. After Thornton allowed Gavin to read from the diary for a few moments in silence, he sat back and waited for the man to speak.

The diary only confirmed all of Gavin's suspicions about the vision he had at the bottom of the staircase, and the talk he had that morning with Noah, who now remembered everything, rounded it out. He handed the book back to the constable and nodded his head in grim agreement. With the policeman, Barry, and Reggie in the room, Gavin took Noah's cold hand in his and began to tell the story.

"We all had part of the answer but none of us could see past our own set of blinders. Only Andrew had all the facts and because he did, he could play us all to suit his own twisted need. He had it planned out even before he killed his father, or I should say, he had his father killed. Perhaps Seth acted on his own in that case, tired of waiting, but I doubt it."

He looked up at Noah while he spoke, as if they were the only two people in the room. Noah was propped up in bed, battered and bandaged with the IV still in his arm. His steady blue gaze never left Gavin's face.

"Your father tried everything he could to stop the family curse, even from the time of his own childhood. He knew that unnatural things were in the house and strange unexplainable things had happened throughout the history of the family. When he inherited the place he did his own research, much like I had McKewen do for me, and discovered the terrible truth. That is when he found out he had a dead baby brother, yet another sign that the family curse was real. He also had access to things I could never find out; family documents and the crypt with its ancient altar in a circular room built for one purpose. That is where the rubbings of the more ancient wolf carvings came from. I noticed them immediately, on the altar and the walls."

"I had been to the ruins earlier," Noah said with a shake of his head. "I had thought the old ruined chapel might hold the key but it never occurred to me that they would not have exposed their secret to the light of chance discovery. They hid it underground, in a place made specifically for that purpose and kept secret for hundreds of years. Seth was with me that day, to watch out for me he said, but really he was there to see that I did not go into the vault and discover the secret crypt."

"He may have had other reasons," Gavin added darkly.

Noah had only that morning told him what he knew about Seth…and about Andrew and Seth.

"In any case, that comes later in the story. The only thing that explains why your father failed to acknowledge you when you were born was that he was terrified of the curse. He thought that by keeping you a secret and keeping you away from the Hall that you would be safe. Helen apparently agreed to that arrangement…for awhile. When her grandfather died, she talked James into marrying her and bringing the both of you to live at the Hall. Because the house had been silent for years, James thought it might be safe. Everything seemed fine for three years."

"Not so fine," Noah said sadly.

"Well, by the time he figured that out," Gavin said, "it was too late for Helen. It never occurred to James that the entity would act through Andrew that night."

"No," Noah agreed, "It didn't. For months I had been suffering in silence with the growing menace in the house. Only I knew Andrew was susceptible to its control. He seemed like two different people to me; a loving older brother who played with me and seemed to care for my company, or a stranger who shouted at me and sometimes locked me in scary dark places."

"Wait a minute. You are saying that Andrew killed Lady Bainbridge?" Doctor Fox-Pitt interjected curiously. "He was how old back then, fifteen, sixteen?"

"It wasn't really Andrew then, at least, not *only* Andrew," Gavin tried to explain. "There are many layers going on in Bainbridge Hall, shadows over shadows. When he came after Noah that night, even nine-year-old Noah understood that it was not his brother. He ran for his life until Andrew caught him at the top of the staircase. It would have ended then except for Noah's mother. Helen came to the aid of her son and paid for it with her life."

"I saw her fall," Noah said softly, having regained the horrible memory. "I had no choice but to leave her. I did what she told me, ran outside and hid."

"The diary states it clearly enough," Constable Thornton agreed with a nod. "Lord James came home late that night from a meeting in Edinburgh. He walked into a mad house with his wife lying dead at the foot of the stairs and his youngest son missing. The servants were in a shambles and had not yet rang for the police. Andrew had oddly enough gone back to his room and was asleep as if nothing was wrong. That was when Lord James knew what had happened. He calmed the servants and sent for the doctor and then they searched for Noah. It was a dark, cold, stormy night and he was out of his mind with grief. It was almost daybreak before they discovered the child hidden in the stables, practically beneath the feet of one of the horses."

"All that explains clearly to me Noah's natural fears of the dark, of horses, and loud storms," Gavin picked up the explanation. "After Noah had been found, Lord James took him to a private hospital where he could hide his identity and get him the best of care. Noah was in a coma and remained in one for weeks. Afterward, his memory of the event, indeed, most of his memories from his childhood were gone, locked away where they could not hurt him anymore. Those missing memories were a huge stumbling block for Noah once he came back to the house of his childhood and the thing in the house that had once tried to kill him."

Gavin paused and gave Noah a long silent look, his naked emotions clearly written on his face. He closed his eyes for a moment to gather himself before continuing.

"Lord James blamed himself for the death of his wife and the condition of both of his sons. The local doctor ruled Helen's death an accident—death by misadventure—and James kept the rest of it hidden, mostly by dismissing the entire servant staff, with large payouts to keep their silence. Andrew seemed to suffer no ill effects and, even if James suspected otherwise, he protected his eldest son from recriminations. He also did the only thing he had left to do to guarantee that it did not happen again. He sent you away, Noah, where you would be safe. He cut himself out of your life in fear that he might inadvertently trigger your memory or show the *presence* in the house where you were. He forbade Andrew from seeing you, from even writing to you for years.

"Unfortunately his tactic strengthened the problem in other ways. He turned his guilt and grief inward and withdrew from life. As the years passed, during which he paid your way and followed your career, his guilt caused him to rethink his choices. Andrew grew to resent and then to hate you for stealing his father away from him...and it made you yearn for that home and family you no longer had. James managed to keep the entity at bay for years, denying his place in clan succession, denying the truth to Andrew. Then Andrew somehow discovered the family secret. It is not so much a curse as it is an...*obligation*."

"Andrew found his father's diary at some point," Thornton said, holding up the book for emphasis. "He had probably discovered the crypt and altar in his youth without knowing what it meant. When he found the diary, the poem, and read the family history, he understood the connection. He blamed his father for ruining his life by not fulfilling the family oath that had promised the death of the younger son in exchange for some vague inheritance of power or wealth."

Noah gave a small shudder. "He knew father had purposely blocked the supernatural element in the house by using his own psychic power against it and later, by trying to exorcise it entirely. By then father had begun to suffer the consequences of his actions."

"We may never know," Gavin continued grimly, "if Andrew, or some of the clan members, or even the *presence* in the house helped it along, but James began to lose control. He went to Father Perrine for help but then changed his mind, perhaps fearful for what his actions might do to Andrew. Then he changed his will."

Gavin paused and looked straight at Noah. "He no longer had the heart to cut you out entirely so he gave you half of what he could and thought he was guaranteeing your safety by compliance with that forfeiture clause in the will. He gave you the proof of your heritage probably to back up your claim in case Andrew tried to take it away from you. Personally I believe he did it simply because he wanted you to know that he was your father…and that no matter what he had done to you, he did love you."

Noah wiped at his eyes. He understood his father better now, but it did not lessen the pain any. Both James and Andrew were dead. He was still alone…at least, until he looked at Gavin and saw the emotion shining in his dark eyes.

"The changing of the will set the entire plan into motion for Andrew. That hole in your heart had eaten away at you for years and when your father died—probably murdered by Seth in a psychic attack similar to the one you experienced the night of the concert—and Andrew reached out, you had no choice but to respond. In fact you leapt at the chance, however small, of a reconciliation with Andrew and a chance to uncover your buried past. The money never did mean anything to you. Andrew had counted on it. And you, knowing nothing of this, chose to believe Andrew an innocent victim of the *presence* in the house, trying to protect him until the end. Your only weakness, loyalty. I have the same problem it seems."

"I was a fool," Noah muttered.

"We are all fools," Reggie stated blandly. "It is the human condition." The doctor turned to Noah, addressing him directly. "Andrew must have been drugging your food and drink from the first evening you arrived at the Hall. I found noticeable amounts of the same drugs I had prescribed for your father when I checked your blood."

Thornton nodded. "Aye, the bottles of pills were in Lord Andrew's room."

Reggie nodded in agreement. "I had suspected as much. Your 'spells' were probably on account of those drugs. A public display of illness fit right into his hand of showing you off to his friends and the locals as a weak, mentally unstable person."

"Hmmm," Gavin said and sighed. "At any rate, Andrew

brought you back to the house with the plan of having the *presence* in the house, or Seth, murder you eventually. Once you *mysteriously disappeared*, he could blame it on your mental state and walk away clean. But like your father, you have a strong psychic energy. The very thing that made you susceptible to the house also gave you the power to fight it. The night of the concert you defeated a direct psychic attack witnessed by Dora and Barry."

"Dora was already suspicious of something," Noah mumbled, shuddering at the depth of his brother's madness. "She just wasn't sure what." He looked up at Gavin. "And then you showed up."

"Andrew really was not prepared for that," Gavin said with a slight smile. "He had to change his plan, slightly risky since he wanted to remain clear of any hint of suspicion. Earlier last night, in the dining room, he tried everything to defeat you; ropes, drugs, even darkness in the room that he knew was the weakest place in the house for you to defend yourself. Even then, you were going to defeat him. He was almost beside himself after that failed. It was his last chance to have the house do the dirty work for him, his last hope of keeping his hands and his conscience clean, so to speak.

"Then something else happened that he had not counted on. I added that final straw, the comment that we were thinking of leaving. That sent Andrew into a rage. The deed had to be accomplished before I could take you away and that was when he remembered the crypt. In the oldest days I have no doubt that fathers actually murdered their sons in that horrible room, maybe even with other male Clan members present or taking a direct part in the ceremony.

"It would be the perfect place to murder you and conceal your body. No one knew the place existed. He could kill you himself or he could leave you there to die a slower, more agonizing death; either way he was relatively sure your body would never be found. I suspected Andrew had tried to kill you, but fool that I was, I did not think that he would try it again, so soon…not with me there."

"I walked straight into his hands," Noah said, shaking his

head. "I still refused to believe that it was Andrew. I had put all my suspicions on Seth. I knew how it was between them. I had seen them together, in the stable one night. I thought…well, I thought that Seth was the one in control. I had no idea what his reasons might be other than he and Andrew had kept their relationship a secret and because of that maybe he had a hold over Andrew. I thought maybe he was jealous that I had suddenly appeared out of nowhere and took Andrew's attention away. Seth had his own secrets, it seems."

Even Noah had trouble believing what Gavin had told him about Seth being the wolf that had attacked him in the meadow. He thought about the flashes of fur and teeth that he envisioned the first night, the day of his father's death, and the image of a wolf-like creature watching him that day at the churchyard. It had been the same psychic wolf creature that attacked him the night of the concert.

And then Noah remembered the bright green eyes and the mesmerizing sensuality that even Seth's sister Moira seemed to possess and it made him wonder. The wounds in Gavin's arm had certainly been made by long sharp teeth; Reggie had attested to that.

"Andrew was a bit out of control after that," Gavin continued in the silent pause. "He might have gotten away with it too if not for your abilities and your stubborn faith in me. I *heard* your silent scream for help from across the estate. It deafened me as much as it scared me, but it drew me to you like a magnet. They were not expecting that you might still have a way to defend yourself. It was Seth who attacked me in the meadow. Without the pick from the stable…things might have ended differently. Even then, without Andrew's blind rage over Seth's death, I might never have gotten us out of that crypt alive."

Gavin had told Noah about Seth but he had kept other things to himself. He told no one about the greenish light that had aided him that night; the front door crashing open, the strangeness with the horse, the glow that led him to the underground crypt. He had his own ideas about that unnatural mist.

"Dora knew what was going on," Barry added seriously. "She woke me up jabbering about wolves and blood and murder. I'll never forget what I saw last night. I'll never doubt that woman again either."

Nor will I, Gavin thought with a shiver.

Constable Thornton scratched his chin. The entire thing was unbelievable but then again, insane people did insane things. The facts would bear out their story...at least the believable parts. Before he left, he made certain that they could all agree on the facts, properly edited for the eyes and ears of Scotland Yard, of course.

He thanked them for their time and wished them a speedy recovery. With his facts sorted and his evidence in hand, he went about his duty. The town and the tourists finished the last day of festival none the wiser.

NINETEEN

The rest is silence.
—Shakespeare

Apparently Constable Thornton's explanations carried a great deal of weight. That, and the remarkably efficient Anthony McKewen, provided a much needed insulation for Noah and Gavin in the chaos that followed the strange death of the younger Laird Bainbridge less than a month after that of his father.

Amid the influx of policemen and reporters that overran the small village in the span of a few hours, the locals were amazingly quiet. Frustrated reporters were met with closed shutters and silent stares. The village, as it had always done in times of crisis, kept their own conscience.

Gavin had telephoned McKewen the evening of the odd, half-remembered day spent in Reggie's little surgery rooms. McKewen had promptly dispatched a team of private investigator and high powered attorney to come to their aid, showing up himself the following afternoon. He took control of the situation like a military commander, relocating his charges to a small private inn at the edge of the sea where he barricaded the doors against all comers that did not pass his scrutiny.

That was all right with Gavin, who was suffering from exhaustion and fighting his own personal demons as well as worrying about Noah. They took Noah away from the hospital as soon as allowed, Gavin carrying him from the chauffeured car up the long path to their new private rooms at the secluded inn. Noah put his arms around Gavin's neck and allowed himself to be carried in silence. Gavin really wanted to carry Noah the entire way to London, away from all the horror and suspicion, out of the nightmare that seemed to have swallowed them whole.

He never wanted to see Scotland again.

Or wolves again…any kind of wolf…anywhere. Ever.

Gavin did not say much once they were relocated to the inn. When Noah could for short moments at a time, he hobbled about on crutches, taking phone calls and speaking to policemen. Gavin silently waited on him hand and foot while dealing with McKewen's people, detectives, and the constant flow of telephone calls. They had precious little time alone, speaking only of necessary things.

Barry Fitzgerald was good enough to arrange for the burials of both men in the village churchyard. All of the Bainbridge family—save one—would now reside there, beneath the cool green lawn beside the sea. That reminded Gavin that Noah was the last in the line of two ancient but haunted families. Andrew had died without a will or an heir, allowing the ownership of the Hall to revert to the only remaining son of Laird James Bainbridge.

Noah wanted nothing to do with the name or the estate, refusing even the inherited title of Lord Bainbridge. He actually turned white when McKewen told him that the title and estate would legally pass to him.

It would not be that easy; Jamis Selkirk seemed to think that part of it should go his way as a distant relation. The legal wrangling might take months. Noah would have simply let him have it except that he wanted no one with Bainbridge blood to ever again risk their lives in the place. As far as Gavin was concerned, they could burn it to the ground; neither one of them wished to lay eyes upon it again.

Duncan agreed to stay on at the Hall until its fate was decided but he was a broken man. He had seen the signs and like so many, had ignored the possible consequences. His statement to the police had been enlightening in many ways and his apologies to Noah and Gavin had been anguished and profuse.

Seth remained an unexplainable mystery. The police did not require that part of the story for their purposes yet Gavin and Noah knew the truth. Neither one of them had the courage to speak out loud what they were both thinking; that Seth could not possibly be the only one. Such things were not supposed to be possible in the light of reason. They left their suspicions about Moira unsaid, but they would never again look in the eyes of someone from the village without wondering.

It all seemed somewhat dreamlike in many ways, people drifting in and out, faces Gavin did and did not recognize speaking words he often did not hear. In those first few days after the event, Gavin had no control over his emotions or the bleak horror that he felt. Tears often came without warning while sitting alone in his room or standing with others. The near constant deluge of rain and wind did not help.

Because he understood Gavin's self-imposed penance, Noah allowed his lover some space to recover. It had not been easy for Gavin to kill, even though the price had been their lives. Noah watched the internal battle in those dark silent eyes, having only conquered his own demons as he sat in his room with Dora, talking about that night on the dark meadow.

With his upper thigh still tightly bandaged, Noah tossed his crutches aside after a couple of days at the inn and hobbled around without assistance, often watching Gavin from a distance. Gavin spend time alone sitting on a wicker sofa on the rear porch, staring out across the sea crashing just beyond the cliffs. Little by little the solitude, cold rain, and endless ocean cleansed his soul and helped him to forget.

On the fourth day at the inn, they began to spend a little time together, often without saying anything, just sitting in silence. During that time, Noah kept the outside world away from Gavin as much as he could, allowing McKewen to be the buffer. Gradually Noah began to talk to Gavin, keeping the short conversations quiet and about nothing in particular, not expecting Gavin to contribute.

Beneath Noah's care and sympathetic nature, Gavin slowly responded and began to relax. They never spoke of the horrors they had recently endured. Instead they slowly learned a little more about each other in lengthening private conversations as they sat looking out across the isolated landscape. Noah began to appreciate the comfortable motion of a padded rocking chair and the crackling heat from a fireplace.

Mostly he just appreciated Gavin. He soaked up every moment they spent together, even the ones spent in silence. He loved Gavin's passion for life and his sense of humor. He loved everything about Gavin, his handsome face and intelligent dark eyes, his strong personality and sense of honor…even his ability to feel sorrow deeply. They shared that sense of sorrow and guilt even if they did not speak of it. Slowly it receded into the background, to a place where they could live with it.

On the sixth night at the inn, Noah went to Gavin's room.

Already in bed, Gavin sat up when Noah walked in quietly and closed the door behind him. They faced each other across the darkness until Noah took the three necessary steps to cross the floor and fling his arms around Gavin's shoulders.

"I'm sorry," Noah told him, finally breaching the unspoken barrier between them. "I'm sorry. If I had listened to you, none of this would have happened."

Gavin buried his face in Noah's shirt with a sigh. "None of this is your fault, Noah. Remember what I told you when all of this started? Some things you just have to follow through until the end."

Noah lifted Gavin's chin with his hand and looked into his face. Gavin's open dark gaze met his, filled with emotion.

"Are you all right now, Gavin?" Noah asked softly.

"I will be."

Gavin rolled him over into the bed and kissed him.

They finally made love, their muted cries of passion lost in the crashing wind and thunder of another autumn storm. Afterwards they wept and talked with whispered tenderness, their hearts filled with gratitude. It was the first step back to the people they were before the curse of Noah's ancestors almost destroyed them.

They were still awake when the first sounds of disturbance

began to disrupt the peace of the dark and sleeping inn. Footsteps hurried down the hallway outside the room, quickly joined by other footsteps and the sounds of men's voices, their words indistinguishable over the noise from the wind. A door slammed and then a woman's voice made a sharp exclamation of surprise.

Gavin sat up on the edge of the bed and reached for his clothing.

"I'm going to see what's going on," he told Noah, not bothering to switch on a light. "Stay here. I'll be right back."

He was gone before Noah could fumble for the lamp on the bedside table. No comforting glow came from the effort; the power was out. In the palest of light coming through the undraped window, Noah searched for his clothes while the sounds of voices grew muffled, coming now from somewhere outside.

Buttoning his shirt, Gavin stepped through the exterior doorway to find several people standing on the long porch. The driving rain had slowed to a drizzle but the wind was still strong, whipping through his hair and clothing. He came to a stop beside the dark figure of McKewen, still in his robe and pajamas.

"What's going on?" Gavin asked, having to speak fairly loud to be heard over the wind.

McKewen pointed out into the darkness.

At first Gavin had no idea what he was supposed to be looking at. Then he could make out the yellowish glow in the distance. It certainly wasn't the dawn rising from that direction, although he had no idea what else it could be. The village surely didn't light up that bright at night. While he watched, a single flash of light reached higher up into the night sky and what sounded like the echo of a far off explosion reached his ears.

"What is that?" he asked, glancing at McKewen.

McKewen did not look at him. "From the location and the distance, I'd say it was Bainbridge Hall going up like a matchstick."

Shocked, Gavin turned his gaze back to the suspicious glow.

Now he could see the flicker of flames that must have been shooting up a hundred feet into the sky to be seen from that distance. A fire that large could only spell doom for the old house. The wind would whip the flames into every corner of the isolated mansion.

"We should see if we can help," Gavin said, grabbing McKewen's arm for emphasis.

"There's nothing can be done," Mrs. Lister, the innkeeper, offered with a shake of her head. She reached up to catch her wind blown hair, turning toward him. "The village is not equipped for such a fire and if it is the Hall, it would be too dangerous to get near it in this wind."

"She's right," McKewen added with finality. "If the fire brigade is there, the only thing they can do is what we're doing; watch it burn."

Gavin looked back toward the terrible and now obvious flames in the distance. The fire was beginning to light up the sky like a false dawn.

"Do you think lightning caused it?" he asked, not really believing that could be the reason.

"Who knows," McKewen said flatly.

"Maybe it is divine retribution," Mrs. Lister added, the wind whipping her robe around her legs.

Gavin doubted that either lightning or gods had anything to do with it. He turned his head and noticed that Noah had silently walked up to stand beside him in the darkness. Noah's blond hair was now cut short but Gavin secretly hoped that one day soon he would be able to run his fingers through its silken lengths. As he thought that, a wicked fork of lightning flashed across the sky overhead, illuminating Noah's hair silver white.

"Let it burn," Noah said softly, so quiet that only Gavin could hear.

"I'll get dressed and go over," McKewen offered. "Make certain Duncan and the women are all right. Would you like to ride over, Moore?"

Gavin put his arm around Noah and shook his head.

"Don't blame you," McKewen said with what could have been a smile in the dark. "Go back to bed. I'll fill you in tomorrow, hopefully on a plane back to London."

The rain started up again, getting them wet even on the covered deck as it blew in with the wind. McKewen went back inside, quickly followed by everyone but Gavin and Noah, who stood just beside the door, somewhat sheltered from the cold wind. The rain made no difference in the intensity of the flames that could be seen through the darkness.

"I hope he is right and we can go home tomorrow," Noah said with a sigh. "Home, to London, where we belong."

"Maybe it is better this way," Gavin replied to the finality of Noah's voice. "Nothing left to remind us…of any of this."

A gust of wind blew rain drops in their faces. Gavin felt somewhat relieved that the physical link to Noah's nightmares would be gone, burned away by cleansing flames. He wondered if perhaps Duncan, or maybe even the blue witch, Dora, had something to do with it. Perhaps seeing it in ashes would give them peace as well.

"I love you," Noah said quietly in the darkness.

"I love you too," Gavin told him easily.

Noah put his arms around Gavin's neck and kissed him. The burning house meant nothing to him but the final erasure of a life and a past that had never really been his. Gavin was all he would ever need, all he could ever possibly want or desire.

Gavin placed his arm around Noah's shivering body and kissed him back.

And Gavin knew that he had found his peace and redemption right there, in the gentle forgiving soul he held in his arms. He was born and he died in that instant, his entire life distilled down to that one kiss. Gavin would always remember him in that moment; the sound of the ocean waves crashing against the cliffs, the scent of Noah's rain-dampened hair, the warm touch of his soft lips and smooth skin.

Beyond them, the ocean continued to move, the rain continued to fall. Morning would come and the sun would rise over the ashes of Bainbridge Hall.

They would be all right.

It was the nature of things.

ABOUT THE AUTHOR

REIKO MORGAN lives with her family in the Pacific Northwest. Influenced by her multi-cultural background, Reiko's stories are often distinctly non-American in nature and hint at a strong belief in spirituality that she presents in many forms. Once employed in the fast moving technology field, she now directs her energy to her family, art, and writing.

THE TREVOR PROJECT

The Trevor Project operates the only nationwide, around-the-clock crisis and suicide prevention helpline for lesbian, gay, bisexual, transgender and questioning youth. Every day, The Trevor Project saves lives though its free and confidential helpline, its website and its educational services. If you or a friend are feeling lost or alone call The Trevor Helpline. If you or a friend are feeling lost, alone, confused or in crisis, please call The Trevor Helpline. You'll be able to speak confidentially with a trained counselor 24/7.

The Trevor Helpline: 866-488-7386

On the Web: http://www.thetrevorproject.org/

THE GAY MEN'S DOMESTIC VIOLENCE PROJECT

Founded in 1994, The Gay Men's Domestic Violence Project is a grassroots, non-profit organization founded by a gay male survivor of domestic violence and developed through the strength, contributions and participation of the community. The Gay Men's Domestic Violence Project supports victims and survivors through education, advocacy and direct services. Understanding that the serious public health issue of domestic violence is not gender specific, we serve men in relationships with men, regardless of how they identify, and stand ready to assist them in navigating through abusive relationships.

GMDVP Helpline: 800.832.1901

On the Web: http://gmdvp.org/

THE GAY & LESBIAN ALLIANCE AGAINST DEFAMATION/GLAAD EN ESPAÑOL

The Gay & Lesbian Alliance Against Defamation (GLAAD) is dedicated to promoting and ensuring fair, accurate and inclusive representation of people and events in the media as a means of eliminating homophobia and discrimination based on gender identity and sexual orientation.

On the Web: http://www.glaad.org/

GLAAD en español:

            http://www.glaad.org/espanol/bienvenido.php

CPSIA information can be obtained at www.ICGtesting.com
Printed in the USA
LVOW041911260612

287753LV00001B/7/P